THIS edition, issued in 1954, is for members of The Companion Book Club, 8 Long Acre, London, W.C.2, from which address particulars of membership may be obtained. The book is published by arrangement with the original publishers, Cleaver-Hume Press Ltd.

Also by
JAN DE HARTOG

Novels
STELLA
THE LOST SEA

Plays
THE FOUR-POSTER
SKIPPER NEXT TO GOD
DEATH OF A RAT

CAPTAIN JAN

A STORY OF OCEAN TUGBOATS

"A blessed companion is a book"—JERROLD

CAPTAIN JAN

A STORY OF OCEAN TUGBOATS

★

JAN DE HARTOG

THE
ENGLISH VERSION EDITED
AND ABRIDGED BY
CARLOS PEACOCK

THE COMPANION BOOK CLUB
LONDON

Made and printed in Great Britain
for The Companion Book Club (Odhams Press Ltd.)
by Odhams (Watford) Limited,
Watford, Herts.
S.654.ZT

CHAPTER ONE

THE rapid promotion of Jan Wandelaar from deck-hand to mate was nothing exceptional in the early years of this century, when Holland's tugboats first started venturing on to the high seas.

The first tugboat service had been established about 1840: a tiny, panting paddle-steamer, pulling windjammers in and out of the harbours of the North Sea and sometimes, as they became venturesome in later years, towing them as far as the Isle of Wight if the wind had failed. Before the advent of this service, the great windjammers had been doomed to wait for a fair wind, sometimes for weeks on end, before they could sail. During the next fifty years, other paddle-steamers joined the service: sturdy, powerful vessels, specially built for towing—but none of these ventured beyond Bishop Rock.

But about 1890 the Dutch "water-builders" had become sought after all over the globe and were building harbours and damming rivers as far afield as Africa, Asia and South America. For these enterprises dredgers, floating cranes, lighters and sluice-gates were needed, which the Dutch shipwrights knew how to build. At the start, these auxiliary vessels were taken apart in Europe and shipped piecemeal to their destinations; but the task of assembling them on the other side of the world with unskilled labour proved to be impracticable. There seemed only one solution left: to tow them in one piece across the Atlantic, despite the gales.

The first captain to make the hazardous trip in his paddle-steamer was called Bakker, and he came back with a grey beard, mad eyes, and hoarse stories of sea-serpents, waves the size of cathedrals and voracious bats the size of windjammers, that had chased him round the Sargasso Sea. But he had always been known as a liar, and the size of the waves and the bats grew with the number of drinks his awed listeners in the harbour-pubs stood him, to hear his

7

gruesome fantasies. Yet they believed him, for the simple reason that the tugboat sailors of the Dutch shore had never been to sea themselves. They had never ventured out of sight of the land for generations, they had never been taught any navigation: all they did was to keep an eye on the shore if the horizon was clear, or take a sounding lead if it was foggy: the sample of sand the lead brought up told them where they were: they just looked at the crumbs of sand caught by the grease and said, "Dogger Bank," and if in doubt they tasted it and knew for certain. To them the last horizon was the faint, glittering beam one saw from Bishop Rock on frosty days; and behind that, for all they knew, lay a steaming hell crawling with sea-serpents, deluged with waves the size of cathedrals, and fanned with the wings of giant bats on the lookout for little white slugs in sailors' hats, which they devoured. The truth was that Captain Bakker had been so terrified the moment his lead no longer touched bottom that he had drunk himself into a coma and stayed tight until his mate sighted South America. In the meantime, moaning in his bunk, he had seen the waves, the bats, and the serpents that are the punishment God metes out to inebriated sinners: he was no liar, but merely an honest drunk.

Captain Bakker was the harbinger of veritable swarms of little water-beetles towing behind them over the ocean their precious loads. Once the telegraph wires had buzzed with the news that the first towed dredger had arrived in Buenos Aires—battered and mauled but in one piece—dozens of new tugboats were ordered from the shipwrights: tugboats specially designed for the deep seas. The first ocean-going tugboat was launched in the year 1892; but that same year thirty-six dredgers, hoppers, floating cranes, and sluice-gates were towed across the ocean, for the ship-owners had not waited for the new fleet. They had transformed their old paddleboats into deep-sea vessels by mumbling over them some formula of seaworthiness to set the childish minds of the crews at rest and by paying a handsome bonus to help the simpletons believe it.

Once this exodus started, the lack of trained navigators became a problem; for not everyone was favoured by God, not everyone could sail across the void with nothing to

8

guide him but a squinting compass and a bottle as the great Captain Bakker had done. Somehow all the transports arrived somewhere, but a generous number of them arrived at very odd spots indeed. Sluice-gates for Rio de Janeiro were proudly towed into the baffled harbour of Montevideo; dredgers for Buenos Aires greeted the natives of Punta Arenas with triumphant squeaks from their queer little hooters; the men of the deep-sea tugs were wonderful sailors, displaying glorious courage in the face of sea-serpents, bats, and waves like cathedrals, but they were worse navigators than the seagulls. The shipping-directors started by adding "captains for navigation" to the skippers of their tugs— most of them late masters of windjammers, a dying trade. But the experiment was not very successful; the rival captains cut each other's throats on the high seas or got drunk together; the only solution was to teach navigation to promising youngsters who had sailed on tugboats ever since they first tasted the salt spray—and Jan Wandelaar was one of those.

Jan Wandelaar was the only child of a fisherman's widow, who had lost her husband to a shark when the colour of her baby's eyes was still undecided. At the age of fourteen the boy had become an apprentice on board the paddleboat *Fortuna*, a slow, goodhearted hulk of a ship, towing windjammers through the North Holland Canal from Amsterdam to Helder. Jan wanted to go to sea, but although his mother in the course of time outgrew the memory of her husband, the idea of the shark still haunted her, and whenever the boy mentioned the word "sea" she had a weeping-fit and would only be comforted by a filial vow and a dose of hot grog. Never, never would he go to sea, he swore; he hated the sea, he couldn't for the life of him understand what people saw in the sea, he'd rather die than go to sea. He'd stay nice and cosy on board the *Fortuna* on the North Holland Canal until he had made enough money to buy a cottage, a couple of pigs and a good, solid wife of the right sort. His mother died one night, with a smile; the happy tears suddenly stopped running down her face after his vow and the half glass of grog grew cold on the bedside table until it was drained down by the doctor, who said, "Courage, my son." Three months later, the

Fortuna was promoted to the status of a deep-sea tugboat; and Jan stayed on board, for he would by doing so keep half of his vow. He had sworn to stay aboard the *Fortuna* and never go to sea; the first half of the vow had, of course, been the more important. He was eighteen years of age, a full-grown sailor, and all he wanted was adventure.

He certainly got his share of adventure during the next four years. Ships in distress; sinking lifeboats saved out of the teeth of murderous seas; comrades sawn to death by scissoring hawsers; but nothing like that would ever happen to him, oh no—never. He was Jan Wandelaar, of the charmed life; other people might die, but he was immortal.

On 16th October, 1906, at ten o'clock in the morning, the *Fortuna* paddled out of the harbour of Helder in a gale, to salvage a barquentine which was drifting towards the shoals with her rudder out of action. The ship was sighted at noon, the tow-ropes fastened at half-past one. But at a quarter to two a hawser got caught up in the *Fortuna's* starboard paddle. The *Fortuna*, paralysed, began to heel over in the heavy seas, and was in danger of capsizing in a cloud of steam if she failed to keep her nose to the wind. Then Jan Wandelaar jumped over the rail, with a line fastened to his belt and a knife in his teeth; after a quarter of an hour the rope was cut and the *Fortuna* paddled, panting, back to life. The hero was dragged back on board, more dead than alive; why he had done it he couldn't say—when he jumped he was just blind, and when they hauled him back on board more frightened than he'd ever dare to confess to anybody; but when he realised that he was lying on the bunk in the captain's cabin, and that the apparition pouring him a drink was the skipper himself, and that the ship had been saved by him and him alone, he got drunk with pride and fell asleep.

On 17th October able-bodied seaman Wandelaar was standing in front of a mahogany desk with old Mijnheer van Munster behind it in a swivel-chair, and he heard that because of his heroism and devotion the Company had decided to pay for his studies, on condition that he sailed with the Company for a period of ten years after he had got his master's certificate. On 18th October he was sitting on a school-bench, stiff and unhappy, a giant among the youngsters. On 21st October he wept in a wind-swept porch, sobbing: "I can't! I'll never do it! I can't!" while Nellie Dijkmans, the daughter of the lock-keeper, awkwardly tried to comfort him, repeating, "You can, you'll see how you can . . ." terribly embarrassed because any moment someone might pass and stop to ask what was the matter with that boy.

On 20th December he walked along the quay in despair well into the small hours; and if there had been a tug starting on an ocean voyage that night he would have stowed away on her—for tomorrow he'd get his first school report, and that would mean, of course, that he'd have to go back to sea as a sailor.

On 21st December he stood in front of Mijnheer van Munster again, grinning from ear to ear, but leaving everything he touched wet with nervous perspiration. He got a pat on the back from a delicate hand smelling of expensive soap, and in the corridor he stumbled over the umbrella stand—well, better than under a bus, even if it set the head clerk cursing so ferociously that he rushed out of the building with shaking knees.

On New Year's Eve he drank ice-cold beer in the drawing-room of Dijkmans, the lock-keeper, under the ice-cold eyes of Mamma Dijkmans, whom he'd see floating over his bed like a hovering bat that night. He was embarrassed, for the beer gave him the burps, which came out through his nose when he tried to suppress them, and he had the awful suspicion that the hairs on the crown of his head were standing on end again, despite the brilliantine. At midnight he spilled red wine on something white, as they clinked glasses for the New Year; and he was so put out by the mishap that he forgot to hold Nellie's hand under the table at the pealing of the bells and the hooting of the foghorns—although it was really the chance of doing this that had enticed him to the party.

On 15th April he got his second school report and went to a dance; but he couldn't think of the three-four time because his head was full of logarithms. He couldn't hear the name "Co!" called without thinking of cosine; and he tried to calculate the variation of the compass for the year 1950 while Nellie, in his arms, babbled about furniture

and curtains for the year 1908. He only came to when he
stood in the wind and the darkness, with the warmth of
her mouth close to his and the scent of her hair so much
nearer than the spray and the seaweed; he sank into another
dream: dark, glorious and terrible, a whirlpool of thoughts
that were no thoughts, an avalanche of surging longings he
had never suspected were lurking in his innocent body; he
kissed her and hugged her and they stood swaying on their
feet in the swirling darkness until hoarse voices near by
shouted something obscene and he was overpowered by a
blinding rage, a hot desire to bang their bloody heads
together—but to do that he would have to let go of Nellie,
and he couldn't do that because she'd fall over when he
took his arms away. He caressed her bonnet, but he didn't
dare to kiss her any more; they strolled slowly to the bridge,
arm in arm, and stood in an embrace on the brink of the
black, gleaming canal until a rat dived with a splash into
the depths and scared them away. They whispered a hurried
good-bye in the porch, with the dead clematis rustling and
chafing in the wind. As he trudged home he cursed to himself at every step. The world was full of louts and rats and
Mamma Dijkmanses, with ice-cold eyes and a mouth like
a scar and a bosom full of uncompromising authority—to
hell with the lot of them.

In July he got two months' holiday from school and sailed
again as an A.B., as if nothing had happened. He tried to
learn his homework by the swinging light of an oil-lamp
in the foc'sle, but his comrades made it quite plain that he
mustn't think himself a gentleman now: "Have you
finished with that bloody mumbling or haven't you? Some
people have got to work, some people need their few hours
of sleep; get the hell out of here with your hymnbook, or
we'll . . ." He swore, and tried to snatch a few minutes
with his books in the lavatory; but they spotted him and
suddenly everybody wanted to go, or they shouted,
"Wandelaar! Wandelaar!" and when he jumped out they
pointed overboard and said: "A mermaid, you're just too
late."

He didn't want to report them to the mate, for that
would be mistaken tactics; he slammed one of them in the
teeth and that was the biggest mistake that he could have

made, for after that one blow the whole foc'sle was full of swinging fists and kicking boots, and someone jabbed a fork in his behind. At night, at the wheel, he could hardly stand for pain; he grasped the spokes as if they were the throats of that rabble; the compass turned into a misty moon as tears blurred his eyes.

But at last the purgatory came to an end; he hadn't learnt much for the school but a lot that would be handy in life. His first report that term was poor, but now he'd show them! He thereupon turned his nights into working days, and even Mamma Dijkmans said she hadn't seen him for a long time, in a tone that implied he was up to no good.

On the eve of his examination he and Nellie strolled along the harbour, arm in arm, close together, their hands tightly locked in the little hot tunnel of her muff. The joy of spring hung over the land already, but over the water the sadness of winter lingered on in wisps of mist and the smell of dead weeds. "Always . . ." she whispered, "I'll be with you always, my love . . ." He could hardly bear it, it choked him and blurred his eyes. It was so silly, this simple happiness, but yet so sincere, so solemn, that he felt ashamed of being just a man: an awkward lout, ruining every caress by his clumsiness, who could only manage to express his love and joy and gratitude by stammering out: "Dammit! God dammit . . . !" When he had taken her home he felt like throwing himself and her into the gleaming darkness of the canal to drown there together, locked in an embrace; for he couldn't wait any longer, yet he knew he must, and he knew, too, that somehow what they had experienced that night would never be surpassed. Anything that happened afterwards would only seem cheap and commonplace, spoiling the memory of this. This would never happen again, never—an odd thought for a man strolling home through the night, towards the morning and towards the rack.

Yes—that's what it was going to be: the rack. He'd never survive that examination, he knew it; they'd get him, the bastards, and he'd have to put an end to himself. He'd lie awake all night and remember his life—no, he'd better rehearse that chapter about Great Circle sailing; or better still, give himself a good wash all over, and in the meantime repeat the ports on the Baltic; the maritime law he might just as well leave alone, for if they should start with the maritime law he hadn't a chance in the world. At home, lying on his back on the bed, with his hands under his head, he noticed for the first time that the knots in the ceiling-boards resembled the Great Bear; he looked for other constellations and suddenly stared with startled eyes right into the sun. He had slept for six hours in his clothes with his shoes on. When he tried to stand up he fell back on the bed, groaning; his feet were swollen and ached so much that he couldn't walk a step without wincing. He didn't eat, he didn't drink; all he did was to smoke a cigar, which he was forced to discard half-way through the train journey. He'd vomit during the exam; no, that would be the last straw. He tried to vomit in the lavatory in the train, but only managed to make himself feel even more sick. He couldn't feel worse, once he arrived for the examination, with his eyes and throat burning like this and a prickly sweat soaking his forehead. The half-hour he sat locked up in the waiting-room before the ordeal started was the worst in his life. He paced up and down, read at least eighty times that smoking and spitting are forbidden; no smoking, no spitting; smoking, spitting, no, no; no gnikoms and no gnittips on gnikoms and . . .

"Mijnheer Wandelaar."

If he passed he'd give that midget of a porter a guilder; if he should fail he'd kill him. With that appeasing thought he let himself be ushered into the examination-room, where cigar-smoke and pale morning light filtering through high narrow windows met the eye, and also a long, green table with a row of faces behind it: faces with beards, with moustaches, with pipes and spectacles—but all of them with hard, suspicious eyes that looked him up and down with hostility. During the first few seconds, which were occupied with the crackling of papers, the scratch of pencils being sharpened and the heartless hammering of pipes on ashtrays, he glanced at the faces, furtively looking for some sign of friendliness or compassion; but before he had been able to discover one, the questions started. And a miracle happened—some unsuspected automaton in his head started giving the answers: quietly, dispassionately, with sometimes

14

a pause after a question with a trap in it, and then, with a faint smile, making the correct reply. The whole thing turned out to be easy, and friendly, almost childish—there was nothing in it; this was just silly, hardly a man's job. When he made a mistake he grinned shamelessly, and it seemed as if the mistake had eased the atmosphere. The faces behind the table grinned back; some of the old fogies started lighting pipes, one of them yawned with a click of false teeth and an apologetic grin to the President. But the feeling of relief set one of Jan's eyes aflutter: a maddening, irrepressible quiver; he tried to master it by setting his jaw, by clenching his fist, by shutting both eyes ferociously for a second; but then the next question made him open them again and the quiver went the moment he thought for the answer. The answer came, easily, correctly; the machine in his head replied without any effort, automatically—and then, like a blow from behind, a spanner in the works, everything went wrong. The automaton answered, but it was one number behind. Every single reply was wrong; the pauses between the questions became awkward and oppressive. He clenched his fists until they went numb, he shut his eyes until the room was full of sparks; he stared at the windows until he saw their chequered lattice in his mind's eye when he tried to pretend that he was thinking. But he wasn't thinking; he couldn't catch one single word that made sense in the whirl of his thoughts: all he knew was a desire, a mad and passionate desire to be allowed to go away before it was too late, away, away: a frenzied desire to put an end to it, dead or alive, an end, an end! Then he got a chance to work off some of the panic that had been piling up inside him: he was asked to give the commands preceding various manoeuvres.

Those commands he had known all his life—he had heard them bawled through the thunder of the breakers and sung in the silence of the mist—they were the commands that had guided his life, the voice of God in moments of danger. He shouted and bellowed until the faces behind the table lost their authority; he waved his arms, shook his fists, started walking to and fro like Captain Bouw of the *Fortuna* on his bridge—and then, when asked to give the command for the lowering of a boat, he suddenly fell silent, and a tiny voice inside him whispered: You are mad, you just can't have forgotten it, that's ludicrous—you are mad! He realised, in one fearful moment of panic and despair, that he had forgotten something he had known all his life, and it made him recover his sense. He knew it, he knew everything—it was just nerves, just bloody girlish nerves. Quietly as before, but now inwardly trembling with rage, he managed to get out the answers. God damn me, nerves! Me, who saved a whole ship, who dived overboard in an icy sea to cut a rope in a gale—nerves! He felt like suicide; after this there was only one course: to die of shame. But he answered; he answered promptly and without hesitation; he made a dead reckoning out of the items given to him, he wrote the numbers on the blackboard with a steady hand, he drew the lines boldly and broke the chalk putting down the cross—but all the time he was cursing himself in his thoughts: idiot, coward, lunatic.

When the examination was over at last, he wouldn't have minded going on for a while—he had almost come to enjoy it. But it was finished; the midget porter took him to the front door and as if he had overheard Jan's silent decision to tip him a guilder if he passed—the little man whispered: "If I were you I wouldn't worry, mate." He gave the fellow fifty cents and emerged into the fresh air with the unpleasant feeling of having been swindled. Everything was a swindle, the whole bloody world was a swindle. When Nellie asked, "How did it go?" he shrugged his shoulders and said, "Dunno."

They ate cheese rolls at a café round the corner; she tried to be cheerful and chatty, but he read the paper. Triplets had been born in Rotterdam, and a lady had chained herself to the post office at the Hague in order to get votes for women. Nellie chatted and babbled and rustled a paper bag of sweets; he shut his eyes and thought, "God, make it short."

The results were announced in the afternoon. They shook hands on the steps, then the midget porter let him into the gloomy building again and he joined a subdued herd of fellow-victims in the big room. The smell of cigar-smoke had gone stale and the breathing of the herd had frosted the windows. One name after another was called; he had to wait a long time before they got to the W's. And suddenly a voice said: "Mate Wandelaar: I have pleasure in announcing . . ."

Mate Wandelaar! He hardly heard the rest; he hurried out of the room, jostled through the crowd in the passage, stumbled out of the door and nearly crashed down the steps when he waved his arms and yelled: "Nell! I've . . ." They kissed in the middle of the street, for the whole world to see; they danced round until the bell of a horse-tram chased them off the rails; they were greeted everywhere with broad grins from the passers-by. It was a glorious moment, dizzy with happiness, pride and triumph.

That evening there was a celebration in the lock-keeper's home. The men puffed cigars and laughed with their heads thrown back at jokes that made the women giggle, and Mamma Dijkmans served punch, stroking the neck of the bottle after each round and sucking her finger. He had passed, he had passed! And yet he didn't understand why: he didn't really care. He would have liked best of all to have a walk with Nellie in the darkness, along the water-front, and to say nothing. But when they went, after the celebration was over, it was a failure. "I'm so glad . . ." she whispered; and he pressed her arm and said, "Sweetheart!" But, hell, how artificial and insincere it all sounded; and that business of waving until he was out of sight, after they had said their traditional good-bye at the porch— dammit, it had better not become a matter of routine, that nonsense.

He didn't go home straight away; he made a detour along the harbour. The *Fortuna* was lying ready with steam hissing from her winches; light was slanting from the foc'sle, some- times darkened by a shadow. So they hadn't turned in yet, the boys. He strained his ears until he heard their voices, and the urge to go on board became so compelling that he realised suddenly that something had happened to him he never really wanted. He had been lured away from his friends, his foc'sle, his ship; he couldn't go on board any longer and behave naturally, for everything had now turned against him. He wasn't wanted any more. Jan Wandelaar, the able-bodied seaman, had a home—Mate Wandelaar was a poor unwanted devil. Another man was sleeping in his bunk now; another took his watch at the wheel; another had inherited the warmth and the cosiness and the fun which he, for one single second only, had turned his back on. He slouched home, his head full of mad thoughts: to run off, to stow away, dammit, if only that paddle had knocked my block off as I deserved. . . .

At home he smoked a last cigar, in his shirt-sleeves, gazing at the stars through the attic window, full of sadness and self-pity. But the immense blackness seemed to overwhelm his gloom, the stars to dispel his brooding thoughts. He forgot that he was standing at the attic window, looking up at the sky. A vision flowered for a moment in the darkness: a deserted beach, silver and blue in misty moonlight, the soft sound of distant surf on the reefs, mysterious, monotonous and at the same time melodious, like the murmur of a shell. He had passed his exam. Now the world lay open to him and the future was in his grasp. It was long ago since he had dared to daydream like this; not since he was a child, listening to the singing of the kettle on the stove. A colossal force seemed to emanate from the spangled darkness overhead, from the very Future itself, he was tempted to believe—the wonderful, mighty Future, boundless, eternal, waiting for him. He stared, motionless, up at the Future, with happiness, power and poetry surging within him. He undressed in the darkness, humming softly to himself. As he lay on his back on the bed, his hands under his head, sleep veiled out from the stars, almost imperceptibly. "What a beautiful death," he must have thought, at some moment as he dozed off, for the next morning he remembered thinking that.

The next afternoon, standing in front of Mijnheer van Munster, he was happy and proud, but somehow wary. He listened silently as he was told that he'd have to stay in home waters as mate on board the salvage-tug *Aurora*, which meant that he wouldn't get past Portland Bill for the time being. But the mate whose place he was taking had been promoted to the *Albatross*, one of the two deep-sea tugs, so he was taking a step in the right direction. Nellie was pleased when she heard that he wouldn't have to sail on a long trip for some time, because that gave them a chance to get married.

To get married! Yes, my friend, women are courageous

creatures. The very thought of it took Jan's breath away. Speechless he entered the lock-keeper's house; speechless he watched Mamma Dijkmans, who suddenly changed into a snuffling jelly and pressed him to her bosom, which was a lot softer than he had imagined it to be; speechless he let Father Dijkmans pump his arm and stammer: "My blessing, boy, my blessing, my blessing!" Only when he looked into Nellie's eyes did he believe it. "Always . . ." she had whispered, that night on the waterfront, "I'll be with you always, my love." He opened his arms and kissed her, so unselfconsciously, so sincerely, that even the awe of Mamma Dijkmans' sitting-room, where she had sat enthroned all those months for a reign of sheer terror, didn't bother him. They stayed together for the rest of the evening and the parents wanted to discuss everything; but he just sat, looking at Nellie, while she poured out the tea and looked at him, with the lamplight shining on her hair. It seemed to him as if there was a mouth-organ humming in the distance all the time, and the sparrows rustled in the eaves.

When they were married in September he was twenty-four and she twenty-one. A lot had happened in the few months between, but on the day it seemed as if it was only yesterday that they were sitting round the table and Mamma Dijkmans started talking for the first time about the linen sheets she had to spare and about a wardrobe that would do very nicely, as long as one knew where to kick it to open. The months on the *Aurora* were hell—worse than he had anticipated after his easy time on the *Fortuna* when he was working for his exam. But he had somehow managed to keep his mouth shut and his fists in his pockets, and his Captain had sent back good reports of him. When he solemnly walked up to the altar, with Nellie's arm trembling in his, amidst waves of organ music and across coloured patches of sunlight which glowed upon the tombstones, Captain Bas of the *Aurora*, his bald head bare, followed the couple as best man and handed the ring to the vicar. It was a simple ceremony, almost oppressive because everybody looked so uncomfortable in their best clothes, but anyone who looked at Nellie couldn't help thinking: God, what beautiful things there are in that little world of yours.

The afternoon was like a nightmare of congratulations

and flowers and hot drinks and surprises in the form of aunts and presents. The evening resounded with accordion music—such tunes as *For He's a Jolly Good Fellow*, the National Anthem and various drinking-songs. When eventually the last of the aunts had been kissed goodbye and the last of the drunks piloted home to his spouse, they fell asleep in each other's arms, dizzy and bewildered with exhaustion and happiness.

The next morning he was the first to wake up, and got cautiously out of bed, to surprise her with a cup of tea. But on his way to the kitchen he looked back at her and forgot about the tea. "Always . . ." she'd whispered: "I'll be with you always, my love." Well—there she was, for always. He sighed with a smile and turned to go to the kitchen, but there was her bridal gown, carefully draped over a chair. He took a sleeve in his hand, looked at it and put it down again. He stroked the veil. It was so soft that he didn't feel it and it caught in the horny roughness of his fingers. He went on towards the kitchen, but stopped at the mantelpiece and stroked it. It was his. And that clock; his too. A good clock, with a lion on it of pressed rice. And those two vases: his also; beautiful bronze vases on brown marble feet. And the china dog . . . He caught sight of himself in the mirror, and couldn't help laughing. He looked a fool, with his startled eyes. "Hello!" he said, with a wave of his hand. And again, "Hello!" Then he discovered that he had his nightshirt on back to front—never slept in a nightshirt before in his life, always in his clothes, or in his underwear if there was no watch to come. And now for the kitchen!

But as he turned away he saw her in the mirror, sitting up in bed, looking at him, and she laughed when she noticed that he had seen her. "Hello!" she said, with a wave of the hand, and laughed again. He went back to her, self-conscious and feeling foolish because she had discovered him being silly in front of the mirror. But at the same time he was immensely happy, for she was beautiful. God, she was beautiful, sitting there in bed. He kissed her and asked: "Slept well?" and she nodded: "M'm, m'm, lovely"; and he got her slippers as she swung her legs out of bed. He looked down on her with his arms folded while she was putting them on, and he couldn't help thinking: She is mine too. Mantelpiece, clock, vases, china dog, furniture, house—they are all mine, and so is she.

"Well?" she asked, looking up. "What about the tea?"

"Yes, dammit," he said; "the tea"; and this time he did indeed go to the kitchen.

Three weeks later the order arrived: "Take over from Mate Donker on the *Jan van Gent,* sailing to-morrow with a dredger for Valparaiso under the command of Captain Siemonov." He asked at the office how long the trip would take. If all went well eight months, they said.

Well, there's your future, my boy, there's your freedom. But when the time came it wasn't at all as he'd expected. In fact, quite a lot of things didn't turn out the way he'd expected. Life was a queer business.

CHAPTER TWO

BAS warned him before he went. But who would have time to listen to the gloomy warnings of an old man when he was trying to pack for a trip of eight months in a quarter of an hour?

Bas stood in the doorway, cap in hand, his bald head gleaming in the sunset, and looked at the two children startled from their honeymoon. He looked at them with soft, swimming eyes, and when he was given another drink he said: "Go easy with that Russian fellow, Jan. A good sailor, but a madman in a gale. Don't let yourself be bullied into reckless stunts: think of this nice girl, waiting for you; think of home."

Jan, his arms full of oilskins, noticed at that moment that he had been packing the tea-cosy. "Don't you worry about me, Skipper," he answered; "I'll manage the brute all right. . . . No, sweetheart! I won't want that sextant—get my boots, there's a good girl." When he came back from the kitchen still laden with oilskins, and tried to remember what it was he had gone to look for, he found Bas and Nellie whispering in the doorway. Bas pointed at her forehead with a stubby finger, patted her shoulder, kissed his glass and gave it back to her; when he turned to vanish in the sunset he said: "God be with you, my boy." But he had set Nellie worrying with his alcoholic gabble.

"Jan, love. . . ." Nellie said apprehensively. "Do promise me you'll be careful with that Russian. Bas says. . . ."

"Bas can go and boil his head," he said. "Don't you let yourself be upset by his gabble!" But she went on: Bas said this, Bas said that, and everybody knew that Sjimmenof was not to be trusted, and Joris's Aaltje's husband had. . . .

"His name is Siemonov!" Jan called; "and if anyone knows that man, it's me!"

Now that was downright rubbish. He had never set eyes on the Russian. He knew plenty of stories about him, as did everybody else on the waterfront; he could even draw a portrait of him, with luck; but that was because he had a beard, which made it easy.

"And what about Donker?" Nellie asked. And for the first time since their wedding her eyes suddenly reminded him of her Mamma's. "Every child knows how Donker got his leg broken!"

He threw the oilskins on the floor and yelled at her in his gale-voice: "And now let me tell you, you nagging drill. . . . Ouch!"—she had given him a well-aimed jab in the stomach, and there he sat, the bully, worsted with his own weapons.

"Don't think I care," Nellie lied. "But if they come carrying you into this house on a stretcher, don't say I didn't warn you in good time."

He moaned and cursed, pretending she had hurt him badly; but she wasn't taken in. She made a derisive noise with her lips and climbed the ladder to the attic to get his boots, her strong calves looking very attractive from below, in the red sunlight.

They kissed fervently when she came down. He could almost feel her shoulder-blades crack as she bit his lip with such delicious ferocity and he swung her on to the bed. But the springs bounced her off and there they stood embracing again, by the window, in full view of everyone. In the middle of that embrace she suddenly looked up, her eyes worried and miserable, and whispered: "Oh, Jan, love—do promise me you won't blow yourself up for that Russian. . . ."

22

"Blow myself up? What do you mean?"

"I have known you longer than yesterday, Jan. You're such a damn swank, when anything turns your head. Please do keep one hand for yourself. Promise me, promise. . . ."

"But look here, sweetheart . . . I . . ."

"No! Don't kiss me, you Judas. Promise me. Promise you won't try and wear the Captain's stripes on your sleeves on your first trip. Keep one hand for yourself—for me, for us. Yes?"

"Yes," he said, "I promise."

Who was the lad who had sworn an oath of that kind once before?

The moment he saw the *Jan van Gent* he felt his heart sink.

He knew that Siemonov had the reputation of a dirty neck—but Good Heavens! That a Dutch tug, and one owned by his own Company at that, should look like this—it was downright unbelievable.

The *Jan* was less than three years old—launched in '05, at the same time as the *Albatross*—but she looked twenty. A tattered, worn-out ship, the wooden fenders splintered, the hull buckled and rusty, the funnel peeling and furred with soot, the whole outfit covered with a thick layer of coal-dust and grime. And the crew. . . !

Standing on the quay, his sea-chest on his shoulder, he stared at the hell brood waiting to receive him with toothless grins. Unshaven, criminal heads, with the strangest headgear; knitted ice-bonnets, balaclavas, naval caps with the ribbon torn off: he even spotted a bowler hat amongst them. The bowler belonged to the cook, for someone called "Coo-kie!" and he shuffled off. To be fed by this dirty halfwit was going to be more dangerous than the sea-bats. It was an anxious moment. When he saw one of these gentlemen take a seat on the rails, pantless, to relieve himself in full view of St. Jan's Church and the statue of Her Majesty, Nellie almost got her man back before she had time to make a lonely bed. After all, he had signed on as a mate on a tugboat—not as a dung-raker on a manure-barge.

But suddenly a giant emerged from the Captain's cabin, a bull, waddling on his hind-legs, with a face covered with hair and a sou'wester on back to front, much too small—a piece of tarpaulin on a hayrick. He knew it was Siemonov, even before the bull had sighted him with watery eyes, and called out: "Who are you? Mate? Come on board, then, damn you!"

He went on board, and noticed that the ship stank into the bargain. But he noticed something else: it vibrated with life. The safety-valve throbbed, down in the stokehold, the stokers and furnace men rattled and scraped their shovels with sometimes a bellowing snatch of song; forward and aft, and from all quarters, hobnailed boots were hurrying across the iron deck: it sounded like a beehive, and the King of the Hive was towering in front of him: Uncle Bull come to life. The Captain grasped his hand; he winced and heard some inarticulate noises like, "So! so!" and "Borother" before the giant swung round. Then suddenly the beard parted and from the red gap there flowed such a staggering collection of outlandish oaths that Jan stood and listened in awe. The stream of curses seemed to be aimed at the bunch of beachcombers fumbling with the ropes on the poop: they fumbled deftly and with an indifference that became almost heroic under the torrent of the giant's abuse. The Skipper waddled to the poop, kicked the idiot with the bowler hat out of the way, and aimed his oath stream down the hatch to the messroom—then he fell silent as unexpectedly as he had begun. He cleared his throat and hawked and spat on the deck. When he bent down to inspect the result Jan felt he had seen enough for the present, and went to the chart-room, to stow away his chest and his oilskins for the time being.

The chart-room was in confusion: all kinds of instruments and junk were scattered about it. The centre-piece was a white chamber-pot reposing on the chart of the North Sea and surrounded by a nest of wood-shavings. The connecting-door to the Captain's cabin stood ajar and revealed a glimpse of the sty beyond. It looked as if a sexual crime had been committed in that bunk. The blankets were hanging out of it, as though the body had been dragged away; and the sheet showed a large rent. The walls were smothered under a load of clothes; the couch was buried under a pile of rubbish, and a single hip-boot jutted from underneath it, like a broken leg. The washstand hung open; in the bowl a pair of socks lay soaking in inky water. The wall around it was a map drawn by a madman, a wild confusion of fingermarks, dried soapsuds and long trailing stains like rivers. The stench of sweat and unwashed male was stifling: it battled for supremacy with the smell of wet wool, soiled underclothes, mouldy leather, gin and stale steam. In the far corner of the bunk a red lamp was pouring soot on to a coloured picture post-card, possibly of some Saint or other.

Seeing himself in the dirty mirror over the washstand with the word "хронометрв" written across its face with soap, he couldn't help smiling, a wan smile, and he muttered to himself: "Well, Jan, my boy—here we are!"

Towards evening they sailed: a small, black ship with whiskers of foam, hurrying down a river that gleamed like copper in the sunset.

There was only a tiny stretch of Holland to say good-bye to between the harbour and the outer buoy, with meadows each side, houses and trees and dead-straight dikes running away to the misty horizon. A mill flashed sunsparks from its whirling sails; seagulls screeched and dived in the liquid fire of the river. To some it might seem dreary—and yet to him it looked moving and homely at the commencement of this long trip. Why sail about on that endless sea behind these dunes? Just a meadow between the dikes, a little house with a tuft of willows and a couple of cows in the field—these are enough to fill a lifetime: why has a man to be so greedy? Some of the crew stood looking aft on the poop; Jan Wandelaar stared from the bridge. He had seen this very same view at least a hundred times without any particular emotion; but then it had always been with the knowledge that he would be seeing it again in the next few days. Now eight months without it lay ahead and made everything appear significant and large; in the light of the setting sun even the smallest things grew giant shadows.

At the light-buoy the pilot was taken off, the last man from the shore. He hurried away, the pilot, like a missionary who has suddenly weakened; Jan stayed behind, alone amongst the cannibals. Listen to those stokers caterwauling down below. As if they were roasting someone, and rejoicing in anticipation. The *Jan van Gent* said farewell to the pilot with a blast from her hooter, a hoarse gurgle, and then a long moaning wail, thin and without echo in the boundless space between heaven and sea. She sailed, rolling with the swell, towards a red feather cloud, high and fiery over the western horizon, like a cock's comb. The shore sank away in the darkness that was overtaking them; now they wouldn't see any more of Holland for months on end, except in the symbol of the flag that fluttered on the mizzen-mast.

He stood looking back for a while, full of sadness and self-pity and love for Nellie. Then he went down below to the mess-room and started a letter to her.

"Sweetheart, everything is going nicely. I have a barn of a cabin adjoining the mess-room, which is a kind of saloon with leatherette seats, and there are lots more innovations on board this ship: a winch for the hawsers (that's going to make a difference all right!), a steering engine, a telegraph to the engine-room from the bridge (instead of the tube and whistle, always getting full of seawater), and a Captain who. . . ." He wrote a lot about the Captain, but crossed it out, adding: "He'll be all right in the end. The ship is not very clean and the crew is a bit out of the ordinary, but they look fine fellows who'll be all right in the end. At all events, I must confess I'm looking forward a lot to this trip. Your photograph I pinned on the wall at the foot of my bunk, so I can look at you when I get up or turn in. Now you have gone. . . ." He thought a lot, but it was not the kind of thing one puts in a letter, and he crossed it out. "When I unpacked my chest I found out that I'd forgotten my razor, but you must have noticed that as well. Don't send it to Hull, where we are to pick up the dredger for Akassa, because it would arrive too late and I need a new one anyhow. I am. . . ." No, not in a letter. He crossed it out. "Don't forget to open the top of the stove, before you go to bed after you have half shut the damper in the flue, for otherwise there is a risk of coal fumes and they are dangerous, especially as you aren't used to this stove yet. Say goodbye for me to Mamma and Pa and tell them I was in such a hurry that I couldn't come and say goodbye myself, and if you should feel like writing to me my next address is Lisbon, in case you should have something of importance to tell; it is our first coaling station. I. . . ." No, no; not in a letter. He sat and chewed the penholder, thinking how to hint at it without Bas or Mamma Dijkmans realising what he was talking about. "I miss you a lot?" "I wish you were here?" "I had better not think of you too much," or "I'll go demented?" Not on your life; it would be as if they peeped through the letterbox and caught them in an embrace. "I consider myself to be a very lucky man, being married to you, and . . . ?"

"Mate!" yelled a voice like the last trump, from the bridge. "Number one! Where the hell. . . ."

He wrote: "love—Jan," and hurried out.

That Siemonov was a queer case. He loomed up now in the middle of the night on the bridge, in his underwear with his oilskins thrown over his shoulders, the sleeves dangling empty. He didn't ask any questions, didn't say a word, didn't even respond to "Hullo, Captain. . . ." He just stood motionless on the stairs that led up to the bridge, staring at the youngster pacing up and down. What the devil else was one to do under the eyes of that ogre, in the middle of the night? And then, like a mirage, he was gone. Vanished into the darkness, and no more sign or sound of him until he came to take over. Jan asked the man at the wheel if the Captain made a habit of that kind of thing: popping up and frightening the hide off everybody with his lunatic stare. The man at the wheel said: "Ay," without taking his eyes off the compass, like a clergyman reading the Bible.

Thank goodness the first engineer (another of the 'fine fellows, who'd be all right in the end') felt like a pipe and hammered on the partition between their cabins with a slipper after the dog-watch, calling: "Hey, sleep-walker! Got a smoke on you?" Jan went along to the man's cabin to give him a pipeful, and there lay the Chief, long, thin and bald, stretched out on his bunk in a cabin like a miniature boudoir. There were pictures and souvenirs everywhere, and knick-knacks crowded the walls; there were also rows of portraits mass-framed or mounted separately. Over the washstand there were photographs of a fat child

in bell-bottom trousers, with a face like the monkeys who
hear, see and speak no evil, and the legend in gilt lettering:
Our Little Sun. He had even got flowers in his cabin,
artificial geraniums in a pot which was suspended on chains
from the ceiling, and which swung about as the ship rolled,
like a censer. A lethal thing, that pot, for its orbit covered
practically the whole of the standing-room in the cabin, and
anyone who hadn't got eyes in the back of his head was
bound to fall sooner or later a victim to those deadly blooms.
A murky, pink light gave the cabin a rather sinister
appearance. The lamp was covered by an orange shade
with a hole in it through which a ray of light caught the
bald head of the Chief. The hole was intended, the scarecrow explained, to provide some light to read by in his bunk
at night, if he could not sleep and felt like some quiet
diversion. The books were lined up on a small shelf at the
foot of the bunk: *The Correct Letter-Writer*; *Your Dreams
Explained*; *Manual of Marine Engineering*; *Woman's Flesh
by Auction*.

They smoked a pipe in the pink dusk of this unfading
sunset; the silence in the cabin was soothing and the only
things that moved were the floral censer and the Chief's
watch, hanging on the wall over his pillow, and sliding to
and fro with the rolling of the ship, like a pendulum
without a clock. The Chief asked him all about himself,
and in his turn told him all about his wife, called Alie, and
his five kids: Piet, Freek, Hennie, Doortje and Zus. There
they were—they looked a bit on the fat side, but the camera
moved. The Chief didn't say much about the Captain; it
was obvious that those two didn't take to each other.
Siemonov was skipper of an ice-breaker, he said, that came
to Amsterdam for an overhaul; when he was there he spotted
the *Jan* on the stocks and fell in love with her to such an
extent that he signed himself up in a permanent contract
with the owners. A master-sailor, undoubtedly, but . . . oh
well, young fellow you wait and see. They gassed on a bit
about Women and Religion and agreed that the Socialists
had all sorts of wonderful plans but were unfortunately
no great shakes themselves. Then, suddenly, the Chief fell
asleep, without Jan noticing the change for quite a while.

He went back to his cabin and fell on his bunk without

taking off his clothes; in another hour he was due for the next watch, so it wouldn't be worth the trouble. While he was lying on his back, alone for the first time since they sailed, the depression that he had managed to keep down all these hours suddenly got the better of him. When he had said that he thought the ship was filthy, the Chief had grinned and answered: "Look at me, young man, and have a guess." Guess what? "Guess my age." Forty-four? "No, sir; thirty-five. Yes, and why? Sailed for seven years, and during that time not more than four months' leave, all told. It's the same with the ships: slave, slave, until they fall apart—and leave? Never. It's a fact, anyone who looks for salvation in the tugboat-service. . . ."

Jan glanced at the photograph of Nellie smiling serenely at the foot of his bunk. It was certainly a lovely photo.

When the *Jan van Gent* came churning into Hull harbour, full steam ahead, all the hands off duty were peering over the rail, in order not to miss the first sight of the tow.

The tow was an important item. For three months on end that bulky carcass would be lumbering in their wake, an object requiring unceasing vigilance and care—the nurses were curious about their new charge. "Another of those poxy cutters, if you ask me," said little Abel the stoker, who collected copies of *Mon Plaisir* and knew the word for love in every language under the sun. The cook squeaked that it was a lighter pregnant with a tiny tug; but Stobbe, the bo'sun, almost as huge as the captain, and with about as much feeling, roared: "A dredger—and get the hell back to your work, you lazy bastards."

"How shipshape that little dredger looks, eh? Look at that paint, just look at it, bo'sun. Good example for us. And that pretty red piping on the waterline; and those elegant little dredger scoops, so neat with their black paint and white edges. But don't go sailing into dirty weather with those little beauties, for then they start jumping about and anyone who happens to get underneath one won't have a chance." Apprentice Henkie, whose hair was so fair that he looked like an old man from a distance, knew a yarn about some chap who once survived a blow from one of those buckets, and who. . . . "Shut up, kid! What are you talking about—survived? Go and tell that one to the Marines." "Honest!" said Henkie, "I saw with my own eyes the dent in his nut, under his hair; you could put your hand in it and he used to hide borrowed guilders there; then challenge people to undress him and find where he'd put the coins. If they didn't find the guilders he was allowed by the rules of the game to keep them." "Made him rich, I suppose?" little Abel asked, with his hand behind his ear. "I don't know about that," Henkie said; "I'm only going by what someone told me." "Ah," said little Abel, "that's a very different story."

Siemonov waddled ashore as soon as the gangplank had hit the quay. He ran off as if he were chasing some elusive prey but all he wanted was to get hold of the owners of that dredger and its papers. "Not a dog ashore!" he shouted at Jan: "Anyone who tries to go to de wimmen you break de legs for him." Jan had known him for two days now, and said: "Ay, ay, Captain." Cook had overheard it (Cook overheard everything), and after a meeting of the committee in the foc'sle he came hurrying along the deck in his carpet slippers, squealing: "Mate, Mate, Mister Mate! The boys can hear a leak down below! Hurry, hurry!" But Jan had danced with the mermaid long enough by now to know her song. He said: "If you don't get out of my sight, you smelly soup-pedlar, I'll let you hear a leak that'll drown you!" Cook grasped his bowler-hat, a flabbergasted man, and shuffled back to the foc'sle with the verdict: no go, boys; he's too wise.

At the messroom-table after supper, Bout, the second engineer, a quiet man who was commonplace and who'd remain commonplace all his life, until the draught from God's Great Cellar blew out his light, said: "Good for you, Mate. They are just like women: the harder you beat them, the more they love you. Look at the Captain: they love him —and yet I wouldn't care to count the bruises he's given them these last few years." It was a homely sight to watch Bout crushing a potato in the gravy-boat after everybody had finished: a good-hearted, fat, motherly chap he was, and never out of sorts or boisterous in his laughter.

The Chief, too, said that he ought to give those brutes

hell; and Jan thought: they aren't so bad after all, these people. Who knows—in a month or so I may find that I don't want to leave this rusty tub either. But, by God, a coat of paint she shall have, whether the Russian likes it or not; and as for that brass. . . .

When Siemonov came back, with a face like a thundercloud, the crew was polishing the brass. He stood a moment taken aback; then he hunted Jan out in the chart-room and demanded: "Where do you come from, borother? A cookery-school?" But borother stood his ground. "From a ship whose Captain knew the smell of paint." The Russian had some difficulty in swallowing the retort, but when he did explode, it was about something else.

Orders had been received from the owners of that stinking dredger, saying she was not to sail because they didn't consider it safe in the present state of the weather. The glass had fallen steadily during the night and looked a bit alarming now. A stiff south-westerly wind was blowing, bringing with it sheets of driving rain. Because everything seemed to point to dirty weather ahead, the Underwriters insisted that sailing should be postponed until the sky had cleared. This meant that the crew would have to lie berthed-up, biting their nails in boredom, for days to come. And to make things worse, there was a fair in town. A blessed fair, if you please! The Captain's curses were like the first rumblings of a volcano on the verge of an eruption. The threatening sparks of that eruption began to fall thickly on the heads of the crew who, quite oblivious to the warning, yearned for the forbidden land of the fair-ground. A fair, a fair! Raucous music blared in the streets; crowds of singing people jostled past—and here they were, like outcasts, with idle hands, eyes glued to the sky, and legs that itched to join the dance. Siemonov prowled about on the deck, in and out of his cabin, like a watchdog; the bo'sun was the only one who was enjoying himself.

The Chief, busy rolling his cigarettes for the next day, remarked, sombrely shaking his head: "To-morrow he may be able to keep the lid on, with luck—but the day after they'll blow it off; and then heaven only knows when they'll get back, and in what condition. Yes, young fellow . . ."— and his large pink tongue glistened in the lamplight as he

31

licked a cigarette—"that comes of all this slave driving. If these people could have a bit of leisure now and again, they would behave themselves." Bout, the second engineer, joined them in the mess-room. He had been writing a letter to his mother in his cabin. "Dear Ma"—and then a weather forecast with an extract from the log—"Your loving son, Thys." "Going to the fair?" he asked. The Chief said: "Well, if I hadn't been slaving so much. . . ." Jan began to notice that the Chief's conversation was a bit too full of slavery; but he was still a fine fellow, who'd be all right in the end.

The next morning the despairing Siemonov lay anchored to a bottle in his bunk, with hell in his eyes and more vodka behind his beard than his breath could soak up. "Anything!" he groaned. "I can stand anything, but not this damned waiting, waiting, waiting." But fate sent a consoling angel in the person of a thin, morose captain with rubbery legs, who came to inquire whether the Dutchman would be willing to tow his ship to South Shields, for scrap. Siemonov embraced this lamp-post of a man, called him borother, gave him a drink and thrust a cigar in his beard (for the man wore one too, like a bunch of cobwebs on his chest). After this they left together to have a look at the ship. The wind whined sadly under the doors when the messroom-hatch was shoved open and Bout came stumbling down the stairs, fleeing from the rain. "You watch," said Bout, "now we're going to do some sailing, chum; now you'll be able to see Siem dancing." The Chief scrambled out of his bunk, where he had been enjoying *Woman's Flesh by Auction*. He looked sinister in his underwear which displayed bits of dangling tape; he was wearing black stockings which gave his appearance a ghostly quality, as if his legs had been sawn off below the knee. He asked if it had come off. What had come off? The deal with that Englishman, fathead. "What do you think?" Bout asked. "The owners will be lucky if old Siem wires them at all, for he's half-seas-over now, believe me."

Well, he was certainly that. He came back on board at a gallop and started cursing even before he'd got the gang-plank down. He bawled the crew out of the foc'sle, kicked the third engineer out of his bunk (a pale, hollow-eyed kid, who had been seasick ever since they left; Jan had hardly seen him yet). He had the bo'sun hint at a tot of rum for everyone if they made high tide. A quarter of an hour later the mooring-ropes crashed on to the deck, in the nick of time, for the telegraph to the engine-room had already rung out: Full Ahead. The thunder of the wash under the stern drowned the squeaking of a seedy youth, who had come running out of the office of the dredger-owners. "When will you be back?" he shouted, and Siemonov bellowed "To-morrow!" The youth went on about something with a harassed face, pointing at the office; but the wash churning up against the quay drenched him with a burst of spray and he backed away. "To-morrow—or never!" Siemonov roared as the *Jan van Gent* swung into the harbour. The youth stood staring after them, apparently fearing it would be the latter.

In the trees the rain foamed and spluttered, lashed by the wind.

Up river lay a tall three-master, high on the water, with a small emergency crew on board—rather an odd collection. The *Jan van Gent* drew alongside, striking her hull with a thud. In contrast to the sailing ship, the tug seemed a mere mongrel of a craft, a dog at the feet of a lady. For less than half an hour the tug lay smoking to leeward of the *Scottish Maiden*. During that time the safety valve screamed beside the soot-belching funnel, the winches rattled, the deck echoed with the banging of hawsers and the clatter of hob-nailed boots. Jan boarded the windjammer by a rope-ladder thrown out by her crew; he took two seamen up with him to secure the hawser. Siemonov's voice was everywhere, bellowing in the distance, roaring through the megaphone to the men above; his oaths cut like the lashes of a whip on bare skin. The deckhands hurried, speechless and panting, dragging hawsers, cables, rope-carriers. The gang of the *Scottish Maiden* looked on idiotically. Good Lord, what a bunch! Jan chased them forward and made them lend a hand at hauling in the hawser: "Get a move on, lads; jump to it, damn you!"

When he went to fasten the end of the wire to the last link of the anchor-chain, Siemonov's voice cut him short

with the order to take the wire through the hawse-hole and
to secure it to the bollards on deck. It was a legitimate
command, for it saved a lot of time—otherwise he would
have had to detach the anchor from its chain and lash it
to the deck—but it was foolhardy. If that wire started
chafing against the bow in heavy seas, it might easily snap
and then good-bye to your tow. Well, thought Jan, this is it;
now let's dig our heels in good and proper. He wanted to
call back; but, holy Moses, if he thought for a moment that
he, poor fish, could rap the knuckles of Bull Siemonov, who
for twenty-five years. . . . The Captain repeated the order,
charged with such a load of abuse that even the panting
slaves below deck looked up. It drained Jan's blood from
his cheeks, but he thought: all right, you big brute, all
right—but you'll be sorry for this. There went the wire,
through the hawse-hole, heavily fendered to lessen the
chafing as much as possible. Even this seemed to take too
long for the Russian's liking. But take care: there are limits.
Perhaps they do their towing in Russia with a bare hawser,
in Holland we're different. Yes, that's right: bellow your
head off. But don't come too near a naked flame with that
big mouth, or you'll be blown to bits, you old boozer.

The hawser had hardly been secured when the *Jan
van Gent* began to pull. The mooring ropes of the windjammer splashed into the water; the thin captain on the
companion shouted: "Hey, hey! Easy!" But anyone who
grumbled at an odd scratch at a time like this was an idiot.
Siemonov paid no heed to his feeble croaking. The *Jan
van Gent* hung panting with a heavy list, like a whipped
horse in the traces. On the river the tow had to be steered
so that, in a continually varying course, the swing of the
vessel was allowed for. It was a tricky business in this narrow
channel with such a high-rigged craft. The wind had
freshened from moderate to strong, with sudden squalls.
To tow a tall vessel like her, fully rigged, right round
between the muddy banks was no light matter. But
Siemonov himself had taken the wheel and he proved himself a master. The manoeuvre was carried out without a
hitch. Now they went down the river with nothing to worry
about; they had made the high tide and the Captain was
all smiles. He ordered the bo'sun to give the crew the rum

he'd promised and whacked Jan's shoulder with a blow that jarred his knees. "Well done, borother, good work. Here, have a drink!" The pilot got a drink too; it was all very matey on that bridge. "Pingg! Your health!" Yes—the tug-boat service was the thing to be in.

Off the Humber Lightship the pilot was dropped, and they set course for Flamborough Head. Because the wind was favourable Siemonov signalled to the *Scottish Maiden* that she had better set some sail. It was a long time before there were any visible results, as if those sea-cooks over there had to decide between themselves what "sail" was, before hoisting a sheet or two of lower canvas—very clumsily. "More sail!" Siemonov signalled, and had the code included oaths he would have run up the lot. He cursed his Mate, but Jan could take it now. He was beginning to take a liking to this monster, forgetting his recklessness and his senseless roaring. The way the Bull skated about on that river was wonderful —something to tell one's children about. There are sailors and sailors. Some know their job and that's all there is to it, but others make an art of it. The way Siemonov negotiated those river bends was a joy; it gave a feeling of beauty to anyone with a sense for such a thing.

Cook brought coffee, with a disgusted face, for it blew a lot by now and a tray can jump the rail before you know what's happened. They drank their coffee in appreciative gulps, looking aft all the time at the bunglers on the tow. They were trying to set a couple of stay-sails, but it looked like a nurse hanging out napkins in a gale. Little Abel, who had come up from the stoke-hole to wrench at the ventilators, which were blowing too much wind down, grinned tooth-lessly at the bridge and shouted: "The Scottish Lass is stripping off her clothes!" But Siemonov didn't think it funny. He looked from the windjammer to the sky and back, gulping his coffee as if his throat were a drain. All the while his face was as black as the western sky. On the *Scottish Maiden* the diminutive men toddled crazily about on the rolling deck, as if they were playing hide and seek. The thin captain was standing at the wheel on the poop, his beard a pennant in the wind. He waved his arms and shook his fists and must have been screaming like a madman, for the other specks hesitated a second and toddled away in the opposite direction. Then the captain—after a pathetic pantomime of arms and legs, comical to look at from a distance—let go of the wheel to go forward where the crew were playing with a stay-sail. The ship went off her course, the sails flapped, and the whole crowd was swept off its feet. Jan roared with laughter, and everybody on deck guffawed, except the third engineer, poor boy, who had just come up from below to vomit and who now hurried back, ill and miserable, thinking he had been the cause of all this hilarity. Siemonov asked suddenly: "Hey, you. Can you sail a wind-jammer?" Jan said, innocently: "Of course!" only to realize what he had said when the hand of the Captain crashed down on his shoulder, with: "Good, borother! Get yourself on board of that barge—and get a move on!"

Well, there we were. This was it. "Promise me, Jan, think of me, of us. . . ." Too late. The crew of the starboard boat had started swinging her out already, to the bloodcurdling roaring of the Captain. "Hurry up, Wandelaar is taking over the tow—Bo'sun! Come on up to take the Mate's place! Brega! Kaap! Collect your gear, you two—you're to sail that jammer! Don't stand and gape, you lubbers, hurry up!"

An order was an order. If Jan was a little nervous as he hastily crammed some things into his spare oilskin, it had nothing to do with fear, or a bad conscience. Oh dear, no. It was the fever of adventure. Yet, it was odd that at that moment he should have forgotten to look at the little portrait of Nellie which was staring him in the face while he was rummaging in a drawer for a pair of pants.

He jumped into the boat, and the deck-hands took the oars. There was an immense swell running; it was quite a job to avoid being capsized by the hawser; for the captain with the cobwebs over there was steering the crookedest course in Christendom, and every time he tacked, the treacherous hawser jumped out of the water with a terrifying twang. But all went well. They got safely alongside and climbed up the swaying rope-ladder to the deck of the *Scottish Maiden*. What looked funny from afar was tragic at close quarters; a man had broken his leg when a flapping sail flung him against the rail. The captain stood at the wheel, with rolling eyes in a face overgrown with beard, as

36

if he were sailing the *Flying Dutchman* round the Cape. Jan didn't know much English, but it was enough. First he had his boat hauled up by his men, Bulle Brega and Kees de Kaap, two heavyweights with the faces of bruisers and the hearts of young girls. The thin captain went wild when told that he had to hand over the command of his ship; he protested in a screaming voice that broke with a sob when he was pushed away from the wheel. Jan put the vessel back upon her course; she pulled hard because of the flapping stay-sail; they had better do something about that or there'd be accidents. He called Bulle Brega, handed over the wheel to him, and, when the captain looked as if he were up to some monkey-business, he said, with a blush: "You keep low sir, or I will put you flat." As he made his way forward he wondered if he'd said the right thing. Of course he hadn't; he ought to have said "I shall." Blimey, that English was full of snags.

The emergency crew of the vessel had watched the boarding party arrive with stupid, terrified eyes; now they stood shivering in a bunch on the foc'sle, a tiny herd of sad mules. The devil might know what they were, certainly not sailors. He split up the bunch into two teams and handed over one of them to Kees de Kaap; then they started clearing the stay-sail, with more kicking and cursing than hauling. But they managed it, and Bulle Brega held that wheel as if the ship were running on rails. Once the sheets and the halyards had been sorted out, the *Scottish Maiden* gave up her antics. She pitched heavily, being in ballast, and her tops swayed ominously against the leaden sky; but she stuck to her course.

As soon as the deck was shipshape, he went down to look for the captain, and found him in his cabin, head in hands, a bottle of solace in front of him on the table. He whimpered about "the wife" and "my kids at home," plucking in his wet beard for a lost cigar-stub. It was bad to see a drunkard like him in command of so elegant a ship; but the sailing trade was dying out and this was his last trip. There was nothing for it, then, but to let him mumble on in that vast cabin, with its fraying plush and the gilt peeling off the mouldy panelling, alone with his bottle and the reflection of his despair in the polished mahogany table—God help him.

The chart-room was a cubicle on the companion; Jan decided to make his bed on the bench to be at hand in case of trouble. He ordered Kees de Kaap to take his belongings to the foc'sle and, as acting bo'sun, to knock some obedience into the mules. When that was done he had the lights trimmed, for they were sailing into the night. The wind had freshened even more. The *Scottish Maiden* must have been a sprinter in her palmier days, for she skimmed the sea, sails bellying, and ran after the tug at a speed of nine knots. He saw that the *Jan van Gent* had a job to keep ahead of her, and ordered the three shivering skeletons of the lee-watch to keep an eye open for signals ahead. In the chart-room he checked the barometer by the flickering light of a match. It didn't look too cheerful—the glass had fallen so much that he gave a long low whistle. But on his round of the deck everything seemed to be lashed shipshape; there was nothing left to do but to sail and keep one's fingers crossed. Let it blow, thought Jan, but heaven save me from those sea-cooks.

Bulle Brega was at the wheel, looking, in the dusk, like a tree rooted to the deck, with his great fat legs. He was a fellow you could trust with anything—there was such simple goodness in his face. Kees de Kaap, though smaller, was almost as broadshouldered as Brega, so he wasn't exactly a baby in arms either. With these two stalwarts he'd be able to go a long way, if the weather wasn't impossible.

And then, all of a sudden, a stranger emerged from the galley like a mole out of its tunnel: a grey-haired gnome, the mere sight of him enough to make one seasick. He wore a little cap, grown to his skull like the cup on an acorn, and a kind of apron covered with grease-smears and blood-stains. He was carrying a steaming pan, and he announced: "Me cookie, here dinner ready." He then put the pan on the deck, waddled back to his hole and disappeared into it again. The pan contained a hash of meat and rice. They called Kees de Kaap and the three of them made short work of this windfall. The gnome was probably filthy, but his grub was all right; it certainly put heart into a man amidst all this gloom. The wind whistled malevolently through the rigging, the swell became choppy and confused, and the sky was full of scurrying clouds tinged with patches of greenish light. It was a queer sky to look at ; it seemed crammed with everything one didn't want. After Jan had gone to have another look at the barometer he lit an after-dinner pipe with the same match he'd struck to see by, just as if nothing were the matter. But the glass hung scowling on the wall. He went out into the wind again, with a streak of sparks flying from his pipe. He gazed at the sea and the sky. The menace he faced was frightening and exhilarating at the same time—for this was his first command.

Jan Wandelaar: twenty-five years old and already a captain—life was good.

At nine the tugboat flashed the order to shorten sail. The order was superfluous, really, for the *Scottish Maiden* caught up with the *Jan* so fast now, with every gust, that they could have hailed one another but for the hell-cat screaming of the wind in the rigging. To take in the lower and stay-sails was no easy task; the emergency crew were too seasick to stand and they needed both hands to hang on to the rails. To chase them up the shrouds and out on to the yards would be like ordering monkeys to put out a fire. With his two deck-hands, and even eventually a couple of the roughs from down below who seemed to have realized that their lives were at stake, Jan managed the foresails, hanging in the foot-ropes over the yards. It was a tough job and after they had furled the mainsail, the stay-sails and the crossjack they were beaten by the spanker. A treacherous squall hit the ship like the blast of an explosion. There was a report like a gunshot, a tearing screech that suggested the death-yell of a monster— and the lashings of the spanker hung flapping in the breast-backstays, like giant birds in agony. That was a bitter blow: to keep this wild horse hove-to without a spanker might well prove to be impossible, They scrambled up the ratlines and were tossed about like plums on a branch that was being shaken by a madman. They clung to the backstays for dear life, and managed to hack and tear the tatters of the spanker out of the shrouds. By the time they had finished, there blew a strong gale that made the *Scottish Maiden* overhaul the tug as fast on her bare rigging as she did with her sails set an hour before.

The night was pitch dark; huge mountains of water battered her hull, leaping sky high and crashing down on the deck with peals of thunder, and with a force that made the masts tremble like flagpoles. The ship pitched and tossed; her toplights streaked like comets across the sky; everything on board that could shift, began to roll about; everything that was hanging loose clanked and rattled. The ship seemed possessed by some supernatural power. The *Jan van Gent* could only be spotted at odd moments whenever a rift was torn in the clouds, and a splash of moonlight came racing across the water, picking out for an instant a foam-smothered black creature, with its ghostly ray, then racing off again into darkness beyond. Gone was the joy and the pride of the first command: there was nothing left in the world but a desperate ship, fighting for her life, and water, water, always more water, and higher and angrier seas foaming, whirling, crashing, seething—a deluge, the end of the world.

Jan tried to hold the wheel with Bulle Brega, he felt that the *Jan van Gent* was pulling at right angles, she couldn't keep the tow hove-to. He heard a shot in the terrific din, but couldn't think where it came from; then he saw, through the deluge of flying water, a glow ahead, a ruddy gleam, flickering on and off, like flames in the wind. Lightning? It couldn't be that—it must be fire from the funnel of the tug. And then—oh the simple heroism of fools!—a man came to the companion, like an apparition out of hell. He dragged himself hand over hand along the rails on the lee side. Three breakers nearly washed him into the beyond, but the man wouldn't let himself be caught and each time he popped up again from his refuge behind the rails, where he had been squatting down patiently, until he could seize his chance. When he finally reached the companion he turned out to be Kees de Kaap, who told them, yelling each word through his cupped hands, that the *Jan van Gent* had been thrown broadside on, that she was tearing her guts out but couldn't heave them to any more. Now the wire towing-hawser was tearing their stem, striking sparks, and within a few minutes they'd be cut adrift.

So that explained the fire-glow ahead: sparks struck off the pitching stem by the wire. The shot he heard must have been the dolphin-striker giving way. The realisation brought one fleeting moment of justifiable pride; he was jolly well right when he wanted to lock the hawser to the anchor-chain. If the Russian had let him have his way this wouldn't have happened. But the fun didn't last long—for if they were cut loose there would be a windjammer adrift in a hurricane with three sound men on board and a choir of seasick landlubbers to sing their requiem. He thought of dropping the anchors, but the idea was knocked out of his head when a shudder shook the ship. The helm spun with the force of a paddle-wheel, and Bulle Brega was hurled, God preserve him, head over heels into the night. The gale howled in the rigging, swirled the ship broadside on and pressed so hard that she seemed to be nearly flattened. The two men, hanging on the eyebolts of the companion that dipped precipitously, looked right down into the raging sea. Then the ship trembled, tried to stagger back on her keel, only to be flattened down once more with an even dizzier list.

Many heroes have found watery graves; but for some men the sea waits in vain. After Jan had been bowled over by a great weight of water he realised, as soon as he could breathe again, that not only was he still hanging on to the deck and the ship had not capsized yet, but that someone was lying by his side, and that someone was Bulle Brega. He didn't think this strange until later; at that moment the resurrection of the dead Bulle gave him back his trust in the indestructibility of life. He dragged himself with his two men to the weather-side rail and tried from there to reach a mast.

When the *Jan van Gent*, more like a half-submerged seal than a ship, lurched past, wheezing and rolling, the *Scottish Maiden* was hoisting stay-sails. Quite an achievement for three men, but a man can do things in an emergency he could never do in cold blood, not even if he could gain immortality by doing so. Those stay-sails meant salvation to the *Scottish Maiden* and to the stokers of the *Jan van Gent* ordeal by fire; for Siemonov yelled for ever more steam—the windjammer raced away on her few rags with such a speed that her toplights, feeble glow-worms in the darkness, threatened to vanish out of sight.

The sea and the gale, robbed of their prey, continued other pranks, including the uprooting of the topmasts. The

Scottish Maiden, with Jan and Kees and Bulle clinging to her kicking wheel like men drowning, weathered the storm, lifting her bows to the sky or plunging them beneath the great waves which burst asunder at her stem with terrific explosions and cloudbursts of spray like a hail of flying glass. But she sailed and she floated and she lived on, she took the giant waves like a steeplechaser taking fences—ally-oop, and she was over. Then came a wave so high that she seemed to stand up on her hind-legs. She threatened to turn turtle, but managed to scramble on to the crest, and was hurled down into a void so deep that she seemed to be flying. An earthquake, a deafening collision, and a thundering avalanche of topmasts, yards, cordage, and tons of canvas, crumpled down upon her deck. Another wave like a landslide, and she went right under from stem to stern. When she emerged again she had a pile of debris on her poop as high as a house, and was dragging a tangled mass behind her. But from the ruins three minute figures wriggled themselves free, and started hacking and tugging and fumbling. Now that all the overhead stuff had come down and been washed overboard she kept a lot steadier. She ran without fuss and obeyed the helm. Bulle Brega had a dislocated arm and Jan had had to cut Kees free from a rope which had caught his leg and threatened to drag him overboard. Of the scratch crew there was no sign. The ship seemed to be deserted except for the three of them. But who was this, crawling from his hole? The mole with the bonnet and the gory apron! He hauled himself along the rail towards the poop with one hand, while in the other he carried—seeing was believing—a kettle of coffee to revive their spirits. He didn't say anything—there was still too much noise in the universe for conversation—he merely handed the kettle to Jan and shuffled back, one hand on the rail. The sea and gale, as if abashed by such a stroke of boldness, let him pass unharmed. Only when the mole had vanished into his hole did they start again to rage and roar. The coffee wasn't half bad, not tepid even. They drank from the spout, three swigs each, until there was no coffee left. Then they let go of the kettle and it flew away. The world was full of marvels, and the cook was one of them.

Anyone who thought the worst was over now was

mistaken. True, the wind didn't freshen any more during the rest of the night, and about day-break it even seemed as if the gale had begun to blow itself out. But the seas became higher as they got farther away from the land. In the end it was impossible to stand, for the ship tossed and pitched so much. But as she kept a steady course and no change of sail seemed called for, Jan and Kees de Kaap lashed themselves to the wheel. Heaven knew where they were sailing to at twelve knots—the avalanche of the rigging had smashed the compass cover and knocked a few spokes out of the wheel, but it still turned, and the ship obeyed. Bulle had gone off to the foc'sle with his dislocated arm, to find out if any of the scratch crew were still sufficiently alive to push the joint back in its place. It would seem not, for he did not come back. However, he might have fainted, for having an arm set isn't everyone's idea of fun, and Kees told Jan, hollering in his ear, that Bulle was a coward, and liable to faint at the sight of blood.

The *Jan van Gent* was nowhere to be seen; perhaps she had thought, when she saw the wreckage floating by, that the disaster in that wave-trough had been the end of them. She was probably fishing among the debris to see if she could find any sign of life. The pitching and rolling became worse the more the wind dropped; an eerie, jerky tossing, with frightening joltings and sickening lurches. Within an hour they were squinting with headache. Queer, mad thoughts obsessed their brains: Don't fall asleep; don't fall asleep; hell what a headache; don't fall asleep; no spokes here; all spokes gone; dammit, don't fall asleep. In front of their eyes little red eels started wriggling and squirming, swimming worms in a streaky fog. Don't fall asleep; hell where's my hand; easy, ship, easy. Lord—what a job it was to open one's eyes. And once they were open they didn't see; they just squinted inwards. It was hours before they saw again, and when they did see, the sight that met them was the day breaking. Yellow and tear-smudged with rain, a faltering glimmer in a storm-torn sky. Then the question came to Jan. How could he possibly see the dawn now they were heading west? He tried to look down and when he had managed it he realised that he was hanging back to front on the wheel, Kees de Kaap hung the other way round, with a rolling head and dangling arms, fast asleep. But the moment a sail quivered he turned the ship away from the wind, like an automaton.

Towards sunrise things were at their worst. The ship swayed so wildly that one of the mizzen-shrouds— the mizzen-top was the only one left—snapped like a gunshot. It was nothing compared with the crashes that had shaken them overnight, but it startled them out of the trance-like sleep that left them dangling limply over the wheel with wide-open eyes. Life was perhaps no more than a feather blown from God's hand—but if you'd struggled for what seemed centuries to keep this side of the grave, you couldn't help fearing for that precious life of yours when bangs of that kind go off. That shroud was a bad business. One more of those lurches and the whole lot would snap, and once the mast got loose on the weather side, it was then good-bye to everything. The only solution would be to lower the topmast in order to lessen the sway. But he hadn't got the courage or the legs, and now that his eye had got fixed on that top-mast it just stuck there, because he was too tired to look away. If only that creaking and groaning would stop, he thought, it wouldn't be so bad; he might even get a wink of sleep. But the creaking and groaning went on with merciless persistence, to and fro, to and fro. He couldn't see what it was without looking down, and his eyes were too tired for that. Yes, yes—he knew of course. Jan, boy, if you don't lower that topmast it will be good-bye. He wanted to do it all right, but just couldn't. Then fate gave him a shove.

The thin captain strutted the deck like a cock, after a night with his head in his feathers, to greet the dawn with drunken crowing. He was so drunk that he walked the swaying deck with an ease impossible to any sober man; he just didn't notice that the world was awash. He had spotted two pirates at the helm of his ship and was making tracks towards them in order to assert his authority. The appearance of this melancholy rooster brought Jan back to his senses, in the same way as Bulle Brega's resurrection had jolted him into action during the night. He detached himself from Kees and the wheel and tried to get hold of the drunkard before he missed a step and found himself washed overboard. But a revengeful wave came swirling over the

44

rail, knocking the captain off his feet and hurling him into a corner, where he floundered in a bath of hissing foam, as if he were condemned for his sins to drown in a flood of beer. The same wave caused another of the shrouds to snap with a twang; now death was strumming the two remaining chords with an ominous sound. Jan forgot the captain and shook Kees, who was so put out by this roughness that he let the ship luff up for the first time since he fell asleep. But the sight of the collapsing shroud cured him quick enough. They lashed the wheel so that it would steer the ship unattended for a while, and clambered up the ratlines.

To lower that topmast might cost both of them their lives; but if they didn't take the risk the end was certain. They were tossed about so ferociously on the mizzen-top that they lost all sense of height and space. After five minutes of frantic work all they seemed to be doing was to cling, desperately, on to the pendulum of a huge clock which was trying to shake them off and fling them into hell—then clock, pendulum and all crashed out of the sky. Surely this was the end. But no, it was nothing. They were still alive. All they had done was to lower the topmast, as they set out to do. They looked at each other with sheepish faces, as they hung on to a pole that turned out to be the cross-tree which was caught in a jungle of ropes. The resinous smell of splintered wood was their first sensation in a new world. "Done it," Kees said, and the thunder of the flapping sails sounded like gigantic applause.

They slid down the backstays, which now could easily stand the tension; when they set foot on deck again the sea seemed to have quietened down all of a sudden, for they could stroll up and down as easily as the drunken captain did. Kees took the wheel again and put her back on her course; Jan went to get help to cope with the devastation. The foc'sle was still cut off by the surf. Jan hammered on the door of the galley. The mole popped his head out and understood everything, even before it had been turned into English; he shuffled to the wheel, with the same disdain for the elements he had shown when he brought the coffee, and took over from Kees with the casualness of a man who had done this sort of thing before. Kees and Jan dragged the captain—still miraculously alive in the shelter of the rail—

to the hatchway of the cabin, opened the doors, and let go
of him. He rolled down the staircase, with a thud and a
splash at the bottom, and having thus got rid of him they
shut the door again with a funereal reverence. Then they
attacked the tangle on deck with a feeling of superiority.

Half an hour later the deck was clear. The sea looked
played out; the swell was subsiding and the gale had dropped
to a stiff breeze. It might be an illusion that the crisis was
over, but for Jan the tension had gone and the indifference
of exhaustion overpowered him. The mole had married
himself to that wheel—no worry there, he'd sail on till
doomsday and never bat an eye. Jan waded with Kees
de Kaap to the foc's'le to look for Bulle Brega, with a lantern.
They didn't stay below for long; the stench of vomit and
human excrement was not inviting. The emergency crew
lay scattered on the floor like corpses—a sorry spectacle of
scared, filthy men whom terror and seasickness had turned
into animals for a night, and who now, exhausted and overcome, lay miserably snoring wherever fate had toppled
them. Some of them looked indeed like corpses—their arms
stiffly extended, their legs crooked and their upturned eyes
leaden and lustreless; but they moaned if they were kicked,
and their fingers twitched, so there was still life in them.
Bulle Brega was found in a lower bunk, where he must have
dragged himself and where, having fainted with pain, he
remained until they hauled him out. His shoulder looked
ugly and they dared not fumble with it; best thing was to
leave him, in case by moving him they made things worse.
The sea might have subsided, but there was still enough
of a swell running to skittle over two men carrying a
third.

Kees de Kaap wouldn't sleep. He stayed on deck to keep
an eye on the mole and the sails. The mizzen-mast was all
right now; the ship was responsive, and there was no need
to dodge the wind. They could head for somewhere now—
but where? The *Jan van Gent* was nowhere within sight,
nor was the coast. The breeze must be south-westerly, but
it was impossible to be certain, for the compass was useless.
They must be making five to six knots, close to the wind;
the *Scottish Maiden* seemed to revel in it. Behind them the
sky was still pitch black. The waves were green monsters,

veined like marble, with sparkling crests of foam. The black clouds held half the horizon locked in their embrace, so that the ship seemed to be sailing out of the arms of a dark power. But ahead, to the west, where the shore ought to be, there was nothing. An endless plain of teeming water, blue, shining, merging into an endless sky, pure with light. No horizon, not a ship, not a bird. Nothing but the sky and the waves; a boundless expanse of waves, swelling, curling and sinking, as far as the eye could see.

Jan wanted to make a reckoning by taking the sun. But in the chart-room none of the instruments was to be found; the sea had rammed in the doors and cleaned it out. A few tatters of charts dangled like weeds from the racks under the ceiling, a chair with broken legs had hidden itself underneath the table—that was all. Lord, he was tired. He swayed on his feet from exhaustion; but, bear up, the show isn't over yet. He lowered himself into the cabin; there sprawled the captain, laid out on the couch, like a corpse. It was quiet in the cabin, eerily quiet; no sound but the singing in his ears and the muffled roll and thud of a bottle, rolling backwards and forwards against the wall, moved by the swell. Seeing the man, he couldn't repress a certain pride, and he said: "Captain, your ship is saved." At first the captain didn't seem to have heard, then he said with a startling authority: "Go home, you fool." As Jan, after a moment of indecision, swallowed down an answer and started opening the drawers under the bunk, looking for a sextant, the captain said: "Once the finest vessel afloat; now better lost. Yes—lost; God, let her be lost; Almighty God, Who art in Heaven, Hallowed be Thy Name. Go home, you fool, go home." And there was no sextant either; better to sail blind, hoping for the best. The tug couldn't stay over the horizon for ever. Next to the coat-hooks hung a portrait with its glass splintered. An old-fashioned woman with three old-fashioned children; her face had been damaged by the broken glass, and sea water had seeped in too. Seeing that portrait he thought of Nellie, for the first time that night. As he dragged himself up the stairs he wondered why that should be. He had always been told that at the moment of death a vision of one's beloved floats before the eyes with a smile of comfort and consolation. He had felt the hand of the dark angel on his shoulder at least three times that night, but there had been no vision of Nellie to comfort him. He wasn't too weary to make excuses for his broken promise; if it wasn't even worth her while to have a fleeting little dream about him, with seaweed in his hair, then there was nothing for it but to do his manly duty, without sentimental restrictions.

Yet it didn't quite work, this sensible reflection; he stretched himself on the bench in the chart-room with an uneasy conscience, until he fell asleep. And that wasn't long.

Towards the evening the *Jan van Gent* caught up with them again. The men on both ships hailed one another, to say: "Hullo, boys." At the third attempt a line was taken aboard and was hauled in without much trouble. When the tug started pulling again, the bo'sun arrived with a boat. "Hullo, bo'sun."

"Hullo, Mate, any damage?"

"Not too bad, thanks."

"Hullo, Kees."

When Jan saw Siemonov again they shook hands. So they should. And they had a drink. So they jolly well should. Bout said: "What! Still alive?" The Chief said: "Now you've seen for yourself what this slave-driver's capable of." But Nellie made no comment; she looked out of her frame with an odd expression. Don't you worry; she'd have enough to say when the time came; lucky fellow to have eight months in which to think up an answer.

Little Abel said: "What did I tell you? Go easy with those Scottish wenches." And Bulle Brega pulled a face as if he were laughing. But he gave a hell of a yell when Siemonov put a stockinged foot in his armpit and did some rope-pulling on his bad arm. "Do you know why the Sultan of Turkey has only midgets to serve him in his harem?" little Abel asked cheerfully. And when Bulle didn't know, he said: "Because they are too small to look in the beds. Ha ha ha." But Bulle didn't laugh; Bulle had fainted. Kees de Kaap had tears in his eyes and went on deck rather than watch that torture. Ostensibly he'd gone on deck to ask cook if he wouldn't rather fry an egg for the casualty, instead of moping over the rail like that. Cook said: "Fry an egg? That man will be out for the count for the next ten hours."

48

Cook was a bit unhappy, for he had lost his bowler-hat. Funny the way one gets attached to a thing like that; in the end it become almost like a dog. Henkie said: "Man! He didn't half feel it; I saw the blood ooze from his eyes and. . . ." "You don't say so," Abeltje remarked, with his hand behind his ear. And then Bout's voice called from the engine-room: "Boys, just hand down a bucket of water, will you?" Henkie exclaimed: "That's the third engineer, sick again!" And the bo'sun said: "You stay out of this, sonny, and go and do what you're told."

Eight months at sea was a long time. Sometimes Jan wept in his bunk, hiding his face in his pillow. But who can blame him? For heroism in itself is no cure for a lonely heart. And for someone as young as he, and so newly married, he hadn't at all done badly.

CHAPTER THREE

IT WAS a strange experience, a long trip like this—so long, that you didn't even try to visualize the end of it, for no one can look halfway round the globe. Endless months on endless water made the ship a self-contained little world, isolated from all the rest. What was Holland? A tiny triangle on the map, so tiny that you didn't even try to picture the tiny house, sitting in the north-west corner. And in that tiny house a tiny woman and in that tiny woman an invisible tiny child. . . . Cook had a tin, once filled with cocoa, now with coffee, and on that tin there was a picture of a fat nurse, in three colours, carrying a tray on which there was a tin with the same picture of a nurse on it. Thus on an ever-diminishing scale the same banal picture was endlessly reproduced in the space of one cocoa tin. Good Lord, it was enough to drive a man potty, looking at that tin long enough: an endless row of fat nurses diminishing into eternity. The monotony of that picture was only paralleled by the monotony of this long sea trip. Better not brood over it too much or try to look through the wrong end of a telescope and drive yourself crazy with sentimental memories. The ship was the first consideration. The men

49

on that ship were your comrades. As to the rest, it was all nonsense; let the world roll by and if the sky crashes down that's the end of us. Siemonov said: "You see, you're getting used to the tugboat business"; Bout said: "The best sailor's an automaton with iron hands and a wooden nut." And then you looked at Siemonov, and you thought to yourself: funny, I know that man better than my own wife by now. All sorts of things that Nellie and I thought were proofs of love happen between that man and me every day without any smiles or hugs: we think the same things at the same moments; we say the same things at the same time; we share one mug of coffee when the other mug has gone overboard; we wear each other's clothes, if our own kit is wet. Siemonov was a wonderful skipper, a wonderful person and a wonderful friend—better than all women, at eight thousand miles' distance, put together. And Bout was another wonderful person and a wonderful comrade; the whole bloody ship was full of wonderful people, better than the rest of the world with all its teeming bastards. And the *Jan van Gent* was a wonderful ship; anyone who had his legs planted on her bridge could snap his fingers at the world. And if she sailed through the universe, or revolved like another planet round the sun, it couldn't be any different from a long trip like this.

Sail, sail, sail, sail. . . . Good Lord, those stories one used to listen to, open-mouthed, as a kid: "And, for more than a month, chum, nothing but sky and water—nothing at all except perhaps an albatross or flying fish once in a while. . . ." Yes, great fun to listen to. Wouldn't mind trying it myself one day. Then the irresistible urge had come upon him to go to sea, to try his luck in that pure world of sky and water which was the birthright of the seaman. Let it happen soon! God, let it happen soon! . . . And now that prayer had been answered. Providence, with what seemed an ironic generosity, had granted all he asked. Now he was condemned to go on sailing till he dropped dead, as the Chief had done.

The Chief gave up in mid-ocean. One afternoon, at dinner. He had been coughing a lot for some weeks; he nearly choked himself sometimes, and then his eyes would be pale with fear. He said he had a diseased stomach and diseased lungs. Jan had thought: I hope you choke, you and your lungs and stomach and all the rest; choke, you bloody old bore. He did.

They were having semolina-pudding with redcurrant sauce, as was customary on Saturdays. The Chief hadn't eaten anything, but when the pudding came, with that lovely thick, red sauce, he let himself be tempted by the sight of it and heaped his plate with it. Suddenly he coughed, and Bout said: "Hey, hey, father: you're coughing currant sauce all over the table!" But when they looked at him he sat white and deathly still, his hands clutched the edge of the table, and what he had coughed up was not redcurrant sauce, but blood. They wanted to put him down on his back on the bench, but he would not let go of the table; when they tried to wrench his fingers away he shook his head and coughed again. Blimey, what a mess; cook had plenty to scrub. Once they had carried him to his bunk he seemed to be better. He even got as far as starting to read again, although he couldn't speak yet. Jan was the last to see him alive: he looked round the doorway and saw him again as he had seen him that first time—the little lamp with the pink shade alight, a gleam on his bald skull; the pot with the geraniums swinging with the swell, and the watch on the partition swinging also. Half an hour later, when Bout went in to have a look, he was lying exactly like that, only he was dead. A political pamphlet about "Strikes as the Road to Liberty, Equality, Fraternity and Justice," lay open on the blankets. Bout said: "Let's hope his soul has taken the right road, now his ticker has struck for good." But he didn't mean it as a pun. Siemonov thought it unwise to shove him over straight away; better to let a doctor have a look at him before doing away with him; one never knew.

They heard of a doctor in St. Paul, a miserable hamlet on a piece of rock at the end of nowhere; it was only two days steaming, which was all to the good. The doctor was a fat Swede with drooping moustaches hanging down both sides of his red, feminine mouth, like a couple of handles. He peered at the Chief over the little half-moons of his spectacles. His fat, white hands hopped like well-fed birds up and down the thin body of the dead man. He wrote a certificate full of blots and sweat-smudges, holding his breath at every word, and finally said, breathlessly: "Away wiz—de cadaver —too long—already."

The Chief was covered with stones in a little churchyard, where he had about half-a-dozen molehills like his own, for company; the ground was too hard to dig a proper grave. The crew stood round him in a circle, the sun beat mercilessly on the rock; it was no joke to stand in that heat with one's head bared, so the ceremony was short. Siemonov read a chapter from the Bible, which nobody understood a word of, and said: "Rest in peace, borother, Amen." It was not a very uplifting or impressive service, and no one had liked the Chief very much, but the ship was silent all the same and everyone had his own thoughts. Towards sundown they sailed again, for there was nothing going on in that island; just the church and a few houses with old women knitting in the doorway, peering at the strangers with impassive faces, and scratching their heads with their needles. The island remained on the horizon for another day—a gigantic tombstone; then it was gone.

Clearing out the Chief's cabin and storing his things was a tough job; but luckily Bout came to give a hand. They packed *The Correct Letter Writer, Your Dreams Explained, Woman's Flesh by Auction, Alie, Piet, Freek, Hennie, Doortje,* and *Our Little Sun,* without comment in a chest and made a list of them; nobody wanted the geraniums, so they went overboard. For a few minutes the little red bunch of artificial flowers floated on the ocean, then it went down: a posy on the grave of an obscure seaman. To write the letter to the widow was Siemonov's task; he had time till Pernambuco and spent at least an hour daily on it; at last the consul wrote it. It was a wonderful letter, full of sincere compassion and gentle consolation. But how was it possible? the third engineer naively inquired. After all, the consul didn't even know the man.

The third engineer was promoted to second for the duration of the voyage, because Bout was Chief now. It brought the good lad a ray of hope and encouragement in the gloom of his worm's life, and he certainly needed it. Before the Chief died everyone, seeing the third, had thought: you won't last out the trip, my lad. He wasn't ill, he just didn't seem to want to live. Not that he ever said as much, or would have confessed it when asked; but he had begun to show symptoms of that contagious disease of the sea—fear. Fear of space: in the end he hadn't dared to go on deck, the sky drove him mad. Fear of depth: he had often sat on his stool by the side of the engine, dead-still, staring down between his knees at the hull plates, as if he looked straight through them and saw the three thousand fathoms of water down there, full of slinking monsters lurking in the deep green vaults between the swaying weeds. Fear of sound: if anything fell on deck he nearly jumped out of his skin, and Bout had once been compelled to kick him away from the engine where he found him screaming, his eyes staring and his hands over his ears. He was so near the swishing piston rods that he would have been drawn in and crushed to pulp the next moment.

But as soon as he was promoted the poor chap got better. It was an odd sort of auto-suggestion, really; for when they got home he would be relegated to a third engineer again. But this temporary promotion helped him to get over the fear. Bout said, a few days after leaving St. Paul, that the ghost of the Chief must have taken possession of that boy's body, for he greased and polished with panting enthusiasm everything that didn't need greasing or polishing, which was exactly what the Chief used to do. Even at the messroom-table he began to look like the late Chief in an alarming way. Sometimes he would suddenly stop eating and listen intently, his fork poised in mid-air. "Hey, isn't that suction-pump missing a stroke?" he would ask, nervously. Or he would sigh and shake his head, saying: "It's a chain-gang, really, this tugboat business—that's what it is." Now if he had used the word "slavery," they would have laughed at him; but because he said the same thing in different words it had something eerie about it, as if the dead Chief had thought: "Well—if I can't stay alive one way, let's try another." It wasn't the third, imitating the Chief; it was the Chief trying desperately to look like the third.

The good humour of the messroom was damped a bit. From now on they sat eating opposite one another without saying much, and when they chatted their conversation tended to be about such things as the future power of the

53

masses, as if the ghost of the dead Chief had taken a grim possession of their tongues.

Rio de Janeiro, Pearl of the South, was certainly a pearl cast before swine as far as the crew of the *Jan van Gent* was concerned. There was no holding back the rabble, that had looked so submissive and subdued during the long voyage. The moment the mooring-ropes had thumped on the quay and the gangplank had rumbled down they swarmed out, like caged birds set free—screeching, hopping, madly flapping their wings. Little Abel was the leader of this vicious pilgrimage. He clapped his hands and a hansom came rattling along, a ramshackle affair on wobbling wheels, drawn by a knock-kneed mule. The whole gang piled itself into the vehicle and when the mule got restive and began striking sparks from the cobbles with its hooves, Abeltje bawled: "A LAS SENORITAS PUBLICAS!" The mule seemed to know the way, for it started running right into the traffic, with the driver chasing after it shouting and holding his hat on with his hands.

"Let them rip!" Bout said. "They'll get themselves into such a mess that they'll soon come running back, to hide from the coppers under the skirts of the skipper." He was right. Bout was always right, because he looked at life soberly, without emotion.

Jan went ashore with him and they strolled through the resplendent city; fountains and sunlight and palms and tramps—and beautiful women, who at close quarters appeared to have moustaches, so black was their hair. They ate a coffee-ice on a terrace; Jan thought it filthy muck and it gave Bout toothache; but they had to pay a lot to the waiter, who bowed so low from the waist that Bout, despite the pain, looked under the table, to see if there was a monkey under it. There were lots of monkeys in Rio whose function it was to amuse the people; but they didn't behave nicely to Jan and Bout. They danced shrieking on the pavement in front of their feet, and when Jan said: "Kscht! Be off!" he seemed to attract more of them, and Bout said: "Better order a bowl of peanuts for them, otherwise they'll make water at you—I've been here before." The waiter brought a bowl of peanuts, which cost even more than the ice; they strolled on through the sunlight and the cheerful crowd, feeling vexed and out of it. There were pigeons, too; and boys who wanted to polish your shoes, and furtive characters with straw hats on, who said: "Come, come, friend sailor, I will show you ze pratty lady." But they preferred the pigeons to the prospect of ze pratty lady, so they sat down on the edge of a fountain and let the birds eat from their hands the bread and rice which they had bought in a little grocery store—odd, how much boredom you could buy in Rio for a pound and how much fun for a penny. Bout became quite sentimental at the sight of the pigeons. "Just look at the beauties," he said tenderly, holding out a handful of crumbs; "they'll peck it out of your breast pocket, if you give 'em the chance." While they were sitting on the fountain they caught sight of the third engineer, who had followed them self-consciously at a distance, and was being accosted now by one of the straw hat brigade. He was very thin and boyish, was the third engineer, but thought himself such a deuce of a chap since his promotion that he was anxious to try his hand with the "pratty ladies," if only to show that character in the straw hat that he was a man of the world. But Jan and Bout went and nipped that in the bud. Even though their feelings towards him were only lukewarm, he was still one of the family, as it were, and in consequence it was up to them to see that he came to no harm. "Take your damned paws off that boy, signor," they demanded, butting in. The straw hat flew into a screaming rage and the third engineer got excited too, with blazing eyes and a trembling mouth; but Jan took the sailors' friend by his arm and strolled away with him, saying: "You clear off, chum, or we'll show you how the butcher makes his sausages." In the meantime Bout stood, with his hand placed earnestly on the thin shoulder of the third engineer, while the pigeons cooed and fluttered around their feet. "Be sensible, old chap," he said; "if you want to know about love, it won't help to land yourself up in the morgue." Some persuasion was necessary before the thing was finally settled. The hat sat unbecomingly low on the brow of the sailors' friend when Jan finally sent him packing. The third engineer, however, wept in a rather unmanly way, and there was a little bubble of rage on his lip as they boarded a horse-tram, the three of them, and let themselves be driven to the outskirts of the town through the noisy streets of the old city. They sat on the roof of the rattling vehicle, which pushed its way through the crowd with clanging bell and curses from the driver, until, at last, they reached the terminus. Then they climbed down and Bout said: "This is Botafogo; isn't it beautiful, boys?"

They strolled through avenues of palms which Bout thought were like broccoli gone to seed. "But wait till you see the Palace, boys, it's terrific." They wandered about, looking for the Palace, for hours; Bout became more and more insistent. He said: "The Palace is over THERE— don't let anybody fool you." He spoke as if he had planned the town himself and now had come back to see how those fatheads had bungled it. When they found the Palace at last, they dutifully admired it, because Bout looked too murderous to be contradicted. A white carriage came up the avenue and Bout was so proud of his Palace that he saluted and whispered under his breath: "The Emperor!" But when two men came out of the front door of the Palace to drag a struggling figure out of the carriage, who shrieked so piercingly that it made one's blood curdle, he became un-easy and asked a passer-by if this was the Palace. The passer-by politely informed him that it was the municipal asylum. Jan doubled up with laughter, and even the third engineer couldn't help smiling wanly. Bout himself man-aged to raise a semblance of a grin, and excused his mistake by saying that the town had been mucked up since he was there last—strike him dead if it hadn't.

They went back to the harbour by another horse-tram, and when they got back on board the third engineer re-ceived a shock, for when he went to his cabin to check his cash he found that his wallet had been stolen. That must have been the work of that dirty pickpocket with the straw hat! He stumbled back on deck, cursing shrilly, and wanted to scramble ashore to get hold of that rat and rip out his guts; but Bout, who had gone to wash in the lavatory, popped out stark naked and dragged back the third engineer before he ran off to meet his doom. The third engineer became quite hysterical. He screamed and dug his nails into Bout's white chest. Jan had to come to his assistance, and only just in time, for on the quay a crowd had gathered: women took refuge behind their parasols, and tiny men, with flashing eyes and flashing rings on brandished fists, called for justice. You wouldn't have guessed it by appearances, but the people of Rio were very pernickety about decency, so long as the curtains weren't drawn. A copper came galloping up, with a truncheon, and a mule stood gaping vacantly at them, its ears directing ghostly traffic; Bout scurried back into the lavatory and Jan kicked the third engineer into the galley. There Mate J. Wandelaar gave an impressive performance of an old salt giving advice to a snivelling youngster amidst the mugs and wooden spoons. The third engineer started to sob under the steady stream of hearty words, and sniffed: "Yes, yes—but it was thirty-two guilders and fifty cents. . . !"

"What are thirty-two guilders and fifty cents," Jan asked, "in comparison with God's free and glorious nature?" In comparison with God's free and glorious nature the third engineer didn't think thirty-two guilders and fifty cents amounted to much, but when they were in the sweating hands of that bastard with the straw hat it was a different story. The moral of it all, Jan tried to point out, was that you should never go ashore with so much cash on you. And that took them back to the beginning of their argument, which came to an abrupt end when cook opened the door and asked suspiciously: "And what can I do for you, friends?"

There was a Dutch colony in Rio de Janeiro, but it consisted of grandees only, of whom even Siemonov was a bit scared. When they invited him and his officers to an informal little supper he tried to get out of it, for he had discovered a Russian tramp ship in the harbour and wanted to eat bortsch and cheat at cards with his feet on the table. But Bout said they couldn't get out of it and Jan agreed; he wouldn't mind the experience for once, a meal with all those exotic birds might be quite amusing.

They washed themselves thoroughly for the occasion, the messroom being cleared for the purpose. The table was put on its side against the wall and a tarpaulin was spread on the floor. Cook provided a tub of hot water and there they stood, steaming in the narrow room, for they dared not risk washing on deck because of the coppers. They helped each other with the scrubbing; Bout joined them, for he loved washing. Jan had never suspected that Siemonov could have had so much hair on his body; he looked like a monkey, and the hot water made the hairs stand on end, so that you could have shown him in a circus. Jan was the most tanned of the lot, though he was the fairest; and the third engineer was chalk white, whiter even than Bout, and he hadn't got a single hair on his body. The third was a bit self-conscious amongst this giant nakedness. He had a narrow chest and a mole on his back the size of a medal. Bout said to him: "I bet you crawled through the bars of the cradle the moment you were born." Siemonov said: "Quiet! Give me a hand with my back, borother." Siemonov had a triangle on his back, between the shoulder blades, that he had never been able to reach, and it showed. Jan scrubbed it with a wad of cotton waste and soft soap; when this proved ineffective, Bout went, steaming, to the engine-room to get a brush, leaving the others sweating in the draught. The brush did the trick, but when the spot had been cleaned blood trickled down between the hairs. Once the washing was over the cook and the bo'sun could clear up the mess, while the gentlemen officers stood singing as they shaved themselves in their cabins. Cook said: "Now you see how much dirt there was under that golden tan." They dragged the tarpaulin up the steps to the deck, with a great weight of water folded in the middle. The messroom was covered from floor to ceiling with smudges and soapsuds. Siemonov stood howling in the doorway of his cabin, for he had forgotten to take his boiled shirt with him when he left Russia twenty years ago. Now cook was ordered to go out and buy him a dicky. Cook went ashore, with a piece of string the size of the Captain's neck. He came back half an hour later with a strange object. It was wrapped in tissue-paper and was labelled "REAL AMERICAN FAKE SHIRT FOR GENTLEMEN." It consisted of a dozen sheets of white paper, in the shape of shirt-fronts, to be fastened round the neck. The gentleman in the haberdasher's shop had recommended it strongly, for it was extremely practical and ingenious into the bargain; if you had soiled one front you could tear it off and have eleven more clean ones at your disposal; as a special attraction a serial had been printed on the back of the sheets, entitled *The Rakish Lover*. It was all right with Siemonov, as long as the damn thing fitted, which it did. Cook had been clever enough to procure a celluloid collar at the same time, and Bout had got a funeral tie somewhere in one of his drawers. The one thing lacking was the cuffs, but cook would help him there, for he had stolen a pair from the late Chief's remains; so you see, a sin may turn into a virtue in the course of time.

When the Captain and his officers were ready to set off for the banquet, they were certainly a credit to the tugboat industry. The party consisted of four gentlemen in sombre black suits, but gay headgear, for Bout had bought four straw hats with coloured bands from an Indian pedlar who was hawking them around the quay on a donkey. The Indian had only one size, but that didn't matter, Bout said, for you had to keep the things in your hand when you went indoors, anyhow. They diffused a manly smell of camphor and soft soap, and their faces shone with scrubbing. When a cab had taken them to the hotel where the banquet was to be held, Siemonov, on alighting, was seen to have burst out of his gala jacket. The porter listened with wonder to the curses of the giant as he tried in vain to grope round the back— Jan appeased him, whispering that there was nothing showing, and that no one would be any the wiser for luckily the lining was black too, and it hadn't torn. They were received by the consul, a little bantam of a man with a goatee beard and covered with medals, who shook them by the hand, delightedly, as if they were his own sons. And sons was exactly what a military greybeard called them half an hour later when he made a speech in their honour— Sons of One Motherland—long live the Queen!

The Dutch colony was larger than their worst fears had led them to expect. There was a long glittering table, like an avenue of candle flames, crowded with silver and crystals and little flower beds, and flanked by rows of boiled shirts and ample bosoms. Heavens, what a lot of fat wenches, and all the males were sitting bolt upright, as if they had swallowed iron rods! Siemonov sat at the head of the table, next to the military gentleman with the whiskers. He stared down the avenue of flames as if he were watching the beginning of a fire in a cargo of explosives, while he was manacled to his chair. He was very hot, and some air must have got in underneath the first instalment of the serial on his chest, for it formed a bulge which his lady partner couldn't keep her eyes off. She was a small bird-like woman, with a flower on her shoulder and a braid of grey hair on her head with another flower in that too. She was very kind and helped the Captain so unobtrusively with the choice of forks and spoons from the arsenal around his plate that no one would have noticed it if he hadn't made such a clatter with them. It was understandable that Siemonov was a bit confused, for during the preceding half-hour all sorts of ladies of all ages and sizes had been putting questions to him of such staggering silliness, that he had ruined the parting cook had so carefully put in his grease-tamed hair, by scratching his head. Jan had been able to overhear a few of those questions in the odd moments that he himself was left in peace. "Now you tell us, Captain—what IS this strange superstition, that makes sailors shoot at the sun every day?" And: "Tell us, Captain—what does your crew READ on long voyages like this one?" The question was not so alarming, but the answer might have been, so Siemonov stammered, in despair: "Er—er—the—the Bible, madam, and—and the newspapers." The lady raised her bushy eyebrows, shaped her mouth to a surprised 'o' and asked: "The newspapers? But how on earth do you get those delivered in the middle of the sea?" Siemonov had looked about him in terror; Jan was afraid that he was looking for the exit. But the first lady had come to his rescue with: "But of course, dear—by pigeon-post! Isn't that so, Captain? You have a cage of homing pigeons on board your ship, haven't you?" At that moment Jan was monopolized by a fat, short gentleman, with aggressive moustaches and an expression which showed he wouldn't be easily put off. The gentleman had grabbed his arm and towed him behind a palm; there he had looked round, grabbed a button on Jan's waistcoat, and said: "Young man—tell me one thing, and one thing only: what exactly do you people do about your manly urges, you healthy, sturdy people at sea?" Jan answered: "Nothing"; and the gentleman looked up at him incredulously, with eyes

embedded in fat, and said: "Come, come, young fellow—
don't be bashful! Months and months on the water, and
no member of the opposite sex in sight—don't be shy about
it, I'm a doctor as a matter of fact; I'm making a study of
the subject." Jan said: "The best thing would be for you
to sail with us for a while, doctor; we haven't got much time
to bother about our urges, you know; one has to be a
specialist for that."

Bout was sitting one seat below Siemonov, between the
grey-haired lady with the flowers and a flat-chested, melancholy spinster with dreamy eyes and a dog collar, who said
nothing, ate nothing, and did nothing but gaze at the silver
knife-rest, with which the white, tapering fingers of her right
hand were continually playing, her left hand cupped under
her very long chin, as if she were musing about some distant
lover. Bout ate very correctly; he picked and probed with
his knife and fork on his plate with cautious movements, as
if he were tackling a delicate job in the engine. His face was
solemn and impassive, his eyes cast down, as if he was reading
a bitter future in the hors d'oeuvre. His composure and
assurance were wonderful. He sat bolt upright and munched
his food with a steady rumination, only betraying his
nerves by occasionally mopping his brow with his
napkin.

The third engineer was sitting next to a lively homely
lady, who laughed uproariously and ate like a horse. He was
completely at ease, this strange boy. After five minutes he
drew a tugboat for her on the table cloth with the point of
his knife, and told endless stories of terror and heroism, in
which he kept himself modestly in the background. But the
homely lady realized at once that everything would have
ended in disaster, during that terrible hurricane, if he hadn't
been there to shut down all the valves at the peril of his
life. And after half an hour she knew exactly what the inside
of a Babcock and Wilcox boiler looked like—yes, yes: lots
of little pipes and flames—but now you should eat something, my dear, otherwise you'll go hungry.

Jan was lucky. On one side there was an old lady, smelling
of lavender and listening only to the military gentleman with
the whiskers. She left him in peace, luckily for him, because
on his other side was a young woman, almost a girl, with

wonderful shining hair and sweet earnest eyes in a white
little face. She had helped him out at the beginning, which
was the most difficult part. She had a soft voice, and slender
hands, and wore a single ring with a green stone in it. He
watched her with hushed reverence at first—she looked like
one of those pictures in hairdressers' shops; he had never
suspected that women like her existed in real life. And, by
Jove, was she alive! She chatted and laughed at him and
looked at him with large earnest eyes and, lord, look at those
teeth—wonderful. At first he had listened politely to the
conversation of the old gentleman and Siemonov, with a
notion that all this must be a crazy dream, but then her soft
voice had asked: "Mr. Mate . . . would you mind telling me
what exactly IS deep-sea towing? I honestly don't know a
thing about it." He had been pleasantly surprised that someone as rich and beautiful as she, should confess that there was
something in the world she didn't know about. He blushed
with confusion and answered: "Nonsense—you know
all about it, no need to tell you." And she laughed and asked:
"Why . . . how do you mean?" And he grinned and said:
"Well—er—you know I'm the Mate, to start with. A moment
ago a lady took me for the ship's doctor." She had looked at
him with a surprise that clearly expressed her deep concern
for all those unfortunate men, and asked: "You don't mean
to tell me that you *haven't* got a ship's doctor on board?"
And he had smiled in a fatherly way and answered: "No—
not a live one, that is. We have got a paper one though." And
she asked, pulling up her chair: "Oh, please—tell me all
about your paper doctor!" And he leaned back and put that
damned knife away for a moment and said: "Well—it's a
wooden chest full of bottles, and each bottle has a number
stuck on, and with it goes a list of the numbers. . . ." And
she went on listening intently, with sometimes a question to
prove that she understood everything and was genuinely
interested. She had laughed at all his jokes, laughed her head
off, and suddenly she put her hand on his because he amused
her so. The hand was light and soft; you could see that it
had never done any heavy work, yet it wasn't weak. While
the meal was in progress—there was no end to the titbits,
and everything came separately—she told him, in her turn,
that her name was Agnes and that the old gentleman at the

head of the table was her father, and the lady—that one with the flowers in her hair—was her mother. Jolly old sport, wasn't he? "Yes, Daddy can be quite fun, and he loves sailors you know; there have been lots of sailors in the family. I honestly couldn't help laughing when you people came in, just like a peasant's wedding—oh! I'm so sorry, I didn't mean to . . . but you don't mind me telling you, for no one has thought it at all embarrassing or funny, honestly, you can be sure of that. Everybody understands perfectly well that one can't carry a dress-suit about in such a teeny weeny ship, and—what's that? You and the Captain change watches every four hours? Good heavens—but that's terrible! How on earth do you manage to get enough sleep? Good heavens, how perfectly wonderful of you! You don't say . . . really? Well I must confess I'm absolutely hushed with admiration for you all, absolutely; and what Daddy says is perfectly true, he said——"

Daddy stood up, tinkled against his glass with his knife, and proposed a toast, in which he called Siemonov a Giant of the Depths and an Emperor of the Ocean, and the others Gentlemen, Worthy Peers. He thought the *Jan van Gent* was the personification of "our own dear Motherland: small in size but GREAT in deeds. Long live the Queen!"

The wine was excellent and there was plenty of it. There was a continual clinking of glasses and in the end you clinked glasses with yourself. The gaiety mounted, the happy informal gaiety of compatriots amongst themselves. At last even Siemonov got up and proposed a toast to the HOSTS, LONG LIVE THE—sorry, ma'am, I didn't mean to splash you— THE QUEEN! Because he put it so forcefully, and because it came so spontaneously from his honest heart, so delightfully nautical, the gathering was enthusiastic and roared: "Up with Orange, Up with Orange, long live the Queen!—Down with the Socialists, long live the Queen!" Cheers! Hurray! Yes, yes—the real Motherland lay beyond the border, across the sea; and the capital of that Motherland across the border across the sea was Rio de Janeiro, the Pearl in the Crown, hurray, prosit, Captain: shake hands, man, let's shake hands. The white whiskers quivered with emotion when daddy showed a passionately sweating Siemonov to the crowd, his hand on the rough shoulder, a manager with his boxing-champion: cheers, hurray, long live the tugboats, down with the Socialists, long live Orange, MUSIC!

After the meal coffee was served in the ballroom, which looked much less forbidding now. A band was playing on a platform at the far end, with red, white and blue ribbon tied to their violins and orange flowers behind their ears. They played national songs, with the tempo and sensuality of the pampas: "I hear the bells of Schokland—Hoppla—ringing—Hatcha, husa!—for my dead love, crash-bang!"—"There is a friend for little children—Crash, bang, pingelingeling!—Above the clouds—Ole, ole! getcha, husha!—he loves our little waifs and strays—Carramba! bang, crash, toodeloodeloo! hurray!" Laughter and shouts and happiness everywhere; by Jove, this was good! Hey, Bout! How do you like this, eh, you fat old baboon? Bout liked it all right; he sat grinning over a tiny coffee cup, the unattached lady by his side. Hey, third! How are things? Things were fine with the third engineer, he was practically sitting on the homely lady's lap, to show her what the stoke-hole looked like. Siemonov was standing in the centre of an admiring circle, his paper shirt bulging now, like a woman's bosom, gruesomely splashed with wine, and his cardboard cuffs protruding far below his sleeve. It looked as if he had fallen at last into the temptation of showing those idiots what a real Russian folk-dance looked like; but he was only explaining how a hawser was hauled in. Agnes laughed with her head against Jan's shoulder and asked if she might call him Wim. Of course she might, only his real name happened to be Jan. Then the band struck up a tune, the *Destiny Waltz*, full of slow, tender sentiment, and they started dancing almost without realizing it. The South American temperament couldn't put up with Nordic sentimentality for long, and the waltz got quicker and quicker till in the end they were spinning through a room full of swirling skirts and ablaze with crystal chandeliers that looked like comets. You either became dizzy or stared stolidly at those eyes and that mouth; you just had to fasten your gaze on that throat and that delicate parting of the bosom or you'd go reeling right into the palms. Lor', what a cosy, cheerful, generous crowd; all those square-rigged frigates turned out to be quite simple people, at heart real compatriots; and you felt at home here

64

as you could never feel at home at home, that's a fact. The only song they refused to sing was "Roll me over in the clover," which proved that they were true aristocrats, and that was good, for the world needed aristocrats. Aristocrats to inspire you to wash yourself after six months of sea-water, coal-dust, and engine-oil; aristocrats to dress up for like a gentleman, after six months of seaboots and oilskins and stinking underwear that stood up by itself with sweat and salt; aristocrats to feed you after six months of kidney beans, mushy potatoes and chicken soup made of seagulls; aristocrats to hold in your arms, soft, tender, warm and excitingly feminine, after six months of stiff manilla-rope and scrubby ship-fenders—and desperate longing. One-two-three, one-two-three—isn't it wonderful? Delicious, one-two-three, one-two-three, you dance beautifully for a seaman. Leave off the "seaman" sweetheart, one-two-three, one. . . . Phew! Let's have a breather, shall we?

On the balcony. A heavy heady summer's night.

"Isn't it funny—in Holland it's winter now."

"Yes, isn't it funny."

"Beautiful view, sweetheart—why are you laughing?"

"It's nothing."

"No, own up: why are you laughing?" How close her face was to his, suddenly.

"Because of the 'sweetheart,' " she confessed. "But I wasn't laughing at you."

"H'm," he said. "You know everyone has his own language."

"I love your language," she answered. "It's so honest, so straightforward."

"H'm," he said, "I don't see you people beating about the bush either."

"That's sweet of you, Wim," she said with a sad little smile, and then she looked at the view again and sighed.

"What's the matter?"

"Nothing."

"What are you sighing for?" How close her mouth was to his when she turned her head and looked at him again. But she didn't smile any more. She looked at his mouth and her own lips were parted, and there was almost a tragic expression on her face. "It's so terribly boring here," she complained, "there are so many people and yet one is so lonely; one never meets anybody whom one can talk with about anything that matters, anybody who is really a friend."

"Is that so?" he said; "I wouldn't have thought it was all that boring here. You ought to try life on a tugboat—you'd find that much worse. On a tugboat there are only a few people, all of whom are your friends, with whom you talk the whole goddam day and the night as well—you get fed up with that too, in the end, let me tell you. In the end you'd like to see something else for a change instead of unshaven chins and cracked lips, and you'd like to smell something more pleasant than tobacco-breaths and gin yawns."

"So you see," she said with a melancholy little laugh, "everyone has his own loneliness."

"Yes," he said, "that's true."

And then they stood looking at the view for a little while. Behind them the dancers laughed and chattered; below them the glittering town murmured in the distance; overhead the great stars sparkled bluishly in the vast darkness of the sky.

"Wonderful view," he said, voicing the thought that was most in his mind. Then she suggested: "Let's go and have a look at it from the roof-garden—there you'll see something you have never dreamt of in all your life."

He hesitated for only a second, then answered: "Yes, let's go."

She led the way—a rustling, shimmering wraith in the darkness—along the balcony, to a set of french-windows reflecting the stars. The stars dropped from the sky when she opened the windows and stepped into the room beyond, disappearing in the darkness. He followed her—it was pitch dark—he groped about, and she caught his hand. She pulled him, gently, through a long passage, smelling of dusty carpets and stale perfume, up a flight of stairs, along another passage, up another flight of carpeted stairs, across a little landing and then up a flight of uncarpeted stairs. Then a door squeaked and he felt the night air flowing in, and when he looked up he saw the stars. She had let go of his hand now, and when he followed her on to the roof he saw her standing at a balustrade, her back to him: a tiny silhouette against the flickering filigree of the town lights. The lights seemed to weave away on to the horizon. Here and there high shadows loomed up, and everywhere waved the pink plumes of fountains. The night seemed larger, deeper, now. In the distance he could see the bay, the sea, the lights of anchored ships and the dark, squatting islands in the creek. The sea and land were separated by a green phosphorescent ribbon, which was the surf. It was a view so strange and so mysterious that he couldn't think of anything else for a time. Something stirred in him, a response from some deep and hidden recess in his memory, unformulated, nothing but a growing feeling of reverence, of awe. Then a puff of wind brought a sound, a far away, nostalgic sound, like the murmur of a shell held against the ear. And then he remembered that night before his examination, when he had stood looking up through his attic-window and saw in his imagination this very scene: a beach, far away, silver and blue in misty moonlight: a boyish vision of impossible beauty. Now that vision had materialized, and the miracle was that in reality it was even more mysterious and magnificent than it had appeared in the imagination of the boy as he stood staring at the sky from his attic-window: this was the real thing at last, this was the splendid truth.

The memory had taken him completely unawares, and he felt suddenly so overwhelmed by this miracle of a dream come true, that when she came and stood by his side without saying a word, he could only make a vague gesture in the direction of the shimmering surf. He couldn't help thinking of Christ standing on the mountain, with the Devil by his side whispering: "All these things will I give unto thee, if thou wilt. . . ."

Then she came closer to him, much closer, and he felt the warmth of her body through his clothes, her slender, yearning body. He smiled in the darkness, and a curious, tired sadness came over him and at the same time a great joy, as radiant and pure as the silver haze on the horizon, and he said: "Come, sweetheart, let's go back." She was silent for a moment, and then she said: "Just as you like."

They went back through all those passages, down all those flights of stairs, back to the din and the lights; later, he asked himself in loneliness and bitter regret: why, oh why didn't I do it, why the hell didn't I do it? I could have done it if

I'd wanted to; I'll never meet a woman like that again, never, never, not in a hundred years; why the hell didn't I do it? The answer was somewhere in that haze on the horizon, somewhere beyond the great expanse of sea: in Holland it is winter now. In Holland, my Holland, with Nellie, my wife.

What a party, what a party! When the four of them were driven back to the *Jan van Gent* they behaved like a bunch of students, so jolly, so hearty, so boyishly merry after all that hospitality. Cook gave a hand at piloting the revellers safely on board, and the third engineer kissed him, for in the dark all cheeks were alike.

But the next morning they sailed again, sailed on towards the ends of the earth. They were seen off by those who had been able to get up that early, and there weren't many: only daddy and the doctor of the manly urges. The whole crew of the *Jan van Gent* felt the effects of their spree when the ship began to pitch again on the swell of the Atlantic. But all the same they cherished the happiest memories of the Pearl of the South, memories which nothing would obliterate, neither sea, nor sour underwear, nor kidney beans. Jan had taken, by way of a souvenir, a tiny wine glass: the glass from which the girl sipped throughout that wonderful meal. A delicate, slender glass—a crystal flower. He couldn't have picked a more evocatory souvenir: whenever he looked at that glass he saw Agnes of Rio de Janeiro.

It stood on the shelf in his bunk for a whole nine days. Then a tragedy occurred. He was busy pulling on his boots in double quick time, for the ship had run into a patch of fog and all hands had been called on deck to keep a sharp look-out. Everything was dead still on the sea and on the ship; only the throbbing below deck disturbed the silence. Then suddenly the fog-horn let out a colossal, long-drawn-out blast, and he heard a faint tinkling noise. When he looked up he saw the glass shattered to pieces on the blanket, with only the foot still standing on the shelf—the stem of the little crystal flower.

He looked at the fragments, speechless, for a moment, as they rolled there on the blanket; then the fog-horn started bellowing again and they vibrated together with a tiny, tinkling sound. When he stood on the bridge in the fog, and Siemonov waddled to and fro, like a fettered ghost, he thought to himself: now that's all over, over for good.

Yes, Jan my boy, such is life. Sail on, and don't look back. On board a tugboat crystal dreams won't last.

CHAPTER FOUR

RIO DE JANEIRO to Montevideo; Montevideo to Punta Arenas; Punta Arenas to Valparaiso: sail, sail sail. The Straits of Magellan: a panting struggle against the wind between yellow plains, a swampy channel without end. It was cold, sometimes bitterly cold, and yet it still was almost summer. Winter clothes were taken out of the storage chest again; the watches on the bridge became endless walks to and fro, to and fro between the rails, in wind, snow, hail and endless, hopeless rain. As the *Jan van Gent* struggled with the wind and the tide feuds were forgotten, homesickness evaporated, desire ebbed and only the basic emotions remained: hunger, sleep and a numb yearning to be curled up somewhere warm and dry. But there was another urge that seemed to lash on not only the men but the very ship itself: Westward ho!

Westward ho! Westward ho! Sometimes the wind held back the dredger with such force that she became almost motionless. Siemonov slept in his clothes; Bout became feverish with exhaustion; the third engineer looked like a lunatic. At first no one mentioned it, then someone hinted it and finally everyone knew it: the ship was short of coal. The jump from Montevideo to Punta Arenas was the longest jump, and it was reckless to attempt it. Siemonov had risked it; Siemonov risked everything and he had never been beaten by fate yet. Siemonov was calm and confident. He didn't take any notice of the general apprehension; he was undaunted, even by the most difficult stretch of water in the world: the Straits of Magellan. After four days of head-wind and only sixty miles' progress, he was sufficiently exasperated to invoke the aid of his patron saint in a manner that would have shocked the ears of any true believer. But this salty and irreverent appeal seemed to have its effect. The wind subsided, and it grew foggy. The remedy turned out to be worse than the complaint. For two days and nights on end they were kept on the bridge: sitting on the bridge, walking on the bridge, yawning on the bridge, beating their arms warm on the bridge, their breaths mist in the mist. They had been kept on that bridge for longer stretches before: they had come through a gale near Cape Corrientes that had cost them as much coal as they would burn in two hundred miles of normal sailing, to say nothing of losing sixty-three hours of sleep. But this peering, walking, yawning, listening—peering, walking, yawning and listening for two days and two nights on end, was worse than sixty-three hours' hard labour, worse than murderous seas and a screaming hurricane. They steamed on at half speed—that cost coal. They sounded the hooter every two minutes—that cost steam. They didn't hear anything day or night except the monotonous, melancholy chant of the men at the lead, the whole God-given night and day: "Five fathom bare—Five fathom full. . . ." They had their meals in the wheelhouse, and ate with their fingers, their plates at their mouths; their hands were too numb to handle a spoon. They dozed off for two minutes, then the fog-horn bellowed again and they woke up with a start, to peer, yawn and listen, to beat their hands warm, to walk a few steps in their hen-coop between the rails, and to peer again and yawn and listen until they dozed off once more, to be woken up anew two minutes later by the howl of the fog-horn.

There was something sinister about this fog on the very edge of the world. Perhaps it was just the curious blankness of the chart, which stared them in the face as they bent over it with their parallel ruler and compasses; perhaps it was just the idea of being poised on the edge of the world, a vague echo of the old sailors' fear of tumbling over the edge into the void. Never before had a fog done such queer things to them. After making them wet and cold, it started to make them jumpy. It brought with it the feeling of eyes peering at them, of huge silent shadows flitting through the clouds with only a swish of wings—almost like the great bats in the alcoholic visions of Captain Bakker. The second night Siemonov suddenly seemed to have turned grey—it was the

70

hoar frost in his beard. The second day Jan seemed to go mad and to start ripping off his clothes—it was only a seagull that had perched on the wheelhouse, taking off. Wailing noises drifted through the night; shrieks of agony burst out and died away. The voice of the man at the lead faltered for a moment when something like claws seemed to scrape the hull; then, with obvious relief, the voice took up chant again as the man realized that what had touched the ship was only a piece of driftwood held fast in a floating mass of weed. After two nights and two days of this ghostly passage the ship had become very still; the silence of the great void had engulfed it. In this deathly silence the men, obsessed by the fear of doom, suffered agonies of conscience and remorse. Terror-stricken, they swore that if they got out of this they would become paragons of domestic virtue, loyal and dutiful to their wives. "God, I promise, when I come back I shall treat her differently. I swear, God, I won't get angry with her again after a week ashore, sick of her nagging and the whining kids and the washing up and the stupid gossip. Merciful God—I won't look at any other woman again; I won't spend my money on drinks and pipes and ties and wenches any more; I'll take every penny home and give it to her and say, I love you, darling, I love you, for ever and ever." Six fathom bare, five fathom full. The final darkness was full of sounds, like the breathing of some sleeping giant. "Let me live, let me live. I'll take up religion again; I'll go to confession, I'll burn gilded candles; I'll build a new grave for my parents. Let me out of this, show me the sun again, let me live, God, a wiser man, a witness of Thy love, a proclaimer of Thy glory." Five fathom full, six fathom bare.

And then the giant sleeper turned. A sigh, a silence, a gust of wind, and the veil parted. The yellow plains, the grey water, the low, sad clouds and the driving rain returned. The engine-room bell tinkled, the engine started throbbing again. The rain swept on over the plains and over the water, but what did it matter? Snatches of ribald song came up through the stoke-hole ventilators, mingled with bits of psalms and other expressions of high spirits. After the first squall of rain the air turned frosty, the horizon became clear, revealing in the distance the scrap-heap settlement of Punta Arenas.

On the horizon it looked like the promised land; from the harbour it looked like hell, the fountain-head of all depression. Grey, everything was grey, with the exception of the vast snow-covered Andes, looming rusty-red and bluish-white in the background. The houses were grey, the sheep were grey, the water was grey and the sky was grey. The bunkering of the *Jan van Gent* was the only sound in the greyness. Sometimes a bird screamed overhead, a gust of rain spattered on the water, or a sheep bleated behind the houses. There was no other sound except the whirring of a steam crane, the rattle of coal being shot into the bunkers, and the clanging and scraping of the shovels.

When they sailed again it was almost a flight, an escape from this cradle of despair, out into stranger waters.

The western half of the Straits of Magellan was another world. The stunted shrubs and the steely-grey marshland had disappeared; instead there were rocks, towering walls of blood-red rock, splashed here and there with brown. The narrow line of the sky overhead gave them, after a couple of days, another illusion. Now they might be fish, struggling against the current on the bed of a river. When they looked up they saw the troubled surface of the stream, the waves, the swirling foam, and, sometimes, towards the evening, the black shadow of a ship. This was the Great Beyond, with no road leading back from these rocky depths to the meadows and the larks, the smell of bonfires and the nut trees of Lovers' Lane. But it was the final stage of a pilgrimage. When they rounded the last bend of the road and emerged in the open Pacific, it was as if they were witnessing the state of things described on the first page of Genesis.

The Pacific Ocean was waste and void, and darkness was upon the face of the deep. The swell was colossal, although the wind was moderate, mountains of water heaved and sank so tempestuously that the dredger was out of sight most of the time. It looked as if they were still sailing among the giant rocks which had melted into mountains of seething liquid. They paddled on laboriously, amidst those ranges of heaving mountains. The universe seemed to reverberate with a colossal laughter. Eight thousand miles of loneliness behind these transparent monsters, with only one way of escape from their smothering scorn: to slide overboard, to become part of them; to laugh with the mountains, weep with the sky; to plunge in a moment from Genesis to Revelation. No gale had ever got the better of Jan, but the breeze on the Pacific finished him. After three hours he tried to behave normally, to chat and to play a game of Black Cat; but the cards dropped from his hands and he collapsed sobbing on to a stool, his face in his hands. Siemonov said nothing; he patted Jan on the back and got up and hauled himself, swaying, along the bunk and the washstand to the corner cupboard, where the bottles were kept. He poured out a glass, grunting "Hey, hey!" and "Now then!" to the ship, which was plunging so wildly that the drink splashed from the bottle. Then he said: "Chin up, borother—here, take this." Jan shook his head, convulsively. He didn't dare to look up; he wanted to curl himself up so small that the sea wouldn't notice him. But Siemonov pulled him to his feet by the collar, and he choked as the drink was poured down his throat. The alcohol burnt his palate, it stung his nose; he coughed and spat and staggered, cursing, between the swaying walls. Siemonov had sat down again, propped up in the corner, his legs on the drawer underneath his bunk —moored there for ever, it seemed, no matter how hard the wind blew. Siemonov played a game of Black Cat with himself, a curious spectacle, seen through a chink in the fingers: a huge bearded man, pretending at each trick that he didn't know the hand lying open on the table. He played with a kind of animal intentness; he fooled himself with convincing dignity. The spectacle was absurd and yet mysteriously heartening: a man, fooling himself in the midst of a threatening and chaotic world, without being the least afraid or even impressed.

It worked; Jan got up with a white face and stumbled to the door. He looked back from the doorway, propped up against the post so as not to be flung across the cabin by the enormous swell. The shadows of those waves rushed across the walls; water gurgled on deck with a sound of choking. He looked round at Siemonov who was playing cards there with his calves on the drawer, and who didn't even bother to bestow a glance in his direction. He looked at the tiny smoking flame in front of the icon, at the sea-boots sliding madly about on the heaving floor, at the oilskins swinging from their hook, like a hanged man in a gale. And a feeling overpowered him—a mixture of many emotions: hatred, love, disgust, friendship. But one emotion was there no longer, it had been eliminated by the gin and the Black Cat: the feeling of loneliness, the fear of life, the yearning for that cradle of the deep. He was so ashamed, looking at Siemonov playing cards with himself and yet hiding an ace in his beard, that he swung himself on to the bridge and faced the sea. He had to hold on to the rail for dear life, and was hardly able to breathe as he peered over the sprayshield. He stood looking at that sea, motionless, for so long that the man at the wheel thought he was asleep. But he wasn't. He was fighting the battle every sailor has to fight once in a life-time: the battle with fear and terror, the battle against the sense of nothingness engendered by this boundless force, the battle between a man and his Creator.

In Valparaiso a cable arrived from the owners. A cable Siemonov could make neither head nor tail of. "DO NOT SAIL UNTIL FURTHER ORDERS." He beckoned Jan into the chart-room and showed it to him. Jan couldn't make head or tail of it either. They agreed to keep it a secret from the crew for the time being, but of course cook ferreted it out and the trouble started. Early next morning Stobbe and Little Abel went into the messroom during breakfast and, as repre-sentatives of the crew, demanded an explanation from the Captain. The Captain was swallowing porridge in one of his grim Russian moods, and informed them that all he could tell them was to go to hell—and double quick too. Jan soothed them a bit when they looked as if they were going to make trouble. He explained that the officers were just as ill-informed about the reason for that mysterious cable as they were, and he advised them to sit and wait like the rest until some explanation was given, in which case they would be fully informed. The two representatives retired, rather disappointed, for if you're hanging about with time on your hands there is nothing like a bit of an argument to relieve the boredom. The officers in the mess talked it over. Bout said the cable was a sure sign that this was going to be a trip round the world which would take at least eighty years. Of course they'd be sent on to Surabaya or Singapore to

take a dry-dock home through the very worst of the monsoon
—that was the kind of thing those bureaucrats loved to
arrange. The third was afraid that the cable was about him.
He thought the owners had found that he had been sailing
above his rank and consequently the ship would have to
wait for the arrival of a new second engineer, now on his
way from Holland. Jan had no ideas; he didn't care a damn
whether they sailed east or west, Valparaiso was as far away
from Holland as any place could be, so if they sailed away
from there they would at least be getting somewhere nearer
home. He had the blues, and stared at each speaker with
vacant eyes, stirring his coffee.

Two days later a cable arrived that explained everything:
the company had ceased to exist. Van Munster's Transport
Company had been merged with the Kwel Tugboat Company and had become Kwel and International Tugboat
Company. Because the rivals of yore were one body now,
Kwel's *Vlieland,* due at Antofagasta with a string of barges
from Surabaya, would be sailing on to Iquique to pick up
a crane and go home via Tandjong Priok, where a harbour-
tug would be added to the convoy. The *Jan van Gent* was
to proceed immediately to Buenos Aires, where the
Schouwen was due with a pontoon in a fortnight's time, and
to sail home from there with a heavy floating crane, in
convoy with the *Schouwen.*

The news came like a bombshell to them, but their
reactions to it differed. Siemonov didn't care one way or the
other. He was even rather pleased for he hated having to
deal with a floating crane alone. As long as they left him
on his ship, the people ashore might arrange whatever they
liked. And he didn't care about his salary either; it always
vanished anyhow. In the foc'sle two schools of thought
emerged in the dispute about that cable. One half thought
it was enough to drive a chap to suicide—that miserable
slave-driver Kwel, expecting his men to pay for their own
grub, paying wages that were a disgrace to the white race;
the other half thought this was how the business should be
run. It was a scandal that five tugboat companies should
be cutting one another's throats on a coastline of barely
a hundred miles; no wonder the wages and the accom-
modation suffered. When the whole tugboat-business was in

the hands of one company, they said, the conditions would improve and the wages go up. And when all the crews were sailing under the same flag they'd have a chance to organize themselves and protest if there were anything that didn't suit them. The leaders of the two disputing parties were Bout and Jan. The third engineer's reaction was like Siemonov's and he didn't care either way; the first thought to cross his mind at the news was: now there's a fair chance that they'll forget all about me in the fuss of merging their offices and administration. With a bit of luck no one will ever twig that my promotion was only temporary. Bout was in favour of the merger. He was delighted at the idea because the engine oil that Kwel's engineers used was at least decent stuff—and just look at their ships, look how they were kept, how their paint shone, and their brass sparkled! Good God, one blushed with shame to lie alongside one of those yachts in a dung-barge like the *Jan van Gent*. And the trips were likely to get more reasonable too, once there were more tugs about to pick up the scattered junk in all these God-forsaken places. No more wearing out the poor old engines until they shrieked with agony; no more pistons knocking like steam-hammers through sheer neglect; no more packing rings getting worn so thin that one had to spend one's whole day nursing the damn things. Now the ship would get a proper overhaul in a decent dry-dock, now. . . .

But Jan was bursting with indignation. He stalked up and down the tiny room, shouting and waving his arms. Jan knew. Jan knew better than anyone else on board this blooming tug. Jan hadn't sailed for nothing in the salvage service for over six years. He'd competed with Kwel and his rascals; he knew how that crook sweated his crews, how he bled them white, how he had them in irons! They'd remember this day and what he told them when they got tied up to old Kwel's chain-gang. A crime, an absolute crime, that's what it was! Of course the idea of a merger was all right in itself; of course the present conditions were scandalous; but with Kwel, of all people! With Kwel, who paid his mates sixty guilders a month; with Kwel, who let the women starve after their men had been drowned or crushed to death in his service; with Kwel, who—you know the story, don't you? You know what happened to that poor wretch Meyer and

the price of razor-blades!" the *Schouwen* shouted back. Another hit; anybody's game now. Cook called: "What about dropping in for supper tonight, gents? We've got kidney beans, with eggs and bacon!" Cook scored a winner, for everyone knew that Kwel's crews lived on a diet of kidney beans only, because they were cheaper. And eggs were far too expensive. But the *Schouwen's* cook stood up to the challenge and shouted back: "You wait, you squinting liar, until I get across and write my name in your dirty pans!" Then a whistle from the bridge summoned them and the whole lot turned like one man, reverently, to face the altar.

An hour later the captain of the *Schouwen* was rowed across in the lifeboat. Maartens was his name. He was tall and plump and had heavy eyes in a large face, red and expressionless as a ham. But he wasn't to be despised; he had earned his laurels in the tugboat business. In '95 he had commanded the convoy that took the first dry-dock across to Africa; he got a medal for it and a testimonial, and his picture had appeared in all the papers. A layman wouldn't have recognised him from that portrait. For the purpose of the portrait he had worn a peaked cap with gold leaves on it, and the artist had given him a collar too, and put a cigarette-holder in his mouth. The man who came on board looked almost as ragged as Siemonov. He wore no peaked cap but an old battered hat, discoloured to a greenish blue by the sun and the brine of every latitude, and he had got a chipped pipe in his mouth instead of a cigarette holder. He spoke slowly with a lazy drawl, while his expressionless eyes wandered around the chart-room. He rubbed the top of the table with his hand and looked at his palm as he was speaking. Jan had planned to be as rude as possible to Kwel's agent, but when he faced Maartens he didn't dare. The man had an authority about him that took one's grin away, although he didn't show any emotion; if this fellow ever got excited one would have to watch one's step. Maartens said that he had orders to command the convoy, and so would Siemonov please be kind enough to be ready with full steam to-morrow morning at six sharp; he'd hear the rest in due course. Siemonov grumbled something like "All right" and offered the fellow a drink. When he drank it was obvious that he was a stranger to vodka. Siemonov offered him

another drink, and Jan realised that this was the beginning
of a treatment; but the fellow was cool and wily and said:
"No, thank you, one will do me nicely." Siemonov was
disappointed and showed it in his pig's eyes which were just
visible in the ambush of hair on his face. Siemonov took a
third one himself, which was unwise. Maartens pulled a
shabby wallet from his pocket, with a rubber band round
it, and after he had fished a pencil stub from his breast-
pocket and put it in his mouth to wet the tip, he asked:
"Horse-power of the ship?—Right.—Speed?—I see.—Length
of the hawsers? — Right. — Number of deck-hands? —
Thanks." After he had written all this down, very slowly
and painstakingly on the back of a postcard with a view of
a tulip field on it, the pencil stub went back in the breast-
pocket, the rubber band was replaced on the wallet and the
wallet was returned to the inside-pocket of his coat. After
he had gone cook said: "And to think that I knew that man
when he was only that high—I wish to God I'd foreseen
this. I'd have kicked him to death." The animosity of cook
against anything smelling of Kwel was overwhelming. The
night before they sailed he went ashore and came back
followed by an Indian carrying three sacks. The Indian
called him "Signor Capitano" and bowed from the waist
after putting the sacks down gently at the bottom of the
gangplank. When cook was asked what he had got in those
sacks he answered: "A nice surprise for Mr. Kwel."

The engineers of the *Schouwen* didn't come over to the
Jan van Gent for a chat, because they had no time. They had
scarcely a breathing space to snatch a meal, for within a
quarter of an hour after berthing the coaling of the ship
had begun and now they had to clean out the boiler tubes,
which would keep them happy all night. The mate was
pretty busy too; he had to go ashore and do some shopping;
and the captain would be busy all night in his cabin, cook
said, shaving his armpits. Jan shut himself sulkily in his
cabin to re-read Nellie's letters. In Buenos Aires he had
found four waiting for him. Dear Jan, and then a lot of
nonsense he was learning by heart: about the baby and
Mum and Dad and Bas; about the weather and the baby and
the *Fortuna*; about the house and the chimney and the baby;
about. . . . Only two more months, sweetheart, just two

months! And to his sea-chest he said: "We're going home to mother!"

As he sat there, happy and cosy with his pipe and those letters, his legs on the washstand, the door suddenly opened and there was Siemonov. Not once in all those seven months had the Captain come to visit him in his cabin: he was taken completely unawares. But after a moment or so everything seemed quite normal; Siemonov had brought his bottle with him and his cards and they played a game on the sea-chest, a swig a point. Neither Siemonov nor Jan mentioned it, but of course the ham-faced skipper was at the bottom of this. It must have been a bitter pill for a man like Siemonov to swallow, who had always held the reins himself, and was now expected to start trotting in someone else's harness. They played with great concentration, as if nothing at all was the matter; but however hard Jan tried, Siemonov lost and that made him very gloomy and Jan got rather drunk. After three games the Captain threw down his cards, tired of it all; it was past midnight and he got up to go back to his bunk. "Emperor of the Ocean—that's what that bloke in Rio called me," he said, as he turned. "Cart-horse would have been a better name." But before Jan had a chance to comment, or perhaps say the wrong thing, the Captain had gone, leaving the empty bottle behind him. On its label two women played the guitar to a dancing goat.

Jan looked at the women for a long time, before he went to bed; somehow they were depressing to look at, for the world of the dancing goat was a world Maartens would never understand. A world beyond that wallet and that battered hat; a world of heroes and giants and icons. For ten minutes or so it seemed as if all the fun and glamour had gone from the tugboat business. Now the clean, sober, routine men had taken over this gamble with the elements, the women with their dancing goat had acquired a kind of nostalgic significance. Farewell liberty, farewell youth. The future had a faint synthetic smell about it, like a factory, instead of the honest-to-goodness scent of tar and spray. Then he discovered that it was the drink that gave the smell when he hiccoughed, and he staggered to bed. Perhaps that was the reason why the Russians were sad; after the intoxicating passion of the beautiful women strumming idly to a dancing goat, the future smelled sulphurous and synthetic. He burned his fingers when he blew out the lamp. In the darkness black spots circled before his eyes: sleep was a great well into which he sank, darkly, to oblivion. Somewhere in the ship he could hear singing. Why should the future suddenly seem so frightening, so lonely and cruel and without joy? If Nellie were with him all his fears would be allayed. God damn that vodka and the stubby pencil, and the postcard of the bulbfields; God damn that hat and those beefy hands. If you lay one finger on my Russian, by Jesus, I'll kill you, Kwel—you and your automatons, and your sham twin-funnelled prams, I'll kill you, kill you. . . .

It was Siemonov who was singing.

The next morning, at six sharp, the mooring ropes hit the water and the two ships steamed into the inner harbour, side by side. It was a proud sight, to anyone who had a feeling for such things; the floating crane was made fast swiftly and expertly under the quiet authority of Maartens, and when they put out to sea, with the towing signal hoisted, Jan was forced to admit that those chaps of Kwel's knew what towing was. They might be crooks, but the way they handled a job was a lesson. Siemonov turned out to be as good a follower as he was a leader; during the first watch he took the wheel himself and responded so accurately to Maarten's signals that their ships manoeuvred together like a parallel-ruler. It was a joy for the eye, an exhilarating spectacle. This was indeed Holland's glory. A crowd had gathered on the quayside as they headed for the open sea. When the ships passed, the people waved, and on the vessels anchored in the bay small crowds stood lined up against the rails, waving too. Once they had passed the outer buoy Siemonov's course was laid down for him by someone else—for the first time in his life. He took it like a man; he didn't even bother any more, for now they were on the job, and the job came first. "Stick to *Schouwen*, borother," he said to Henkie, who took over the wheel, and Henkie grinned for this was the first time he had been called borother, so now he was a man.

After the meal, when Jan went on deck for a breather before turning in, he found out what was in those sacks cook had brought on board at Buenos Aires. When the fat

82

cook on the *Schouwen* waddled to the rails to chuck a load of potato-peelings overboard, his opposite number on the *Jan van Gent* came out with a pail. He banged two frying-pans together and when the cook on the other ship looked up, he showed him the pail triumphantly, then he tipped it over the rail with studied deliberation, and out slithered a load of empty egg-shells. The cook on the other ship stood one second, flabbergasted, before turning hastily away and waddling back into his galley, a beaten man. Every blessed day at the same hour cook turned over a pail of egg-shells into the Atlantic Ocean. When Jan said in St. Vincent: "Come on, cook, stow it. This has lasted long enough. One more go and that poor brute over there will have a stroke," cook grimly shook his head and replied: "Never in my life have I had so much fun for sixpence—I'm going to get my money's worth."

In St. Vincent a cable lay waiting for "Mr. J. Wandelaar, Mate, Tugboat Janvangent." It was a week old, and when Siemonov handed it to him Jan went as white as a sheet and ripped it open with trembling hands.

"June 7th son Bart all well Nellie."

Siemonov whacked his shoulder with a resounding thud, and Jan was so moved that he burst out crying, the fool. Cook knew about it first of course, and they all got hot dripping toast for tea, and Bout said: "By gum, if this is the result let's tell the boys to get going. Let's propose that the owners give a premium for every child."

No one admitted to spreading the news, but at sea rumour travels with the gulls. They had only been sailing for a quarter of an hour after the news had arrived when a signal was hoisted on the *Schouwen*. It was a curious signal, quite out of the ordinary, and it caused a minor panic on board, because until it was decoded from the book Siemonov was convinced something had gone wrong. When they discovered that it meant "congratulations," Siemonov cursed the blasted fools, but Jan stared at the signal with tingling eyes and a curious feeling in his stomach.

God knows how he managed it, but it was one of the most cunning things Mr. Kwel had ever done. He had tamed a potential rebel with just two flags on a bit of string. No dictator ever quelled a revolution at smaller cost.

CHAPTER FIVE

In his imagination he had pictured the scene a hundred times over. First the darkening haze on the horizon, then the dunes emerging from it, yellow and white under a blue sky. Then the pilot's cutter with Nellie on board, waving in the distance; then a longboat with Nellie in it, carrying a small bundle under her arm; then the rope-ladder lowered overboard and then that face, that face that had been smiling at him all those months, radiant as the rising sun on the horizon; that face that now looked up at him from the swaying cutter, smiling and weeping at the same time, longing to get on board and yet frightened for the sake of the child, and then. . . . Hell, he couldn't stretch his imagination any further; but when that wonderful day did come, he'd be able to press her in his arms and feel that she was still alive, and not just that he had sold his soul for a ghost.

A hundred times he had lived through all this, and when it actually happened it turned out to be quite different. An old bo'sun was reported to have said once that to be home was all right, but coming home was the very devil. And that's how it was with Jan: the nearer he got to home the more agonizing it was. When they got within the sight of land he was having a drink in the chart-room, the bottle in one hand and the glass in the other. The door of the cupboard squeaked as it swung to and fro in the swell. As he drank the glass rattled against his teeth and he took another drink to steady his hand. There were the pilot's boots clumping on deck. There was cook's voice, saying: "Hullo, old man, how's home?" And there was the pilot's voice answering: "Morning, cook; morning, men. Welcome home."

There were the calls of the men on the foc'sle to the oarsmen in the boat: "Look who's here! How are you? Want a rope?—Hey, look out with your blooming oars—new paint!"

Where was Nellie's voice now, that should be asking: "Where's the Mate? Where is Wandelaar?"

The door of the cupboard swung and squeaked. On deck

a voice hollered: "Mate!" Good Lord, he couldn't get his feet to move, and when they did start walking, the coward in him whimpered secretly: I don't want to, I don't want to; I don't want to go away from that cupboard. Give me another drink, just one more. I don't want to go out of the chart-room. I don't want to get off the ship!

When he climbed the stairs to the bridge with slow steps and a head that felt like a balloon, all he saw was the pilot, gabbing with Siemonov, and no one else except the man at the wheel. His mind had been a blank as he climbed on to the bridge. He had only repeated to himself, now it's going to happen, now it is happening. But nothing did happen. The pilot shook hands and said: "Hullo, Mate, welcome home."

And he answered mechanically: "Thanks, pilot."

So she was dead, she was dead! For God's sake don't mess about—out with it!

But the pilot went to the engine-room telegraph with Siemonov. He saw the man at the wheel peer at him in a curious fashion. What had been said on the bridge before he was called up? The pilot said to Siemonov: "We hadn't expected you so soon—had the wind behind you, I suppose?" And Siemonov replied: "No, no—we just stoked her up a bit; the trip had lasted long enough." And the pilot said: "I see." Then to the man at the wheel: "Port a little, Pete." The man at wheel echoed: "Port a little."

And the pilot again: "Keep her so, Pete."

And the man at the wheel echoed: "Keep her so."

Of course, you idiot, Jan thought, we're early. How the devil was the girl to know that? He reprimanded himself for his foolishness by a series of inward reproaches. You're out of your mind, he told himself. Why should Nellie come out on board a cutter? Who do you think she is—the Queen? Come on, keep an eye on your work, you blithering idiot. Look at Siemonov, he hasn't got any nerves, and he's just as thirsty. "Cheers, Mr. Pilot." "Your health, Skipper." Just a blooming waste of money, taking on a pilot, if you're going to set him reeling with neat vodka from a tooth-glass within five minutes of his coming aboard.

There was the jetty, with people waving on it. Little boats scudded about in its lee. Look out, you ass! Nearly went overboard that time. You and your staring! Pick up your feet, look where you're going!

Siemonov called: "Hop, hop, borother—the hawser!"

And he hurried down aft, his ears hot with shame. What a disgrace for a Mate to be called out of a dream by his Captain at the moment they entered port—a blooming schoolboy. He took his revenge out on the hawser, that had to be shortened for the manoeuvring ahead. It was scorching hot on the poop. The sun beat down mercilessly on the black iron and sweating bodies. He stripped off his shirt and threw it behind the main bollard. The sun beat down on his naked back like a fire when he bent down to undo the springs. The big winch hissed angrily, with Stobbe at the control cock. They had to wait for a signal from the *Schouwen* before they could start hauling in. Then it came. A crest of steam from the *Schouwen's* whistle; a few seconds' silence, then the long-drawn wail. Siemonov called: "Haul her home, boys!" Jan shouted: "Home!"

Stobbe opened the cock and pulled the handle, and the winch started its mad stampede. The heavy rope came coiling in, a giant snake, slimy with seaweed. They kept it amidships by forcing their chests against it. Five panting men, cursing at the slithering monster, were barely enough to keep it in check. The water poured down their backs and chests; it ran down into their trousers. Knots of seaweed flopped on deck, slithered down the rests. The winch clattered and hissed in a kind of St. Vitus's dance with Stobbe on its back, his figure blurred by the vibration. The *Schouwen* wailed again, Siemonov shouted down: "Make fast!" Jan repeated: "Fast!" And the winch ground, gnashing, to a standstill. They struggled with the loops that had to be taken round the main bollard. As the men coiled the rope in place, Jan and Stobbe battered the loops home with sledge-hammers. Then the *Schouwen* wailed for a third time, the engine-room telegraph rang out below decks, and when the hawser was pulled tight water spurted from it in flashing jets. Cleaning up the part of the rope they had hauled in and tucking it home took his mind off what was happening beyond the rail, until he heard a woman scream in the distance. He looked up, panting, his arms twitching from the strain and the seaweed dripping down his back and saw a boat with a woman clutching the gunwale. She screamed: "Who's the flag for? Who is it? Henk! Where's Henk?"

Henkie shouted from the foc'sle: "Here I am, Mum—here!"

The woman cried: "Henkie! My baby . . . !" And she sat down like a sack, laughing stupidly, trying to wave and blow her nose at the same time. Henkie didn't like it, he was furious with his fat mother and yet so moved that he paced about nervously, muttering: "The silly old fool; Christ, she might have known that it was meant for the Chief, I sent her a letter all about it."

Jan had forgotten all about the flag, flying at halfmast. No wonder that that woman got the shock of her life. Fancy Nellie standing on shore and thinking. . . . He hurried up the stairs to the bridge, turned halfway, ashamed of his dirty body and his soaked trousers, and jumped to the deck between the stoke-hole ventilators. At this point he started waving his arms madly, so that she could see him if she happened to be somewhere amongst the crowd lining the river. He felt the heat of the deck through his shoes. The funnel, huge and black behind his naked, gesticulating figure, radiated a terrific heat. He waved and shouted, running from port to starboard, waving at the crowd, shouting at the rowing boats swarming round them. Christ, what a lot of women! How the devil was he to recognize Nellie in that crowd? He got panicky when they all started waving back and cheering and dancing in their wobbling boats. It looked as if his Nellie had hidden herself among thousands of other waving Nellies, of all shapes and sizes. And of course she'd be furious if he didn't wave back. He waved his arms above his head and shouted: "Hurray!" like everyone else on board. He waved with the shred of cotton waste which was tucked in his belt. He cried: "Hullo! Hullo!" with tears of misery running down his face. She wasn't there, she was nowhere. Yet she seemed to be everywhere. Oh, Jesus, I wish I had been spared this, he thought. I wish we'd made that trip round the world after all.

The convoy sailed slowly up the river. To judge by the noise the people made, it was quite an event to have their men home again. The *Schouwen* had been away for seventeen months, the *Jan van Gent* nine. Yes, those van Munster crews made nice short trips; but those days were over now, Kwel had got them under his thumb. Kwel's argument was: "I'm paying these brutes to sail, not to lie in bed with their wives," and of course, he was right, in a sense. Where that crowd had sprung from at such short notice was a mystery; but they were obviously delighted. They cheered so loudly that Little Abel emerged from the stoke-hole to find out what the noise was all about. "Listen to them, the fools," was his muttered comment. All the deck-hands stood waving at the rail and shouting, pushing, cheering, stumbling. It gave one a feeling of giddiness to watch them.

When at last the *Schouwen* had moored at the quayside and Captain Maartens went ashore, he was met by a lot of gentlemen who hung a garland rather like a funeral wreath round his neck, and then he was photographed for the papers.

Nobody understood what all this fuss was about—Maartens himself least of all; but when one of the gentlemen started making a speech, he gathered that he had made the longest towing voyage in history: he had beaten Captain Barger's trip by four hundred miles. Three cheers for Captain Maartens! The gentlemen waved their hats in a congratulatory manner. Maartens shook hands with them all, amiably, and let himself be patted like a horse without moving a muscle in his hammy face. But the gentlemen seemed to forget that Maartens hadn't seen his wife for seventeen months, and was naturally anxious to find her.

She turned up at last, a tubby little woman with a flat hat filled with fruit. Her face was red and shiny and her white dress had smudges under the armpits after all these hours of waiting in the glaring sun. The gentlemen called bravo, bravo, when Maartens bent over her to kiss her; but the wreath was in the way and so was her hat, and in the end they just shook hands awkwardly. All she could find to say was: "Hullo, dear; how are you, dear?" But the gentlemen cheered so loudly that they couldn't hear one another speak.

The longest towing venture in history wasn't over yet, however. The gentlemen had their rights too. Yet another one started reading a speech from a paper. Maartens stood motionless and impassive, by the side of his wife who wasn't able to hide her own emotion any longer. She sniffed, hiding her face underneath the brim of her hat. The gentleman went on mouthing out words like "hero," "dauntless" and "immortal" over Mrs. Maartens' hat. Sometimes he became inaudible, when a cart rattled by over the cobbles of the quay or a horse-tram shrieked round a bend. When the speech was over Maartens shook hands with the speaker and said: "I thank you for the pleasant reception on behalf of my officers and men; it has been a pleasant ending to a pleasant trip." When the same gentlemen said farewell to him three weeks later, at the start of a voyage with a tin-dredger to Banka, and from there to God knows where, he would express the hope, on behalf of his officers and men, that this might be the pleasant beginning of a pleasant trip. Bravo! Bravo! Bravo! This was the stuff that nautical heroes were made of.

The crew of the *Schouwen* were given leave, and filed ashore, loaded with their belongings. Some of the wives were quarrelling already. "Can't you look where you're going?" one mother scolded, and another mother scolded back. Later, workmen of the wharf took possession of the ship which had to be docked that afternoon. An engineer from the works had arrived in a launch to check up on the condition of the engine. The Chief couldn't help waiting on the ship until he had had a word with the barbarians who were about to lay their paws on his engine. When the works-engineer came up the ladder he said: "I would like to warn you that the grease-cups. . . ." But from the quay a woman's voice called: "Chris, Chris! Where are you? We've got to catch the ten fifteen!" And he hurried off with a worried face.

When he had gone, the engineer said to his foreman: "Well—I must say she doesn't look too bad, the old junk-box."

No wonder. Those piston rods had been polished five hundred and sixteen times during the course of the trip, for the Chief lavished on his beloved pistons the paternal love which his family had to go without.

The *Schouwen* was taken to the dry dock, and that afternoon she was lifted slowly out of the water, her hull covered with weed and barnacles from the seven seas, and she looked like an old sea wall at low tide. By this time the *Jan van Gent* was pitching home on the choppy waters of the North Sea—on her way to her home port. Jan was happy, but the rest of the crew hated it. Most of them lived in Amsterdam, and their only worry was to catch the last train from the north. Down below, in the stoke-hole, curses and furious scrapings and clatterings rang out all day, for the stokers were flinging as much fuel under the boilers as the furnaces could take without getting choked up. Bout had to check them, shouting over the din of the engine in the doorway between the stoke-hole and the engine-room. "Are you out of your minds?" he yelled. "The safety-valve is blowing off." The deck-hands, now the job was finished, were making themselves presentable for the shore; a sudden passion for cleanliness had overtaken them. They spluttered and splashed and scrubbed in the lee of the midships on the poop, stark naked and very noisy. Stobbe washed them down with the fire hose; the heavy jet glinted in the sunlight and flattened itself into a fan of sparkling spray as it played on the back and chests of the scrubbers. Jan, too, had himself sprayed clean by the bo'sun. The jet hammered on his chest and tore at his legs; he scrubbed and splashed, and couldn't get enough of the hard cold water. He sang out at the top of his voice until the bo'sun managed to hit him on the mouth and made him choke. After they'd finished, the bo'sun inspected them like a humourless matron, to make sure that there were no more dirty toes and artificial shadows in the ears. Then cook treated them to a shower of fresh water, so that their wives wouldn't pull a face at the taste of salt. The trip was over; the fresh water he had watched over like a demon for weeks ran down their faces and went to waste. After the bath, he stood them a round of farewell coffee; they must take a happy memory with them of the ship to which they would be coming back in a fortnight. They drank the coffee slowly, luxuriously lying naked on the hatch to let themselves be dried by the sun.

Jan gazed at the shore, his chin on his hands. There was the gap in the dunes, the big dike between Camperduin and Petten. Another hour or so and he'd be home. He thought: tonight I'll sleep in a bed. That was difficult to realize. He thought: tonight I'll sleep in a bed with Nellie, and that was somehow so startling that he jumped up and ran down to his cabin to dress.

Siemonov stood on the bridge in the light of the sunset. He was happy, the ship was his once more. She was free of an alien master, obeying no one but him now. But it was not for long: already the dike between Camperduin and Petten loomed on the horizon. In an hour or so she'd be lying alongside the quay, and there'd be no one else on board except himself for days, perhaps weeks on end. Those are the hardest moments for a sailor: to be alone with his ship. A man likes being alone with his wife, but a sailor alone with his ship feels as lonely as the grave. He looked round on the deck below to find some fiddling job to give the ungrateful dogs who seemed to think of nothing else but ratting off the ship as quickly as possible—the faithful ship that had carried them safely through all those months of hazard and hardship. There were plenty of jobs left to keep them on board one night longer, so that he'd have one night less of loneliness and silence. . . . But Little Abel saw him peering and hurried below to get his accordion. He had a lot of things to pack yet, but this was something of greater urgency. He scrambled back on deck, ran to the corner below the bridge and started working to squeeze a song out of the accordion. The song was so nostalgic, so hauntingly Russian, that Siemonov, within three minutes, was spellbound like a snake. He stood gazing at the sunset, his hands clasped behind his back, his beard stuck up like a moon-attracted bear; then he started swaying to the music, humming the tune. The little charmer peered up at him and when he saw the first tears trickle down into his beard, he grinned and began singing under his breath: "We've got that train— we've got that train. . . ."

In the grey evening haze a spark flashed out suddenly on the horizon. Jan saw it from his porthole and whispered to himself: the lighthouse, the lighthouse. . . . Bas used to say on spotting it: "Well, boy—it's time you filled in the log." At that Jan used to jump down the stairs to the chart-room to light the oil lamp over the table, whistling as he went. Then, still whistling, he would take pen and ink from the cupboard and sit down to his task. Only when he began writing did he forget to whistle. Then concentrating on the page in front of him, he would write such entries as: "To-day after sailing at 5.30 a.m. heading for the lightship *Haaks*, we passed at 6.30 p.m. the bark *Heliade* of Norwegian nationality, which, struggling hard with a S.S.W. wind, asked us by means of the usual signals to tow her into the port of Ijmuiden. . . ."

Having filled in the log, he would put the book away, and return, whistling, to the bridge—a tall, fair boy, with untidy hair, and an old peaked cap on the back of his head —and there he would stand looking at the spark of the light-house and the flash of the lightship like a fiery question and answer glinting to and fro in the night. As he whistled he would think to himself: another day wasted crawling up and down this blessed coast; when would he get out of sight of these confounded lights?

Never had that boy suspected how long, how terribly long, that little stretch of time would seem, between the first glimpse of the lighthouse and the final putting into port, on one occasion in his life. The whole journey of sixteen thousand miles seemed nothing in comparison, a mere pleasure jaunt.

When at last he dragged his sea-chest up the stairs of the messroom and on the deck, a wave of joy overwhelmed him; mad, ecstatic joy, but tinged nevertheless with an unexpected sadness—and even a lurking fear. He was sad because this journey was over for ever, and a little afraid because the arrival of the child might put a barrier between himself and Nellie, and all the old familiar things might have changed. But the most curious thing of all happened when he took Nellie's portrait off its hook to pack it in his bag. He looked at the portrait which had been his inspiration and solace for nine weary months and he felt, as he put it away in his bag, as if some dear friend had died.

The *Jan van Gent* backed in against the quay. As her stern approached the wall a line was thrown ashore, and one of the beachcombers lounging about among the crates and the barrows caught it and hauled it in. When finally the loop of the mooring rope was hitched over the bollard Jan's job was done, and he looked up. And there confronting him were Nellie, Mamma Dijkmans and Father Dijkmans and a pram. Oh hell, what a to-do they made with all their waving and beckoning! Father Dijkmans jumped up and down on the quay, the old fool, and Mamma Dijkmans waddled panting to the gangplank, like a human jelly on the move. But Nellie stayed where she was with the pram. She had forgotten to take her hand down when she first caught sight of him, after having waved at no one in particular for quite a while. There she stood, one arm in the air; and there he stood, the loose end of the rope still in his hands, and they just gaped at one another. Then suddenly he yelled "SWEETHEART!" and jumped over the rail like a monkey. He frightened the life out of her, his twelve-stone bulk descending on her without warning, like a bolt from the blue. She was so startled that she couldn't help making an instinctive move to protect the pram. There were tears of joy in her eyes and she was almost too moved to smile. Jan grabbed her and swung her off her feet as he caught her in his embrace.

Meanwhile old Dijkmans stood gaping at them and seemed afraid that his daughter might be crushed to death before his eyes. He wanted to shake hands with Jan; he tried to loosen his arms to shake hands with him; he even hammered with his fist on Jan's arms and said: "Hullo, Jan! Hey! Don't you know me any more?" But Father Dijkmans couldn't get them apart. However, something squeaked and stirred in the pram and that did the trick.

Nellie took Jan by the hand and let him look into the pram. He stammered: "By jove, what a lovely kid!" But he was only guessing, because as it happened he couldn't see anything for tears. All he made out was an eiderdown and a tiny pillow with what looked like the top of a coconut on it. Nellie and he looked at each other, smiled, sighed, and once more embraced.

But they had to come down to earth sometime, and it was Mother Dijkmans who brought them back with the sensible suggestion: "You help Jan pack his things, love; Father and I will go ahead with the baby." It seemed that she remembered the ways of lovers better than Father Dijkmans, who started to protest loudly, until she slapped her hand over his mouth and hissed an explanation in his ear. So they went off in the sunset, with the pram wobbling over the cobbles on the quay, while Jan and Nellie stayed behind. Jan and Nellie went on board the *Jan van Gent*. For Jan it was a solemn moment, though he couldn't quite say why. The fact was that the presence of Nellie made him incapable of any clear thinking. All he could do was to keep looking at her.

Nellie had shaken hands with Siemonov and the cook and Stobbe and Little Abel and everyone else who came shuffling hurriedly past, eager to get away. Bout popped out of the engine-room and he had to shake hands too, after he had wiped them hastily on the seat of his boiler suit. It was funny how self-conscious Bout was with women. He grinned and coughed, and only managed to keep his end up with: "Pleased to meet you, and it has been a very nice trip and what nice weather we have had lately, very nice."

Then the third engineer arrived and made quite a stage affair of it with a courtly bow and his hundred-per-cent man-of-the-world smile. "Well, madam, bursting with joy now your husband is home, I take it?"

Poor Nellie had not got much knowledge of human nature. When she and Jan were safely in Jan's cabin she remarked: "Nice fellow, that young engineer; the fat one seems a bit silly."

Jan said: "The fat one is, bar Siemonov, the finest chap in the world; the third engineer is a washout."

"Is that so?" Nellie said, "just fancy. Who'd have thought so at first sight." And Jan said: "That's why you should never judge a person's character at first sight, but wait until you have got to know them a bit."

Nellie looked at him with tender eyes. "Sorry, Mr. Mate; I won't do it again," she said. That was a direct invitation to a kiss. Bout came in in the middle of it, blurting out: "Sorry. . . ." and bolted like a rabbit. Jan jumped up and opened the door again and called: "Come on, don't be silly; what do you want?"

But Bout muttered: "No, no, it's nothing," and escaped through the door to the stoke-hole, the odd cove.

Well, there they sat, in his empty cabin. Woman-like she began nosing round, opening all the drawers—she whose

94

portrait had kept him company there all those months. She had got a bit fatter and her nose seemed a little out of the straight, but that was probably the portrait's fault. Curious, after all, to know the portrait of your wife better than your wife herself, to believe almost that the photograph is the real thing, and she only the copy. "What's this?" she asked, holding up a pair of socks he had left behind in a drawer for the cook to throw away. He said: "Oh, a pair of socks from Rio; they are finished."

"Good Heavens!" she exclaimed. "Who on earth would leave filthy things like these behind?" And she inspected them with a wrinkle in her nose.

O Lord, O Lord, they hadn't seen each other for nine months and now with hundreds of things to talk about they needs must discuss a pair of dirty socks. He tried to say something; he started: "Love, Nellie, I—I. . . ." But so much emotion was released by those few stammered words that he took refuge in the socks and started to tell her breathlessly where he bought them and for how much and for what purpose, and how nice a party it was, and what a wonderful view there was from the roof. . . .

He babbled and babbled with her hand in his. And she listened, gazing at his eyes and mouth. The cabin got darker and darker. At last it had got so dark that she could hardly see him any more, and as she had only been looking, not listening, she suddenly asked with a start: "What's the time?" He hadn't the faintest idea, and, after all, who would bother about the time after nine months of. . . .

But she said: "I hope it isn't past ten, I've got to feed the baby!" Oh Lord, the baby! Yes, of course, right you are. He struck a match to look at his watch in his waistcoat over the washstand, and lied. "Quarter to ten—but you MUST see the cabin with the light on." But she couldn't sit still any longer, and that lovely, humming silence with only one's voice softly murmuring in the background had been swept away. They went out and as Jan shut the door of the cabin a feeling of sadness caught him unawares. Goodbye, cabin, goodbye. . . .

"Come on, Jan," she said.

"Oh well—let's go." It was hopeless trying to get at the bottom of all those emotions anyhow.

The evening didn't pass quickly; it seemed rather like the evening of their wedding day. It was mostly Mother Dijkmans and Father Dijkmans and gossip and giggles and grilled herrings and come on, boy, tell us something, and come on, Jan, take some more. And then the showing of the child, whom Jan thought downright ugly, but whom Mother Dijkmans pronounced to be the bonniest bairn she had ever set eyes on. Mmmm, I could just eat you, though little Nellie was bonny too when she was as small as that. The child yelled its head off, lying on the table, while its napkin was being changed. Look at those leggies, just look at them, and those little thighs; oho, I could eat him, so I could. The women fussed around the child, and Father Dijkmans tried to make it grab his pipe-stem, but Mother Dijkmans chased him off. Jan had to say it was sweet and ducky and fat and healthy till his jaw ached with saying it. After that he was allowed at last to go and lean against the doorpost of the backyard for a moment, to peer out into the night and relight his pipe. He was dead tired after all this fuss, much more tired than after a stiff watch at the hawser; and the swell still seemed to be under his legs; he had to lean against something to get a feeling of steadiness. Well, my friend, now you're home. Now you have got at last what you have been hankering after all this time. You had better be truly grateful now for all the blessings Mother Dijkmans has counted for you; because if they should ever suspect that you're longing for the *Jan van Gent,* longing so badly that it makes you groan, they. . . . Good Lord, listen to that child screaming, as if it were having a fit!

He hurried back, deeply alarmed, to find his son red and convulsed with rage in the lamplight, with a mouth as large as his head, and shrieking so piercingly that the women were hardly able to make themselves heard. But after a moment or two the tantrums passed and all was peace again. "The little darling," Jan tactfully murmured, and hurried off again to the blissful solitude of the backyard.

When the old folk had gone and Nellie was washing the tea things in the kitchen, singing and clattering; when the child was back in its cradle, making little sucking noises and grunts—only then could he sit down in the horsehair

chair, his stockinged feet on the table, and light a fresh pipe
—home at last.

It was a nice room, really, he decided—high and spacious.
And all those nice knick-knacks on the walls and mantelpiece
—just as it was the day they married. Only the lino had been
worn down a lot in so short a time; those women just barged
about in their clogs as if it cost nothing. He sat with his pipe
purring, and examined Nellie's housekeeping book which
he had found behind the clock on the mantelpiece. How
quiet it was in the house now, how cosy. Memories pervaded
that little room, memories as delicate and as precious as the
little crystal wine glass he had brought from Rio.

The lamplight made a kind of circular horizon line in
the smoke which floated in drifting veils about the room.
For nine long months that lamplight had shone on Nellie's
hands while she was making little sheets or sewing vests that
wouldn't cover a man's hand, or writing in this housekeeping
book. A small, black book, dog-eared and covered with
smudges. He turned the pages cautiously with his hard
fingers. Yes, she certainly wrote a beautiful hand. He had
shown her letters to almost everybody on the ship after a
month or so. Look, doesn't she write a beautiful hand? he
had said. And then the others had shown their letters too,
and they had compared them; and, oh well, after all they
might as well read them too. He had read the letters of
everyone on board, and he had been often amazed to find
how alike they were. All of them were about the children
and the weather and the milk that had gone up a farthing
a pint, and do you know about him and her? And then:
Well, I must finish now, for the baker is at the door or the
baby is crying or Annie has come to fetch me for the choir
practice. Cheerio, dear; everybody sends their love and I
hope you'll be home soon.

But not one of these women wrote such a beautiful hand
as Nellie did, so even and flowing and with such lovely
flourishes, and never a word crossed out, never a blot. Even
in this little book she had written with that even, flowing
hand, and those elegant flourishes although it was intended
for her own eyes only and written in pencil, like a log. It
was in fact a kind of housewife's log, this little book.

October 7th: bread 11 cents; soda 3 cts. When she wrote

this, he was dangling in the rigging of the *Scottish Maiden*. Or perhaps he was dragging that drunken captain to the hatch of his cabin with Kees, or battling with the splintered wheel. Funny that the woman whom he loved more than anyone else, who was really part of himself, should have been writing down half a loaf and a pound of soda, or letting the cat in.

November 12th: ½ lb. bacon 8 cts; 2 eggs 10 cents. That day she had been extravagant and treated herself to pancakes and bacon, the darling. And he—let's see—he must have been walking to and fro on the bridge in the rain in the Bight of Benin, or helping Bout to haul Siemonov up, who had been too weakened by malaria to walk. The ship had been like a madhouse in that endless downpour; screams and wild howls from the foc'sle, where the men lay tossing and sweating with fever in a stench like a goat-house.

March 22nd: 4 yds. flannel 80 cents. That must have been meant for the child; she knew by then she wasn't alone any more. Perhaps little Bart had already started kicking her knitting off her lap whenever she sat down for a moment to rest, as she described in her letter. And that was the day he sat in Rio de Janeiro looking at the monkeys with Bout on that terrace, or had been strolling with the third engineer under the royal palms of Botafogo.

April 18th: cough-mixture 16 cts; fever pills 1 guilder 25 cts. Fever pills? God Almighty—she had never written to him that she had been ill! It made him angry; he wanted to call and ask what she had got to say for herself. But he listened to her humming in the kitchen, with a tiny tinkle every time she put down a tea-spoon after drying it. Never mind, it was a long while ago, anyway. But let's see just how long she has been ill for. . . . *"April 23rd"*; that's another hand, not nearly as beautiful; must be Mother Dijkmans'. *Butter 24*, with a blot; *Doctor 2.50;* the doctor, even! Good Lord, what a touch-and-go business life was—this might just as well have read, "Hospital twenty guilders"—the book might even have stopped there. And while she lay dying, perhaps calling his name, he would have laughed just as lustily with the boys in the dark long-room of the training ship in Valparaiso, when the couple crashed off the platform or when the red-faced officer was hit on the head. The

thought made him so uneasy that he wanted to go and join
her in the kitchen, but when he lifted his legs off the table
they were so stiff that he groaned and stayed where he was,
rubbing the backs of his knees. Yes, that was the price of
luxury; one had to get used to everything, even sitting
still.

June 5th—that was a strange page. First: *4 bowls, 86 cents.
One rubber sheet, small, 50 cents; 2 yds. navel ban——* and
then it stopped. The rest of the page was covered with
scribbles and funny little drawings, like the ones he made
himself in the rough log as he sat thinking, or had to wait
until the ship settled down a bit before going on with his
writing. A dot, and then a spiral round it, and at the end
of the spiral a little figure with rakes for hands and its nose
on the side of its head, and then, in shaky letters, growing
larger and larger *Jan, Jan, Janjan—JAN, JAN, JANJAN-
JANJAN.* There was a blot as if a drop of water had fallen
there; she had been dabbling about in it with her pencil,
had drawn little tails out of it, and then a heavy scratch,
running right off the page. What a strange page. When he
looked at the next one he recognized Mother Dijkmans'
writing again in ink. The entry for June 6th had been lost.
The book went on with *June 7th; veal cutlets 30 cts. Potatoes
12 cts. Midwife 7.50. Cable Jan 9.20.* Lord, he had been more
expensive than the midwife!

He sat looking at that odd page for a long time, and then
turned to the last one. *July 12th.* That was yesterday. Did
she know by then he was coming home? She couldn't
possibly, and yet it said: *Bread 33 cts. 1 oz. Hurrays 15 cts.*
He flicked the pages back, and saw that for over a week she
had been taking three times too much bread, and every other
day an ounce of Hurrays. He had had them for tea that
evening: biscuits with red, white and blue icing and
"Hurray" written on them. They weren't living in a seaport
for nothing. There were also biscuits with orange icing and
"Cheerio" printed on them, but these weren't nearly as good.
Yes, she must have known that he would be coming home
to-day, for the last entry in the book was: *½ lb. flour, 15 cts.
4 eggs, 20 cts. 1 basket of raspberries, 25 cts.* She had known
it before the others had an inkling. He remembered how his
mother used to say: "My legs are so funny to-day, and my

head's so dizzy—I bet your Dad'll be coming home tomorrow."

He understood now why she wouldn't let him in the kitchen when he offered to help her with the washing up. When a little later the door creaked open and she came in, shuffling cautiously, carrying a raspberry tart fresh from the oven, he was greatly surprised and said: "Well—I never!" with wonderful sincerity. By that time the little book was back behind the clock on the mantelpiece, exactly as it was before: upside down with the pencil sticking out of it.

When at last she had finished fussing around with the plates and spoons, and the tart stood steaming in the lamp-light with a huge corner missing, and he was picking up the crisp crumbs from his plate with his thumb, she sat down herself. She uttered a sigh of contentment and her heart was full of things that no words could express. Jan put his open hand on the table and she laid her hand in his. "Now let me look at you," he said. She brushed a straggling lock of hair out of her eyes with her other hand, still red and damp with the washing up, and smiled at him. There were the eyes, the sweet, earnest eyes that had haunted his memory all those months, and there was the sweet, soft mouth. "Well," he said, "here we are at last, love."

She laughed and her lips trembled a little, and when she rubbed her eyes with the back of her hand she said: "Fancy the smoke stinging like that; I'll have to get used to it again, I suppose."

They went to bed at midnight. At four o'clock in the morning he woke up; the routine of the watches hadn't got out of his system yet. It took him a little while to realize where he was, but when he heard her breathing on his shoulder he kissed her forehead, stared into the darkness for a moment, and was asleep again before he knew what had happened. When he dozed off again he dreamt he was looking up at the grey sky of the Straits of Magellan, where a swarm of white birds wheeled about, crying softly. And a seagull swooped down at him, screeching, then soared up again into the sky, its cry fading. He opened his eyes and saw the early sunlight shining through the curtains. From the open kitchen door came the soft splutter of bacon frying in the pan; in the cradle the baby cooed.

He opened his arms and stretched luxuriously, as if he were lying in the sun, and as he heaved a great sigh of content the sigh formed itself into a word: HOME.

CHAPTER SIX

NEAR the harbour of den Helder was a pub, with a fat landlord in it called Timmer who had a bald head, three chins and three fat daughters, constantly smiling like their father. This Timmer had been doing good business of late, for more and more of Van Munster's deep-sea tugs were coming home from their long voyages, which was a good thing from Timmer's point of view. When the crews of these tugs got home they found a printed notice waiting for them, announcing the conditions that would prevail as to salaries and food now the fleet had been merged with Kwel's.

The men read these notices with indignation and set the flower-pots on their parlour tables dancing as they banged the tables in their rage. Snorting with fury, they went out to share their grievances with their pals. At their pals' homes they shouted and cursed and belaboured the tables until the children woke up howling. They were then, of course, chased out by their pals' wives before they had even started to discuss the scandalous business in coherent terms. In these circumstances it was natural that a protest meeting should be held to define the general attitude of the employees of the late Van Munster's Transport Company towards the Kwel regime.

And where could a protest meeting be held better than at Timmer's? He had an oblong ballroom, with creaking chairs and hissing gaslight and a rostrum where speakers could vent their indignation and shake their fists at the ceiling. After about three speakers had roared themselves hoarse, and the smoke had become so thick that the last speaker could hardly be seen, an interval was called. When the doors to the saloon were opened, there were Timmer and his three fat daughters standing by the beer-engines, with glasses at the ready, just waiting to stimulate the feelings of hate and indignation if they showed any signs of flagging.

The interval lasted rather a long time, for there was a little man there with a club-foot and a broom, called Piet. He wore a white coat and was called a waiter; but all he did was to wipe the floor of the meeting-room. For during the first half of the meeting there had been so much spitting and ejection of tobacco plugs on the floor that the speakers might well have slipped and broken their necks, and then who would have saved the seamen's children from the vicious exploitation of Kwel and his gang? Because Piet had a club-foot and did his job conscientiously with a yellow broom taller than himself, it took a long time for the meeting to be resumed. But after Timmer had been in there three or four times to have a look round and to abuse the dilatory Piet, the leaders of the protest meeting decided that they had waited long enough. They kicked Piet out and called the members in, and the shouting was resumed. It was a good thing for Mr. Kwel that he wasn't present at those meetings, because he would have been drawn and quartered every time. But Mr. Kwel had sense enough to stay at home and employ agents to do his work for him.

During the meetings one of these agents was present in a far corner, writing busily in a little book, unconcerned by the mounting indignation which eventually expressed itself in a decision to send a telegram of protest to Kwel. This was the only practical measure that emerged after four hours of roaring, stamping, whistling and applause—the one grain of wisdom sifted out from all the dross of verbiage. The telegram stated that the officers and crews of the deep-sea tugboats *Albatross*, *Medusa*, *Seahawk* and *Hercules* protested most vehemently against the lowering of their wages and the arrangement by which they would have to pay for their food themselves, and that they were resolved to resist these unilateral decisions of the owners with all the means at their disposal. A reply was expected before the meeting closed.

One of Timmer's daughters had the kindness to take this telegram straight to Pauw, the postmaster, who'd have to be dragged out of his bed for it and that was a woman's job. But she was so fat she couldn't go very fast, and she squinted as well so she took the wrong turning occasionally. In the meantime the meeting had to be kept going, and how could this be done better than at the counter in Timmer's saloon? In there the poor panting Timmer could hardly cope with the orders, for now he had only two daughters available, and Piet wasn't much use because he frequently stumbled and spilt the drinks, and when he got a kick under the counter he stumbled further and spilt more.

But the other daughter, now ploughing her way doggedly through the night, was doing a magnificent job, for the answer arrived just one minute before closing time; she had waited for it in the post-office. In tense silence the envelope was ripped open by the first man who happened to get hold of it and he read out hoarsely that Mr. Kwel had taken note of the protest and would give the questions raised his earnest attention at the earliest opportunity. In the meantime he urged the officers and crews of the tugboats in question to resume their work and await the outcome of his deliberations without impairing the efficiency of the service. The protest meeting roared and whistled and made uncomplimentary noises and so on; but it was a long telegram, painstakingly worded, so the meeting had not been without results. Kwel had had to get out of his gilded bed to send an answer, and this was only the beginning of what they'd do to that bastard, if only he knew it.

The meeting was adjourned with a few last fiery words from one of the more ardent spirits, and the men went home noisily through the empty streets, to tell their wives that they'd let that slave-driver have the truth for once, by God, not half, and to hit the table until the children woke up howling, and that was the end of the fun. At that point the wives voiced a protest of their own, and the men went hiccoughing to bed and an historic day was brought to a close.

The next morning everything was as usual except that Mr. Kwel had received from his agent a list of the ringleaders whom Mr. Kwel would deal with in due course with all the means at his disposal. Those means were a lot more effective than the ones at the disposal of the rebels. When the men had sobered up they realised that their only weapon was a hunger strike by their families and this wasn't much good if mother didn't happen to fall in with the idea. And when mother refused to die of starvation for the justice of the cause, the only thing to do was to wait until Mr. Kwel had completed his earnest consideration of the grievances in question. And that's what he was still busy doing when the tugboats sailed again with the same crews and the same captain, who had been handed a slip of paper containing the names of the ringleaders, with instructions to keep them under close observation.

Yes, Mr. Kwel knew what he was doing all right, and so did Mr. Timmer. There were certainly some clever people in the world. And they must have some place in the scheme of things, for no thunderbolt descended from the sky to hurl them to perdition, as happened in biblical times, and the pastor said since the Bible was written nothing had changed in the eyes of God. So Mr. Kwel and Mr. Timmer must in some mysterious way be forces making for good, which was exactly what Kwel's agents said. "It's all for your own good, boys—and if you can't realize that it's because you can't see beyond your own noses."

On the night of July 20th, 1909, they were all very busy at Timmer's, for another protest meeting was about to start. It was the fifth one, true; but this time it looked as if it was going to be a particularly noisy affair, for the most recalcitrant section of the rebels was due to have its say—the crews of the *Hydra*, the *Galebird* and the *Jan van Gent*. Those were the ships that had been away longest, the *Jan van Gent* as long as nine months, and nothing fostered bad feeling and recklessness like a long trip. The chances were that tonight there would be some pretty strong language flying about.

Timmer had been told that people were coming from as far afield as Amsterdam to attend the meeting; and although a seaman's word isn't always gospel truth—for he likes sometimes to take a rise out of people, especially if they're the fat, profiteering sort—Timmer had ordered his daughters and limping Piet to fit out the loft as a dormitory. The loft could hold fifty people, if the mattresses were properly arranged, and the cost of a night's lodging would be a crown, with a good breakfast thrown in. It was Piet's job to make sure that the rat-traps were emptied before the guests went to bed, in case the sight drove the guests off in search of other lodgings.

Kwel's agent had taken his precautions too; now that the riff-raff of the *Hydra*, *Galebird* and the *Jan van Gent* had been stricken with the contagious disease of protest, reinforcements should be kept ready for any emergency. The policemen whom he asked to keep an eye on the meeting were not very eager; most of them had been flung out of the windows before. If the gentleman was afraid of being molested, they said, he had better stay away. So outside aid had to be enlisted in the form of thugs of various kinds, including some huge fair-haired boys with white teeth and carnivorous grins. During the meeting the boys would be having a beer at the counter, like ordinary peaceful citizens, so if anything should go wrong they'd be near at hand. But the agent impressed on them that they weren't to turn up before he called them. He had handled situations like these before, and knew that things would go off all right as long as there was no provocation. He'd make himself as inconspicuous as possible in the corner nearest the door, so that he could slip away at the first sign of real trouble.

At about eight o'clock the men started crowding in. Their boots rumbled on the floor, their bulky shapes obscured the light, the smell of their rain-soaked duffels thickened the air. The hired bodyguard had arrived earlier, but they attracted no attention because the men had eyes for nothing but the glasses and bottles behind the bar. With thirsts already mounting, Timmer and his daughters could start smiling and pulling the handles straight away. The men raised their glasses to Timmer's daughters with such uncomplimentary remarks as: "Your health, tubby," or "Here's to you, my buxom sausage." Timmer's daughters smiled affably enough; they were paid good money for these rather crude endearments and they weren't self-conscious about their figures either, for wasn't the human figure God's handiwork? When one of the men pinched Alie's arm to find out if that vast expanse of pinkness was real she didn't object; and Miebet giggled coyly when an ogre with rings through his ears, a nose like a loganberry, and a glass eye, tickled her under the chin with a black-nailed finger and roared: "Now aren't you well upholstered, ducks! What about a double gin for Uncle Jimmy?"

At first Jan Wandelaar, the young Mate of the *Jan van Gent* hadn't felt like going to that meeting; but when he got a letter saying his wages had been cut by half and that he would be free in future to choose what food he liked and pay for it himself, because so many complaints had been received about the monotony of ships' rations, he was wild with indignation. He had got the wind up. He had nearly had a row with Nellie because after cursing and shouting he had started banging on the table until the cups danced, and that set the child yelling, which had the effect of transforming the sweet and docile Nellie into a towering virago.

He had gone out in a rage, slammed the door, and marched on board the *Jan van Gent,* where he found Siemonov still in his bunk at three o'clock in the afternoon in a stifling cabin. The blankets and the floor were covered with paper shirtfronts because the Captain happened to be reading the serial printed on the back of them. Siemonov had had a letter from the owners too. But why bother? If that was the way things were going to be, what the devil could a simple sailor do about it except shrug his shoulders, and clear off to sea as soon as possible. Back to sea, my boy; where we have the sky and waves for company, which is a much better bargain than Kwel's itching palm. Mr. Kwel couldn't buy the happiness of a free man on a bridge in the sunset for a million meals of kidney beans; Mr. Kwel was a madman and all one could do was to pity him. Siemonov said he'd rather live for the rest of his life on ship's biscuit and stale water in an open boat, than sit down on Mr. Kwel's cushion and scratch his head and ransack his brains to devise a way to screw another penny out of those grinning seamen who possessed some secret happiness that he, Kwel, hadn't got. Jealousy, that's what it was: the old devil was eating his heart out with jealousy. And, by God, he was right—let him choke in gold, he'd never have enough of it to make a sunset.

But Jan let loose all the indignation he had worked up at home, and after a while Captain Siemonov came to like the idea of a good old row with some healthy shouting, and he promised to go with Jan to that meeting, just for the fun of it. After all, as Captain he ought to acquaint himself with the complaints of his crew.

When they entered the saloon it was as full as Mr. Kwel's purse and the atmosphere was electric. The whole crew of the *Jan van Gent* were there; and there was Wolters, the Mate of the *Hydra*, and Boer, the second engineer of the *Galebird*. Jan stood a moment bewildered on the edge of the crowd, but there was Bout, the engineer, waving his arms to attract his attention, and Little Abel, who shouted: "Cheers, Mr. Mate! Death to Kwel and his rabble!" That toast was too good not to be seconded by anyone who happened to hear it; fists shot up with flashing glasses, and the lamps vibrated with the roar. Thus the meeting started by consigning Kwel and his swine to blazes, and everyone was happy. On this note of unanimous hostility the meeting began; a shrill voice asked the comrades to take their seats in the meeting-hall, and they complied with a shuffling of feet that sounded like the rumble of an earthquake. When the hall was full and the doors had been shut on Timmer's daughters and their nervous giggles, a man mounted the rostrum and screamed for silence in a piercing voice. Jan recognized the speaker to be Verwoert, the second engineer of the *Terschelling*, who had come to see them on board the *Jan van Gent* in Brest and who had made him a present of a book called *The Right to Strike*. Jan was amazed to see the man here, for he had sailed for Kwel all his life. But an engineer of the *Galebird*, who was sitting next to Jan, told him that this man Verwoert had been fired by Kwel on the grounds of subversive tendencies, and now he made it his business to plague the life out of Kwel. Verwoert, in the meantime, had started a speech in which such words as Freedom, Slavery, Proletariat and Capitalist bulked large in his oratorical scheme. But after he had been declaiming for a while with a whole range of frantic gestures, a rival speaker hoisted himself on to the platform, pushed Verwoert aside and lifted both arms for silence. The meeting threatened to split into two parties, one yelling: "Verwoert is speaking—let him have his say"; the other shouting: "Good boy, Janus, kick him off the platform!"

Janus stood with his arms upstretched, like Moses, utterly unperturbed. He even shut his eyes while he waited there in serene confidence, as if his whole life had been devoted to the suppression of revolutions. But it hadn't. He was in fact the bo'sun of the *Hydra* and he was married to a negress. Of course the meeting had to chew over this information after it had been broadcast by the opposition, and a few questions were shouted at him about black Venuses and khaki children, but he kept his arms up and his eyes shut and in the end he won, though he had to wait some time. At last the meeting quietened down, or rather the noise subsided sufficiently for him to make himself heard. He opened his eyes first, then his mouth, and the voice that came out of it was so deep, that the opposition fell silent in amazement.

"Boys," he roared, "I won't say anything to get excited about, only this: we are here as free men, in a free country, to protest against. . . ."

By this time the opposition had recovered from the shock of the voice and started heckling him: "Get on with it! Don't muck about, say something!"

But the speaker roared on, without moving a muscle of his colossal ape's face—"against Kwel and his tricks, but that is not a social issue, it is merely an affair between ourselves and Kwel. We don't need any professional agitators; we aren't sitting here to be mouthpieces of the Socialists; we are FREE men who have got only ONE thing to decide: what are we going to do about Kwel? And if this gentleman here has nothing else to offer but a world-revolution, then I must say that it seems to me as nonsensical as shooting sparrows with a blunderbuss."

There were cries of "Hear, hear!" The opposition became confused, for this speaker could at least be heard. "And that is why," the speaker concluded, "I should like to propose that this meeting makes it plain to the Socialists that we are not going to be led by the nose by a man who is paid for putting us up against our owners. For if we are indignant, it's our own business and nobody else's."

That was man's talk. Thunderous applause and more shouts of "Hear, hear!" proved that Janus had succeeded and that the first speaker had failed. Afterwards Verwoert tried to convince the meeting with a few business-like arguments that they'd have to start by organizing themselves into a trade union, if they wanted to get any results at all. Within a week they'd be at sea again, and if they had to organize a trade union first before going to Kwel, they couldn't afford to waste precious time in useless talk.

Scores of new speakers emerged from the din and the smoke, all of whom thought that they weren't understood because they weren't speaking loud enough. One said that a trade union was nonsense, for most of the men were at sea all the time, and you couldn't organize people who were scattered all over the globe. Another started a speech that was completely unintelligible, and the audience shouted: "Take that quid out, chum, can't hear what you're saying!" But he mumbled on till the next speaker got up and shoved him off the platform. The new performer declared that he had only one thing to say: They must send that crook a telegram; it must be short and unequivocal, and it must point out to that crook, in a few short and unequivocal words that they, being free men, wanted to make it unequivocally plain that he, that crook, must not think. . . .

The fourth speaker leapt on to the platform like fury incarnate, roaring: "Yes! A telegram, men! Let's make it rhyme! "To the bloodsucker of the tugboats, on behalf of the boys of the fleet: Damn your wages, bloody skunk, we shall roast you in your bunk!" Cheers greeted this gem of poetry, and the next speaker. . . .

It was a depressing business, really, this spate of ineffectual, incoherent verbiage. When at last the time came for the interval and the honoured gentlemen were received with open arms by Timmer and his fat daughters at the counter to have their flagging ardour revived by gin, Jan realised sadly that Verwoert was right. These lunatics wouldn't achieve anything worth while this way. All they would do was to get roaring drunk, perhaps knock each other's teeth out, have a hell of a row with their wives and then sail again, with splitting heads, leaving Kwel still holding the trump card. Wonderful boys on board ship and at the hawsers; but in this business they were mere children. He strolled dejectedly towards a corner of the saloon when the crowd at the counter showed signs of coming to blows, good-humoured and friendly blows, of course, at this stage, but later on it would probably be a very different story.

In the corner Bout was sitting at a table with a couple of strangers. Siemonov stood making wild gestures in the tobacco haze, his cap on the back of his head and his stomach stuck out, with the thin skipper, Zuurbier, of the *Hydra*, racing him like an undertaker. Bout introduced Jan to the engineers of two other tugs and to the mate of the *Galebird*, a young chap like Jan, who had just come out of a nautical school in Amsterdam. The officers grumbled to one another and shook their heads as they discussed the nonsense that had been talked before the meeting adjourned for this breathing space. As they talked they kept glancing at the counter where the crowd was getting more and more bellicose. Bout thought the whole affair was a depressing business and the others agreed with him as they sat there sipping their drinks; when Van der Gast, the captain of the *Galebird*, and later Siemonov and Zuurbier joined them, the full staff of the three tugs were sitting together in one corner, as if a signal had been hoisted: "Let's keep together for mutual assistance."

After half an hour the bo'sun of the *Hydra* clapped his hands in the doorway to the hall: "Come on, gentlemen! Let's start the meeting again and be quick about it— decisions have to be taken!" Yes, by God, and no light decisions either. The glasses were drained in a hurry and thrown on the floor, as there suddenly seemed to be no room on the counter to put them down. The crowd packed into the smoky hall, and a few moments later limping Piet was thrown out and the doors banged to. But the officers didn't move. They stayed where they were round the table in the corner of the saloon, and ordered the same again. "This round on me," Zuurbier insisted. Behind the doors the shouting and cheering started all over again, but somehow it sounded even more depressing and pointless from this distance. They listened in silence for a while to the roaring, the stamping and the applause, while Timmer and his daughters and limping Piet were washing glasses behind the counter. Then Bout sighed: "Yes—such is life," and tapped on the table with his glass. "This one's on me," said Bout. "It doesn't happen every day that you find yourself with fourteen colleagues round one table."

No, it certainly didn't, and that was why they should use

the occasion, Jan said, to decide what course the officers should take in the matter. Or were they expected to take everything lying down? Siemonov flicked at a gnat and said: "Oh, what the hell."

Zuurbier shrugged his shoulders and Van der Gast said: "Oh, well. . . ."

"What's the point?" Bout asked. "There's nothing we can do. The tugboat-business is a monopoly now."

But that young mate of the *Galebird*, Vitter or Gitter or whatever his name was, thought they certainly could do something; they could go to another company. Apart from Kwel there were four other tugboat companies in Holland: Meulemans in Flushing, Herder in Maassluis, the National in Ijmuiden and Kiers in the Isle of Terschelling. So it was wrong to talk about monopoly.

"That's right," said Zuurbier, "but only the National does deep-sea work, the rest are just harbour-tugs, which do an occasional salvage job. And once you've done a long voyage you won't ever get used to that coast-work again."

Van der Gast said: "That's true enough, and what's more you'll never get into those others. They don't build any new boats themselves; if they took over another ship from someone else they'd promote one of their own crowd. They'd never take on an outsider as a captain."

"To hell with them," said Siemonov, hammering on the table. "Borother, the next round's on me!"

As if they suspected that there was something going on in the saloon, first Verwoert and then Kwel's agent slipped in from the hall, bringing with them a wave of noise and smoke each time the door opened. Verwoert approached the table with glistening eyes and an attache-case full of pamphlets. Here, at last, would be people who would understand him. Now he really could. . . . But he made a sad mistake. Zuurbier pointed out to him curtly and firmly that they had no use for his talk and they didn't care for his company. Verwoert, however, put up a brave show. "Oh, I'm sorry, chums; I thought that I, as a colleague. . . ."

"Colleague be damned!" grunted Bevers, the chief of the *Hydra*. "If you've plotted yourself out of the service that's your affair. But now you're paid to make trouble, don't call us colleagues. We're not one of your sort."

111

Red spots of anger appeared on Verwoert's white cheeks; he said in a shrill, quavering voice: "Where the hell did you get hold of the ridiculous idea that I'm paid for this! Not a cent do I get, not a cent! I'm doing it only because I want to help you, because I have come to realize. . . ."

"Tell that to the marines," Boer of the *Galebird* said. "You wouldn't be creeping about the quay with that bag full of that stuff for nothing. What do your wife and children live on—paper?"

Verwoert's lips began to tremble. He looked ill, the poor devil. "Not a cent do I get," he whined again. "I make a living as a plumber; that's all I can do. But I'm not a criminal, not me! I've always done my work honestly, haven't I? I. . . ."

But Van der Gast interrupted him. "Clear out," he said, indicating the door with his thumb. Thereupon the salesman of the proletarian millennium disappeared into the rain, taking his attaché-case of pamphlets with him.

Jan pitied the fellow. But the men were right. It was his own fault; he had sailed with Kwel all the time, so he had no business to start complaining now. . . . "Listen here, chaps," the mate of the *Galebird* was saying, "why shouldn't we draw up a protest of our own, or go to see Kwel ourselves, the fourteen of us?"

Kwel's agent placed himself in the background where he could hear every word. Up till now only a few officers had been to these meetings: to have all the officers of three boats round one table was a chance not to be missed. But he wasn't surprised that they should have turned up here in full force. These boats had been away longest, so the men had all the grievances of a long trip in common. The crowd in there was easily dealt with, but these fourteen men were more dangerous. He ordered a drink, unobtrusively; when it came he leant back against the wall with his eyes shut, as if he were asleep, his hat on his forehead and his feet on a chair. His bodyguard of yokels wondered why the hell they were there. They had been bored to death the whole evening in that empty saloon; now they strolled into the hall on the off chance that something might happen in there presently. The agent, with his hat over his eyes, didn't notice them going in. Van der Gast asked: "Who are these chaps?"

And Boer answered: "Don't know." The agent, however, didn't hear it because of the sudden din that broke out when the doors were opened.

"Believe me," said Boer, "you can't do anything except pack up and clear out. For you youngsters who haven't got a family to look after, there may be some chance. But for the rest of us there's not a hope. So for God's sake let's work for a few cents less; at sea we are among ourselves and that's the main thing. What we choose to do about food when we're out of sight of land is nobody's business; if Mr. Kwel wants to find out he'll have to swim."

It was too dangerous for the agent to start making notes, even though his fingers itched to do it. He had a good memory, but to keep an accurate record of what fourteen men said. . . .

"Maybe it's more difficult for you than for us," the young mate said (Jan knew now that he was called Bikkers); "but Mr. Wandelaar will agree with me that we'd rather starve than let ourselves be stripped and robbed by that crook without lifting a finger!"

The agent risked it. He yawned, pushed his hat back, cast a sleepy look round, called for another beer and started flicking over the pages of a dog-eared railway guide, like any commercial traveller might do.

"I must say I agree with him," Jan said, "even though I've got a wife and child to provide for." It was wonderful to be able to mention that casually; he felt something of the quiet authority of these old family men come over him. He added up secretly how much he had got left, then knocked with his glass on the table. The next round was on Mate Wandelaar of the *Jan van Gent*.

Why shouldn't a commercial traveller jot down the times of trains for the next day? When the dim little man in the shadows started scribbling no one gave him a thought.

Timmer brought the glasses. The men were silent as he passed them round, but once his back was turned Zuurbier said: "Yes—if I was young and single like Bikkers here, I think I'd get out. By God, I would. It's not just a matter of shrugging our shoulders and saying 'To hell with him.' The fact is we've got to stay and swallow whatever insult that bastard cares to fling at us. It's all very well talking about the free life of a sailor and the pride of a command—but the grim fact is that we're all at the mercy of that—that—well—he's the scourge of the tugboat-business, that's what he is and so—your health, Wandelaar, and we know what we're all thinking."

They raised their glasses, and Jan proposed: "The liberation of the tugboat-business!" The others hesitated for a second, then Van der Gast said: "All right—I'll join you. 'To the liberation of the tugboats and the downfall of Kwel!'"

The agent wasn't by nature a sensitive man, but this quiet demonstration did something to him. It was much more menacing and alarming than the bellowing behind closed doors which was now reaching another incoherent climax. If these burly seamen should find out that one of Kwel's spies was eavesdropping on them within a yard or so. . . . Only then did he realize that his bodyguard had vanished. He looked apprehensively round the room, glancing towards the doors.

"You're right, Zuurbier," Van der Gast agreed. "We're just a lot of bloody slaves, that's what we are. He could cut our rations down to chicken feed, and our wages to a kid's pocket-money, and we wouldn't be able to do a thing. There is, damn him, nowhere to go; he has blocked every single loophole, the swine. Let's admit it, even if we can't do anything about it. My God, I've been wanting to say this for a hell of a long time. I've been wanting to yell it from the bridge, to shriek my throat hoarse, like those fellows are doing in there now. Sometimes it is a curse to be a skipper; the moment you raise your voice, you're finished."

"I'll tell you what," Bikkers said. "I think I'll cock a snook at him and go to the merchant service. Why the hell hang around in the tugboat-business when it's the monopoly of that crook? I bet you the merchant ship owners will be glad to have me, for everyone knows that the tugboats breed good seamen."

And then Van der Gast looked at him with his knowing old eyes and laughed softly.

Jan asked: "What do you mean?" He had been thinking on the same lines as Bikkers: better a mate on a tramp than let himself be bled white by Kwel. He felt the indignation, stimulated by the gin, tingle in his fists, and obsess his brain, and he thought to himself: easy, Jan, easy, my boy—you're heading for a good old row. Yet that indignation was somehow dangerously pleasant—almost sensual. It was wonderful to see yourself just for once as a poor, misused slave, kicked around by a boss in a silk hat. In some dark corner of his mind an irrational fury was slowly uncurling like a snake. What started as a kind of drunken bravado became a primitive and alarming impulse, something that was not directly inspired by his own personal experience. It was as if all the ancestors who had ever been ground under the tyrant's heel had risen from their graves and infected him with their accumulated hate and indignation. "Why shouldn't we go over to the merchant navy?" he asked, hoarsely.

"Don't you know?" Van der Gast asked. And when Jan, Bikkers and the engineers confessed they didn't, he told them something that was listened to in breathless silence. He told them, in fact, that they couldn't go over to the merchant service because according to nautical rules the time served on sea-going tugboats didn't count as the practical experience necessary for a mate's or master's certificate in the merchant service. Anybody wanting to pass his examination as a mate or master must have at least three hundred sea-days' experience before the mast; but sea-days on a tugboat were not sea-days according to that rule; they were "canal-days," valid only for certificates of master or mate on the inland waterways.

Canal-days, by God! On no ship sailing the seven seas could a man get greater or more varied experience of seamanship than on a deep-sea tugboat—a tugboat with its four-hour watches after four hours' rest; a tugboat where you stood up to your waist in water most of the time you were on the bridge, a tugboat where. . . . "But no! We aren't allowed to claim those as sea-days, because they're officially rated as canal-days. Lord help us! We, who drag dry docks of vast tonnage from one end of the world to the other, are pronounced unfit to sail a pleasure steamer from Amsterdam to London! We, who deliver pontoons, floating cranes, dredgers, sluice-gates (and is there a more difficult tow than a sluice-gate?) safely to the remotest parts of South America, are unfit, according to that rule, to hold the wheel of a coaster! We, who are tossed between sea and sky for fifteen or perhaps twenty months on end, with thirteen souls on board who start cutting each other's throats with claustrophobia after being at sea less than a fortnight, we who rub our eyes with wonder every time we deliver those lunatics back safe and sound to their wives, knowing that it's an absolute miracle that we haven't had our throats slashed or our skulls bashed in months ago—we tugboat officers aren't considered to possess sufficient authority to tell the messroom boy when to wash up his dishes, or to superintend the polishing of the brass! And who do you think is responsible for this rule? Who do you think bribed the members of Parliament one by one, with the help of the big capitalists in Rotterdam, whose names and addresses I could write down for you on a piece of paper? If you want to know who's behind it all I'll tell you—it's the same Mr. Kwel who's bought us lock, stock and barrel, as if we were merely fittings that go with a ship."

"That's a lie!" cried Jan. "I won't believe it! You can't tell me that our Parliament would let itself be bribed like—like the French customs!"

"Strike me dead if it isn't true! You tell them, Zuurbier! Is it God's truth or isn't it?"

"It's true," Zuurbier said, "it happened a couple of years ago, when we were running away from him in our dozens, we captains and mates, because we wouldn't stand for his nonsense any longer."

"That's right!" said Van der Gast hotly. "When the big boom started, when he couldn't get enough staff to man his coffins, and the merchant service offered us gold—gold, mark you—all the captains, one after the other, ratted on Kwel and on the other owners too, although they weren't so bad. But the others weren't as sharp as Kwel. They started improving their ships and raised the wages to keep their men; it cost them a hell of a lot of money and that's why our Van Munster went broke. But Mr. Kwel knew something better; he and his cronies in Rotterdam—the wharf-owners, the coal bosses, the big ship-chandlers, spent half the amount the others laid out and bought over some stinking little party in our incorruptible Parliament, and that law about tugboats was passed without a murmur. And so here we are, bound hand and foot."

The agent could hardly keep pace with it all; his fingers were aching with the pressure of his scribbling. But presently there was a slight lull when that boy—what was his name?—"Wandelaar"—smashed his glass on the table and roared that the next round was his again. The boy seemed to be rolling in money and rather drunk—but that was all right: drunken people spoke the truth, and the truth was what Kwel wanted to hear: nothing but the truth.

"Men!" Jan Wandelaar cried, getting shakily to his feet and spilling his drink; "you may be too old, too timid or too tired to cut that crook's throat, but as a seaman I've had my dose of him. I have seen Meyer blow up in his *Marken*. I have known old Van Munster as if he were my father, and I owe him more, in fact, than I owe my father. You and my children shall witness my oath, that I won't sail another mile under his bloody flag except as his sworn enemy. I swear that every beat of the ship's screw shall be the sound of another nail driven into his coffin, and every command I give shall be a wish to see him burn in hell. Who'll drink with me to the damnation of that bastard Kwel? Here goes!"

But even though they were drinking at his expense, the rest of them thought this was going too far. Only young Bikkers got up, with blazing eyes, and their glasses clinked so hard that one made a noise like the twang of a snapping string. "Here goes, Wandelaar!" Bikkers shouted: "To hell with Kwel!"

"Easy, Bikkers. . . ." Zuurbier said, dragging the boy down by his belt. "To-morrow you'll regret it, for Providence sometimes takes a rash man at his word."

Van der Gast emptied his glass and shook his head. "Wonderful boys," he said, "wonderful boys—I wish I wasn't sixty. With such mates"—and his gnarled finger pointed shakily at Jan and Bikkers—"with such mates the tugboat business has grown into Holland's glory; and once these youngsters become skippers Mr. Kwel had better hide himself in the attic, for they'll ram their bows through him, though they have to scuttle their ships to do it!"

He threw the glass over his shoulder and it rolled across the floor with a bumping sound until it hit the skirting. He kicked the table with a drunken boot, making the glasses wobble and finally topple over with a crash on to the floor. Then he shouted: "Timmer! The next round is on Skipper Van der Gast, the damned soul of the *Galebird*!"

And Timmer hastened to fill the glasses for the fourteen damned souls, breathing a little prayer of thanks to the mysterious Mr. Kwel who did so much to stimulate the liquor trade. He didn't quite know who Mr. Kwel was, and he had certainly never set eyes on him, but if he ever entered this pub, and made himself known, Timmer was willing to present him with a bottle of his best gin, without even asking a deposit on the bottle.

When Timmer carried the tray to the table the broken glasses crunched under his feet, and the sound wrung his heart. But even those glasses would repay their cost with interest, for Karel Timmer, though he wasn't much to look at, had a better eye for business than the mates and skippers of the deep-sea tugs. In fact Timmer and Mr. Kwel had this in common: they knew that two and two made four, and the man who knows his arithmetic is the man who gets on in this world. Certainly Mr. Kwel knew his arithmetic, though he didn't know how to sail a dinghy and the movement of a ship made him turn green. But it's amazing what a man can do with just a pencil and a piece of paper.

Mr. Kwel knew who was worth paying and who wasn't; Mr. Kwel was a great student of human nature, a great businessman, a great patriot. He was the creator of the tugboat business which earned the name of Holland's glory. When the first dry-dock had crossed the ocean and arrived safely, with only three deck hands drowned, a cabinet minister had become quite lyrical at the banquet organised to honour this Captain of Industry. "Mr. Kwel!" the minister had cried, almost weeping with emotion, "I think I am even justified in saying Brother Kwel, for we face each other at this moment as brother patriots, as sons of the same illustrious motherland—Brother Kwel, in these historic heroic days the people of Holland, of Europe—nay, of the whole world, look up to you as a lonely giant rising from the ocean, which you have bound with your chains of steel, which you conquered as St. George conquered the dragon . . . the people of the earth, I say, see you towering from this ocean like a legendary figure, a lone survivor of the Great Flood. . . ." At this point the minister dropped his spectacles and was unable to read any more of his speech until they had been found again.

When at last the minister had his spectacles handed back to him by a lackey wearing the Order of the White Elephant because he had served the Emperor of Siam's breakfast in bed, he continued to cover his brother patriot, this son of the same illustrious motherland, with the flowery garlands of his eloquence. But of the seamen who had slaved, and sweated, and starved, and died for Kwel, not a word was said. Posterity might have supposed that Kwel's career had been a shining example of uprightness and square dealing. There was, however, a letter in existence which might have made a future historian raise his eyebrows. In this letter the father of Holland's glory wrote to his son: "No business becomes great without a little sharp practice now and then, but the blessing of God must rest upon it."

At all events, Mr. Kwel was a pious man. And he had every reason to be.

Little Abel, the stoker, was the first to spot the bodyguard. He jumped on his chair, agog with excitement and indignation, and yelled: "Men, we're betrayed! There are spies in the house, Kwel's spies—there they are!"

This was the clarion call the restive and frustrated crowd had been waiting for. As at a command, the chairs flew off the floor and into the air, and chaos descended on Mr. Timmer's precious ball-room. A great weight of masculine fury hurled itself on the traitors with a bloodthirsty roar. The bodyguard, completely overpowered by this avalanche of wrath, defended themselves desperately; but a hawser was something quite different from a plough, and a sloop out of control was a lot more dangerous than a bolting horse. The bodyguard was flung into the saloon and the doors went with them, to the accompaniment of the roar of splintering wood, and howls of rage from the infuriated seamen. Timmer's daughters dived behind the counter like disappearing puppets in a Punch and Judy show; Timmer himself ducked away to safety; the agent at the table, afraid of being crushed to death, flitted out of the door into the night like a bat. The officers in the corner jumped up and tried to check the panicking herd, tried to bring them to their senses by shouts and commands, and even by kicks and blows from their chairs; but they might as well have tried to check a landslide. The walls of the saloon cracked under the weight of the crowd. A great cheer broke from the throats of those who had shouted themselves hoarse to no purpose at all that evening. One by one the groggy guards were lifted overhead on the sea of waving arms and thrown through the windows into the street. There were six of them and only four windows, and there wasn't a splinter of glass left in the panes after the enemy had been finally cast out and peace restored. Mr. Karel Timmer was restored to an upright position by a beer bottle being broken across his hindquarters, and his daughters were dragged, screaming, from beneath the counter by their plaits. The four of them, almost demented by fear, started pouring gin into beer glasses and beer into trouser-legs, with hands that trembled like aspen leaves. The orgy lasted until well past midnight; by then not even the tables were left whole, although they were made of iron. The police came to have a look at last, showing pale faces for a moment in the black holes of the windows, but they were wise enough not to interfere.

No one quite knew how they got home—whether it was Bikkers who piloted Jan, or Jan Bikkers, or Siemonov the two of them. But in the end they found themselves in the chart-room of the *Jan van Gent*, with lumps on their heads, and sentimental tears rolling down their scratched cheeks. They had a glass of vodka to celebrate the good results and to swear eternal friendship, with glasses that seemed to elude one another when they tried to clink them, until at last they met with a resounding crash. When Siemonov dropped his cards in the middle of a game of poker, they dropped theirs too, and lapsed off into unconsciousness straight away, and when they came to they found themselves surrounded by sodden paper shirtfronts and puddles of vodka. Siemonov was still sitting upright, huge and motionless, like a dead baboon. Jan threw a shirt front at him, which missed, and another one which missed too, and when the third one grazed the crown of his head he toppled over, crashed on the floor like a falling factory chimney, murmured "Mother," and slept on.

Nellie said nothing when Jan came home, torn with remorse and a headache. She was boiling milk in the kitchen, very pale and very composed. She said nothing when he babbled: "Sweetheart, little girl, I. . . . You must understand, we. . . ." She only backed away from his reeking breath with a gesture of disgust. But when she came in and saw him sitting in the horsehair chair with his elbows on his knees and his head in his hands, gazing miserably at a hole in the oilcloth like a despairing angler staring at his float, she said: "Go to bed, you big boozer." And when he lifted a hand in weak protest she grabbed him by the arms and dragged him to bed. Having taken off his boots and a few of his clothes, she pulled the blankets over him and left the room without even looking back.

But a little while later she returned to put a wet sponge on the lump on his forehead; and he opened his eyes and mumbled: "Sorry, old girl. Forgive me."

At first it seemed she would go away without a word, but she sighed and said: "I've got nothing to forgive."

"Yes," he said thickly; "yes, yes, you have. Please forgive me."

"I haven't got anything to forgive," she repeated. "But Kwel has—and let's hope he will."

Kwel didn't. Two days later Jan got the sack.

CHAPTER SEVEN

YES—that old Captain Zuurbier of the *Hydra* had been right enough when he said: "God sometimes takes a rash man at his word." And often things said in an unguarded moment alter the course of a man's life. That's how it was with Jan.

After Jan had read the letter which Nellie found on the door mat that morning there was silence for a while in the little room. In the pink light of dawn they read the letter together, read it again and again. *". . . Having taken note of your opinions, as expressed on the evening of the 11th inst., we consider you unfit to command a vessel flying*

the flag of Kwel & Munster's International Tugboat Com-
pany, and in consequence we regret to inform you that as
from the first of next month your services will no longer
be required."

Unbelievable. A piece of downright nonsense. He, the best
mate of the fleet; he, the boy whose study had been paid for
by old Van Munster himself, given the sack! No, it was
impossible. It was all a mistake, or just a threat on the part
of the owners. When he went to Rotterdam himself and
apologised nicely everything would be all right again. Of
course. "Come on, sweetheart, don't cry. What's the matter
with you? Of course it's all nonsense. You don't know these
owners; this is the way they teach their rebels a lesson. Come
on, stop snivelling. Now you've started little Bart off too!
Tomorrow I'll go to Rotterdam and put things right in a
minute. In a day or two I'll have to sail again with the
Jan van Gent, so don't let's waste our last days together with
this kind of nonsense. . . . Tomorrow I'll go, and in the
evening everything will be as right as rain. Yes, sweetheart,
I know it is an expensive journey to Rotterdam, but that's
the price one has to pay for being foolish, don't you see?"

Mr. Kwel had many more ways of making his rebels pay
the price. There was some salary owing to Mr. Mate, and
Mr. Mate claimed it after the clerk with the greasy hair,
who presided behind the counter, had at long last convinced
him that he was indeed absolutely and irrevocably dismissed
on the grounds of hooliganism and subversive language.
What proof had the owners? He would like to know. "My
dear sir, if you don't mind. . . . What did you say? You do
mind? All right. In that case we'll read out to you the
offending statements."

The clerk rang a little handbell, and another clerk with
a little moustache appeared. "Would you be so kind as to
bring me the files on Wandelaar, J.?" the first clerk said.

The man with the moustache vanished again. The other
clerk flicked over the pages of the ledger in front of him and
Wandelaar, J., stood near the desk, whistling bravely and
drumming his fingers on the ink-stained wood while he
wondered to himself exactly what they had got against him.
There was the little moustache again, bringing a yellow
envelope. The first clerk flicked through a wad of papers

with fat white hands. "Mr. Wandelaar—now let me see, yes —perhaps you would be kind enough to tell me if it is correct that during the course of a meeting last Saturday night at the inn of Mr. Timmer in the Harbour Street of your town, you spoke the following words: 'You and my children shall witness my oath that I won't sail another mile under his bloody flag except as a sworn enemy. . . .' Excuse me! Let me keep that paper, please! 'I swear that every beat of the ship's screw shall be the sound of another nail driven into his coffin . . . ?' I notice you do not try to deny this, and I'm glad you don't—it saves us a lot of trouble with lawyers and so on. Who told us? My dear Mr. Wandelaar, a good captain knows what's happening on board his ship and a good owner also knows something about the men he pays. And, Mr. Wandelaar, I hope you'll forgive me for saying so, but in my modest opinion the owners have treated you leniently, very leniently indeed, by just dismissing you and not. . . . But, my dear sir, is it so difficult to understand? What's that? I know, I know—but you must see that it is not the point! You may have salvaged wind-jammers single-handed; you may have saved dredgers; and taken over command when the whole ship was down with malaria—that's not the point! You must realize yourself that any company that values discipline and good relations on board its ships cannot—one moment please! I'll thank you to let me finish what I have to say—cannot, I repeat, employ anyone in a responsible position who, in the presence of the officers of three ships and their respective crews, pro-poses a toast in the following terms—yes, here it is, a report of the actual words, a toast to 'the damnation of that bastard Kwel.' "

The former Mate of the *Jan van Gent*, Jan Wandelaar, shuffled through the twilight gloom of the office to Desk C, where the accountant would give him all the particulars relating to his salary. A tall man with a bald head, like an egg, and with spectacles that looked as if they had been painted into his face by a child, presided at the desk. "Who? Ah, yes, Jan Wandelaar."

The accountant put his pen behind his ear, which seemed pushed out of its normal shape by the habit, and a blue spot of ink showed on his temple, like a mole. The stool creaked and his skeleton-hand grabbed a little bell. At this summons the clerk with the moustache reappeared from the other side. "H'm—the h'm files of Wandelaar, Jan, h'm please." The skeleton-hand went on totting up figures on a page while the moustache collected the files again. Ex-Mate Jan Wandelaar, standing in front of the desk, didn't whistle this time, nor drum his fingers on the ink-stained wood. He just stared at the accountant with big, worried eyes and a boyish mouth —young Jan again, cap in hand, waiting to be scolded. What a mess—what the devil was he to do now? Lucky thing they owed him that salary; it gave him a week in which to look round for another job, before Nellie's little housekeeping book began to show a deficit. And that expensive journey! Nellie was quite right, it was more than a week's wages.

After the clerk with the moustache had brought the same envelope again, and after the accountant's bloodless fingers had rummaged through the papers for a long time, like the white snouts of pigs delving into a trough, the second stage of the torture began.

"Mr. h'm Jan Wandelaar?"

"Yes, sir. . . ."

"I have h'm unpleasant news for you."

"Yes, sir. . . ."

"We owe you h'm fifteen guilders sixty-three cents for services rendered and bonus."

"Yes, sir. . . ."

"I am sorry to h'm have to tell you that this amount is insufficient to cover your debt to the Company."

"Beg your pardon, sir . . .?"

"Look, Mr. h'm Wandelaar: here is a h'm contract dated October seventeenth, nineteen hundred and six, signed by Mr. van Munster on the one hand, and you on the other. In it, Mr. van Munster agrees to pay all your expenses until you have passed your examination for the Master Mariners' certificate, ocean-going tugs. Remember that contract, Mr. Wandelaar?"

"Yes, sir. . . ."

"Well, it stipulates that you, on your part, agree to serve for a period of ten years as either mate or skipper with Mr. van Munster's company, and that, in the event of your wanting to leave his service before the ten years have elapsed you shall pay back a reasonable proportion of the expenses incurred on your behalf. This service, Mr. Wandelaar, started, according to these documents, on July twenty-third, nineteen hundred and eight, and it consequently terminates on July twenty-third, nineteen hundred and eighteen."

"Oh Lord, sir, I didn't know that! I. . . ."

"Here you are, Mr. h'm Wandelaar. Here is the contract, duly registered and stamped; and do you recognise this as your signature?"

"Yes, sir, but. . . ."

"One moment, Mr. Wandelaar. Let us get this clear before we enter on a discussion. Paragraph D of this contract says, that you shall pay back that reasonable proportion of the expenses incurred on your behalf in case of voluntary retirement, or—and this is the clause to which I should like to draw your attention—or 'in case of the probationer's dismissal from the owners' service as a result of incompetence, insobriety, immorality, etc., as specified in the Charter as grounds for dismissal.' There follows something about lawyers and arbitration, but I think this—h'm—is sufficient for the time being."

For Jan it was more than sufficient for the time being. He stood gaping dumbly, while the accountant rambled on about Kwel and Van Munster's International Tugboat Company having taken over all rights and responsibilities of the late Van Munster's Transport Company. But he had ceased to listen. The voice seemed to come to him from a dream, and it reminded him somehow of the droning talk of the stokers when they came out to get a breath of air in the lee of the bridge. Only when the accountant, with a cough like a pistol shot, drew his attention to the calculation he had made did Jan rouse himself up. How the man had arrived at this result Jan didn't know, but the upshot of it was that after his salary had been deducted he owed the owners the sum of one hundred and thirty-three guilders eighty-five cents.

He said nothing. He didn't even look at the features of the accountant behind the desk who had started talking to him as man to man. He gazed through him at the square patch of blue sky, framed by the window, and at the white cloud that sailed majestically across it, borne along by the soft summer's breeze. The accountant pointed out to him as man to man that the owners had h'm treated him exceptionally leniently, in view of the fact that the merger of the companies had come into operation over two months ago, and so, legally, he would be entitled to only—h'm—let us see—nine guilders twenty-three cents instead of h'm fifteen guilders sixty-three cents; but when the lucky man didn't seem to be impressed by this unexpected windfall, when he didn't even seem to be listening but remained gazing in silence at the cloud moving across the window, the accountant felt duty-bound to point out that paragraph E of the aforementioned contract stipulated expressly that a restitution as described in h'm paragraph D could not be claimed from the heirs and assignees of the signatory party in the case of death, with h'm suicide, of course, excepted.

In the end the signatory party was so crushed that when he left, cap in hand, he even said "Thank you, sir," to the accountant, and also to the hall-porter, who looked a lot more seaman-like than the famous Captain Maartens who made the longest tugboat-trip in history, for the porter had silver stripes on his coat and silver anchors on his collar, and he wore a peaked cap decorated with silver braid.

Outside the sun was shining brightly and great clouds sailed in splendour across a deep blue sky. Jan strolled along the embankment into the park. There the tramps loitered in the shadows of the chestnut trees; the gravel crunched under the boots of nursemaids who wheeled prams, with wobbling canopies, beside banks of flowers and through the transparent green of the shadows. What the nursemaids hoped to find was a bench where some respectable gentleman sat reading the paper with sparrows chirping at his feet; or perhaps a ship's officer with his cap on the back of his head and his legs outstretched, recovering from the perils of the deep.

It was like a stroll through another world to walk slowly along the paths and through the shadows, past all those benches full of happy, lazy people; to escape from heat into coolness. Even the tramps sleeping in the grass, with their heads propped up and their hats on one ear, looked like resting animals in paradise. The nursemaids threw sidelong glances at the tall, tanned boy strolling along with the supple, rolling gait of a young sailor, but he was unaware of it. He sat down on a bench at the edge of a lake where stately swans, angry and insulted, tried to chase away any intruder who trespassed on their stretch of water. Jan abstractedly watched the play of light and shade, and when a little old gentleman, with thin legs and flat feet and spats like horses' hooves sat down by his side, he didn't make room—even when peered at indignantly over the tiny half-moons of the old gentleman's pince-nez, nor yet when a straw hat, with a hollow sound like a box, was slammed down ostentatiously on the other side of him. Presently the old gentleman started talking about the swans, and how they had their wings clipped by the park-keeper to prevent them flying away. He was indignant at the barbarism of it and denounced the tyrannical streak in man that sought always to deny other creatures their freedom, attempting even to quell the proud and regal spirit of the swan. The word 'quell' startled Jan out of his reverie. He jumped, frowning, to his feet, as if he had recognized someone he knew, but disliked, on the other side of the lake. The old gentleman was puzzled when he failed to see anyone in that direction, after having put on his second pair of glasses expressly for the purpose. By that time, however, the young stranger had disappeared round a bend of the path.

Just before closing time Jan rushed into the post office in the Beurs Square and sent a telegram to Nellie: COMING BACK TOMORROW. LOVE JAN.

Nellie didn't understand what it was all about when she got the telegram just before going to bed. But she was alarmed, and not without reason, for some men had been to see the house and had looked at the furniture, without giving any explanation. And they looked sinister despite their oily politeness. She had never before been afraid when alone, but after getting that telegram and seeing the men turn the chairs up to look at the bottom of them, she gave an urchin a penny to run along to Dijkmans, the lock-keeper, to ask if Mrs. Dijkmans would please come at once. For half an hour she wandered about the house, dusting the mantelpiece, nipping the dead blooms out of the geraniums, feeding the canary and stroking the cat. And all the time as she did so, she wondered if that boy had put the penny in his pocket and not bothered about the message. She wanted to put the baby in the pram and go to the lock herself, but the evening air was so raw with sea mist that she didn't dare take the baby out in it. Nor did she dare to leave him at home by himself after those men had behaved so strangely in the house. But at last Mother Dijkmans came running along, with her slippers flapping on the cobbles—because she had been in too much of a hurry to put on her clogs.

The two women stayed together for the rest of the evening, doing their knitting in the lamp-light. But the knitting was a little ragged because they dropped so many stitches. "You ought to rub the wick with a cork occasionally, child," Mother Dijkmans said, "the light is very uneven."

"Yes, yes, I will; and now you taste that tea, and have a guess how much I save by buying it."

Mamma Dijkmans tasted it with pursed lips, while the shadow of the fringe round the lampshade fell upon her face, making her look as if she was peering through the bars of a prison. Just when she was about to speak Nellie silenced her by lifting her hand and asking: "Shh—do you hear something?"

But there was nothing to hear but the rustle of the sparrows under the eaves, the purr of the lamp and the eternal sound of the surf in the distance. "A pity Father couldn't come with me," Mother Dijkmans said. "But they are draining tonight, so he couldn't get away."

They heard the roar of the water when the lock gates were opened. A dark, foaming rumble, drowning the distant sound of the surf. Luckily, by that time the baby was sound asleep. Although he couldn't get away for long, Father Dijkmans came to have a look at them just after midnight; the sound of his clogs gave them a start, and Nellie jumped up when he was still some distance off. But when she opened the door she recognised his cough and went back wearily to her chair. The weather seemed to be breaking now. Lightning flickered behind the horizon, and sometimes the sound of distant thunder could be heard above the roar of the water pouring through the lock gates. Father Dijkmans wanted Mama to come home with him, but of course she refused. "Come home with you when there's a thunderstorm coming on! Are you out of your mind? And surely you understand that I can't leave the child here all by herself in a storm." Father Dijkmans understood all right, but where was Jan, he wanted to know. And when he heard that Jan had gone to Rotterdam to sign the articles for a new trip because the company had been taken over by Kwel, he grumbled and somehow didn't quite believe it. "Dammit, there's something queer going on here. Hendrik the policeman behaved queerly too, when I offered him a beer tonight to celebrate his daughter's birthday. He wouldn't even accept it." To save further argument Mother Dijkmans told him to get back to his lock at once and to stay there, in case the gates got washed away.

What a night it was—with thunder and lightning, and deluges of rain. When the storm subsided a bit the women tried to get some sleep, but didn't succeed very well; they merely tossed and turned while the lightning flashed purple between the curtains until it died out in the red flush of dawn.

That day nothing happened. The street was wet and the watery sun shone in the puddles; only a few people passed by, and when someone knocked on the door it was only the baker.

And then, suddenly, Jan stood there. God what a face he had! The shoulders of his blue coat were sodden black with the rain. He came in slowly, and she helped him off with his coat. He patted her arm, but didn't say a word. She looked up at him and said: "Well?"

Well, there was nothing to say. He'd got the sack from Kwel's, and had been seeing other owners today and yesterday—de Herder in Maassluis and the National Company in Ijmuiden. But as there was no immediate vacancy they had put him on their list—a rather long list—because a lot of men were trying to get away from Kwel. He had written to Meulemans in Flushing and Kiers in the Isle of Terschelling; they'd answer him soon, he thought. He didn't mention his debt to Kwel, and she didn't mention the men who had been looking at the furniture. It was marvellous how they managed to cheer each other up by talking and laughing together.

A few days later Meulemans' reply arrived: he was fully

manned, but he had added Jan's name to the waiting list. A day later a reply came from Kiers: he happened to have a vacancy and remembered Jan's name in connection with the salvaging of the *Scottish Maiden*, for the affair was much talked of in shipping circles. A simple, generous letter it was, written by Kiers himself on a rather dirty piece of paper. Old Kiers was known as a wonderful old boy, very good to his men, and he sailed one of his tugboats himself.

Jan and Nellie danced with joy, clapping their hands and crying like a couple of fools. Little Bart was taken from his cot and hugged and pinched and shaken by way of celebration. God, what a miracle, what a relief! How they loved each other, how wonderful the world was again! It was a lesson, Jan said, which he'd never forget, never, never, as long as he lived. And he was sure now that everything had turned out for the best and that he'd be free and happy with old Kiers, that wonderful old grouser—much happier probably than he would ever have been as just one of Kwel's chain-gang.

They stayed up into the small hours, chatting and making plans. "Terschelling must be a lovely island with wonderful people—look at Kiers! Show me that letter again, Jan."

"Why? You must know the damn thing by heart now; you must have read it at least eighty times."

"No, do come on, show it me; there's something I want to see."

Jan then confessed that he didn't mind looking at it again himself. The old chap writes a very clear hand for his age, doesn't he?—You bet, old Kiers is a queer bird. Over sixty, he's as lively as a cricket, and they say he'll give a hand with the ropes himself, if need be. The sharks can wait for him till the sea goes dry. Even those Terschelling shoals have never been able to get him. . . . But, Jan, honestly, are they dangerous, those shoals? I've heard. . . Nonsense, sweetheart, old wives' tales; I've known those shoals since I was a kid, nothing to them. They just show a bit white in a gale, that's all. But most of it is only foam, you can see them miles ahead. . . . Then why does everybody say. . . . Don't listen to what everybody says; they don't know what they're talking about. Believe me, I know those shoals like the inside of my purse.

His purse at the moment didn't take much knowing, for it happened to be empty. The baker, the grocer and the milkman looked a little unfriendly, but they did admit that it would be a wonderful step up for Mr. Mate to be going to the Isle of Terschelling, to sail for old Kiers.

Three days later a second letter arrived from Kiers. It said: "I'm sorry, young man, to have to tell you that I have made enquiries about you and what I have learned is not very favourable. If I am to take it on hearsay that you are an excellent sailor, I must take the rest on hearsay too, and that part I don't like. I have no use for a mate who is in debt, and as you are about to be declared a bankrupt I certainly can't employ you, for I have grown old and wise enough not to start meddling in Mr. Kwel's affairs. So I'm sorry, but I have engaged someone else. Greetings, Kiers."

"Now that you are about to be declared a bankrupt. . . ." Where the devil did the old fool get that nonsense from?

A fortnight later Jan Wandelaar, was declared insolvent by the provincial court, and his estate was ordered to be sold by auction for the benefit of his creditors, Kwel and Van Munster's International Tugboat Company.

A month later they were out in the street. The clock, the vases, the horsehair chair—everything had gone, and even the pram was pushed away empty. All they were allowed to keep were the clothes they stood up in, and one napkin, one dress and one blanket for the child. The *Galebird*, the *Hydra* and the *Jan van Gent* were out at sea again, otherwise this would never have happened—the boys would have seen to that. But now there was nobody to come to Jan's aid, and everything had to go to the highest bidder. The sight of his stuff being sold like this reduced Jan to tears. Luckily for him, he had a heroic wife in Nellie. Though she had plenty to worry about herself, she could always find a word of comfort for him, and spare him further anxiety. She kept her own troubles to herself. She didn't tell him, for instance, that there was another child on the way. She just kept going as best she could and put a brave face on it.

The night after the auction they sat under another lamp

yes. Now, WHY did Kwel pick on you, instead of on Van der Gast, or Boer or Bikkers? Because you were an exceptional case: your study had been paid for by Van Munster, you. . . . How do I know that? Comrade, the Cause has its disciples everywhere, even in Kwel's office. Comrades who'd give their very lives, their very souls to further the great Cause: the liberation of the proletariat!"

Jan got up. He was very sorry, but. . . .

But Verwoert hung on to him like a leech and wouldn't be shaken off. He even insisted on going with Jan as far as the ship. "Of course I'll come along with you, old man. I don't mind a bit—this is important." He followed Jan up the road to the quay, stumbling and coughing as he shuffled along through the red beech leaves which were whirled about by the wind that blew from the direction of the harbour and brought with it the scents of the spice wharves. "You see? Because you were in debt to the Company to the tune of a paltry hundred guilders he was able to use you to teach the others a lesson. Tugboat people are honest, generous and impulsive, but they're not realists. That is our main difficulty in starting that union: we lack a sense of realism. We. . . . Oh, are you going that way? Hey, wait a minute! I'm coming with you. See? Kwel may be a scoundrel, a murderer, a slave-driver, but there's one thing you've got to give him credit for: his knowledge of the tugboat seaman is second to none. He KNEW that they'd never realise that what he did to you he could only do because you were an exception. He KNEW he'd scare the wits out of them, that they'd think: I'd better watch my step, for THAT's what's going to happen to me if he catches me saying, to hell with Kwel! I'll. . . . God, Wandelaar—sorry—but could you please not go quite so fast—my chest, I. . . . That's right, I'm sorry. I mean: this whole rigmarole of having you pronounced bankrupt, of organizing that sale, of giving it all the publicity he gave it—do you think the price he got for that lot of junk of yours covered one tenth of his expenses? Sorry, old man! Of course I didn't mean that your things were junk. All I meant was, that in comparison with what Kwel spent on the business, they were only a trifle."

At this point Jan shook him by the hand because they had reached the ship. The *Young Lily* was a coaster of about eight hundred tons, rather small for a long voyage, but there are times when you've got to take what you can get. "Good-bye, Verwoert," Jan called. "Thanks a lot, and good luck."

"Think it over!" Verwoert shouted after him. He stood there on the quayside, a thin man in rags, among the fluttering gold of the autumn leaves. "Think about it, Wandelaar, think. . . ." And the last Jan saw of him when he turned at the top of the gangway was a scarecrow-figure gasping in a paroxysm of coughing. Better to sail as a bo'sun on the *Young Lily* at forty-five guilders a month than to starve as a plumber-martyr for the liberation of the slaves on ocean-going tugs.

The *Young Lily* was not a bad ship although she was old. She was a good-natured ship, a ship without moods. Her Captain was a sour Northerner, as unfriendly as a porcupine, but he was honest and outspoken and as sharp as a needle when it came to business. The ship was his property; he sailed her at his own expense and hoarded his profits with miserly care, considering he had no one in the world to provide for. His stinginess made the meals on board rather monastic and the ropes had been spliced so often that they looked like strings of sausages, but life was bearable. The routine was easy: four hours watch and eight hours off—a rest-cure for any tugboat seaman, and he'd have got fat on it if the food had been more plentiful. The crew was composed mainly of old and experienced hands, who did their work without fuss, and smoked their pipes. As bo'sun of this easy-going lot he felt at first the lack of any outlet for his own strength and vitality. But after a couple of days it seemed as if he had done nothing else all his life but drawl: "Hey, Uncle Klaas—would you mind coming back here with your brush for a minute?" or "Well, Baas Kuitert, what about knocking out your pipe and helping old Knelis to scrape the rust off the poop? But you'd better start on the far side, in case you disturb Mr. Mate who's trying to sleep with a stomach ache."

It was curious how many of the crew had stomach trouble on board this ship. They could hardly take any food at all and ate even less than the sufferers from lumbago, of whom there seemed also to be a large number on board. But Captain Minnema preferred moody grumblers to cheerful athletes with appetites like horses'—even if they could hardly do any work at all. The point was that they were cheap, and the ship could almost sail herself.

The *Young Lily* had plied from Amsterdam to Savannah, via the Azores and Bermuda, so often with her hold full of cheese, that now she seemed to find the way herself, like a milkman's pony. To a man who had been used to a life of adventure this monotonous routine was sheer torture. Nobody said anything that wasn't boring; nobody asked anything unless he was bored. Nobody went ashore for a spree in St. Michaels or St. Georges; when these old salts went ashore they merely gazed about them like cows confronted with new pasture.

When Jan went for a stroll in the High Street of St. Georges he spotted Captain Minnema sitting alone at an iron table in front of the Hotel Ultima Esperanza, ruminating on a cheese roll, as if he hadn't smelt enough cheese as it was on board his own ship, with a glass of goat's milk beside his plate. Jan greeted him by touching his cap and then tried to get away as quickly as he could from that monumental figure of boredom, but the Captain beckoned him with his fork and pulled up another chair with a screech of iron on the tiles. Now he had to sit down, whether he liked it or not. He took off his cap and joined the Captain, who had gone on eating without a word. They were the only ones on the pavement; as far as the eye could see there was nothing to look at, not even a girl passing by, but only a dog, and that had a limp. The sky between the gables was colourless and nondescript, and the waitress who appeared when Minnema called out "Allah!" was as devoid of physical attractions as a nun. Minnema asked what the bo'sun would have: he himself recommended the goat's milk; it was excellent here. But though as a matter of policy a subordinate should always agree with his superior, Jan on this occasion asserted his independence and ordered a glass of beer instead. Minnema and Allah were quite amazed—beer at this time of day?

"I would take something nourishing, young man, instead of wasting my money on liquor which does nothing except confuse the brain." So Jan ordered goat's milk after all, because Minnema's reference to "my money" had made him wonder whether he meant his own cash or his bo'sun's. If this was going to be a Dutch treat, he had better order the cheapest thing on the list, for every penny he saved went to Nellie.

After the goat's milk had been served, and Minnema, munching and swelling, had remarked that this trip had been quite satisfactory so far; and after a black cigar had been pulled from the breast-pocket and its top bitten off by amazingly large, yellow teeth, Minnema asked: "Well, bo'sun, tell me: how do you like this trip yourself?"

Jan hesitated a moment. The words "pleasant," "smooth" and "satisfactory" didn't come to his mind without a good deal of effort. He felt like a child repeating the catechism it had learnt by heart the night before. But when Minnema, glancing at him with his cunning little eyes, asked if he hadn't enjoyed the beautiful weather, he couldn't hide his impatience any longer, and blurted out that to someone used to the tugboat business this kind of sailing took a lot of getting used to.

"So, so, young man, well, well; and why is that?"

"Well, because nothing ever happens. Because there's nothing to see, nothing to hear. Because when you look round you expect to see something in tow at the stern and when you don't see it you feel somehow incomplete. Because . . . well, skipper, just because a tugboat man on board a freighter feels like a sailor on shore."

So, so, so, young man, yes, yes, Minnema quite understood that, quite—but why on earth didn't he stay in the tugboat business if he felt like that about it?

Ay, he'd talked himself into a nice mess there. Now he would have to wriggle himself out of it as quickly as he could. He mumbled something about more money, and shorter trips, and more leaves at home and that kind of thing, twirling his cap nervously; while Minnema slowly lit the black cigar which had to be lit with the necessary ritual.

Minnema let him stammer out a string of lies until he got stuck, then extinguishing his match with a waving motion he said: "Is that so?" It was obvious that he smelled a rat, and whenever Minnema smelled a rat he liked to track it down, even though he had to take the house to pieces, brick by brick. He questioned and prodded till at last Jan put his cards on the table in sheer despair, the sweat running down his face. Yes, he had been sacked. Yes, he had been sacked because of misconduct. Yes, he had been looking for a job for over two months before he got this one, writing to everyone under the sun. Yes, yes, he had got a wife and child and another one coming in six months' time. It was indeed his intention to make enough sea-days as a bo'sun to get his mate's certificate for the merchant navy. But there was something Minnema didn't understand. He didn't understand why the bo'sun hadn't got himself that certificate long ago; he must have had plenty of sea-days on the ocean-going tugs, enough in fact to get his master mariner's certificate. And when Jan told him about the law that decreed that the sea-days spent on board ocean-going tugs were only to be counted as canal-days and were not valid for the officers' examinations for the merchant navy, Minnema raised his eyebrows and said: "That's wrong, that's very wrong."

And when Jan said: "There you are, skipper. Because I dared to say that I got the sack." Minnema frowned and said: "So, so, so."

When Allah brought the bill and Jan wanted to pay for his share Minnema wouldn't hear of it. "Don't bother, bo'sun, this is my party," he said. Jan heaved a sigh of relief when he found that the scowl on the Captain's face was intended for the iniquitous tugboat law and not for him.

During the trip to Savannah the Captain stopped Jan occasionally on his way to the poop, to hear the ins and outs of that law. At first this interest seemed to Jan a rather pleasant surprise, but after a while it got as boring as everything else on the ship, and it recurred with the monotonous regularity of the sunset. When the skipper, towards the end of the homeward run, asked him to have a look at a paper, and to tell him if the facts were correct, Jan thought to himself, Heavens, what am I in for now!

But he was amazed when he read the letter. It was written in the majestic style of the Old Testament, and was addressed to the President of the Christian Historic Party of the Second Chamber of the States General of the Kingdom of the Netherlands. In this letter the President was asked, in terms that conjured up a vision of a black-coated preacher in a whitewashed church smelling of wet overcoats and goloshes, if he would oblige the undersigned by looking immediately into a most scandalous law concerning sea-days on tugboats which had been passed by his party some years ago. The undersigned had always depended upon the integrity of the Christian Historic Party as upon a rock. If the President had in fact been instrumental in passing the law in question, the undersigned would feel as though the solid world was collapsing under his feet. For did it not say in chapter seven, verse eighteen, of the Third Book of Moses that. . . .

The letter went on for three pages, and it won Captain J. Minnema, of the freighter the *Young Lily*, a life-long corner in his astonished bo'sun's heart.

The home-coming, after two months with the *Young Lily*, was very different from the one after his journey with the *Jan van Gent*, five months ago. After they moored in Amsterdam he got a week's leave; Monday next they'd sail again at six a.m. sharp. Not a soul on the quay, only a nurse with two children who pointed at the ship, and the nurse said: "Well, isn't that a lovely big ship? If Benny is a good boy, he'll get one like that when he's grown up."

Nellie wasn't at the quay to welcome him. Even though he didn't expect her to be there, her absence inspired him with gloomy feelings. This sense of depression remained with him while he sat in the train, looking at the landscape. It seemed only yesterday since he had seen it last, and the whole trip seemed merely a boring kind of dream. While the train stopped constantly, with screeching brakes and clanging couplings, to pant on again after a few seconds' halt, he sat in the corner, his legs on the opposite seat, peering gloomily at the darkening polder. This is your future, Jan, old fellow, he told himself. This is what you'll be doing for the rest of your life—in and out of port, with no consolations except a nap after lunch and a black cigar. When the train stopped with a final screech of brakes at the terminus, he gathered up his kitbag which contained only his dirty linen and a shawl from Savannah for Nellie. As he got ready to leave the train he felt a curious nostalgia in his heart, a nostalgia that had nothing to do with Nellie, the child or the land of his birth, but sprang rather from the memory of Siemonov, Little Abel, Bout and the colossal swell of the Pacific Ocean, and the wineglass of Rio de Janeiro, and for the dangers and hardships of the tugboat world.

He heard someone tap on the window, and there was Nellie, her nose flattened against the glass. After they had managed to open the door of the compartment, despite the fact that they were both pulling opposite ways, she threw her arms round his neck and they kissed. At that moment life began to mean something again, and as they strolled slowly homeward, she pushing the pram and he with his kitbag on his shoulder, they were both very happy. Yet it was a bit quieter, this home-coming, and somehow also a bit more restrained than last time. The child had grown during those two months. It lay on its back now and looked up at the road-side trees as they loomed over his pram. Nellie told Jan how beautifully Bart could sit up and kick, and when he thought no-one was looking he would try and sit up by himself. But now he had to be still, nicely covered with his eiderdown, for it was chilly and the November wind whistled round the corners. When she asked Jan what the trip was like he had little to tell her; but he mentioned the letter Minnema had written to his member of Parliament, and they smiled about it, in a wan mechanical way, like old people who tell a joke, without looking up from their Bible or their knitting. Yes, they had grown older, much older. They even showed it. Nellie looked thinner in the face than when he went away, but that was because she was expecting another child, and she had rings round her eyes too. She said Jan hadn't changed a bit—how could he in the space of only two months? But he felt she wasn't speaking the truth, and when Father Dijkmans greeted him in the doorway and grunted: "So, youngster, welcome home, but goodness how washed-out you look!" he knew he had altered in some way, but he wasn't quite sure how.

Here at home everything was much the same, Mamma Dijkmans told him as she laid the table. The sluice had been tested and she went on about having all the bother of making tea and even toast for the workmen and the engineers. And she told him about a cobbler who had come to live in their old house, and a very nice family too. She took her Sunday-best shoes there to be resoled just to see how those people had furnished the place, and she had to say it was all very nice and respectable, and he seemed to be a good workman too, for she had walked in those shoes for over a month and. . . .

But Jan couldn't stand any more of this trivial talk. He pretended that he had heard Father Dijkmans calling him, and on that pretext he sauntered out into the night with his pipe. Nellie called after him from the kitchen window: "Supper in a quarter of an hour!" and he waved back at her without looking round. A quarter of an hour would just be enough time to have a look at the harbour. When he reached it, after struggling along against the wind, there was nothing to see. There weren't any deep-sea tugs in, only the old *Aurora*, and the *Achilles*, the one that belonged to Kwel. He sneaked past the *Aurora* and stopped to look at the *Achilles* because nobody knew him there. But he had forgotten that the crews had been shuffled after the merger, and he noticed too late that someone was spying at him from the porthole of the galley. When he turned hastily to go, he heard laughter and someone's jeering voice calling after him. He resisted the temptation to go back and start a row. He didn't even look round, or show any sign of annoyance. But it wasn't really a victory for self-control. Jan the Mate of the *Jan van Gent* would have rung that rat's neck; but Jan the bo'sun of the *Young Lily* drank goat's milk and put up with anything. Yes, he thought to himself, even my old town's fed up with me. We'd better move to Amsterdam, once I've got my mate's certificate and can pay rent again. Amsterdam will do just as well for Nellie, with all those shops and brass bands in the parks.

But, of course, it was childish self-deceit. A man needs a town to get attached to and to think about when he is at sea. Anyone without a home of his own should at least have a town, for without some roots ashore a sailor turns sour. Sour, that's what Jan was, at supper that night, though he tried to be cheerful and chatty. Father Dijkmans inquired about his plans for the future and he answered with convincing assurance that everything was going along splendidly. The *Young Lily* was a grand old ship, and after one more trip to America he'd have made enough sea-days to be

141

able to register for the mate's examination. He had an idea that Minnema might like to take him on as his second officer, because the one he'd got now had a bad stomach and spent most of his time in his bunk vomiting. "Looks as if you have a bad stomach yourself," Mamma Dijkmans said when he pushed his plate away half finished. He laughed and answered: "I'm not hungry tonight; must be the excitement of being home again."

After the meal they sat together cosily for hours; the men chatted and smoked with their stockinged feet on the stove and the women brought in the tea when they at last finished fussing about in the kitchen. Bart was put to bed immediately after supper by the whole family—quite a performance, with grandpa playing the star part.

Dijkmans said: "Come on, boy! Tell us something about the trip; you sit there looking as if you had got the tooth-ache." "Do I?" Jan laughed. "It must be because I'm drinking it all in; it's wonderful to be home again."

"Well," said Dijkmans, blowing his pipe stem clear, "we must thank God that everything has turned out all right. Another couple of months and you'll have your certificate for the merchant service, and, if you ask me, the day will come that you'll thank your lucky stars you got away from those stinking tugs in time to start something decent."

Jan couldn't agree enough. In fact he agreed so fiercely that Father Dijkmans stopped filling his pipe for a moment, so taken aback was he at the sudden outburst of violent language. "My God, that stinking, bleeding, blasted tugboat business!" Jan exclaimed. He couldn't wish his worst enemy a tugman's life. By God, that was no life—it wasn't even an existence. By Jesus! how could he ever have been so silly, so utterly blind as to think that life on a tug was bearable! Things were very different on the *Young Lily*. Regular meals, regular rests, regular leaves, everything regular! That's what made life worth living—regularity. No more trips of months on end; life on the *Young Lily* was paradise, compared with the hell he went through when he was on the tugboats. What a relief it was to have escaped finally from that nightmare of slavery, filth and physical exhaustion.

"Yes," Father Dijkmans said, slowly filling his pipe while

he gazed sadly at the little red glow of the stove, "yes, our Lord sometimes blesses a man in unexpected ways."

Nellie agreed, too, that night when they were undressing under the slanting ceiling of the attic, where they shared the cupboard bed. When she stood in her petticoat and he was taking off his boots on the stool, she said that she thought everything was on the whole working out for the best: a captain on a tramp commanded more respect than a skipper on a tug, and it would be nice to know exactly when he was coming home and for how long.

Jan answered: "Yes, of course," and wondered why he hadn't the courage to tell her the truth, to confess how caged and thwarted he felt at having to work on a ship that seemed as dull and lifeless as a convalescent home. If only he could tell her the truth she'd understand everything and help him to find a way out. But he couldn't. The same false self-control, the same cowardice that kept him from running back and starting a fight with the fellow who called after him from the *Achilles,* now kept him from breaking down and confessing to her his inmost feelings. He pulled off his boots and his socks, opened the windows and blew out the candle, a quiet, composed, slow-moving man. And the worst of it was they were drifting apart by this very silence, a gulf of misunderstanding was growing between them. But when he sank back in the bed, when his head touched the pillow and he pulled the blankets over them with an old man's sigh, peace of mind returned—the peace that belonged to weariness, boredom, regularity, comfort, security.

Of course, his experience on the tugboats wouldn't be forgotten in a month or even a year, but the memory of it would gradually fade, like a ship disappearing over the horizon. Soon the only memories he would have of those wild years would be a few faces without names, some sights and smells faintly remembered, and a little photograph frame at the bottom of a drawer, framing a ghost of a memory. But it was so demoralizing, this soothing feeling of security that when Nellie asked him: "Jan, what's the matter with you?" he could only answer vaguely: "Nothing, sweetheart; what could be the matter?"

But it didn't end there. She told him he mustn't think she hadn't noticed how miserable he was. What on earth could be the matter . . . ? But he kissed the question away, and in doing so he almost succeeded in achieving his own peace of mind.

For the first time in his life he was frightened because he couldn't come to terms with himself. He knew it was bound to end in disaster, yet he couldn't do a thing to help himself. Once he thought he might have a heart-to-heart talk with Nellie as they walked together along the dike and the harbour wall. But she chattered and laughed so much there was no need to answer or even to listen. The more he tried to reason with himself the more frustrated he became. At last he took refuge in a kind of savage gaiety. Everybody was taken in by it except little Bart. The child was frightened when Jan began romping with him. "Funny," Mamma Dijkmans remarked when the child began to scream hysterically, "he's never done that with anyone before."

Nellie took the screaming child into her arms, with a glance at her husband sitting miserable in his chair. But her glance told her nothing, nothing at all.

After the scene with little Bart Jan wandered off to the harbour again while the women were cooking supper. This time Father Dijkmans came with him, panting: "Hey, easy, boy! Easy. . ." Without realizing it, the old man nearly drove Jan to distraction by his senseless chatter.

In the evening they played a parlour game together in the lamplight, with the revolving beam of the lighthouse flashing between the curtains. It was a gay evening and the fun was so uproarious that Father Dijkmans, choking with laughter, had to point at the ceiling to remind them that little Bart was asleep upstairs. It was a really jolly family evening, made more cosy by the sound of the wind howling outside.

The wind had freshened even more by the time they went to bed. It thundered in the chimney which ran through the wall behind the cupboard bed, and it rattled the window shutters. Jan and Nellie lay listening to the noise of the wind for a while. There would be a regular gale tomorrow, by the sound of it. When, however, Nellie turned to Jan and said: "Now, love, tell me honestly: what IS the matter with you? Are you miserable?" she realized from his breathing that he was already asleep. He must be tired, the poor chap; he's been overdoing it today, she thought as she snuggled up against him and listened to his heart thumping under the roughness of his vest.

In the middle of the night she woke up with a start because he was making strange moaning noises like the wind outside and when he started hitting out with his arms as if he were chasing something, she shook him and asked what was the matter. He woke up, murmuring something about the number one hold and five rivets gone. When she pulled the blanket over him and stroked his hair he mumbled the word "cook" before dropping off to sleep again.

She lay awake in the darkness for a while, listening to the wind battering the roof and banging the shutters, but she was too tired to think; she merely felt very lonely and worried, and wished she had a hot water bottle. She decided to get up and get herself one, but somehow she couldn't make the effort. When she woke up with the first yellow streak of dawn the idea of a hot water bottle remained in her mind till the sound of the milk cart clattering through the gale dispelled it.

That morning the weather was even worse: terrific gusts of wind, bringing with them fragments of broken branches, lashed against the doors. The tugs in the harbour chafed and groaned against the jetty walls. It was just the kind of weather that brings disaster at sea.

Sure enough there was a shipwreck after dark that night. A flare: a helpless flicker of smoky light from a wilderness of seething water. The *Aurora* went to render aid. Jan heard the shrill hooter he knew so well as Captain Bas nosed his way out of the harbour.

They were sitting under the lamp again, silent now and close together under the onslaught of the gale that hammered at the walls. Father Dijkmans read the paper with his glasses on the tip of his nose, narrowing his eyes as the smoke of his pipe got into them; Mamma Dijkmans knitted for the heathens with plump, fumbling hands; Nellie was darning Jan's socks in readiness for the next trip, with the lamplight making a shimmer of gold on her hair. Jan was swotting up a book for his examination, his hands over his ears and his eyes cast down. He didn't look up when the *Aurora* blew her hooter; didn't even hold his breath to listen. Nellie glanced

145

at him in surprise. She recognized that hooter all right because she had so often listened for it in the days when Jan was on board. Father Dijkmans heard it too; he said: "There must be something going on the shoals—listen!" But as no one moved or listened he went on reading the paper with a frown, his cough drowned by the colossal thunder of the gale. Even the lamplight flickered and the flame of the spirit stove danced under the simmering tea kettle. When, following the whistle blast of the *Aurora,* there came the booming note of the *Achilles,* Father Dijkmans was certain there must be a shipwreck. He wanted to go outside to have a look, and asked Jan to come with him, but Jan grunted and shook his head. Father Dijkmans grumbled and rustled with the paper and sneezed and cursed under his breath when he had to grope on the dark floor for his spectacles that slipped off his nose. Mamma Dijkmans sighed and yawned, patting her open mouth with her hand. "Ah," she said, "what a wonderful thing for us all that you won't ever have to go out again in this kind of weather, boy —not ever again—think of it!"

After an hour with no other sounds except the thunder of the wind, the rattling of the window-panes and the sharp click of Mamma Dijkmans' knitting needles, the sound of running clogs was heard approaching the house. Jan jumped to the door and flung it open. Mamma Dijkmans let out a scream, for the wind rushed in like a mad monster. The flame of the spirit stove was blown out and Father Dijkmans' paper flapped up like a bird. But the clogs ran past and vanished in the stormy darkness. Who ever it was must have been going to fetch the coxswain, for when Jan shut the door he shut out the far-off tolling of the alarm bell, calling the crew of the lifeboat. That meant there was a ship in distress on the shoals, out of reach of the tugboats. Now Father Dijkmans was damned if he would stay indoors any longer; he'd go and find out what was going on, Jan or no Jan.

He went and stayed away for hours; hours in which Nellie became more and more worried. During all this time Jan had kept his book in front of him, with his hands over his ears; yet he hadn't turned a single page since the hooter of the *Aurora* sounded in the harbour. Mamma Dijkmans didn't notice it; she knitted away happily, with occasional bursts of chatter. There was no sound from outside, except the wind and the rain. The lamplight quivered and the blue flame of the spirit stove kept up its incessant dance. It was long past midnight, but Mamma Dijkmans didn't seem to notice; she knitted and knitted, chattering all the time about Sally Honing whom she saved from falling out of the swing when they were both children.

She was in the full flood of her reminiscences when the door burst open, making the curtains fly up and quenching the lamp flame. "Heavens, man," she exclaimed, "can't you at least ring or knock at the door, before you frighten the life out of us like this?"

But Father Dijkmans had no breath for arguing; he collapsed into his chair with water streaming off his oilskins. "My God, you've never seen anything like it, this is the worst gale of a lifetime. It was the *Achilles* they were after. The *Achilles* got a rope caught in its screw when it was trying to swing round and make fast to that Norwegian ship on the north shoal. But the lifeboat couldn't get at them for ages— almost on top of the dike she was, but they got most of them off with a line from the shore. Only two of the crew are missing, and if that's not a miracle then I don't know what is. If you had seen that ship, like a dog drowning in a whirlpool, you'd realize what a feat it was. Within ten minutes the ship broke up—first the funnel, then the foremast. I saw two of the poor devils drown in front of my own eyes."

When he was asked for the men's names, Father Dijkmans couldn't quite remember them, though he heard them clearly at the time. All he knew was that one of them was a seaman, something like Jansen or Hansen, and the other was the mate, with a name that sounded like Sickert or Wickert, or something with a B in it. Yes! By George, that's right: Bikkers! How did you know? Oh, yes, of course . . . !

"Hey, Jan! That must be the boy, you remember, the boy who was so drunk that night at Timmer's, the boy who said even worse things about Mr. Kwel than you did, and who was kept in the service without so much as a scolding—by George, there's justice for you! Fancy if you'd been kept on like that boy was, fancy if you'd become mate of the

Achilles—Jesus, boy, it makes my blood run cold, the very thought of it; if we were worthy of our blessings we'd kneel on this very floor right away and thank the Lord for His wisdom and mercy. Tonight we can all sleep sound in the knowledge that a special blessing of Providence rests upon us."

But Jan and Nellie didn't sleep at all. Once the candle was blown out and they were alone in the gale-shaken attic, Jan started to talk. He talked quietly and softly, but in such a mad, rambling way that she became alarmed and begged him for God's sake not to talk and shake like that. But he rambled on, relentless as the storm that frequently drowned his words with the roll of thunder and the howl of wind. When, at last, Nellie fell asleep she was so upset that she hardly remembered a word of what Jan had said; it was all so weird, so unreal.

The next morning, when she came down late, thinking he'd be gone because he had got out of bed before dawn, she found him writing at the table, surrounded by half-written sheets of notepaper. She didn't say anything, and he didn't even glance at her when she picked up one of the sheets of paper and read:

Mate Jan Wandelaar to Mr. H. Kwel: "I beg to state that I now realize that my conduct was reprehensible and I feel it is my duty to apologize. . . ."

Mate Jan Wandelaar to Mr. H. Kwel: "After the recent shipwreck of the *Achilles* I cannot help feeling that I was entirely to blame, and I would like to offer my apologies and at the same time respectfully ask for. . . ."

Mate Jan Wandelaar to Mr. H. Kwel: "I hope that in the course of the last few months you have reconsidered the question of my dismissal and have come to the conclusion that. . . ."

Nellie looked over his shoulder and watched him signing his name to a rather unconvincing letter in which he applied for a post as mate on one of the ships of the united tugboat fleets, in case there should be a vacancy.

It was madness, sheer madness! She could only gasp: "Jan, Jan. . . ."

But he gave a kind of forced laugh and said: "No, sweetheart, it's not because I can't do without the tugboat any longer. It's because of that boy Bikkers, and the oath we made that night. Now he has gone, it is my turn to. . . ."

She burst out sobbing and he did his best to comfort her. But his voice was still hard when he said: "You have seen yourself, tonight. Bikkers had sworn that he'd hunt Kwel to his death, and now he has failed in his attempt. I have tried to back out of it, but now my eyes have been opened and I. . . ."

She didn't have to tell him that she knew he was lying. It was so obvious that he must have known that she wasn't deceived. "You're lying, you're lying!" she exclaimed. "It's the tugboats you're in love with. They mean more to you than your wife and your children. And Bikkers was the same. They meant more to him than his very life. I know the truth now—it's the tugboats that have come between us." But when she had calmed down again and was buttering the bread for breakfast in the kitchen, with only a faint sob now and then, she forgot her hatred for Kwel. She didn't hate anybody because she felt no one was to blame for what had happened. It was all a nightmare, a mad dream. When the baker tapped on the window she smiled and opened it and heard his version of the shipwreck.

It was Verwoert's fault really. If that man hadn't opened Jan's eyes he would never have been so mad as to offer his services to Kwel again. He'd have tried to wangle his way on to one of Kiers' ships or one belonging to the National Company, if only as an ordinary seaman, or merely as a deck hand. But Verwoert had insisted that Kwel had nothing against Jan personally; that he had only used him as an example. If Verwoert was right, Mr. Kwel wouldn't mind taking him back now. On the contrary. It would give Mr. Kwel a chance to prove how benevolent he was, how ready to give anyone a second chance if only the offender confessed the error of his ways. And Jan considered himself a jolly good mate, worth his weight in gold, especially as the tugboats happened to be short of staff. It was no good just taking a beachcomber on the quay and making him second in command on an ocean-going tug. Even a first officer in the merchant service would be a square peg in a round hole if he tried to work on a tugboat. People like Jan Wandelaar, reared in the business and trained from childhood for this highly specialised job, were as rare as black seagulls. These were the conclusions he had arrived at since that occasion when he'd heard Verwoert, a scarecrow figure among the golden autumn leaves, calling to him from the bottom of the gangway: "Think it over, Wandelaar—think it over!"

But when he had posted the letter, he suddenly realised the stupidity, the shameful weakness of the whole thing. He even went so far as to call in at the post office to ask Pauw if he could have the letter back which he had posted that morning, because it was all a mistake. But the letter had just gone on the ten-fifteen train to Amsterdam, so it was impossible to retrieve it.

That afternoon, walking with Nellie along the quay in the sombre, grey light of the wild day that followed the storm, he was so completely cured of his madness that he promised her he would take his text-books with him on board the *Young Lily* and authorized her to tear up any reply Kwel might send, without telling him even what it was. The old tub, he confessed, wasn't so bad after all, and even if she was a bit boring and dull, there are lots of other ships for him to pick and choose from once he'd got his certificate. . . .

He told her endless stories about Baas Kuitert who let that fender slip in St. Michaels, and old Knelis who owned an Indian jersey with a pair of canaries embroidered on it. He talked so much about the ship and those wonderful old shipmates of his that he got carried away by the yarns he told. When, during supper that night, Nellie asked him to tell her again about Uncle What's His Name's canaries they laughed so much that they made the lamp rattle, and everyone thought the *Young Lily* was a wonderful ship after all, manned by sturdy sea-dogs of the old school.

When on that Sunday night his train was about to take him back to those jolly old shipmates, and that decent old Captain Minnema, it was a gay and happy goodbye. Those two months would be over before you could say knife.

He went on deceiving himself until he was back on board the *Young Lily*. He even managed to put a brave face on it

150

until they reached Ijmuiden, panting and coughing their way through the North Sea canal. But when the swell started rocking them and Minnema, smoking his pipe on the bridge, stopped him on his way to the hatches, saying: "Tell me, young man—I have been thinking about that law, and I wondered whether it would be a good idea if I wrote to the Synod of the Reformed Church of the Netherlands. . . ." he knew he was faltering. Before the day was over it seemed as if he hadn't been away at all; everything was the same again, so uncannily the same, that it gave him the creeps. The boredom, the dullness, the killing sense of being dragged round the world in a kind of floating bath chair, were depressingly familiar, so familiar that his morale collapsed after two days and he started worrying again. Up to the time they reached St Michaels he made an effort to read his books instead of nodding over them until he fell asleep. But after that he succumbed to tedium of the routine and Mate Wandelaar became again the Sleeping Bo'sun who did his work slowly and mechanically, confident that the ship could sail herself if needs be.

The *Young Lily* crawled from St. Michaels to St. Georges, where Jan drank another glass of goat's milk with Captain Minnema in front of the Hotel Ultima Esperanza. Then on from St. Georges to Savannah where Jan bought another shawl for Nellie. In the meantime he was so drugged with boredom that he didn't even think about Kwel any more. Life was so much a matter of routine that he found himself anticipating things, as if by second sight.

In St. Georges, on the way back, Minnema said: "The second mate was a bo'sun too, before I promoted him."

"Yes," said Jan. "I knew that."

Minnema raised his eyebrows. "That's curious; I didn't tell you, did I?"

"No," said Jan, "I just knew it."

Minnema said: "So, so, so." He waved out the match with which he had lit his cigar, and called "Allah!" When Allah came with the bill and Jan fumbled in his hip-pocket, Minnema said: "Don't bother, bo'sun. This is my party."

Lucky thing that nothing unexpected ever happened on board the *Young Lily* for Jan hadn't even bothered to take his purse ashore.

In Ijmuiden a telegram had been waiting for Jan for over a week.

OFFER YOU POST MATE TUG "AMELAND" FOR TRIP ST. JOHNS NEWFOUNDLAND UNDER CAPTAIN VAN DER GAST STOP SIGNING ON FROM FRIDAY NEXT AT FIVE P.M. HARBOURMASTERS OFFICE ROTTERDAM—KWEL.

This was Thursday.

He tore the telegram up and threw it overboard into the sluice. He took the train from Amsterdam. He got out three stations short of home. On the windy platform he wrote a postcard. "Sorry, sweetheart, but I can't come home now. Kwel has offered me one more chance and I'm going to take it. I won't see you this time, but as the trip is only as far as Newfoundland, I expect to be home within two months. Don't be angry with me, or upset; I would never have been any good on a freighter and you know it. I love you very much, sweetheart. Break the news tactfully to your parents and perhaps they'll understand then. Keep smiling and don't let this worry you; it is all for the best. Much love and a kiss for Bart, Jan."

When he had posted the card from the station master's office he had to wait another hour before the next train was due in. Two more trains stopped at the station on their way north, but he let them go.

What a rotten thing to do. Nellie would be waiting at the other end, and worrying her head off. He was beneath contempt—a coward who didn't even dare face his wife and tell her to her face that he had chucked away a salary of seventy-five guilders for one of fifty, and exchanged a quiet, easy life for a slave's existence and pittance. He told himself all this again and again and yet, for the first time since that day when he came home from Rotterdam with the news of his misfortune, he felt alive again.

CHAPTER NINE

"THE WHITE WHALE" HOTEL,
ST. JOHNS, NEWFOUNDLAND.
APRIL 23RD, 1910.

SWEETHEART,

I JUST got your telegram, and I can't tell you how happy I
am. How wonderful that it should be another boy, and
such a sturdy one at that. I think the name Jan is all right,
although we didn't discuss it before. I love the idea of having
another son, though it takes some getting used to because
during the trip I have been imagining it would be a girl
whom I would like to have called Mary after my mother,
who was a good soul after all.

You may be surprised to get such a long letter from me,
but if you've got my cable you'll understand why. Such a lot
has happened, and at the moment so little is happening.
Bulle Brega (you remember he was one of the deck-hands
on the *Scottish Maiden*), bo'sun Janus (the one who married
a negress and was one of the speakers that night at Timmer's),
Flip de Meeuw, three more of us have taken a room together
in this hotel, which is called the White Whale and is full
of skeletons of sea-monsters. On the tables are whale's
vertebrae for ashtrays, white things that sound hollow when
you knock your pipe out in them.

Yes, sweetheart, a lot has happened and I don't know quite
where to start, that's probably why I am perhaps gabbling
a bit. But I'll start at the beginning and see where we get.

That night when I sent you the postcard from Alkmaar
station and went to Rotterdam instead of going home, I had
a difficult time, as you will probably have guessed. I kept
thinking about you and little Bart and the new baby that
would be arriving soon. I thought a lot about Father and
Mother Dijkmans and Minnema too, and my conscience
pricked me. Yet I knew I had done the right thing, as I
pointed out to you on that postcard; without the tugs I am
sure I would have gone crooked. Apart from all this, however, I had another worry on my mind: the moment I got

Kwel's telegram I knew there was something fishy about his offer; I was sure he hadn't been able to find anyone else for the job. So when I arrived the next day on board the *Ameland* I was prepared for almost anything. I had expected an old, ramshackle ship, one of those floating coffins of his which lie rotting away in the estuary and which he refuses to break up for scrap, nobody knows why. I expected this even more after I met the crew at the signing of the articles: the whole lot of them were rebels who had been publicly cursing Kwel, and who even now were saying quite openly the most outrageous things about him, while his representative tried to behave as if he didn't hear. Most of the staff I had met that night at Timmer's—Van der Gast of the *Galebird*, the skipper; Bevers, Boer and bo'sun Janus of the *Hydra*; cook Hazewinkel of the *Albatross*. The third engineer, Van Gulik, who came off the *Wieringen*, was the only one I didn't know, and he had never sailed with Van Munster.

The moment I saw that crew I thought: that's an odd collection; supposing something should happen to the ship —Kwel would be rid of fourteen of his worst enemies at one go. Rather an unpleasant thought, I admit; but we've had enough experience of Kwel to know that he isn't quite the paragon his supporters make out. I was prepared for anything, and the curious thing about it was that I didn't feel at all worried or depressed. I felt strangely calm and yet very alert. At least I knew what was coming, and I was certain I would get the better of him, just because I knew what to expect. I decided to keep my eyes and ears open, and to act on the assumption that he was trying to do us in. That seemed the only chance of coming out all right in the end.

You can imagine my amazement when I found the *Ameland* was a brand new ship—so dazzlingly beautiful that I thought at first I had come to the wrong quay. But she had the name on her stern all right, in bright new gold lettering, and I rubbed my eyes. She was a magnificent ship; not big, but with the kind of line that made one fall in love with her at first sight. She combined strength with elegance in a way I had never seen in any tug before; there was none of the clumsiness and squatness I had come to take for granted in a tug. She had a very low stern, ending almost level with the water, and though her bow was very high, it had been cut away to give her prow a grace that would have made you understand why sailors talk about ships as though they were women. Really, never before in my life had I set eyes on such a gem of a ship—and when I went aboard I must have looked a fool, for it wasn't at all as I expected. I had prepared myself for anything, I thought, but not for this.

In the messroom I found Boer and Bevers (the chief engineer), and Bevers showed me round the ship. First the engine-room, of course, and although I am no expert on engines I understood his excitement the moment I was through the door. The works looked like nothing I had ever seen before; everything covered and simplified; no awkward corners one couldn't get at, no greasepots in impossible places. You could walk right round the engine, which was smaller than any I had ever seen before and yet, so Bevers told me, she had a cruising speed of eleven knots. Eleven! As you can imagine, I refused to believe it. But the big surprise came when he showed me her bunkers. You know that a tugboat has more coal-space than a liner, because she has to develop practically the same amount of horsepower when towing, and yet crawls along at about one-tenth of the speed. And as a tug is so much smaller in size, most of her available space is taken up by the bunkers. When I saw the *Ameland's* bunkers I blinked, for they looked like a warehouse, divided into cubicles. Bevers explained, very excitedly, that she could take almost twice the amount of coal any other tugboat could, and that her engine was about twice as economical, so that she could steam, without a tow, up to twelve thousand miles! To give you an idea of what that meant: if she bunkered right up in Rotterdam, she would be able to sail to Melbourne, round the Cape of Good Hope, in one stretch! He explained that the partitions were intended to keep the coal from shifting about in tough weather, and to distribute the weight evenly over the ship, but I had stopped listening. I had expected a coffin, and instead I found the most beautiful ship I had ever seen; and when Bevers told me that she was the flagship of the fleet, I thought: well, either Kwel is mad, or I am.

After Bevers had shown me the fire extinguishing apparatus, the pump for salvaging sinking vessels, the searchlights on the bridge and over the main bollard, the ash-elevators from the stokehole to the deck; and after we had had a cup of coffee in the galley, where cook Hazewinkel sat dazed by the glamour of all his glittering new utensils and the frightening new steam-cooker, I couldn't keep my thoughts to myself any longer. "Why the devil should it be us who have to sail this ship on her first long trip?" I asked.

Bevers didn't answer at once; he took me out of the galley first and then to his cabin. Obviously he didn't want the cook to hear. After he had shut the door of his cabin—looking round in the messroom first to make sure there was nobody within earshot—he whispered: "You mustn't think you're the only one to be punished by Kwel for what we said that night. Van der Gast has been taken off his old *Galebird*, after sailing her for over fifteen years, and given a river job that nearly drove him frantic with boredom and home-sickness. Boer has been kept waiting ashore at half pay for over six months. Hazewinkel was given the job of painting the passage in the office, and I had to stoke the central heating. Everybody on board this ship has had his knuckles rapped, and I don't think there's a spark of the old fire left in any of them, in spite of all their talk. They are all dying to make good; they'll put up with anything, literally any-thing, in the way of food and wages and working hours, now they've got this chance to prove their worth in their proper jobs. And, if you ask me, that is exactly what Kwel has been after. He wants to break all records with this ship. He wants to make this a trip the whole world will talk about; he wants to knock hell out of his rivals, and not the local ones, for he has got them tamed long ago, but the Germans, the Norwegians and the English, who are trying to catch up with us on the deep-sea work. If you ask me he picked this crew as long ago as last year, when this ship was on the stocks, and he picked us on our records. I won't blab about the reputation I got when we were stationed in Greenland for nine months, and had to live on boiled fish until we grew fins ourselves; but look at Van der Gast, look at yourself. That affair with the *Scottish Maiden* has made you the best known mate in the business. This crew is a prize crew. I don't think you could find fourteen men in the whole world who could beat us at this job. But if we hadn't been given the treatment he has given us for the last six months, we might have taken one look at this ship and told him to go and boil his head."

"Why?" I asked.

"Look at this cabin—look at the messroom; it's all very nicely painted and leather seats and that kind of thing, but have you ever had less space to move about in? Look at the angle this bunk is put in at. The blooming hole is a pure triangle, for your bunk next door fits into this one, see? The whole thing has been arranged like a tin of sardines; all the space has been sacrificed to the bunkers. We're just fourteen mice in a coalheap—you lie down in that bunk and try to stretch your legs!"

I did, and he was right. I couldn't stretch them; and when I sat up I hit my head on the ceiling even before I had got up on my elbows. Bevers grinned, and said: "We'll have to sleep with our knees under our chins, and eat with the plates between our feet—that's all. But, by gum, that old crook has brought it off; I'll be damned if I'll as much as whisper a protest. He might have stuck me in a matchbox, I still wouldn't have complained. Never say again that Mr. Kwel doesn't know how to handle a sailor."

I had to confess that he had me licked, the scoundrel. Bevers got a flask from under his palliasse, and we drank to Mr. Kwel, rather cock-a-hoop, for we were sure we had seen through his little game. The wicked old rogue, we said—why does he have to do everything in a crooked, indirect way? Why can't he ever scratch his left ear with his left hand, instead of using his right round the back of his head? I liked Bevers, and he liked me; but we would have liked anybody that day—we were as exhilarated as boys. We even liked Mr. Kwel, in an odd way.

But while we drank more geneva than was good for us; while we joked and tried to laugh heartily without hitting the backs of our heads or bruising our elbows, a little thought kept spoiling my sense of relief. It wasn't even a thought, it was nothing but a feeling. A nasty feeling that I am sure I wouldn't have had if I had only been punished the way Bevers and Van der Gast and Boer and Hazewinkel had been punished. But after being sacked, and having our house taken away from us, and all our things sold and our whole marriage nearly wrecked by Mr. Kwel, I couldn't help having that feeling, I suppose.

I felt that there was more in this than met the eye. I just couldn't visualize Mr. Kwel collecting his worst enemies on one ship, just because the ceiling was so low.

When I was alone in my cabin I felt a bit dizzy and stood for a while with my back against the washstand and my eyes closed, thinking. No, not thinking, really—just feeling. Feeling the danger in the air. But although I racked my brains, trying to see through Kwel's game, I couldn't see anything wrong with the ship. He had got me licked, the bastard; I knew he had. But only God and Mr. Kwel knew how.

I am writing this by the light of a candle in the hotel kitchen, for it's the only place that's warm at this time of night. I don't know what has got into me, sweetheart; I have never written such a long letter in my life. But somehow, while I am writing this, I feel nearer to you, and that's what I want. I would give a year of my life just to be with you, if only for a night. Curious that this trip should have taken me that way. I dare say you'll be thinking to yourself: he deserted me for those blooming tugboats, so he can keep his explanations and excuses. But that's not true any more; I doubt if I would have done this if I had had the experience I have had now. For the greatest adventure hasn't been outside, it has been inside during this trip. But I'll have to tell you what happened first, before you can believe me.

After I had unpacked my kitbag, that first day, and hung your portrait at the far end of my bunk and changed into my seaman's clothes, I went up to the chart-room to see if Van der Gast had arrived. Bevers had told me that the old man had gone ashore to collect the chronometer from the Met. Institute. When I entered the chart-room he was busy unpacking it. The chart-room, and also his cabin which I could see through the open door, looked as neat and new as all the rest, and it was obvious that Van der Gast was a lot tidier than Siemonov. He seemed sincerely pleased to see me, shook me by the hand and refused to let it go, grunting: "Wandelaar, my boy, wonderful to have you with me, wonderful."

His voice sounded a bit shaky and I thought he looked

a lot older than he did that night at Timmer's. His hair was whiter and his whiskers didn't bristle half as proudly as they had done on that occasion. He looked like an old tom cat who'd come out of a rainstorm. When he stopped pump-handling my arm at last, he rubbed his eyes with the back of a very old hand, and I discovered that there were tears in them. It was a curious way to behave for a skipper of his age and record, for I knew he had always been considered the toughest captain in the business. He had even thrown an admiral off his bridge once when he tried to prevent him bringing in a dry-dock in Singapore against the tide and the full monsoon. I felt again that curious emotion which I had experienced when I first stepped aboard this ship: there was something fishy here; Van der Gast's welcome seemed, somehow, part of the danger that I smelt but could not trace.

But it was only a passing feeling; it soon gave place to something like pity. For while Van der Gast stored the chronometer away and unrolled the chart before discussing the trip, he chattered like an old woman, almost breath-lessly, and all he chattered about was the *Galebird*. If I had only *seen* that ship, he said; if I had only known her the way he had come to know her after fifteen years, I would agree that there was no finer, sweeter, more reliable ship in the world. Faithful, that was what she was, good-natured, gay, willing to do anything with a smile. Honestly, if I hadn't known what he was talking about, I would have thought he was discussing his late wife. He had been married, but his wife died twenty years ago. A picture of her was nailed up in his bunk. He didn't take me into his cabin to show me that, however. What he wanted to show me was a photograph of the *Galebird*, hanging by her side and three times as large. Well, I expect you know the *Galebird* by sight; an ugly square box of a ship with a flat nose, a stern like a stove, and a funnel as straight as a chimney. I wouldn't have called her any of the things that he did, but then love is blind.

I glanced round his cabin; it looked like an old woman's room, only tiny. Geraniums, a canary, framed picture post-cards of Switzerland, polished copper knick-knacks lined up on the top of the wainscoting; little kettles and frying pans and a footwarmer. And over the porthole, next to a cuckoo-clock that would stop running, of course, the moment the swell upset the pendulum, a framed motto: *From East to West Home's the Best*. He fiddled about with these toys while he chattered, shifting one, polishing another with his sleeve, tickling the canary's cage and making kissing noises at it. There was a pipe-rack, too, with some gnomes on it, and a newspaper-rack. I remembered having heard of Van der Gast's cabin, and while the man was still the rough and ready old salt he used to be, this note of cosy domesticity must have surprised his crew. But now domesticity seemed to have overwhelmed him. Not only did he live like an old woman, he behaved like one. It gave me the shivers.

It was quite plain, after seeing his cabin and listening to him for five minutes, that he was lost without the old *Galebird*. As far as he was concerned this show boat could go and smash herself, and he wouldn't care. He didn't say so. On the contrary, he went out of his way to impress me with the colossal honour that had been bestowed on us, how fortunate we were to have been picked to sail this gem on her first long trip. But while he said it his eyes looked uneasy, and he talked rather loudly, I thought. When he was interrupted by Kwel's agent arriving with the papers I knew that he had seen the man coming, the cunning old rat. And that was when I guessed that Van der Gast was probably for the first time in his life a frightened man.

After the representative had gone we shifted the ship to the Lek-harbour and moored alongside the hopper *Titan*, our tow. We weren't to sail until the morning, and so I asked Van der Gast if he'd like to go ashore for a drink, after we had made fast, for that was what Siemonov and I used to do. But he refused in a rather frightened way. "God, no," he said. "I'm not going to booze on this trip, too much depends on it."

I didn't feel like going ashore all by myself, so I thought I might just as well have a look at the tow at my leisure now instead of taking a hurried survey of her tomorrow.

The *Titan* was a beast; I sized her up the moment I caught sight of her from the bridge. A hopper, as you know, is a ship into which the dredgings are emptied if they can't use barges for any reason. It has an engine of its own, but only a small-

powered one which is used to take the vessel to some out of
the way spot, where the load is discharged by opening a row
of shutters under the water-line. When it is empty a hopper
is an awkward tow, hard to steer and with a tendency to
swing even in a moderate wind. This one looked particularly
nasty. But it was a lot better than a dry-dock or a sluice gate,
and as the *Ameland* seemed to be powerful enough for the
task I didn't see why the trip shouldn't be as cosy as a tea
party, even on the North Atlantic in the gale season.

In the foc'sle I found the deck-hands, all quite sober and
busy on little jobs of their own: darning socks, writing to
their wives, polishing their boots, mending their underwear.
I wouldn't have believed my eyes if I hadn't seen some pretty
queer sights already on this trip. Usually the deck-hands
have to be carted on board just before sailing, roaring drunk,
and generally some dockside loungers have to be signed up
in a hurry, because of last-minute vacancies. The explanation was, I thought, that even the deck-hands had been
hand-picked.

Bulle was their captain, and a mighty captain he was. He
looked vaster than ever in that poky foc'sle, and the pipe he
smoked would have done nicely as a club. He introduced
his crew to me by pointing at them with his pipe and roaring
out their names with a short account of their personal
history. The brutes went on darning, writing and mending,
with their heads bent as if they were a girls' sewing class and
I a visiting inspector. One of them looked like a child, but
when Bulle pointed his pipe at him, he roared: "Flip
de Meeuw, twenty-three, fresh from naval college, God have
mercy on his soul." I tell you this because you'll hear more
about this Flip later.

Bulle told me, after he had sent his girls to bed and
produced a bottle of gin from underneath his mattress, like
Bevers, that the *Jan van Gent* was sailing round south
somewhere. He had sailed on a trip with her to La Coruña
with fourteen lighters and during that fortnight Siemonov
had knocked his mate unconscious twice because he was so
stupid. But although it sounded quite possible, I somehow
knew that Bulle lied to give me heart.

"The owners ought to be pleased to have such a mate,
Mr. Mate," he said. And that was the moment I knew that

Bulle himself, Bulle, was frightened and that I must look pretty scared too.

It had started to drizzle, and when I stood in the wet darkness looking at the yellow rings the lamps made in the mist the uneasiness had really got me. I hurried across to the *Ameland* and down to my cabin, and when I looked at myself in the mirror over the washstand I got a shock: I looked like a lunatic. I could have kicked myself for not having taken a good flask on board for myself, and I was about to go and knock on Bevers' door and ask him for a drink, when there was a knock on mine.

I called, "Who's there?" and Van Gulik, the third engineer, poked his head in. You remember I mentioned him at the beginning of this letter; he was a Kwel's man, I had never set eyes on him before the signing of the articles. He said he was sorry to disturb me, but could I spare him a box of matches. I gave him a box, and then he offered me a cigar and so we sat down for a chat, which was obviously what he'd been after. We started by talking about the ship and Newfoundland, and he asked me had I ever been there. And when I said "No" he looked surprised and said: "I thought you were on your way to St. John's that time we met in Brest."

I hummed and ha'd a bit, thinking where the hell I should have met him and as he chatted on I realised that he had been third engineer under Verwoert on the *Texel*. He started discussing Verwoert, saying what an excellent crafts-man he was and how much he had taught him. I couldn't help remarking: "He must indeed have taught you a lot, considering you're on this ship now."

He looked at me in an alarmed way, and asked: "What do you mean?" And I answered: "Well, we all seem to agree that this crew has been hand-picked, don't we?" Then he said: "Hand-picked, yes—but what I would like to know is this: have we been picked because of our merits?"

I said: "I'm blowed if I understand what you mean," for I thought he might be a spy of Kwel's, and I was anxious not to tell him too much. But when he talked on I realised that he couldn't be a spy; he was too silly and too honest. It was strange, but it came as a shock to me that he couldn't be a spy. Somehow I had hoped he was. I wanted him to be. I

162

was sick of all this beating about the bush, and I intended to get hold of the truth at any cost. If Kwel had had a spy on board there wasn't likely to be anything wrong with the ship or the trip. But Kwel hadn't put a spy on board. Van Gulik was as harmless as a glass of milk.

He jawed on a bit about his girl friend and his plans for marriage and so on, while I sat looking at him in what must have seemed a rather sombre way.

Suddenly he blurted out: "I'm sick of it! I think it's nonsense! What the devil is the matter with all of you? Why don't you get out of it if you think that?"

I told him to take it easy and ask me one thing at a time; he was nearly crying with rage and nerves and said that it was a wicked thing to do, to try and scare someone who had only just entered the service and drive him nearly out of his wits. "Who the hell is trying to scare you?" I asked, damned annoyed by this display of nerves because I was nearly in the same state myself.

He shouted: "You, and Boer, and Bevers, the whole bloody lot of you! Who the devil is this Bas anyway? One of those bloody salvage skippers, who doesn't know a compass from his trouser seat. Why Kwel started by giving that jackass the command of this ship is a mystery to me!"

I did a Minnema on him, say "So, so" and "Well, well" until he shut up. Then I asked: "Which Bas are you talking about?"

At first he thought I was taking the rise out of him because he seemed to think that everybody knew about Bas and what he had gone through with this ship. But after I explained to him that I had come in from the merchant service only yesterday he told me that it was common knowledge that a certain skipper named Bas, one of Van Munster's coast-huggers, had sailed this ship to New-castle and back and nearly scuttled her, and when he came back he had told Mr. Kwel that he'd rather tie a stone round his neck and jump into the sea than sail this death trap again: her centre of gravity was too high, and only because Captain Bas was God's greatest sailor had he been able to bring her home the right way up. Now Van Gulik asked me, with flaming eyes: "And who the hell is Captain Bas?"

Well, I don't think he could have put that question to

anyone more entitled to give him a straight answer, but I kept quiet. "A coast-hugger, as you call him," I answered. "So you know him?" he enquired with something like a gasp. "I do," said I; "I've sailed under him as a sailor for the better part of three years."

The silence that followed was strained. After a long pause he asked: "Is he capable of judging a ship like this?" I looked at him and I think I even smiled when I said: "He certainly isn't. He's a nice man and all that, but a rotten sailor." I was in such a state myself that I had no compunction in telling him this lie.

I have always had the tendency to worry more at night than in the morning. That night I worried so much that I nearly gnawed my knuckles through. It is difficult to write to you about how I felt; it almost seems comic now that everything is over. At this moment, recalling that night to my mind, I can only smile when I picture myself worrying in that bunk. It seems silly now when I see that there were so many worse things to follow. But perhaps I worried so because I had a vague inkling of what was to come. I know that somewhere around midnight I was certain that I had either to escape or never set eyes on you again.

The reason why I didn't pack it up and let Kwel and his blessed ship go to hell was precisely the reason why I chucked away a secure and profitable future with Minnema and his *Young Lily*. Out of the tugboat-business I was no good, and this was my one and only chance to worm my way back into it. Even if I was to die in the process, it was better than the living death I would face if I went back to Minnema and his like. This is the part you may find difficult to understand: that a man should leave wife and children and everything he loves to sail on a tugboat with the threat of death hanging over him. I am not quite sure I understand that part myself, but anyhow that's the way it was. That night on my bunk I made my choice.

It wasn't easy, as you may guess. I hadn't done any praying since I was a child, but that night I knelt in front of the washstand and prayed. I had to kneel in front of the washstand, for the bunk was too low and the space beside it too narrow; Mr. Kwel had not made any provision for kneeling when he planned his flag-ship.

My prayer was not very effective. I tried to ask God to show me the way, but before I had achieved any sense of communion I heard a ship's hooter on the river. It was a tugboat, and at that moment it seemed almost like a sign. It may give you an idea of the state I was in, that I should take a ship's hooter for a sign from Heaven. I shut up after that, not sure if I should say amen or try to go on praying for guidance. It was, I think, the worst moment of the whole day. I felt a fool, a coward and a weakling; for the first time in my life I understood why people go and do themselves in.

The river rippled along the water-line and the *Ameland's* fender crunched against the quay. I heard steps overhead and voices; then something fell in the water with a splash and there was silence. The voices seemed nearer when they started speaking again. "You're mad," one voice said; "couldn't have been a rat, there're no rats on a ship as new as this one."

The other voice grumbled something, I couldn't make out what, and the first voice laughed. "Ha!" it mocked—"a bird on the moorings at dead of night. You must have your little joke, I suppose."

The steps went on and the voices trailed away. I realised that these sounds came from the quay. It may seem silly to you, but the idea that the rats were leaving the *Ameland* decided it. Instead of praying, or saying amen, I resolved then and there to stick it out.

I fell asleep with a feeling of peace. Perhaps because I was at last certain, after what seemed an eternity of doubt, that Kwel had planned this trip to do us in, and somehow that was better than uncertainty.

Next morning we sailed. There was nothing special about it, only one little incident: Van der Gast wanted to take the *Titan* out on the short hawser, then tow her on the full bight once we had passed the light-buoy; but I said: "Don't you think we'd better take her alongside, skipper? There's a hell of a current running and if we had to stop we might easily get her on our stern."

Siemonov would have knocked my head off, Bas would have said: "No, boy, because . . ." and given his reasons. But Van der Gast said: "Oh, yes, yes, to be sure, by all means. Right you are; let's take her alongside, that's much safer." I tell you this because it was the beginning of a very curious situation. Nominally, Van der Gast was in command, but after a few days it was I who took the decisions. He left everything to me, down to the smallest details, though he didn't mention it in the log, of course. When he took up his pen it was "I decided" and "I ordered" and "I concluded" all the time. Even the choice of the menus for the messroom was left to me (and that was really important in a way, for, as you know, Kwel made us pay for our own food, so we had to be as economical as possible). To all intents I was the captain, and he merely a silly, apprehensive old passenger. He was very jumpy. When anything was dropped in the ship it startled him out of his wits; he would look up with frightened eyes and ask: "What was that? Who did that?" If someone scratched the paint or varnish he would fly into a rage and abuse them right and left.

I tried to find out what he was after, what reward he would get if he brought this trip to a successful conclusion. Another thing I tried to find out was what exactly he was afraid of. The answer to the first question was plain after a couple of days: Kwel had promised him that he would get back his *Galebird* if the voyage was carried out to Kwel's satisfaction. The second question was more of a mystery, and old Van der Gast was as cunning as a monkey the moment he felt I was probing for an answer. The only clue he gave me was an indirect one: he relied on me in everything, left all decisions to me and didn't really care what I did as long as the paint and varnish didn't get scratched. But there was one item he was the very devil about: the coal consumption. Every day, every watch, and finally every hour or so, he wanted a report from below decks as to the amount of coal left in the bunkers. He made the engineers as irritable as tired housewives with all his fussing questions. Whenever he got the report he started to do sums on a piece of paper, and after he had seen me watching him on one occasion, he locked himself in his cabin and did his calculations there. Even during meals he often looked vacant, his lips mumbling, and I knew he was doing sums in his head.

I asked Bevers: "Is there anything the matter with the coal?" Bevers shrugged his shoulders and grunted: "If you ask me, he gets a bonus on it, the bloody old nagger."

Bevers' face was so ominous that I didn't press the matter any further, for fear he'd throw the gravy boat at my head. The atmosphere on board was getting more and more strained. If the crew hadn't been hardened to long voyages there would have been trouble after the first week. In that time I had come to the conclusion that Bevers was probably right, and that Van der Gast's preoccupation with the coal had something to do with the bonus he'd get on every hundredweight saved. For whenever the consumption had been low he rubbed his hands and slapped my shoulder and larked about with a semblance of his old humour. But if we happened to have a spell of headwind, and consequently made less miles to the ton, he got in a terrible mood. He'd shrivel up like a dead leaf, then suddenly burst out in one of the vilest tempers I've ever seen in anybody. He'd start a row about nothing, shout me down and nearly spit at me in incoherent rage. It was quite a strain on my self-control, but I think I managed to keep my temper all right. I used to think: "Poor old stick, for a man of his age this job is too heavy. In his imagination he's still sailing the *Galebird*." He invariably groped on the left-hand side of his cabin door for the knob, before he remembered that on this ship it was on the other side. He was always displaying this kind of absent-mindedness. No wonder he got jumpy on board this ship chock full of patent fittings and labour-saving devices. Even I took some time to get used to them.

After that week I began to wonder if my misgivings had been unjustified. For however much you distrusted this ship, you had to admit in the end that she was a gem. She ran like lightning and responded to the helm so quickly that sometimes you had to shout at the helmsman because she was bolting while he blew his nose. The atmosphere on board began to improve after a fortnight or so, for the high spirits of the ship were infectious. Her verve and her buoyancy were somehow exhilarating, and she had the stamp of a thoroughbred. She was indeed a gem. To watch her lift her bows and cut the waves in curling sheets of pure silver, sometimes as high as the bridge, was sheer joy. She used to quiver like a race-horse, before she rode a heavy roller, and when her bows plunged into it she seemed to leap up with a perfect gliding motion that hadn't a trace of pitching or bucking about it. She helped us to forget the kidney beans that reappeared at every meal and the foul potatoes that had to be chucked overboard halfway across the Atlantic because even the maggots were sick of them. Bevers, Boer and Van Gulik were lifted out of their gloom by the liveliness of the ship. After that first fortnight they used to come down for their meals beaming and rubbing their hands. And they were ecstatic about the qualities of the ship. No wonder old Kwel insured her so heavily, they said.

I didn't know that, about the insurance, and it brought back the old suspicion which I'd almost forgotten under the ship's high spirits. "Is she as heavily insured as all that?" I asked. "As heavily as a mailship, my boy," Bevers informed me. "If this jewel should go west Mr. Kwel will make a hell of a profit."

"You're a dirty slanderer," Boer protested. "Who put that idea into your head?"

"I have got my own sources of information," Bevers answered with a grin.

I tried to pump him about this insurance, but they both began ragging like excited boys, and I got no further.

The deck-hands and the stokers were equally happy in their work and were singing and larking most of the time. They called the ship names when she tried to throw them off their feet and giggled like women when they had to hold on to the rails for dear life. She was swinging more boisterously every day, but she dived and rolled so gracefully that it felt like dancing. The only one who was immune to her charms was old Van der Gast. He peered gloomily over the sprayshield at the splashing silver, and his hands clutched the rail with a desperate tenseness. I offered him a drink once before I took over the watch because he looked so gloomy. But he refused again—even more vehemently than he had on the first occasion. "No, no," he said; "no spirits, Wandelaar; it's bad for the work. And if you take my advice you'll leave it alone yourself."

I laughed and said: "Come on, skipper, that night at Timmer's you weren't exactly a teetotaller." His face became so miserable that it almost frightened me. He suddenly looked more like an old woman than ever. "Yes, yes," he said, "and I dare say that night cost me enough to keep off it for the rest of my life." He turned away quickly and peered over the sprayshield again, although his watch was over. I went to the wheelhouse to check the course, and when I came back he was still standing there, his hands clasped round the rail. I wanted to say something, but I saw him blinking and realised he was weeping. It was most embarrassing, and all I managed to blurt out was: "Look, skipper, how nicely she takes them. . . ."

He turned away again and hurried down below deck, avoiding my eyes by keeping his own fixed on the steps as he climbed down backwards.

But I stopped worrying about Van der Gast's queer behaviour; the ship's exaltation was irresistible. The deep hum of the engine sounded more and more like the purring of a cat; the stem rose and fell with the grace of a seagull— proud and slender and beautifully feminine. She took the tow along like a toy—the ugly hulk just behind us didn't get a chance to play any tricks. I enjoyed my work more and more as the days went on. Everything I did was done with care, almost, I might say, lovingly. Yes, I think I had begun to love that little ship *Ameland* as I had never loved a ship before. There was something almost human about her. She seemed to give her life into your hands when you took the helm and kept her on her course under the stars. And she would dance over the sea sometimes, like a girl with a skipping rope on a summer's morning, her skirts fluttering.

Her pranks got wilder, but they weren't in any way vicious. She knocked bo'sun Janus's pipe out of his mouth when he was measuring the bilge-water. She tossed water into old Pleun's paint-pot when he was touching up a scratch inside her rail, and he scolded as if she were his mischievous grand-daughter; the engineers down below would call: "Hey, take it easy, will you?" when she tried to fling them in the works with a sudden roll of her slender body. Like a child she was, a child on a swing—higher, higher! A mood of reckless gaiety took possession of the crew. The stokers and the sailors got completely above themselves. They sang and yodelled and stamped in the stoke-hold, beating time with their shovels. The messroom at night sounded like a pub on a Saturday with so much singing and laughing that sometimes when I was on the bridge I couldn't hear what the helmsman said. It made Van der Gast as nervous as a hunted chicken. I began to pity him more and more, for the gaiety of the ship got me completely. I hummed on the bridge, whistled as I filled out the log, and coming down to my cabin after a watch I winked at your portrait and said: "Hullo, Nellie!" Then the ship would make another of her sudden dives and throw me against the washstand. After I had kicked off my boots and tried to remove my trousers she would make me hop round on one leg for hours, trying to keep my balance, and I would end up on my back in my bunk with my feet in the air. I'd scold her and grumble, rubbing my spine. But once I lay in my bunk like a child in a rocking cradle, I'd fall asleep with a smile and a curious lightness in my heart—a lightness I had never felt since the days you and I were courting.

Yes—she worked on us like a woman, a wayward, wild, be-witching woman. That's perhaps why we seamen, who knew ships as thoroughly as our own conscience, never noticed the warnings we got of what was about to happen. The warnings got more obvious every day. In the end, only blind men could have ignored them—or men in love.

That must have been it; she had bewitched us all. The *Ameland* was a wicked ship.

I must try to finish this letter before the morning, for tomorrow I'll have to start work. I've got a plan which I think will come off. I'll tell you all about it in a minute. It must have been second sight that made me ask Bulle this morning to get me a dozen candles; I wouldn't be surprised if I spend the rest of the night writing, for there is still a lot to tell.

I don't know why, but I feel a lot older. While I was writing about the *Ameland* last night I couldn't help think-ing what a child I was. And yet it happened not more than a month ago. I think I've discovered something about life: it is not the adventures, the big events that make a man feel older. It is the thoughts that suddenly pop up in his mind while he's doing something ordinary; filling a pipe or tying a shoelace, or trying to thread a needle. I had a moment like that just now when I realised for the first time that I am a captain now. It is not at all as I had expected it to be; it is rather a lonely feeling. Life seems a lot darker since we last met, sweetheart. If you weren't there behind the horizon I would get frightened. It feels like sailing without a chart towards a shore on which all the lights have been put out.

Until about ten days past the Scillies everything went well. That's to say it really got worse every day, only we didn't notice it, because the process was so gradual. Van der Gast had packed up altogether in the end. I used to take his watches as much as I could. He grew older almost every hour; his shoulders drooped; his eyes became watery, and he used to mumble to himself, chuckling sometimes in a childish way. And he had even given up bothering about the coal. I didn't mind taking over his watches as long as all went well; but when it started to blow I got worried.

We had seen it coming for a day or so: heavy, rolling cloud from the south-west and a choppy swell. But the big wind wouldn't come; it only seemed to gather strength behind the horizon. I didn't like that horizon at all; but rough weather was to be expected in these latitudes at this season. Nobody on board the *Ameland* worried about it. A ship like this could take any gale in her stride. I wasn't worried about the ship either; I was worried about the watches once the gale should break loose. I might have been able to sail the ship by myself for a while, but if it became a matter of spending days and nights up to my waist in angry water I would have to be relieved for an hour or so from time to time, and the chance of that seemed remote. The moment the horizon began to darken Van der Gast locked himself in his cabin. On the evening before the storm the helmsman—who had gone below to call the Captain for the next watch—came back on the bridge alone and said: "The Captain doesn't answer, Mr. Mate. Would you mind going to have a look?"

I went below and knocked on his door. When he didn't answer I went round to the chartroom and tried the communicating door. It was unlocked. I opened it and found Van der Gast lying on his bunk, fully dressed, and the lamp smoking. I asked: "Anything the matter, Captain?" and then he turned his head and looked at me. He gave me a shock, for never before in my life had I seen such fear in human eyes. It was hardly fear any more, it was nearer madness. But it may have been partly because the light was queer, for when he spoke his voice was quite ordinary. "I thought I might as well have a lie down before the thing starts," he said. "Would you mind carrying on until I'm needed?"

I couldn't help thinking: I can do quite well without you, thank you—a boyish thing to think. But I just answered: "Aye, aye, sir," and went back to the bridge.

I had made all necessary preparations for the gale before that; but as now I was certain that I would have to cope with it alone I checked up on them again. I had the engineers knocked up, and the full deck-watch. They brought up the small hawser in case it would be needed as a check; doubled the lashings of the springs; gave the sledge another coating of grease and parcelling, and put the steel skylight-coverings ready for the engine-room and the stairways. I even had the boats put ready and the blocks tested. After that there was nothing left to do. It may look a quick job on paper, but in actual fact it took us quite some time, for the swell increased steadily and the ship pitched violently. While I was checking the navigation lights she lurched so unexpectedly that I nearly went overboard. Before the fun started I signalled to the *Titan* to enquire if they were ready for it. Flip de Meeuw signalled back with the morse lamp: "All set—let it blow."

Well it blew, believe me. The North Atlantic is a nasty spot for a storm. Not so deadly as the Pacific perhaps, but a lot trickier. The gusts that hit us were so strong that the ship heeled over like a windjammer and the big waves that rolled across her struck home like tons of bricks. Van der Gast stayed well out of sight, and after an hour or so of nervousness, I forgot him. The nervousness was not just because I was in command; I was alarmed because the ship behaved so queerly. She lunged like mad, and in the face of every breaker that came rushing at us she seemed to shy away, heeling over and trying to turn her flank to it. When we got her back on her course by pulling hard on the helm, she seemed to take fright and slammed her head in like a wild bull. At first I thought that it was our fault. Every ship has her own peculiarities in heavy weather which you have to find out before she obeys you easily—but it wasn't us, for whatever trick we tried she seemed to heel over at a more dangerous angle. One mountain of a wave hit us before we had been able to bring her quite round, and I shall never forget that moment as long as I live. The ship seemed to shriek like an animal in terror; she tried to plunge away from the rolling wall of water with a movement that was more like that of a living creature than an inanimate thing. The wave struck her under the bow. She reeled back, and there was a terrible noise below decks, a sound of heavy things shifting, of little things scattering, of men screaming; and I was more terrified than I have ever been on any ship before. I felt her lose her balance. For one moment the whole thing seemed to be suspended, shivering before the crash. Then I heard a voice, a voice that startled my ears like the crack of a whip. "Hard to port!" it cried. "Port, you goddam fool!"

I looked up and saw Van der Gast at the top of the stairs, and, my God, he looked a sight. I hardly recognized him. Instead of the dotard I had come to pity, there stood the Van der Gast of the old days with whiskers like a demon's and eyes that would have frightened a lion. Bo'sun Janus and I let the wheel spin to port with our hearts in our mouths, but before we had her hove-to we were kicked off the wheel and flung against the wall. Just then I thought she was going, but when nothing happened and I crawled to my feet again, I saw the old man at the wheel, and he was the most impressive sight I've ever seen. For over a fortnight I imagined I'd been sailing with a dotard, a snivelling weakling whom I tried to pity, but whom, in my secret heart, I despised. The giant who took the wheel of the *Ameland* that night and kept her afloat in that gale by sheer authority was a greater sailor than I can ever hope to be. The moment I saw him, I knew that we were saved, and it seemed as if the ship knew it too. For although she kicked and reared and rolled like a horse stung to madness by a swarm of hornets, she never let herself go again the way she had done before he jumped and grabbed her by the scruff of her neck. I have seen some pretty good sailing in my time, but what Van der Gast did with the *Ameland* that night was little short of magic.

Fourteen hours on end we seemed to dangle on the very edge of hell. The seas were terrific, and although I am sure they can't have been much worse than those that wrecked the *Scottish Maiden* they seemed a lot worse because I knew that the ship was unseaworthy. I had felt it the moment she nearly capsized; and if I hadn't felt it then I would have known it by the time Van der Gast had finished with her. For he treated her differently from any captain I had ever watched handling his ship in heavy weather. He treated her as an enemy. He even shouted at her in his rage. "You goddam bitch!" I heard him yell when she was trying to heel over again as she had done before. It may sound silly to you, this old man shouting abuse at his ship, but if you had heard it you would understand a lot. For one thing, you would understand why he managed to keep an unseaworthy ship afloat for over fourteen hours, the same ship that would have shaken me off like a fly if I had attempted to do the same.

They used to call Van der Gast "the grandfather of the tugs." The man who held the wheel that night was more. He was like some old ancestor called back from the grave to save his progeny from annihilation, to save them, not from the sea or the gale, but from the devil who sought to get the whole tugboat business under his thumb. Van der Gast fought that night for the cause of the tugboat men and the enemy he fought was Kwel.

Well, here I am back with my candles in the kitchen, after sending the boys to bed. I had to promise them that we'll start tomorrow, or there'd have been trouble; so I suppose I'm in for it. I'll have to cram the rest of the story into the smallest space I can.

That morning, when the gale was over and we had seen the worst of the seas, we found that we had lost a deck-hand without even noticing it and that two stokers had been injured. Then the *Titan* signalled: "VESSEL LEAKING. CANNOT MANAGE ALONE. SEND ASSISTANCE."

It was no joke to row a boat in that sea, and besides, there was the difficulty of making fast and boarding the ship. But the crew that manned her were no weaklings, and if they asked for help you could be sure they needed it, and quickly too. At first I wanted to go across myself with the men, but

Van der Gast ordered me to stay on board and take over. He had suddenly gone limp and tired, and his face was so pale that it made his whiskers look yellow. "I'm going to bed," he said huskily; "after you've seen the boat off come down and report to me. I want to talk to you."

I said: "Aye, aye, skipper," and watched him grope his way down the steps. He looked very, very old, and halfway down the steps he stumbled. I jumped to help him, but he nearly hit out at me and growled: "Lay off! Go back to your work!"

He may have looked old; he certainly had not turned into an old woman again.

I went back to my work, and that entailed more than just seeing the boat off. The chief engineer wanted to use the interval for fiddling about with his engine; something had dropped into the bilge and he wanted to fish it out before we sailed on at full speed again. Could he stop the engine for a quarter of an hour, or even just ten minutes? I told him to go ahead as we were marking time anyhow. Once the engine was stopped bo'sun Janus came up to the bridge to ask if he could use the interval for fiddling about with the springs that kept the hawser amidships; two of them looked unsafe after the night's mauling. I told him to go ahead and when he was gone the cook came along to tell me that the beautiful steam-cooker had broken loose during the night and what did I want for dinner making allowances for the fact that he'd only got his emergency oil-stove to cook on. I was pondering this problem, when I suddenly noticed that the ship felt queer under my legs. It may strike you as strange that it was my legs that first told me there was something wrong with the ship, but, after all, one's legs are the contact point and in the course of time they become as sensitive as feelers. When I looked round to find out what the trouble was the megaphone in the wheelhouse caught my eye. It was swinging with the movement of the ship which was considerable as we were then lying cross-seas. I wanted to have a further look round, but my eyes were attracted again to that megaphone. There was something strange about the way it was swinging. I had to watch it for quite a while before I realised what it was: it was swinging further off the wall and nearer me every time—nearer and

175

nearer. The shock I got when I realised what was happening paralysed me. I heard the cook ask: "What about soaked biscuit hotted up with jam? Sort of jam-roll?"

I realised that the ship was capsizing; a couple more waves and she would turn turtle.

A voice made me jump. A feeble old man's voice, wailing from the cabin below: "Wandelaar . . . !"

I made the telegraph in one leap; rammed down the handle to "Full Speed Ahead." It seemed an eternity before they responded to it, but actually it was only a matter of seconds. The engine began to throb, then revved up with a mounting whine. The ship crawled ahead. I leaped at the wheel and let it spin. After a minute the ship lifted.

I can't tell you the infinite relief I felt at that moment. The first thought in my head was: "Wrong. You were wrong to let the bo'sun muck about with the hawser while the engine was stopped. But for an old man, blind as a bat in his cabin, you would have turned her over before you knew what you were doing." For what had happened was simply this. Because the engine had been stopped the ship had been thrown cross-seas; and when the guide springs that controlled the hawser were slackened on one side the hawser slid off the stern. The full weight of the sodden rope started dragging at the main bollard amidships and it would have weighed the ship down if Van der Gast hadn't realized what was happening. I saw now that what I did was a grave mistake, considering that I knew only too well what an unstable ship she was. Thanks to Van der Gast and the speed with which the engine-room responded, our doom was averted once again.

Our doom I call it, for I was convinced now that the *Ameland* had been badly designed. She was certain death for anyone sailing her for more than two hundred miles. And Kwel knew it.

Of course there was a lot of fuss afterwards. Bevers came up, cursing and swearing. What the goddam hell did I mean by that goddam foolery? He had nearly been caught by that goddam engine when Boer started it up. I explained to him what had happened, but he didn't seem really to understand. "Oh, well," he said, "any fool would have realised that she'd be more difficult to handle after losing the

176

ballast weight of all that coal we burned last night. Why the hell didn't you warn us in time?"

Was I to tell him how near capsizing we had been? Before I had made up my mind, the cook screamed and pointed at the *Titan*. When I looked in that direction I got another headache. She was listing heavily, and signals were going up as if she was dressing herself. We had to lower another boat and race out to her, for now she was going.

I had no choice but to go with them. Cook took the wheel with the order to keep her hove-to, even if I had to be off the bridge for a week—and never mind his jam-roll! On board the *Titan* the dickens of a job was waiting for us. Her stern-anchor had torn its moorings and was battering her stern to pulp. She had no steam and was leaking like a sieve in the aft hold. The men had not been able to haul the anchor back because the poop was awash at every wave and it was impossible to get a foothold anywhere. We managed to get the thing under control after an hour or so. When at last I was rowed back to the tug it was dark. I was soaked to the skin, and dog tired; but when I came on the bridge there was no sign of Van der Gast. Cook was still holding the wheel with a face like a disgruntled woman's. "I hope you've had a nice time," he said. And I would have swiped him one if that voice hadn't called again. "Wandelaar. . . !"

It cried, far away, with such a sound of despair that I hurried down the steps and stumbled into his cabin without knocking.

He was lying on his bunk, still in his oilskins, and looked so deathly pale that I thought he had lost consciousness. But he had heard me come in and asked: "That you, Mate?"

"Yes, Captain," I said. "How are you feeling?"

He sighed and moved his hand, that hung limply over the edge of his bunk. "Tired," he answered.

He was silent after that. The hand had gone limp again. It was dark in the cabin, for the lamp was turned low. I leant with my back to the wall and my legs apart to steady myself against the ship's heavy rolling.

"How much coal has it cost us?" he asked in a whisper.

"Sixteen tons, Captain," I replied.

Then he turned his face towards me. The shadows may have made his cheeks look more hollow than they were. He was ghastly to look at, as if the grave had claimed him already. Only his eyes retained a spark of life. They were as compelling as they had been that night, only much paler, almost white. "Sixteen tons . . ." he whispered. Then his whiskers quivered, and he gave a gulp.

I said nothing, and there was silence between us for a long time. The only sounds were the purring of the engine, which made the lamp glass tinkle, and the swishing of the waves outside. After a while I couldn't stand that silence any longer. "Skipper," I said, "let's be honest. There's no point in hiding the truth from one another any more."

He didn't move; he didn't answer. He just looked at me and for a moment it seemed as if the old woman's fear was coming back into those eyes. But when I went on it vanished; and sometimes the flickering of the lamp made it seem as if he was smiling.

"The ship has been constructed wrong," I said. "Her centre of gravity is far too high. When we left she felt all right, but now we have burnt up half her coal she starts to list at a touch. It won't be long before she turns turtle. What are you going to do about it?"

He looked at me for a while, then he shut his eyes. I saw that he tried to turn his head away, but he couldn't. Then he smacked his lips, as if he was tasting something, and whispered: "Bas warned me—didn't want to—couldn't do anything." His voice was so faint that I had to bend over him to make out what he was saying. I wanted to ask him a lot of questions, but his voice grew fainter. "Coward," he murmured. "Old. You young. Children. Better one. Not all. Scuttle her."

Then he opened his eyes again as if he had woken up, and said, loudly and clearly: "Scuttle her, Wandelaar, or you'll be a murderer!"

"But, Captain, . . ." I began.

He made a gesture with his hand that gave me quite a start; it had been motionless for so long. "Now let me sleep," he said. I asked if he wanted something to eat, or if there was anything else I could do for him, but he made no answer. I went out, closing the door softly. When I came back on the bridge I saw by the clock on the wheelhouse that I had been away for only five minutes. It seemed much longer.

I went back three times that night to look at him. Every time he hadn't moved, but was lying exactly as I had left him. I didn't know whether he was awake or asleep, so I just went out again quietly.

The next morning, at six, just before sunrise, I went to have a look again. The first thing I saw after opening the door cautiously was that he had managed to turn himself on his back. His hands lay a little bit apart on his chest, as if he had tried to fold them to pray and not succeeded. His face was very old, and his eyes were half closed; he would have been almost beautiful if his mouth hadn't hung open. I stood looking at him for quite some time, and the longer I looked at him the more it seemed as if he was smiling. He certainly had reason to, for he had not died a murderer, which was the thing he had dreaded all along.

I haven't seen many corpses in my life. I suppose I had the thoughts every one else has had about the frailness of the body and the brevity of human life. While I stood looking at him, not daring yet to move away with the burden he had shifted on to me, it seemed childish to worry about Kwel and my future. What I had to do now was to call a ship's council and to tell them what I knew. The decision to scuttle a ship could hardly be taken secretly, and certainly not carried out without a lot of preparation if I wanted to save all hands. During those minutes I was sure this was what I was going to do the moment I got back on deck. But when it came to the point of taking action I found that burden of responsibility much heavier than I had imagined.

Bo'sun Janus, who had taken the wheel, didn't say a word when I told him that the Captain was dead and that the flag should be lowered to half-mast. He only stared at me with an expression of incredulity which slowly changed to one of fear. Then he went off to carry out the order.

The sun had come out and the sea looked beautiful, shining and alive with colour. I attracted the attention of the *Titan* with three blasts on the hooter. When they had all come running to the foc'sle I instructed Janus to hoist the flag before lowering it to half-mast. They looked at us and waved and tried to make their hollooing reach us, but it was too far. I made the bo'sun signal: "Captain died. Mourning." Then they understood. For the whole day a couple of them stood looking at us from the foc'sle; they had hoisted a flag as big as a house in the foretop and lowered it to half-mast. It looked very gay in the sunlight for the weather had brightened. There was a lot of blue in the sky and big drifting clouds.

Bevers and Boer and Van Gulik were very impressed and so were the men. It was curious that it should take them that way, for they had hardly had a glimpse of him since the trip began. But somehow they must have felt that there was more to it than the mere loss of their Captain.

I called a ship's council all right, but all we discussed was the death-certificate, and all we decided was to bury him at sea the next day at noon. As I could not keep all the watches, a temporary Mate had to be appointed, and we chose Flip de Meeuw because he had his certificate. Old Pleun would take his place on the *Titan*. I didn't mention the last order Van der Gast had given me; I thought I had better wait a bit and think it over. There seemed nothing to worry about at the moment with the weather as fine as it was.

Flip de Meeuw was very impressed, and very excited. He called me "Captain" straight away, and listened to everything I said with big, wondering eyes. I made him read the chart, not because there was any necessity, but because I wanted to size him up. He worked quickly and correctly, and after I had ordered him to fill in the log, he knocked on the door of my cabin and said miserably: "I am frightfully sorry, Captain—I have made a blot. Does it matter?" I couldn't help laughing as I answered: "With God's help we'll overcome that blot, I hope."

It gave me a curious sensation, for I remembered that five years ago Bas had said exactly the same thing to me. It was out of my mouth before I realised it.

It is disconcerting, you know, to find that with the years nothing changes in the game, except the players.

If my letter seems a bit wordy here and there, it is probably because I have been trying to put off saying what must be said now.

As long as Van der Gast's body was still on board, I thought it proper not to discuss the unseaworthiness of the ship nor the plan for saving ourselves when the time came. After Van der Gast had been buried I thought I had better wait until I had made some calculations for myself. After I had made the calculations for the first time I reckoned she would turn turtle after one hundred more miles at the furthest. When I'd worked it out six times and made all the allowances I could, I estimated that we might do a hundred and fifty miles, which would just enable us to make St. John's, if the weather stayed as calm as it was and the wind remained easterly. The long and short of it was that I kept my mouth shut and hoped for the best.

I don't want to whitewash myself, but at the time my argument sounded rather convincing. Here I was, trying to make a new start in a job that was for me the breath of life. If I began by scuttling the flagship on my first trip as a temporary Captain, I might as well go down with her. For even if I had the full backing of the council, even if the log proved without a shadow of a doubt that the ship was doomed to capsize after her centre of gravity had crept up high enough with the emptying of the bunkers, Kwel was clever enough to manipulate the enquiry which would follow such a happening so that in any case I would get the blame. Don't forget that the ship had been certified seaworthy before she sailed, and no one could foresee the tricks she'd play without the most intricate calculations. She would have been perfectly all right by herself; with a tow she was a death-trap.

That was another solution: to cut the *Titan* adrift, and head for St. John's ourselves. But to abandon the *Titan* would certainly mean that my career was ruined for good. We tugboat men have a tradition that makes it just impossible for us to cut adrift from a tow; we'd sooner go down ourselves. That is the essence of the tugboat business.

I don't want to blather about it any longer. I tried to make Bevers say it himself, but he didn't seem to realise what was involved. If you ask me, he realised it as much as I did, but kept his mouth shut because he was as anxious about the future as I was. If you ask me, we all knew it and kept our mouths shut by tacit consent. This is the only consolation I have when I realise that to all intents and purposes I am a murderer.

Of course I thought up scores of plans. I thought of ferrying the coal to the *Titan* in our boats to look as if we were giving her some fuel in case of bad weather. The engine would be stopped for that and I could see to it that the springs were slackened, so that the hawser would shift amidships again and the weight of the bight would pull her over, as it had done the day before old Van der Gast died. I thought out even better plans. I thought like mad and didn't quite know which course to choose. I was fooling myself and succeeding. I was convinced that I would scuttle the ship the moment I had found the best way to do it.

I still hadn't decided which was the best way when the glass started falling. I hadn't even decided when the storm-covers were put on the skylights of the engine-room and the mess. It was like putting the gravestones on a tomb. Bevers waved at me before he vanished, shouting: "See you later!" He was quite cheerful but his eyes showed the truth. He knew the facts as well as I did, and so did everybody else. It was like a nightmare. We all knew, and yet we shut our eyes to it instead of being sensible. My God, if only Siemonov had been there, or even Bas: we would have taken to the boats like lightning, ferried as much coal to the *Titan* as we could, and let the damn ship sink. It wasn't even impressive or dignified, this crazy show of courage. It wasn't courage at all. It was just plain cowardice; Kwel had frightened us into suicide. The tiny straw of false hope we clung to was the possibility that it wouldn't really happen to us. Perhaps it was our youth; Van der Gast, who was old, had no such comforting illusions.

For my part, there was, I know, a still deeper reason which I only dare divulge now because I am all alone at dead of night, out of sight and earshot of everybody. The fact is I shall have to fight Kwel, whether I like it or not. There's no other way out; it's a matter of who kills the other first. Yet my very nature, my whole being revolts at the idea. I don't want to do it. I want to sail and be happy, and see you happy, and give little Bart and little Jan a good education, and enjoy a peaceable old age. Why the devil should I be forced into a battle I detest? But I know I must, and I knew it all the time—can it be that I wanted to make it impossible for myself to back out? That I wanted Kwel to commit this last, unforgivable crime, so that I couldn't go fawning to him any more, wagging my tail? For if the *Ameland* went down because I couldn't make a decision, the real responsibility rested on Kwel, not on me.

The gale that hit us this time was much less severe than the one we encountered before; but the ship responded badly to the helm. I don't know why; perhaps because she was that much lighter. I just couldn't keep her hove-to; she wanted to throw herself cross-seas all the time. The hawser got slack and the *Titan* was blown cross-seas, too. I gave her everything I could, shouting down the tube to the engine-room for more pressure all the time. Bevers asked me, when this proved ineffective, if I wanted him to tighten the safety valve. "Are you mad?" I answered. "I'm damned if I'll have us all blown up."

It was all part of the game, this counterfeit indignation. Blow ourselves up for Kwel's benefit? Not bloody likely! It somehow made it less obvious that we were about to let ourselves be drowned for his benefit. I tried desperately to get the *Titan* back in the wind. The *Jan van Gent*, or even the *Aurora*, would have managed it in the end by sheer doggedness. The *Ameland*, with all her new-fangled contraptions, all her power and shapeliness, was as much use as a child's toy. I had never realised before how much depends on the centre of gravity in a tug; in fact stability is a greater asset than horse-power. The *Ameland* pulled the hawser to shreds, but she pulled to no purpose.

I stood with Janus on the bridge, while he held the wheel. I felt the ship going even before she listed. I shouted: "Jump!" I heard the clatter of glass as I ran for the submerging starboard-side, and a rumble like thunder as the boilers broke away from their fixings. That finished her. She turned completely over like a seal. I managed to fling myself over the rail, slither down her side, and get hold of a bilge-keel. I thought: that's the end of her; now the boilers will explode. I didn't think of you, nor even of myself; all I thought of was those cursed boilers.

What happened after that I'm not quite sure of because I've only heard other people's accounts. The last thing I remember is clinging to that bilge-keel like grim death, thinking of the boilers. One of the boats apparently got clear of the wreckage; I suspect Janus saw to that: he was eminently practical. I think he must have made a little plan of his own, just in case. Anyhow, he got into that boat and so did Flip de Meeuw. They told me they saw me hanging on to that bilge-keel, but they wouldn't have spotted me in the whirlpool if I hadn't shouted and waved. They say that terrific explosions hurled up tons of foaming water and when the ship plunged and sank she sucked a hole in the sea as big as a crater. They say that Janus jumped with a rope round his chest and grabbed me just in time, and that Flip hauled us in while the boat circled round that hole with the speed of an express train. It sounds like an exaggeration to me, but that's their story.

Next thing I remember was being woken by a boy calling "Captain." I'm sure if he had called me "Mr. Mate" instead I wouldn't have bothered to rouse myself. It was the "Captain" that made me come back to life, and somehow it seemed to leave a pleasant taste in my mouth. After a while I realised that what I could taste was gin. They were standing round me in a little group, with Bulle and Flip kneeling by my side. Bulle was giving me the gin and Flip was calling me "Captain." Between them they brought me round. They say I murmured: "Boys, you shouldn't have done this." But it sounds too much like what Janus thinks I ought to have said, and I'm sure he made it up.

Now I can't get Bevers' face out of my mind. I see him wave his hand at me and hear him call, "See you later!" The terrible thing is that ten good men were lost. I feel that their ghosts follow me about wherever I go. They sit round this table in the light of the candle, watching me write this confession. And somehow it's no longer a question of what I am to do—am I to make the facts public? It's now a question of accusing Kwel in the name of the ten men he murdered.

I must settle this account with Kwel before my conscience will ever let me have a moment's peace. I hoped that writing this letter would put me in an easier frame of mind, but the faces of those drowned men still haunt me. The wind, sighing in the crevices, the flame of the candle fluttering, the cockroaches scurrying about, the reaction after what has happened—I feel I can't go on living with this crazy notion obsessing me; surely when once I get back to work again I'll be able to laugh and forget.

I had already undressed and put out the candle when I decided to light it again and write these last lines, I won't read the letter myself, I'll stick it in an envelope and post it first thing tomorrow.

I won't even bother to tell you all about the plan. All it amounts to is that I have decided to sail an old lightship across to Denmark with some rigging I bought off a wrecked cod-fisher. Probably I'll be done in before we're half-way. But I just couldn't stand sitting here feeling those ten watching me any longer.

You know the truth now; you know what I am and what I have done. If you still love me, don't ever mention getting this letter.

Love,

JAN.

P.S. NEXT DAY. A hitch in our plan, so I thought I might as well tell you a little more about it before posting this. Also, I realised this morning that I shall probably arrive before this letter does, if there are no more delays.

About this lightship: I spotted it the first day we were here (we got here, by the way, by hoisting a couple of emergency sails on the *Titan*). It lay in the old harbour, red with rust. Janus came back with the story that it had been sold to the Danes by the Canadians; but they had been haggling for over a year now as to whether the buyer or the seller should bear the cost of getting her across the Atlantic. The idea that we might sail it across ourselves was Bulle's; I didn't give it any consideration until I got a reply from the office to my cable asking for orders.

The office replied: "HOME BY CHEAPEST ROUTE." This I found to be by windjammer to Ireland, and from there by usual route to Rotterdam *via* London. But that windjammer wasn't due to leave for another month.

Bulle got the idea about the lightship because the beachcomber who told Janus and him about the deadlock between the Canadians and the Danes had remarked: "If you ask me, now they're waiting until she sails across by herself."

It got on his mind, and he went on nagging me about it. We had sailed that ugly box of a *Titan* for over a hundred and fifty miles with nothing else in the way of rigging but a broomstick and a duster—why couldn't we sail that light-ship across, provided we could find some decent sails to hoist? I told him to find out if there was any sail to be bought, just to be rid of him. He came back the same day with news of that cod-fisher's rigging.

The homeward voyage for the lot of us would have cost over five hundred pounds, and the cod-fisher's junk cost a hundred. Victuals, instruments, papers and so on would cost another hundred. So I made Kwel a clean profit of three hundred pounds to start with. When I made my offer to the Danish consul, he got stuffy. But the Canadians said: "Go ahead, it's worth a thousand pounds to us to have the damn thing out of the way." So that settled it. Tomorrow we sail.

No other news, except that today a telegram arrived for Van der Gast. I decided not to open it, but to take it home with me to the office. They had better deal with it. I can't say I am looking forward to the trip; but I'm certainly looking forward to the thousand pounds. Kwel will rub his eyes when he sees the men he planned to drown sailing home on a lightship, and getting a handsome profit into the bargain. That alone makes it worth my while—that, and the idea that I'll be home again soon. I love you, Nellie, whatever happens. Goodbye.

P.P.S.—*Three days later.*

I had better stop this P.S. business, for we are now at sea. I just didn't post this letter; partly because of the hurry, partly because I couldn't make up my mind. I seem to have a lot of trouble making up my mind lately. I thought: as I'll arrive before the damn thing anyhow, why not take it with me and give it to you? Then, before I'd answered the question one way or the other, we sailed. Secretly, I think I wanted to go on writing. I got quite used to it, and somehow I'd miss it. It is night now, and I am writing in what is called the Captain's cabin—a poky affair reeking of mildew and bilge-water.

The wind is fresh, the swell confused. I said the *Ameland*
lunged; compared with this ship she was as steady as a rock.
By the way, the name of this thing is *Cape Breton* and it is
difficult to make out what is fore and aft on her. (I've just
had to interrupt this because I was called on deck. The jib
had been blown out of its leeches. The rigging I bought off
that cod-fisher may have seemed cheap, but it's turning out
to be dear at the price. This trip is not going to be as funny
as I thought.)

Three days later. Heavy weather, the third day of it. Sorry
about the smudges. The water flies higher than the mast-
heads. Haven't changed clothes since the day before yesterday. Couldn't stand it any longer without a moment with
you. I've bitten off more than I can chew. It looks grim all
round. And don't shake your head and say, "It's your own
fault." I did it to be with you sooner, otherwise I'd have
made Kwel pay for a cabin. At the moment the ship seems
to be breaking up. More later—or maybe not.

Next day. Weather better now, but let me tell you if I'd
known what I was letting myself in for, I wouldn't have
touched this tub with a barge pole, not for a hundred Nellies
I wouldn't. I don't mind rough stuff; it's part of the job.
But this is sheer folly. If I'm floating upside-down tomorrow,
it will be my own fault. Sorry to trouble you with this, but
I've got to tell the truth to someone. How's the feeding of
little Jan getting along, I wonder? I thought of him, even
when it seemed all up with me. Lord, I am really tired. . . .
And one thing is certain: I'm not going to take this crazy
tub of a ship to Esbjerg. To Rotterdam she goes and not an
inch further. If they want her, let them come and get her.

Here we are, becalmed in the middle of the Atlantic, and
our course is already too far to the north. Flip spotted the
first ice floes a quarter of an hour ago. By the way, I don't
know what the date is, because various things have got lost
since my last entry, the calendar and the log among them.
A big wave which sounded like a fat man crashing through
a crate, carried away the chart-room.

I love you. If I hadn't loved you so much I would never

have tried to take this sieve across the ocean. The boys have been pumping for forty-eight hours now, and the water seems to be rising.

If anything should go wrong, keep on loving me. I'd be sick with loneliness if I had to hang about in Heaven without you. Do you honestly think the hereafter is as ghastly as it looks on the coloured print in Parson Gripper's Sunday-school class?

I wish I could tell you honestly and seriously how bad things look for us, but I just can't. I have to joke about it all day, because of the others. And I just can't get out of it.

Old Pleun has lost his ears and looks pretty grisly without them. Why the devil didn't he keep his stocking on like I told him to? He is behaving strangely of late. This morning he pointed at me when I came on deck and said: "No box so small but there's room for the devil in it."

Quite nicely put, but rather alarming for anyone who's had experience with lunatics before. Just to be on the safe side, I'll keep a marline-spike ready in my pocket as well as under my pillow.

No other news but pump, pump, pump. The water remains at the same level as long as the pumps are kept going ten hours out of the twenty-four. No wind at all; only a strong northerly current. Whenever there's a breath of wind it's southerly. As this unspeakable thing only goes sideways on, like a crab, up to wind force 7, all this means that we are heading for Nova Zembla.

I know I haven't been writing much lately, and I think the real reason is that I hardly dare face the facts. I realise now what a fool I have been, what a bungler. If ever I should get back to you by the grace of God, I'll try to do better—but I wonder? I mean I wonder if, when we meet, I'll ever do any better. For now, after re-reading that stuff about the *Ameland* I am pretty fed up with myself. I am fed up with every-body, except you—and Kwel. Now isn't that strange? I somehow can't blame that man any more, for we didn't deserve any better.

Flip has a boil, he wanted me to lance it but I told him he'll have to wait another day. He sat down on the floor as if he wanted to wait right here, and started to babble about his girl friend. I tried to push him out, but he wouldn't go. I had never noticed before how curious his voice sounds; you can hear all sorts of things in it: the cackle of chickens, the purring of a cat, and the curious bubbling sound that eggs make when they're being boiled. The eggs brought back the memory of Kees de Kaap, cooking for the crew of the *Jan van Gent* when they all had malaria. I started telling Flip about it and I enjoyed it. It was like going through an old album of family photographs. After a minute or so he started to snore.

At first I was so angry that I wanted to kick him out, but the sight of him affected me. He looked about ten years old, with his mouth half open and his eyelids blue with tiredness and hunger (we lost a lot of the victuals during the rough weather of the first week). I looked at him for quite a time, and wondered what the hell life is all about. Why should this youngster be afloat in the North Atlantic dying of fear and exhaustion, babbling feverishly about a girl with thin legs and protruding teeth, who made the pastor's bed in the morning and sang "Hark, Hark, the Lark" in the evening, while her brother accompanied her on the mouth-organ. Where were they bound for, these child-souls on the fringe of the ice floes, slowly going mad with religious mania through lack of beans and water? When I reprimanded Janus for abusing poor old Pleun, he snarled out in a nasty sort of way: "The bastard says he's Christ."

"Let him," I answered, "What do you know of Christ, you blasphemous heathen?"

He glared at me and growled: "It ain't natural." I almost saw the stripes of the tiger flicker through the rags of his shirt.

They'll all turn into animals now the drinking water is finished and the food spoilt—Janus a tiger; Bulle a gorilla; Pleun a very old goat. Only Flip will remain a faithful dog. He's lying on the floor now, behind my chair, curled up, snoring.

Lord, we are done for, I feel.

Pleun is dead, and it was nothing to do with my marline-spike. I think he is dead, that is, for he's disappeared.

Vanished mysteriously during the night, without a splash in the dead calm sea, which I would have heard. I am glad he is gone, even if the way he went is a bit of a mystery, for last night I overheard part of a conversation between him and Janus. "All right," Janus said, with a malice in his voice that sent a shiver through me; "If you're Christ, let me crucify you, you son of a bitch."

I wonder how Janus did it? He must have lowered him very gently. In the log I wrote: "This morning at the change of watches A.B. Seaman P. Molenaar was reported missing. Probably he has jumped the rail while his mind was deranged; see yesterday's entry."

I am sorry for the poor brute, although this is by far the best solution. It seems possible now, just possible, that we may escape the fate of the fishing smack *Scheveningen 66,* which has been haunting me ever since this business started. You'll remember her crew got a form of religious mania in these waters some years ago. They crucified the cabin-boys and pickled them after cutting them up. The whole crew is now in Meerenberg Asylum. Let's hope Janus is not demented enough to see Pleun following the ship at night, walking in its wake, like Jesus walking on the waters. That's the kind of state the skipper of the *Scheveningen 66* had got into. It was Bas who told me all this: his brother is a male nurse at Meerenberg. I loved those gruesome stories; I couldn't hear them often enough when we were lying in harbour, with the rain lashing the deck and the teapot spout steaming in the lamplight, while we ate fried fish off a bit of newspaper. I made him repeat them again and again for my benefit.

What is one to do when one knows almost for certain that one member of the crew has murdered another? What I did, I suppose—fill in the log and mention his abnormal state of mind.

The strangest moment, though, was when I myself knelt down in prayer just before I started to write this. It is over now, so I can tell you without the dread of having to go through it again. I just wanted to pray in what must have been a moment of despair, that's all. But when I knelt down I felt as if the whole crew of the *Scheveningen 66* had entered my body at that moment, and the spirit I evoked was not that of the God of mercy, but the god of the jungle. When

I staggered from my knees I was more frightened than I have ever been in my life, I grabbed this pencil, as if it were a weapon to release me from the horror of that dream.

I think we have come through. This morning we met an Englishman bound for Montreal. We exchanged signals and I went across with the dinghy to get water and something to eat. The faces lined up at the rail were a sight to behold: they gaped at me as if I were the Flying Dutchman in person. But the Captain was much less startled by my appearance than I myself when I happened to catch sight of my face in the Captain's mirror. I nearly jumped, for the man I saw there had the eyes of a lunatic, cracked lips and a beard, and looked like nothing I had seen before.

"Hullo," said the Captain. "Do sit down. Had a nice trip?" When I just stood and blinked he started to complain about the weather. It took hours before he asked: "And now, sir, what can I do for you?" First I had to drink a glass of sherry, and give my opinion on the Mexican situation. He gave me more food than I dared hope for, and five crates of beer and a suit of clothes into the bargain. But the amazing thing was he didn't make the gift too obvious. He behaved as if it was something I had left behind on board his ship when I left in such a hurry last time, and he almost thanked me for letting him use it in the meantime. I felt it was good manners carried a little too far, but God bless him all the same. When I came back on deck his bo'sun had a parcel ready with clothes and tobacco for the boys. When we opened it afterwards we even found threads, buttons, needles and five pieces of soap. But when we sailed and waved our adieus to them they didn't wave back; they just jerked their heads sideways, almost imperceptibly, by way of goodbye.

When I had washed and put on the Captain's uniform, eating a loaf by little mouthfuls at the same time, in order not to upset my stomach after these weeks of starvation, I went on deck and was taken aback by the sight that greeted me. The crew looked like a child's grotesque drawing come to life. We stared at each other speechless for a while; then someone started to laugh, and that broke the spell. We laughed until we wept; we fell on one another's necks with laughter, and the very sea seemed to hold its sides. For the mad English had given us their Sunday suits, which made us look like a lot of overdressed scarecrows.

The change it brought over us was miraculous. The animals vanished like magic and the old shipmates I had known so well took their place. There was some singing in the foc'sle, and when Janus took the wheel at night during my watch my muscles didn't go tense with anxiety as they had done for the past ten days. He was no longer the sinister figure who had cost me sleepless nights, but merely a lumbering giant of a man with the mind of a child.

Well, love, the end is in sight. The day before yesterday we caught the light of the Butt of Lewis. An hour ago we left the last of the buoys of the Pentland Firth behind us; and now, while I am writing, I can see the light of Duncansby Head winking through the porthole. This is virtually the end of our voyage, for the last lap across the North Sea is child's play.

Now I come sailing home with more love in my heart than I would have thought possible for any man to feel. I don't know what is in store for us; I don't know what other adventures we'll have together before we grow old and settle down, but one thing I know, Nellie—no man could love you more.

JAN.

CHAPTER TEN

WHEN the crew of the *Cape Breton* arrived at Esbjerg they were received like heroes. A landau met them at the quay and they were driven in state to the Town Hall where they sat between high-bosomed ladies at a table full of delicacies in the form of champagne, sour gherkins and jam tart. Outside the girls' faces could be seen flattening themselves against the window-panes; inside, the burgomaster made a speech turning round all the time like the needle of a compass, as he tried to chase the reflection of the chandelier off his notes.

They drank the champagne glumly, and munched the

gherkins and the jam tart with the air of martyrs. A waiter
came in and drew the curtains, and the faces of the girls
were banished out of sight. Now there was nothing to look
at but the burgomaster. The Captain had to answer the
toast. He looked red and self-conscious as he thanked the
gentlemen very much for their welcome; it was a pleasant
ending to a pleasant trip, he said. Only Janus was wise
enough to stick a tart and two bottles up his jersey when
they filed out, free to go home at last.

They had to take with them in the train all the bouquets
they had received on this occasion, and the compartment
smelled like a florist's shop. When the train had got clear
of the station, however, all the bouquets were thrown out
of the window. After their official welcome the crew seemed
thoroughly depressed, but their high spirits came back when
the Captain told them the outcome of some calculations
he had been making in a corner with a pad on his knee:
out of the thousand pounds there were eight hundred left,
which meant one hundred pounds per man.

A hundred pounds! Bulle was going to spend his money
on having a good time; Janus on ear-rings for his negress
wife, Bibi; Flip on tickets for grand dances. The Captain
only thought about home. He sat staring out of the window
in the darkness where there was nothing to see but the
reflection of Bulle and Janus playing cards, yet he smiled
and sometimes chuckled, shaking his head. The boys didn't
ask him to take part in their game; they ignored him
reverently. He was the skipper and therefore a law unto
himself.

After a day and a night they arrived at the Dutch frontier.
The latter part of the journey they spent snoring on one
another's shoulders. But the Captain didn't sleep. He stared
out of the window, looking at the wind-mills, the cows, and
the colossal expanse of the sky over the flat polders. He was
blissfully happy. This was the vision that had kept him sane
during those nightmare days at sea. Strange, he thought,
that a man should go chasing the will o' the wisp of happiness, only to find it in the very spot he set out from—in the
rich and peaceful meadows of his homeland. Four hours
and thirteen minutes more, and his happiness would be
complete.

In Amsterdam, thank God, there was no reception committee and no speechifying burgomasters. The crew with whom he had shared so many hardships and dangers vanished like magic in the throng of travellers rushing to the exit; only Flip wanted to come with him in the train to the north, and refused stubbornly to be shaken off. When Jan asked: "But what about your girl-friend?" the boy looked very fierce and answered: "Haven't got any girl-friend. I gave her up."

It was really rather a touching confession, but the boy's indignation made it seem so comic that Jan couldn't help laughing. The laughter did it. Before he knew what had happened Flip had vanished too. He called "Flip! Hey, Mate!" until the staring of the porters made him give up. Now at last he had his wish: he was alone.

In Alkmaar he had to wait an hour for his connection. He sent a telegram: HOME IN TWO HOURS, JAN, and did some shopping in the town: toys for the boys, a tea-cosy with a parrot on it in gold thread for Nellie, a knitting basket for Mamma Dijkmans, a pipe for father and a bag of sweets to be shared by all. When the train pulled out of the station and no one else had come into the compartment, he stretched his legs on the seat in front of him and rested his head on the wooden partition behind. "Home, home, home," the wheels kept saying as they hummed over the rails. The dusk softened the bleakness of the landscape; the moon travelled with him along the canals. These hours of anticipation were the best hours of his life. Terror, shipwreck, murder, madness—all these things seemed the price that had to be paid for a reward of such sublime happiness.

When the beam of the harbour lighthouse began flashing on the carriage window Jan got up and looked out for the station, his hair flying and his eyes screwed up against the wind.

When the platform came in sight—a dimly lit island in the darkness—there seemed to be only one person waiting, a woman. She was dressed in black and looked small and pathetic in the unsteady gleam of the station lamp. As the train got nearer, Jan strained his eyes towards the end of the platform, where the gates were, but there was nobody there except the ticket-collector. No one had come to meet the train but this woman in black. When the train drew in and the doors were flung open, Jan saw the woman going from compartment to compartment, standing on her toes at each window to look in. People kept pushing past her. Then she came into the circle of a lamp, and he saw it was Mamma Dijkmans.

Mamma Dijkmans—what had happened? Why was she in black? Was somebody dead? Father? One of the children? And where was Nellie? Why hadn't Nellie come?

When Mamma Dijkmans saw him, she stopped dead, as if he had given her a fright. But after a momen she hurried towards him and looked up at him with red eyes and a nervously smiling face. "Oh, Jan boy, dear boy," she began. And when he asked: "What's the matter?" her face looked so distressed that he felt his heart thumping.

"But—but don't you know . . . ?" she asked, her voice failing.

"No," he said; "what's the matter?"

She couldn't answer for tears; she shook her head and fumbled in her bag to find a handkerchief to wipe her eyes. "I—I—can't—understand it," she said. "I just can't understand . . . we did send a telegram, didn't we?"

"Telegram?" he asked.

"Yes . . ." she said. "We sent it to your Captain. . . ."

The ticket-collector went along the train, calling "All change!" and slamming doors. Jan went back for a moment into the compartment, the compartment where he had spent the best hours of his life. He lifted his sea-chest off the rack, the parcels, the toys, the bag with the sweets. As he did so his mind was an utter blank, incapable of thought. When he had the things down he took his wallet out of his pocket; the wallet with the long letter he had never sent, and the cable to Van der Gast which he had never opened. He took the rubber band off and the oiled silk wrapper, and there was the telegram, dry and safe after all those hazardous weeks: CAPTAIN VANDERGAST, DUTCH TUG AMELAND, ST. JOHNS, NEWFOUNDLAND. He opened the envelope and read: PLEASE INFORM WANDELAAR HIS WIFE DIED OF PUERPERAL FEVER APRIL 17 DIJKMANS.

He stood looking at that telegram for quite a time, his head bowed under the quivering gaslight. Then he folded it again and put it in his pocket. When he turned round he found Mamma Dijkmans's pale face staring at him. They stood a moment like that, looking at each other, then he handed some of the parcels to her and she took them in her black-gloved hands. Outside the voice of the ticket-collector was still calling: "All change, all change." A locomotive clanked, hissing through the dark, as Jan and Mamma Dijkmans left the station.

They walked home through the darkening evening, now almost night. The west was a red streak in the dark, and strings of little lights dotted the road. The gables of the houses glimmered at every sweep of the lighthouse beam. It was raining softly. The only sounds were the splash of rain in the gutter and the echo of their footsteps, dead and monotonous on the wet street. The rain pattered on the paper bags Mamma Dijkmans was carrying, sometimes it drummed against Jan's sea chest with the sound of blown sand. Neither of them said a word. When they got to the harbour Mamma Dijkmans tried to talk, but as he didn't answer, she realized he wasn't in a mood to listen and she was silent until they got home.

There, Father Dijkmans sat waiting with little Bart, who had been allowed to stay up, on his lap. When they came in he tried to get up with the child held awkwardly under his arm and a sheepish grin on his face. He put out his hand and tried to say something, but Mamma Dijkmans shook her head and he sat down again awkwardly. Jan came into the room and looked at the child and stroked its hair; but little Bart didn't like it. Jan had been away so long that the child had forgotten him. "The baby is asleep," said Mamma Dijkmans. "Would you like to see it?"

They went upstairs to the attic, where the cupboard bed had been made up for little Bart. A night-light glowed on the bedside-table and a cradle was placed underneath the sky-light. They entered on tiptoe and when the door squeaked Mamma Dijkmans said "Ssh!" with a finger to her lips. She cautiously pulled aside the curtain and Father Dijkmans lifted the nightlight; Jan saw a tiny head on the pillow and a tiny fist by its side, very pale; but Mamma Dijkmans whispered that all sleeping babies were pale. He touched the tiny cheek with a finger; it was as soft as Nellie's bridal veil had been that morning, long ago. The baby moved, and sighed. After it had settled down again they tiptoed out of the room.

Mamma Dijkmans put little Bart to bed and the men were left sitting in front of the stove. Father Dijkmans talked about the children, slowly, groping for words. Jan didn't say anything, not even when he was asked a question. When Mamma Dijkmans came down at last and started laying the table the parents talked as if they were alone in the room. Later there was a knock at the door, and Mamma Dijkmans asked, with a frightened face: "Who can that be?" When she went to answer the door a voice said: "Could I see Captain Wandelaar for a moment? I am from the *New Amsterdam Courier* and would like to ask him a few things about. . . ." Then Mamma Dijkmans whispered something, and the voice said: "Oh, I'm so sorry—I didn't know that. . . . Good night."

When the food was put on the table and Mamma Dijkmans asked: "Wouldn't you like to sit down and have your meal, Jan?" he shook his head and stayed in front of the stove, while the parents pulled up their chairs without a word. After a minute or two he got up and went towards the door. "Where are you going?" Father Dijkmans asked. Jan mumbled something about "That rain. . . ." and pulled the door shut behind him.

Everything seemed vague and far away. The road along the harbour where he and Nellie had strolled so often at night because it was so pleasantly dark, didn't make him sad or lonely; he was too numbed for that. He felt as if he had been stunned by a blow the moment he read the telegram at the station. He had the same stunned feeling when he recovered consciousness in the foc'sle of the *Titan* after the shipwreck of the *Ameland*.

Baas Bongerds, the grave-digger, was sitting with his wife and three noisy children at an untidy table under a fan-shaped oil-light when Jan came in. Bongerds put down his spoon and took him into the passage, pulling the door shut behind him. "How do you do, Wandelaar?" he said. "It's a bad thing, boy, it's a bad thing. I'm damn sorry for you, damn sorry. What is it you want? Have a look? Now—at this hour in this weather? There's nothing to see."

197

But when Jan didn't answer and made no move to go away Bongerds had another look at him in the half darkness and opened the door again. "Won't be a minute, Mother!" he called, "just going across to the yard." He put on oilskins and lit a lantern. Then they went into the rain together to the churchyard.

The churchyard was a plot of ground flanked by dripping trees that rose high and vague in the darkness. They stopped at a small patch of ground that lay against a hawthorn hedge at the end of a path. "Here we are," said Bongerds. The lantern shone on a small piece of wood at one end of the patch, like a tiny signpost:

CORNELIA WANDELAAR, BORN DIJKMANS:
12 MAY 1887—27 APRIL 1910

She was lying in a good neighbourhood, Bongerds said— surrounded by the crew of the *Stentor* that was shipwrecked last month. Captain Raat himself had a tombstone of grey marble with black lettering.

REMEMBER ME BUT DO NOT FEEL SAD
I AM WITH GOD AND I AM GLAD

it ran. The headmaster had composed that verse, Bongerds said and the cost was very reasonable. Mrs. Raat didn't pay more than ten guilders for it, lettering and all. But the stone itself was expensive—pure Italian stuff, though of course not so durable as granite.

When they came back to the house Bongerds chased his children out of the room and told his wife to bring the ink, for Captain Wandelaar wanted to order a stone. A white stone it had to be, and that meant marble. A very expensive thing, pure white marble, the most expensive of the lot. But the Captain would pay the very same night, in advance, and never mind the cost. Well, in that case a pure white stone is of course the very best; only the wife of the burgo-master has got one like that, and between you and me it isn't nearly the same quality as the one Mrs. Wandelaar will have, for a special new lot has just arrived from Italy, as white as snow, without a single blemish in it. And what would the Captain like on it? Only what was inscribed on that temporary thing? Didn't the Captain think that a little inadequate for a big stone like that? All right, all right, just as you please. And the lettering white too? Not even gold? But the burgomaster's wife has . . . all right, all right, please yourself. I only give you my advice; but of course. . . . Very well: white all round, no colouring whatsoever. Not even an angel on it, or a pair of hands reaching across the grave. That seems to be all then. Let me see how much that comes to: Burial fees, rent of plot—upkeep—ground tax—parish rates—digging—marble—transport—labour—extras and sundries. That'll be five hundred and eighty-six guilders seventy-five cents. Because Captain Wandelaar *is* Captain Wandelaar, Bongerds will waive the extra cost usual in the case of plain lettering.

When the Captain wanted to pay him in English money Bongerds started by refusing to take it, but when he realised that fifty pound notes would be worth six hundred guilders at the bank, he said he would shut an eye to it, because Captain Wandelaar was Captain Wandelaar after all. His wife asked if the Captain would like a cup of tea to keep the cold out, but the Captain hurried away.

He walked through the rain along the harbour, past the bandstand, along the top of the dike, until the road became so muddy that he couldn't go any further. He turned round and went the same way back. He walked round the church-yard, but the hedge was too high to see over, and his feet sank into the wet, sodden earth.

Why this senseless wandering? He was getting wet and cold and to slog on in the rain just because she was lying in the rain too wouldn't do any good; it wouldn't change any-thing. He started walking again, growing more tired all the time. When he found himself at last looking at the little house where Bart was born, and where his happiest days had been spent, he sat down on the other side of the road on a milestone with his head in his hands.

When he got up at last the dawn was breaking, and he was so stiff and tired that he could hardly walk. He managed to drag himself home by imagining how blissful it would be to sit by the stove and go to sleep. But when he entered the house quietly by the back door and groped his way to the chair in front of the stove he found it already occupied by old Dijkmans, who was sitting asleep. He was so weak and dispirited that the loss of the chair made him weep like a child.

He went back to the kitchen, lit the lamp, ground some coffee and put a kettle on. As he did so he couldn't help thinking: "This coffee-mill—how often has she ground coffee with it? And, that kettle—how often have I seen her putting it on the stove? It was so heavy that she used to carry it with both hands, and I never got up to help her."

The steam from the hot water misted the windows. He sipped the hot coffee slowly, warming his hands round the cup, while the familiar sounds of early morning—the clanking of buckets in the distance and the rattle of cart wheels—came to him from the world outside. He decided he couldn't stay in the house any longer. He picked up the kitchen slate and wrote a message on it for Mamma Dijkmans: "DEAR MAMMA, I have to go to Rotterdam by first train to deliver the log and the papers at the office. I'll let you know when I'll be back. JAN."

The first train didn't leave for an hour, so he had all that time to wait. The station wasn't open yet, but there were men on the platform, loading a goods van. He sat down on a bench opposite the station and waited there. Half an hour later the first passengers began to arrive, and the station gates were opened. Jan was the first to book a ticket. The man at the window was only half awake, and made a mistake in the change. The train was already in the station, but there was no engine coupled to it and the lamps were unlit. Jan walked to the end of the train and sat down. The smell of stale cigar-smoke and musty steam was sickening. He dozed off in the corner seat, feeling ill.

When he arrived at Rotterdam he made his way to the Company's offices like a man wandering in his sleep. It seemed as if nothing had changed there; again he stood helpless and lost among the desks, with the same incoherent rage boiling up inside him. The clerk with the shining hair looked up with the same insincere smile, and congratulated him on his success in an off-hand manner. The superintendent, he told Jan, was waiting to see him.

When a door was opened for him and he was ushered

into a high-ceilinged room, he expected to see Kwel; but the tall man getting up behind a desk to shake hands with him was bland and suave and introduced himself as Rykens, superintendent of the nautical service. Another door in the room was marked "Private." Jan guessed that behind that door Kwel was sitting—Kwel who was responsible for everything. It was all Kwel's fault. He thought: if I don't get out of here quickly, I'll lose my self-control and there'll be trouble.

Mr. Rykens asked for particulars about the voyage and the shipwreck of the *Ameland*. It was a sad business, he said: such a gem of a ship, the Company's proudest possession. He asked about the trip with the *Cape Breton* too—very friendly, suave and full of compliments. "So? One thousand pounds for taking it across? That's not much, is it—spent it all, I expect? What did you say? Still eight hundred left? But that's incredible. . . ."

He got up from his chair. "If you'll excuse me for a moment—" he said and disappeared through the door marked "Private." When he came back his face was as bland as ever. He merely remarked: "You'll be in some day soon to settle the account, I expect?"

Jan thought he was referring to the wages due, and said: "I would rather take the money with me now, if that's convenient to you."

But he seemed to have mistaken Mr. Rykens' meaning. Mr. Rykens went on to explain that the profit of eight hundred pounds belonged to the Company as Captain Wandelaar was in their service. Of course his salary and the wages of his crew would be paid up to the day of delivery, but the eight hundred pounds would have to be refunded. When Captain Wandelaar, utterly taken aback, told him that the money had already been divided among the crew and that the trip with the *Cape Breton* had saved the Company more than that sum in passenger fees, Mr. Rykens smiled suavely and admitted that the terms of the contract which the Captain and his crew had signed might seem a little harsh in this particular case, but he was sorry to say that the sum of eight hundred pounds would have to be deducted.

All the mad fury that had been boiling up in Jan for

months erupted now like a volcano. In a moment he had pushed his way through the door marked PRIVATE while Rykens shouted helplessly: "Captain! Mr. Wandelaar!" At the other side of the door a little bald man was sitting at a table. He looked up when Jan burst in, and snapped: "I'll thank you to ask. . . ." His voice failed him when he saw what was coming. Jan kicked the door shut without turning round. "Get up, Kwel," he shouted. But the little bald man didn't move; he just sat and gaped, speechless at his desk. When Jan grabbed him by the collar the little man screamed and struggled and tried to reach for a bell on the table. Jan lifted the screaming figure as easily as a terrier picks up a rat, and hurled it with a thud into the far corner of the room. Then he threw on top of it every stick of furniture within reach—the chair, the table, the desk, shouting as he did so: "I'll kill you! I'll kill you!" Before they finally managed to overpower him he made Kwel's office look as if it had been visited by an Atlantic storm.

Four constables were needed to drag him into his cell; but once he was under lock and key he quietened down. He sat motionless on his stool with his hands folded, gazing at the floor. Every time the warder spied at him through the peephole he was in the same position, his hands folded, his eyes fixed on the floor.

The morning brought a new life, a new conviction that he was right in doing what he had done. He had nothing more to lose. Now he'd tell the world the whole shameful story of the tugboats, a story of murder, exploitation, tyranny and greed.

He began walking to and fro in his cell, like a caged bear. He rehearsed the speech he'd make to the court, the speech that would rouse the nation, and improve the lot of all his mates in the tugboat service. He'd tell the court everything; he'd prove that what he had done was to kill, under provocation, a man who had victimized scores of simple, honest folk, who wanted nothing else but to sail and do their job well. He knew he'd be condemned to spend the rest of his life in prison, but he didn't give a second thought to it. He had done his duty: that was all that mattered. He was so elated at having overcome at last his weakness and indecision that he began shouting: "Let me out! Let me out! I want to confront the judge! I want to be taken into court!"

The warder came shuffling along and opened the door with a loud clanking of keys. He was old and had white whiskers, like Van der Gast. "Take it easy, man," he said, "take it easy. Your turn will come."

After the warder had re-locked the door with the same loud clanking of keys, Jan fell on his mattress, exhausted. Soon, however, a mood of utter despair took hold of him. He roared like a wounded animal, banging the walls with his fists. But this time nobody answered, not even the warder. He cooled his temples on the cold, clammy walls when the hammering in his brain became so violent that he felt his head must burst. At last he exhausted himself again, and fell into a heavy, drugged sleep. When he woke up his fingers were swollen and black with beating against the walls.

He stayed locked up for over a week. Then, one morning, a gentleman with gleaming glasses and a brief-case arrived, who said he was Jan's lawyer. But Jan didn't want a lawyer; he was determined to undertake his own defence. The lawyer came back three times to hear if he had changed his mind. In the end he shrugged his shoulders and said: "All right, just as you please. It's your own funeral."

The old warder, when he brought Jan's food at night, shook his head and said: "You made a mistake there, my friend. They don't like prisoners taking on their own defence. You'll be so sorry you let the lawyer go, he's one of the best."

But Jan didn't worry. He was certain he had only to speak the truth and all would be well.

The day of the trial dawned at last. The old warder brushed Jan's clothes and put a parting in his hair, fussing over him as if he were an animal going in for a show. All the while Jan was rehearsing in his mind the great speech he would make to the court. . . .

When, at last, he was led into court and given a seat in the dock, he was more nervous than he had been when he took his first examination in seamanship. The strong light blinded him and the presence of so many people, after his days of solitude, terrified him. His hands stuck to the rail of the dock, and he had to keep wiping them on his trousers to remove the perspiration. It needed an immense effort of will to prevent himself from breaking down and whimpering like a child. He looked round at the blurred faces, the dingy walls, the portrait of Her Majesty, the bench opposite—and then he got a shock that knocked the breath out of him, that made his hands stop trembling and his mouth fall open. On the bench in front of the dock the little bald man was sitting with a bandage round his head, peering at him with one malicious eye, while the other was hidden under the bandage.

Kwel was not dead! That was the first blow, and it nearly floored him. Not so much because he wanted Kwel to be dead, but because his whole speech had been prepared on the assumption that Kwel was. Now everything would have to be changed. The shock of that almost unnerved him.

He was allowed no time to panic, however, for a sudden stir in the court-room announced that the legal functionaries had arrived. Everyone stood up as five dreary old men with wobbling caps on their heads made their way down the centre of the room, preceded by an official in silver uniform who bowed as the dreary old men tottered to their seats.

When Jan's name was called he got up with a sense of renewed courage. He felt that the eyes of all the tugboat crews were upon him, the dead as well as the living— Bevers, Van der Gast, old Pleun and cook Hazewinkel of the *Ameland*, Meyer and Barf who were blown up with the *Marken*, Bikkers who lost his life in a shipwreck: all these men seemed to be there in the court, encouraging and applauding him.

A voice asked: "What was your motive in assaulting Mr. Hemelman?"

Mechanically Jan began his speech, the speech he had rehearsed a hundred times as he paced up and down in his cell. "When as a boy I sailed on the tugboat *Fortuna*. . . ."

But suddenly the name *Hemelman* seemed to rob him of his words. He realised with a sickening sense of his own stupidity that he had tried to kill the wrong man.

The verdict of the court was that after taking into consideration such extenuating circumstances as there were— the extremely exhausting voyage, and the death of his wife

—the court sentenced Captain Wandelaar to three months' imprisonment for his assault on Mr. J. H. Hemelman, chief accountant of Kwel and Van Munster's International Tug-boat Company.

During the first week of his sentence Jan hardly moved at all. He lay on his mattress, in a state between sleeping and waking. Then one night he really slept for the first time: a deep, healthy sleep. When he woke up he called for the warder with such a note of authority in his voice that the old man came shuffling along the corridor as if his life depended on it. He had even sorted out the right key from the bunch before he reached the door, so that there wasn't the usual ceremony of fumbling for it.

"Hullo," he said. "How are you feeling now?"

"I'm all right, thank you," Jan answered. "What day is it?"

"It's Monday."

"Monday the what?"

"Monday, June the twenty-first."

"What's the weather like?"

"Fine, but a bit misty."

"How much more of my sentence have I got to serve?"

"Two months, my boy. Nothing worth speaking of—it'll be gone before you know it."

"Is that so?" the Captain said, looking at him good-humouredly. "All right, that'll be all."

The old man grinned, showing for the first time the gap in his front teeth. "Thanks," he said. "Any time, old chap." After the key had turned in the lock, he stood looking through the spy-hole for quite a while.

During the following weeks the old warder often came shuffling along the passage to have a look. He stayed and chatted when he brought Jan's food. He told Jan there had been visitors to see him: a certain Mr. Verwoert, and a boy who came regularly every day—De Meeuw his name was. Did he want to see them?

No, he didn't. He didn't want to see anyone. He preferred to be alone till he'd made peace with himself. In the solitude of his cell he recognized his past mistakes. He saw how silly it had been, all that dreaming and blathering about Kwel and revenge; how childish to imagine that a man like that

205

could be ousted by lashing out at him, as if he were a mad dog. Kwel's great weapon was his cleverness, his powers of calculation. Anyone who wanted to get the best of him would have to beat him at his own game.

One day the old warder came to tell Jan that there was a gentleman to see him, a very important-looking person who'd arrived in a carriage. Here was his card: MR. J. B. BEUMERS VAN HAAFTEN, PRESIDENT OF DUTCH HARBOUR-WORKS COMPANY. Jan did not know who the visitor was, but he said that he would see him. The old warder shuffled away and returned presently with the visitor at his heels.

"Captain Jan Wandelaar? How do you do?" the important person began, speaking to Jan through the prison bars. He apologised for disturbing the Captain, as if the Captain were taking a rest and had given strict orders not to be disturbed by anybody. But his reason for calling on the Captain was not a trivial one. That trip of the Captain's with the *Cape Breton* had impressed him and in consequence he was going to put forward a proposal to the Captain. As the Captain undoubtedly knew, the Dutch Harbourworks Company used a great number of dredgers, floating cranes, hoppers and so on for constructing harbours and dry-docks all over the world. Up till now the Dutch Harbourworks Company had had these things towed to their destination, mostly by Kwel and Van Munster, despite the fact that the majority of them had their own engines and would be quite able to sail across under their own power, if expertly handled. Mr. Beumers van Haaften wondered if Captain Wandelaar would consider experimenting on behalf of the Company by sailing a dredger across to Norway in three weeks' time, with a crew of his own choice and at twice the salary his former employers had paid him.

Captain Jan met the eyes of the important-looking gentleman peering at him through the bars. "I won't be free to undertake anything until six weeks from now," he said.

"Don't you worry about that, Captain Wandelaar," the visitor assured him. "I'll arrange that for you. The question is, are you willing to undertake this or not?"

"I'll consider it," the Captain said, whereupon the visitor

pushed another of his cards between the bars with a precise little gesture. "A great chance awaits you, Captain!" he said. "This may be the beginning of——"

"I know, I know," the Captain answered, interrupting him; "I'll think it over."

The visitor stared back with bewildered amusement, as the old warder led him away down the corridor. Both he and the warder shook their heads over Jan, amazed at his hesitation in accepting this golden opportunity.

But Captain Jan had grandiose ideas of his own. One day, he thought, the whole tugboat business will be in my hands. Therefore I mustn't do anything that may upset my plans. From now on every move must be carefully thought out if I am to realise my ambition.

It was a strange thought for a man who, six weeks later, was to be dragged out of his cell by force, screaming: "I don't want to go! I don't want to go! I want to stay here!"

It was a harrowing scene, but the old warder wasn't unduly perturbed. A lot of prisoners behaved that way, but they soon got over it. He knew from experience that prison sometimes gave men strange delusions.

CHAPTER ELEVEN

To FLIP DE MEEUW and bo'sun Janus belonged the credit of having nursed Jan back to life. They waited for him outside the prison-gates, and when he came out they took him by the arm and wouldn't let him out of their sight again. Both of them had gone through their hundred pounds without anything to show for it, only bitterness and boredom. Their sole interest in life now was Captain Jan Wandelaar, and they clutched at him the moment he came out of the prison-gates with the desperation of drowning men.

He came out weak and unsteady on his legs, and when he saw his two old comrades waiting to greet him, his first impulse was to run away. When the bo'sun slapped him affectionately on the back he leant weakly against the wall, coughing and gasping, till they took him under the armpits and piloted him to the temporary lodgings they had taken for him. It was obvious that the man was ill—probably nerves, most of it. What he needed was a proper rest, a holiday in the country, with plenty of good food and perhaps some fishing to amuse him. He needed to go away for at least a month; the only trouble was the money. Flip and Janus hadn't got a cent left between them. However, the Captain produced two ten-guilder notes from his wallet, which seemed to Flip and Janus quite a fortune.

The next morning the Captain had recovered some of his strength and spirits, though he was still helpless enough to need the assistance of Flip and Janus. Under their care he was shepherded on board a barge that was about to sail to the Estuary. The Estuary was a magic place for anybody needing a rest-cure: nothing but sky and clouds, and a sea of reeds, with here and there a farm or a fisherman's hut or an odd tree on one of the thousand swampy islands. The skipper of the barge said he knew of a couple living there, an eel-fisher and his wife, who would certainly put them up if they mentioned his name and offered a guilder a day for board and lodging.

The eel-fisher lived in a house like a haystack—a huge thatched roof, peeping out of the reeds, with a couple of rooms beneath it the size of linen-chests. It was a remote and mysterious place, with nothing but reeds and sky as far as the eye could see, and no sound except the croaking of frogs, the shrill, wailing cries of spoonbills and the lapping of water against the jetty poles.

They stayed there for weeks, doing nothing but eat, fish and sleep, hardly speaking a word. The eel-fisher and his wife seemed to have lost the power of speech after having lived so long in such a silent place. It seemed strange at first, but after a couple of days Jan and his companions became silent too. They lay basking in the sun in the little rowing-boat, chewing a young reed, gazing at the clouds, listening to the lapping of the water, the swishing of the wind, the occasional metallic clapping of ducks' wings behind the bracken, or the splash of a jumping fish. One of them fished, usually Flip. He had never caught anything except under-sized whiting; but after a week he walked with a fisherman's swagger and took to chewing tobacco and tipping his cap over his forehead to shade his eyes, in the way the old eel-man did.

It was a life that seemed more real, more sane than the kind of existence they had known before. After a week they felt as if they had never lived anywhere else but here among the reeds and the spoonbills, listening to the ducks' wings and the splash of the fish, and watching the sunset redden the great expanse of water, while the blue smoke of their pipes drifted in the wind.

One morning, after a week or so, when Jan got up on his elbow to fill a pipe after lying on his back in the boat motionlessly for hours, Janus asked him: "Feeling better, Captain?"

"Yes, thank you," he said, filling his pipe. "We'll soon be going back to work now."

"Ah," said Janus. "Work, did you say?"

"Work," said the Captain, and struck a match. "Sailing dredgers under their own power."

"Ah," said Janus. "Under their own power, you say?"

"Yes," said the Captain, lighting his pipe. "For Dutch Harbourworks."

"Ah," said Janus. He wanted to hear more, but the Captain was silent, and Janus didn't like to pump him. He felt that the Captain had suddenly assumed again that aura of authority which set him apart and made him a superior being.

As if to mark this transformation in the Captain, the weather itself changed. The first sign of it was a gathering of clouds on the horizon, at first no bigger than your fist, but rapidly expanding into a range of black mountains. The thunderstorm broke at night, and drove the eel-man and everyone else out of their beds. They sat, the five of them, round a smoking candle, listening to the terrific claps of thunder and the drumming of the rain; at every flash that lit up the cobwebbed windows the eel-man's wife cried "Hup!" and rose in her chair, as if she were urging a horse over a fence. The eel-man, with his steel-rimmed spectacles on, was reading the Bible and didn't seem to notice the lightning, except as a hindrance to his reading. When a blinding flash illuminated the window his finger ceased tracing the words for a moment, but resumed again when the lightning was succeeded by the roll of thunder. The storm lasted for a long time and the noise and fury of it seemed to act as a spur on Jan. "I think we had better go back tomorrow," he said; "the nice weather seems to be over."

Flip asked about the dredgers, and the Captain told him, slowly and quietly, while the lightning flashed its fiery ferns across the clouds and the thunder crashed and roared, like the din of windjammers colliding. When the Captain had finished Flip looked thoughtfully at the flickering candle flame. "Sounds all right," he said, "but is there a future in it?"

To that question Captain Jan gave a strange answer. "It is the first step," he said, "on a long, long road."

"A long road?" Flip queried.

"The road to. . . ." But at that moment there was a clap of thunder that shook the house. It drowned Jan's words, and Flip and Janus were left wondering where the long road would lead. But they were content to wait, confident that Captain Jan was the man to follow.

When Jan returned to the world of ships and men he found himself completely changed, but it was a change for the better. When Jan first became a Captain he assumed a certain manner and behaved as if he were a slow-thinking, quiet man who merely possessed that peculiar brand of wiliness which old skippers display in their dealings with the world. The great tug captains he had known were not intelligent men. Siemonov, Bas and Maartens were, in a way, almost stupid. But they had something about them, an invulnerability, an unshakable confidence in themselves, which might well have been sprung from their very lack of intelligence and imagination. Somehow their stolidness gave them a colossal authority, and enabled them to rule, without a trace of hesitation, the turbulent little world their lot was cast in. Once they had made up their minds nothing could stop them.

Jan found that his crew accepted without question this feigned air of authority. Even he himself was at times deceived by it, and curiously enough it was in these moments of self-deception that most of his wrong decisions were made.

For this false self-confidence had made him decide things too hastily. He had never realised that it wasn't their unshakable will that gave those old sea-dogs their power; it was the infinite pains they took in weighing up a situation.

Now, he found that he had acquired by necessity this same slowness of decision, this cautious wisdom which hitherto he had only made a pretence of possessing. It was a strange thing to discover through his own experience that the old sea-dogs were at heart very cautious men. Not cautious in their dealings with the elements, but cautious in judging themselves and other men. When Jan went to see Mr. Beumers van Haaften in his office, he went with his eyes fully opened, a self-possessed, sagacious man, not easily deceived. The person behind the desk, smiling expectantly and fiddling with a paper-knife, was just one of Kwel's type, a bit kinder perhaps, a bit less obsessed by greed and the determination to exploit the simple, honest folk who worked for him, but nevertheless a shrewd business man. It would save him a lot of money if he could sail his equipment to its destination under its own power. It would also break Kwel and Van Munster's monopoly of the tugboat business and force them to cut their prices.

One of Mr. Beumers van Haaften's characteristics was his uncanny insight into the mentality of the seamen. He spotted at once the difference in Captain Wandelaar. He didn't trot out any of the blather about "experiments" and "pioneering" this time. He took one look at his visitor and said: "I haven't bothered you since our last meeting, Captain, because I didn't want to rush you into any decision. I left the next move to you."

Jan didn't answer straight away. "Let me hear your offer again, sir," he said at last.

Mr. Beumers van Haaften's offer was very straightforward. The suction-dredger *Python* had to be transported to Marseilles; if the Captain would undertake to sail it under its own power, the Dutch Harbourworks Company would pay him and his crew double the salary Kwel and Van Munster paid them, plus a bonus of one per cent on the value of the dredger if it was brought to its destination without mishap. Further, in the matter of goods, clothing, instruments, charts, and so on, everything would be left to the

Captain, without any limit to expenditure. The Captain would be required to take the whole project over straight away. He would have to decide how many men he'd need and also to pick them. In fact he'd have to decide everything except the amount for which the ship would be insured.

Mr. Beumers van Haaften mentioned the question of insurance with a significant smile. No man could have been franker without actually pronouncing himself a scoundrel. He even went as far as to say: "If you want me to be frank, Captain, I have put the chances of a dead loss at four to one. So it all depends whether you are sure enough of yourself or hard up enough to risk your neck at these—you must admit—rather unfavourable odds."

Jan, pondering there in front of Mr. Beumers van Haaften's desk, couldn't help thinking: how cunning they are. How hopeless it is even to suppose that one can outwit them. At the back of his mind an idea was taking shape, the vague dream of possessing one day a ship of his own and being independent of Kwel and all the rest of them.

To find a crew was easy enough. All the men of the *Cape Breton* were still about, though they took some tracking down. The sad fact was that they had spent every penny of their bonus money and were now kicking their heels in disillusioned boredom around the bars and lodging-houses in the seamen's quarter of Amsterdam.

But the greater their disillusionment, the more eager they were to sail away from it all, and try their luck again. So Jan had no difficulty in signing them on for the *Python*. The engineers, however, were a greater problem. There were plenty of stokers to be had, but all the officers Jan knew were at sea. In the end he called on Verwoert, to ask if he felt like taking the job. Verwoert crowed with delight when he recognised Comrade Jan Wandelaar; he shook him by the hand, slapped his shoulder, and at once worked himself into a fit of coughing. Between the gasps he invited Jan to come upstairs where his wife would prepare some treat for him. But the woman said she wasn't going to prepare treats for anyone, especially as it meant letting her washing water get cold. When Verwoert pleaded with her she made some coffee which tasted of chicory and soapsuds, and slammed a piece of stale cake on the table. A crowd of children watched the proceedings open-mouthed. While the washing was going on Jan told Verwoert about the trip, and asked him if he would like to join them.

The offer moved the poor man to tears. He was hard up, he said, as the Comrade must have realised, and he would love to have come; but he couldn't leave his business at such short notice, nor abandon his work among the comrades. At this point the woman interrupted shrilly, telling him not to be a fool, as they hadn't paid their rent for weeks. The business was a washout. He wouldn't get an offer like this again as long as he lived, and it was his duty as a father and a breadwinner not to refuse it. But Verwoert got to his feet and declared in a piping voice that he was pledged to serve the Cause and he wouldn't desert it now for the sake of personal gain, especially as so many of his comrades were still living in poverty and squalor. The woman became hysterical with rage, and abused Verwoert and the Cause in the most violent language. At last Verwoert fled out into the street, followed by his wife's screams and curses.

In a café at the quayside he came to himself a little. He greedily gulped down the soup he had asked for instead of the drink Jan offered him. When he was offered a meal he refused. He wouldn't eat without his family, however hungry he might be; one had to practise solidarity down to the smallest things in life, if one wanted to keep one's integrity. Instead of accepting that meal, he wanted to make Comrade Wandelaar a member of the *N.U.D.E.R.W.O.G.T.*, the National Union of Deck and Engine Room Workers of the Ocean-Going Tugs. The entrance fee was twenty-five cents only, plus ten cents per year membership fee. That was five cents less than the meal Jan had offered him. He nagged and insisted so much that Jan let himself be enlisted in the end. Flushed with triumph, Verwoert entered Jan's name in a shabby notebook, and Jan couldn't prevent him from standing a drink, in honour of the occasion. "A turning point in your life, Wandelaar!" he said, raising the glass in a trembling hand. "May you become a crusader in our Cause for the sake of our wives and children!"

In the end he started talking such ranting nonsense that

Jan realised with alarm that that one small glass must have gone straight to his head. He piloted him gently home, and when they got there Verwoert was so sleepy that Jan was able to slip his wife a twenty-five guilder note without the Prophet of the Revolution noticing it. The woman accepted the money with a blush and not at all gratefully; she obviously thought that Jan had made Verwoert drunk on purpose and had come to pay for his fun.

His last hope of getting an engineer was in a bar down a tiny alley behind the harbour. Piet, the innkeeper, ran a kind of private agency. He knew everybody in the business and whenever a captain was hard up for a crew he took a dog-eared ledger from under the counter and started flicking its pages over, but only after his palm had been greased. When Jan asked him if he knew of a tugboat engineer who happened to be free he said: "No, sorry, Captain—not a soul." But after six of the most expensive drinks he produced the ledger. He had got two at the moment, now he came to think of it: a certain Klaas van Donk, a first-class man. Surely the Captain had heard of him? The Captain had, and so had everybody else in Holland; Klaas van Donk was the most notorious drunkard in the business. The second man was not much good, really: a fellow named Bout, who used to be second engineer with Kwel's. But if the Captain would take a piece of sound advice he would steer clear of that man; he was no good.

Bout? Jan could hardly believe his ears, surely there must be some mistake. But there was his name in the ledger. And when Jan got some more particulars there was no shadow of doubt. Piet was put out to the point of rudeness when the Captain went on questioning him about Bout, and wasn't the slightest bit interested in van Donk, who, according to Piet, was such a first-class man and such a jolly companion to sail with too. All he knew about Bout was that he was living with his mother and was reputed to be a sea-lawyer of the worst kind. Besides, he couldn't be much good at his job, otherwise Kwel wouldn't have given him the sack, at a time when engineers were so hard to come by. But after a couple more drinks he grudgingly gave Bout's address, and the Captain hurried out. He knew how private agencies of this kind worked. People like Piet didn't help their customers to get a job free of charge; they had to spend ten guilders at the counter first, before they were even entered in the ledger, and after that there were grades of priority, according to the number of pints consumed.

Mrs. Bout lived in a respectable workmen's quarter in a tiny flat like a bird-cage at the top of a very steep, very narrow staircase. She at once pulled up a chair for Captain Jan and started mumbling about her son Thys straight away. Thys should be home any minute, he had gone to an evening class. When at last tired footsteps were heard mounting the staircase, dusk had fallen. Mother Bout shuffled towards the door, and when it was opened Jan heard a voice say: "Hullo, Ma." He would have recognised that voice any-where. "There's a captain here to see you, Thys," the little woman said. "Shouldn't you comb your hair first?"

"A captain?"

When Bout entered the room, an unfamiliar figure without his eternal boiler-suit, he was frowning suspiciously. Then he exclaimed: "Jan Wandelaar—man, where did you come from?"

The little room was suddenly filled with the sound of men's voices talking and laughing. It took Jan unawares, the impact of all those memories. Bout was part of a lost life, a better life. How gay and young and carefree everything was in those days; you just didn't notice the shadows because the horizon was so bright.

Bout told Jan something of his own story. He had been on his beam ends for a bit, because of a difference of opinion between himself and the owners over Little Abel, who had an accident and lost an eye, and whom Kwel sacked without a cent to live on. But it was not really just Little Abel; it was high time he had a change anyhow. He was just about sick of Kwel and his tricks. Now he had had a wonderful opportunity to devote himself for a couple of months to a course in wrought-iron forging and another in a world-language called *Volapuk*—two things a man would never regret knowing. He was all for that trip with the *Python* straight away, if only to get rid of that dry cough that had been bothering him for over three months now—yes, a body is a bother, as the old Chief used to say.

They wanted to go out, to talk more freely and to have a

215

look at that dredger; but Mother Bout refused to let Thys go out without a meal, and she insisted that the Captain should eat something too, saying that where there was enough for two there was enough for three. And yet for Jan there was a sadness underlying it all. This peaceful little island under the lamp, the odd things that make a house a home, the clock and the cat and the smell of furniture polish, the very pattern in the linoleum, brought back an emptiness, a loneliness he had almost forgotten. It was like being brought back suddenly to a warm, light room, after bracing oneself to go out into the cold and darkness. Although he enjoyed every minute of it, although it was the first really happy evening he had had for God knew how long, yet he wished he had never come. For now he didn't want it to end. He stayed chattering at the table until the little woman started piling up the dishes, having listened to his fantastic stories for hours.

After he'd said good-bye to Bout and his mother he wandered through the town for more than an hour. He paused at shop-windows, hesitated in front of bars, listening to the sound of billiard-balls and music; but he walked on when the doors were opened and people came out, night-blind in the darkness. Then, suddenly, he came to a decision. He called a hansom, and told the man to drive him to the station. He was too late to make the connection to the north: the furthest he could get was Amsterdam. Well, he knew a hotel there.

It was late when he arrived. He was cold and tired, and lay on his back on the bed with his boots on, staring at the square of green gaslight on the ceiling and the shadow of the window-panes. In the harbour a hooter boomed and the echo vibrated through the town. He heard someone talking in his sleep in the next room and a bed creaked overhead continually.

In the end he turned over and fell asleep, his head under the pillow.

He had sent a telegram to warn them he was coming; when he came they were prepared. Mamma Dijkmans opened the door; Father Dijkmans was at the sluice. They shook hands, and she asked him to come in. The children were doing very well; it was a pity they weren't at home just now—they had gone to stay with Nellie's Aunt Anna in Heiloo. No, no, not for good—only for a week, while the top floor was being painted.

She tried to be friendly and motherly, but when Father Dijkmans came in and greeted him sourly, and asked if he had had a good time, he realised they had finished with him. In their eyes the children were orphans, and in a sense they were perhaps right.

He sat in the parlour for an hour, with a cigar and a cup of coffee. He said he was sorry he couldn't stay for dinner, but his train was leaving in half an hour's time. When he went at last, it came as a relief to all of them. If it hadn't been for the children they'd have asked him not to come back, probably. He told them that he'd ask Beumers of the Dutch Harbourworks Company to send them his weekly wages; they'd find the money ample to cover all expenses.

Before going to the station he passed the churchyard to have a look at that stone. He bought a bunch of white flowers on his way, and took them with him to lay on the grave. It was high summer; the trees were heavy with green. Here and there roses were blooming and some of the rowan trees had berries already. It was worse than he had expected and he almost turned back half way. Though he completed the pilgrimage by a supreme effort of will, he felt like a man swaying on the edge of an abyss.

It was only when he went aboard the suction-dredger *Python* that he began to feel himself again.

CHAPTER TWELVE

THE *Python* was a crate of a ship: ugly, clumsy and slow. But Bout said they'd manage all right on her little engine, if only the weather was moderately decent. In any case, there were lifeboats on board. Bout had got himself a second engineer, a shy, pimply youth with a high collar and a brown jacket covered with buttons. He was called Chicken, and for some mysterious reason was christened Coba by the crew straight away. Once he had got his boilersuit on and a spanner in his hands he really looked quite efficient.

Everybody on board prepared himself for a long, dull trip. Bout had taken his books on wrought-iron forging and *Volapuk* with him, and Janus an album of *Marvels of the Congo*. A week before the ship sailed, Flip de Meeuw had put this advertisement in a matrimonial paper:

> Young naval officer with small capital; tanned, handsome appearance; Reformed Church of the Netherlands, yet of modern principles, seeks the acquaintance of a suitable young lady with matrimonial intent: cheerful temper essential, not older than twenty-three, dowry of secondary importance. Letters, with details and photograph, to be sent, c/o THE EDITOR, to "LONELY SINDBAD".

When the *Python* sailed after a sentimental farewell from Mr. Beumers van Haaften, who returned with the pilot, nobody was sad or elated. The fact was that they had succumbed to boredom already.

They remained bored until they reached Marseilles; there they found a miniature dredger, waiting to be taken back to Amsterdam. The sea was calm, the weather beautiful. There was nothing to it really, sailing ships like these under their own power; Mr. Beumers van Haaften had a vivid imagination, that was all. The only one who was a bit put out was Bout, because now he had no engine to call his own or get attached to. The moment you began getting to know one little set of works, off you went to another one. But Jan consoled him by saying: "You wait, Bout, my boy—you wait; one of these days we'll have our own ship, and then we'll really live."

Their own ship—it was a wild idea. But as they couldn't live without the tugboats, and as the owners had so little use for them, there seemed to be no alternative but to try and buy one of their own. It was crazy, of course; even if they saved all their wages and never sent a penny home, it would take them seventy-five years to collect enough money to buy a tug, and not a new one either—one of Kwel's discarded hulks rotting away in the estuary.

But "our own ship" was a wonderful topic to chat about during the long watches and after meals in the messroom. In the end the crew amused themselves by imagining the kind of ship she'd be. They decided she'd have to be small and sturdy, something like the *Aurora* but with the comfort of the *Jan van Gent*. Big bunkers; a simple, powerful engine; a hull that would stand up to rough treatment and was graceful to look at at the same time. And, once they got her, she could go anywhere and tow anything there was to be towed. "Believe me," said the Captain, "there's a lot of money in it." The Captain knew the tricks of the trade by now; he knew the ins and outs of such transactions; once they were their own bosses they'd be rich, for they'd have a share in the company. Flip began scribbling in the log, trying to work out a design for the company's pennant; and Janus ordered catalogues from paint manufacturers in order to choose a nice set of colours. They were all such children that "our own ship" gave them as much pleasure as dressing up.

The only one who didn't approve of this kind of day-dreaming was Bout. "Bah!" he said, cleaning the gravy-boat with a potato; "if you want to earn that boat with the odd jobs we are doing now, Captain, you'll have a beard with cobwebs by the time you've got the money." But then, Bout had always been a practical man, believing only in the Trinity and the future of *Volapuk*. When the Captain started talking about a mortgage he pulled a wry face and said: "Mortgage? That'll mean you won't be your own master even then. You'll merely be sailing for a bank instead of for Mr. Kwel. And, honestly, I can't see any point in starving myself for ten years, only to fall out of the frying-pan into the fire. No," he said, licking the spoon and putting it back in the gravy-boat, "the only way you'll ever get yourself a ship of your own is by a bloody miracle."

Only a miracle, that was true in a sense. But miracles had happened before. Unlikely, improbable, but not impossible.

Captain Jan's dream was no idle phantasy. It was a certainty, an unchanging goal; and Captain Jan was as set in his aim as the compass-needle was to the north. In the end he ceased to discuss his plans with anybody, not even with Bout. He locked himself in his cabin and unrolled the charts of distant seas, looking for coal-stations and the prevailing winds. The tugboat business had bewitched him; it was the only life that meant anything to him now. He sailed his dredgers, his cranes, his barges and his pontoons through snow and hail, through ice and fog, and never doubted he would bring them safely into port. Bulle, under the swinging lantern in the foc'sle, span the fantastic yarn of how young Jan Wandelaar saved the *Scottish Maiden* that night when the gale howled through the tangled rigging with a sound as terrifying as the last trump. Jan had been exactly as he was now—confident and steady. Kees told the story of the rain in the Bight of Benin and the malaria. Mate Jan Wandelaar had been the only one to stay on his feet, and eat like a horse right through the epidemic. Flip painted lurid pictures of the hell of the *Cape Breton* in which Captain Jan Wandelaar figured as a rescuing archangel. But the best story was the one that Janus told, of the Captain standing on that bridge of the *Ameland* and saying "Jump!" as quietly as if he were saying: "A little to starboard." Only those who had seen him at that moment knew what he was really like.

The men respected him and relied on him, but they didn't show him their letters from home, or the portraits of their wives and children. He stood lonely on the poop, respected, but aloof. Bout was the only one he could talk to and be friendly with, Bout who was dull and reliable, and nothing else. Bout talked about the future of wrought-iron forging and asked Jan if he would be so kind as to hear his verbs of *Volapuk*—as it would be a pity if all those expensive lessons were wasted. They shared their meals in the messrooms of all those different ships: every trip another table, another messroom, another cabin. But wherever Bout was, there was a friendly pipe and stockinged feet propped on the couch. In the company of Bout the long evening hours were not so unbearably lonely. For the evening was the time of homesickness, and dejection. To look up at the stars was to think: worlds beyond worlds, eternity stretching to eternity—what's the good of wandering like this with not a soul to care for? Only the men who knew Jan best, the old hands of the *Cape Breton*, guessed, from the way he walked, that he was worrying. When one of them was at the wheel, he would ask: "Well, Captain—when do you think we'll have our own ship?" Then the pacing stopped and Jan would grunt: "I don't know—some day, perhaps." After that it wouldn't be long before Captain Jan lit his pipe again. When he did, the helmsman, glimpsing his face in the flickering light of the match cupped between his hands, would smile proudly and think: he's got over it, thanks to me. Now he'll be happy dreaming about that ship of his own he's going to have one day. . . .

It was two years before the miracle happened.

CHAPTER THIRTEEN

THE transport of the dredger *Cyclops* from Rotterdam to the Isle of Terschelling was on paper no great feat, but in actual fact it took them four days and three nights, and it was about the worst trip they ever had.

A gale on the home-shore always has something sinister about it; on the other side of the globe you somehow don't realise so acutely what's at stake. A man who has never hung at the pumps between the lightships of Schouwenbank and Noordhinder doesn't know what it takes out of you to look, as you might say, death and your old woman in the face at the same time. When at last they arrived at West Terschelling they were as keen to go home as if they had been away for years. They crowded on board the ferry without waiting for a meal even; all of them suddenly felt the urge to get away. Jan waited until the ferry had left the harbour; then he went back to the dredger alone.

He was tired. Their last long trip had been a trying one, more so for him than for his crew. They had got lost in the Niger estuary—the boys never realised there was anything wrong, but he spent some unpleasant hours in that jungle. This little trip from Rotterdam to Terschelling had about finished him. All he wanted to do now was to stay quiet and rest. The dredger wouldn't be taken over by the harbour authorities for another week, so here was the chance to get the peace and quiet he wanted.

Before immuring himself in the dredger he made some purchases in the village—bread, tobacco, tea and sugar. Coffee, beans and potatoes were on board, as there hadn't been much eaten on the last trip. The narrow streets of the village stretched empty in the wind. Not a soul in sight. His footsteps were the only sound apart from the whining of the gale in the telegraph-wires and the banging of a loose shutter. Not at all a bad little place for a rest cure. No loafers shouting on the quay, no small boys scrambling on board, no idiotic old men peering through the portholes. Just what he wanted.

His first task when he got back on board was to rearrange the cabin. He carried two sacks of coal for the stove down the stairs, two armloads of food, a jug of drinking water, and when he couldn't think of anything else to do he pushed the table out of the way. It blocked the steps to the deck, but he wouldn't be going out for the rest of that night, so it didn't matter. He rubbed his hands; it felt like the beginning of a wonderful treat. The little stove soon burned up, and when its friendly glow spread to the walls of the little hold, he judged the time had come for a pipe and a nice hot cup of tea. Outside it was raining cats and dogs and the wind howled in the rigging. He pulled off his jersey, his boots and his wet trousers. It was lovely, just to muck about in your underwear, with your bare feet in carpet slippers. The secret of a really good pipe was to smoke it in peace, reclining on a nice leather seat, while the sweat glistened on the iron ribs of the roof and trickles of moisture ran down the steam-frosted portholes. The very idea of being able to smoke this pipe to the last puff without being called out into the wind or the rain was itself a treat. To taste the salty smoke and let it curl lazily towards the ceiling was wonderful after a sleepless week spent in clothes heavy with sea water. That's a thing people ashore would never realise, what a luxury it was to sit in an armchair, to shift the lamp, light a pipe and settle down comfortably to read about murder, earthquake, fire and shipwreck while the kettle sang on the stove. One such evening was worth more than having your portrait in the papers with the headline SAFELY HOME AFTER HAZARDOUS TRIP; or to be treated by Beumers to a meal in the Industrial Club, with a waiter to push the chair up for you when you sat down. Jan had wondered once why old Van der Gast had the motto "From East to West Home's the Best" nailed up in his cabin, with nothing to go home to but a rusty old ship. Now he understood perfectly well. He understood, too, what the geraniums and the canary symbolized.

He had borrowed some books to while away the time. One was Kees' Bible: *Marvels and Curiosities of all the Seas, Rivers, Lakes and Waters of the World, their Origin, History and Legends;* compiled, edited and commented upon by Samuel de Vries; printed by Willem Spruit at the Ox's Head behind the Round Church at Amsterdam in the Year of our Lord 1687. This was the book Kees had taken with him on every trip since he was a boy, and he had been nearly drowned several times in his efforts to rescue it. The stories he quoted from it were the most horrific Jan had ever heard; now at last he had a chance to read them for himself.

The weather was most appropriate for reading the *Marvels and Curiosities.* After Jan had poured the boiling water on the tea and made the couch more comfortable by bringing the blankets and the pillow from his bunk, he relit his pipe and let himself be buttonholed by Samuel de Vries for a discourse on the horrors of the ocean.

The rain lashed the deck and cascaded down from the roof of the galley. Under the buffetings of the weather the dredger strained and creaked at her moorings. Suddenly Jan remembered that he hadn't slackened the ropes. The tide was running out, and if she was left high and dry her mooring ropes would break. But he had plenty of time yet. Samuel de Vries was describing the taste of human flesh:

"Often has it happened that Men, forced by Hunger, have taken to Human Flesh. Those who have eaten it assure me that its flavour is most delicate. A Young Man from TER GOES in ZEALAND was taken prisoner with thirteen others by the WEST INDIAN SAVAGES. Hunger forced them to eat one of their Fellows almost daily as no other Food was Brought to them. The aforementioned Young Man testified later that he was repelled by this fare at first, but after he had overcome his first disgust he ate as heartily of it as of a well-fattened pig. The Toes of the Feet and the Fingers of the Hands were Toothsome Morsels, most succulent to nibble." Kees had underlined this paragraph; a cook is always a cook, and a man who has his heart in his job is never too proud to learn.

He read for more than an hour, about INSECTS, as large as RATS and with the bite of a SNAKE; about a WEATHER VANE, consisting of a dead NEGRO skinned and stuffed, suspended from a POLE—very rare; about GIANT TURTLES, so large and old that SHRUBS grew on their SHELLS, and made them look like little islands, and about the MUTINOUS SAILOR who was marooned on one of them, and discovered that his island turned on its back in strong sunlight. And then, in the middle of the story about the MERMAN OF SAALFELD, who knocked at the door of a MIDWIFE at dead of night to call assistance for his WIFE in LABOUR, he heard a faint cry in the wind.

Night had fallen; the portholes and the skylight were black in their brass frames. He listened, his head lifted. The rain and the hail crackled on the deck, like the sound of fire. But when he was about to read on, thinking that he had been imagining things, he heard it again: a wailing call, faint in the tumult. At first he wanted to stay where he was, telling himself it was none of his business. But when the voice called again, quite near, the cry perhaps of someone drowning, he threw the book aside, thrust his swollen feet into his boots, swearing; put on his oilskins, pushed the table aside and stumbled up the steps to the deck.

When he lifted the iron hatch off the stairway the rain and the hail stung his face. He stood there for a moment, with only his head exposed, listening. Even though he couldn't hear anything, the feeling of uneasiness was too strong to ignore. He climbed on deck, his oilskins flapping. He had to put a rope round his waist to prevent his coat from ballooning out in the gale. Groping in the wet darkness he knotted the loose end and called out, "Ahoy there!" his mouth cupped in his hands. There was nothing to be seen. The light from the portholes made whirling beams in the rain. "Ahoy there, where are you?" Jan called again. The rain gushed down his face, down his neck, down his chest.

Then he heard the voice again, very weak and far away, almost drowned by the savage noise of the storm.

"Help, help."

It came from the direction of the sea, from the far side of the harbour. Good Lord, all that way, in this weather, in this darkness? But he had already shouted, "Hold on! I'm coming."

He jumped back to the cabin, hastily lighted a lantern and scrambled back on deck. Luckily the lifeboat was hanging ready in the davits. It was a tricky job for one man to lower it in this weather. First the stern-pulley jammed, then it slipped, and the boat dived rudder first into the water. But after a few seconds she was afloat again. Jan had to use all his strength to push her free of the dredger to which the wind glued her. But then the tide caught her and she swung out. The oars splashed in the water, and she crawled, bobbing, away into the night.

Although Jan was still well within the lee of the breakwater a nasty, choppy sea was running. The waves drove hard against the bows and splashed over the gunwales, and within a few minutes the footboards were afloat. After every ten strokes Jan rested on his oars and called. Every time he heard an answer; a flickering circle of light from his lantern revealed nothing but rain and water; and it was difficult to make out whence the shouting came in this roaring wind.

He rowed on, groaning with strain. He called out, "Ahoy there! Answer! Where are you?" But the noise of the sea was so loud that he sometimes scarcely heard his own voice. The boat was getting more swamped every minute, and his feet slipped. Once he pulled himself right off the seat and landed on his back in the bilge water. But at last, when he was thinking of going back because he was getting too near the open sea and the tide was dragging him out fast, he suddenly spotted a glistening object in the beam of his lantern—a capsized boat. As he was swept past it he caught sight of a face in the water; but only for a moment for it was almost immediately submerged by a white-capped wave. He managed to pull his boat round and edge his way alongside. It needed a prodigious effort, for the tide was running more strongly than he thought. When he pulled in his oars he had to pounce to catch hold of the wreck before it was washed out of reach again. He clutched blindly in the darkness and got hold of something flimsy and slippery—hair. He held on to it like grim death, while the rolling shell of the capsized boat vanished in a second. The drowning man had let go his hold. If Jan lost his grip, too, the drowning man would be swept away. Jan managed to seize the collar of a pair of oilskins, then an arm. With the water pouring wildly into his boat as she listed at a dangerous angle, he dragged the body over the gunwale.

It was no time for curiosity; yet when the body had slumped down on its back in the bilge-water, he risked a precious minute to lift the lantern and shine the beam on the dripping face. By God, he was right—"it" was a woman.

His surprise soon gave place to anxiety about his own situation. He might consider himself lucky if he managed to get home with his own craft afloat; for with this current and wind he had no time for baling, and the boat was shipping water as wave after wave jumped the gunwale. He rowed for dear life, in the direction of the dredger. When, after almost an hour, the wet, glistening hull of the *Python* loomed up again and he lifted the body on to the deck his boat sank from under his feet like an ice floe. He had to pull himself up by his hands, the rope between his teeth. When at last he belayed it on the rail he found he had only got about six inches to spare. If he wanted to save that boat he would have to bale her out like lightning and haul her back in the davits, otherwise she'd be smashed to matchwood by morning. But the first thing was to get that body down below deck. Soul came before timber, as old Bas always said.

Jan dragged the limp thing to the hatchway. He pulled the legs over the edge, lifted the shoulders and let the body slither down the steps like a sack. It hit the floor with a thud. When he had lowered himself and shut the hatch behind him he had his first good look at this creature he had rescued from the seas.

She was a young woman, still a girl. Her cheekbones were as high as a Russian's and, wet as it was, her hair was very fair. She lay motionless, her mouth slack, her eyes half open, the irises upturned. She had a nasty cut on her forehead, but there was little blood; it looked like another mouth, limp and bloodless. When he lifted her to put her on the couch her head fell back with a frightening looseness, as if he had broken her neck when he grabbed her by the hair. As he turned her round, her limp arm knocked the lantern off the table. It crashed on to the floor and went out. Luckily the lamp was still going. He was relieved, when he looked at her closely, to find that there were some signs of life. He tried artificial respiration; but when he felt how cold her hands were he thought better of it. She seemed to breathe all right;

what she needed was not artificial respiration, but warmth.

Jan got a rough towel and started to undress her. She was wearing men's clothes down to her underwear. When she was naked she looked even younger, for her body was almost like that of a boy.

When he started rubbing her down with a towel her skin felt like ice. He felt her cheek with the back of his hand. Like a stone—he would have to get a doctor. He couldn't have her die here, without a stitch on, and then run out in the morning and call the local policeman. If he left her now she would be done for. Although commonsense told him to get out of the boat, to hand over the mess and the responsibility to someone else, there was an instinct stronger than mere commonsense, an instinct bred from the tradition of the tugboats. "Hold fast!" Whatever happens, hold fast. A man who abandons a tow is a weakling and a coward. Yet her presence there disturbed him. The sudden impact of her femininity seemed to destroy in a moment all the iron restraint he'd put upon himself.

He hadn't grown out of the longing for a woman, just any woman. He had somehow managed to forget it in ruthless activity. Of course that was the reason why he was so shy ashore, why he ran away after only a few days in a town, like a man hunted by the devil. At sea he was safe; there was no temptation there, no obsession. Up till now he'd been happy enough to live alone on the dredger, enjoying the advantages of both sea and shore—the safety from temptation and the luxury of idleness.

She lay exactly as she lay before, only her eyes were open. She looked at him with a deep wonder, and he stood gaping at her for a long time before he realised that she had actually regained consciousness. When at last, he managed to open his lips and ask: "Are you all right?", she had dropped off again, and lay as still and unresponsive as before. But now for some reason he was no longer afraid of her. In fact it seemed incredible that this pathetic little shrimp should ever have made him feel like St. Anthony wrestling with temptation. He felt her cheeks, her neck; they were quite warm. She was all right. Now what? Wait until she came to? God knew how long that might be. Probably her father and the neighbours must be looking for her in the rain, armed with pitchforks.

227

In the meantime he had better make himself a cup of tea, fill a fresh pipe, and start clearing up the mess in the cabin. He mopped the floor with his wet clothes, put the table back in its place, and, as she stayed slumped on that couch without moving, he collected the pieces of the broken lantern on a plate, put on his oilskins, and opened up the hatch-way. The moment he stuck his head out the wind hit him like a bucket of cold water. He heard the creaking of an overstrained rope and remembered suddenly that he hadn't slackened the moorings to allow for the fall of the tide. He found the ropes as taut as bow-strings, with no hope even of undoing them, for not only had they been pulled so tight that they were nearly severed, but they had swollen with the rain as well. All he could do was to get out another set, make fast with a little slack, and cut the other ones before they tore the rivets out.

It took him half an hour to do this, and another half hour to bale out the boat and haul it back in the davits. While he was trying to swing it in, he turned round at the sound of footsteps. The girl was half way out of the hatch before she realised he was looking at her. She stood quite still for a second, her hands on the hatch frame. She had her own clothes on, and her hair was done up in an untidy knot on top of her head. She looked so preposterously young and comic with that drake's tail over those cheekbones, that he couldn't help laughing. The laugh did it; she scuttled out of the hole like a rabbit, scrambled across the deck to the rail, and with a wild leap that made him shout "Hey! Are you mad?", she landed on the quay on all fours.

He called after her "What about saying 'thank you'?", but all he heard was the sound of running feet, and after a moment there was nothing but the wind and the rain again, and the aimless clanging of the dredger buckets.

The first ferry went at four a.m. He sneaked on board, like a fugitive. Why, for God's sake? All he had done was to bring someone back to life, break a lantern, and ruin a set of moorings. Why flee like this—he had done nothing to be ashamed of.

That night Jan sat in a bar again, alone at a table, revolving his beer-glass on its paper mat. An orchestra started playing after nine o'clock, and the bar filled up with a

crowd of laughing, chattering people. The waiter took the
empty chairs away, one by one, until he sat as he had always
sat and always would sit, utterly alone.

CHAPTER FOURTEEN

WHEN Jan called in on Mr. Beumers van Haaften to hear
what their next job was to be, he was cordially received by
the great man and given a cigar. "This time, Captain, I
should like you to take a bucket-dredger to Pernambuco,"
Mr. Beumers said.

Pernambuco. Well, to put it mildly, that was a long, long
trip. When the hall porter saluted the Captain on his way
out and turned the revolving door for him, the Captain
presented him with Mr. Beumers' cigar. "Thank you very
much, sir," the hall porter said, discreetly placing the cigar
in the red fire-bucket behind him. On his way to the quay
Jan decided it was about time he finished with Mr. Beumers
van Haaften, who seemed intent on finding out just how
much the human frame could stand. Pernambuco, by God.
What a trip!

But the voyage turned out to be quite pleasant and uneventful till they reached St. Paul, the island where the
chief engineer of the *Jan van Gent* was buried. There it
began to blow with the force of a typhoon. The bucket-
dredger stood up to it quite well, but when the weather was
at its worst the Captain gave orders for the superstructure
to be lightened, so the *Frisia* became a bucketless dredger.
A pity, but to have kept that chain of fifty buckets overhead
—each weighing a ton—would have been asking for a nasty
death. When the worst was over the *Frisia* became quite a
manageable craft and pursued her course with zest. Bout
was delighted. "What an engine!", he said, "I wish we could
do something to show what she's really got in her". Bout,
however, was the only one who was delighted, for in spite of
the removal of the dredger buckets, the swaying superstructure tore out a number of rivets and the rest of the crew
had to crawl about in the flooded depths of her hull to stop
the leaks.

They were busy doing this when all hands were suddenly

piped on deck for an emergency. When they had scrambled up into the daylight and were holding on to the rail, blinking, they were informed that a flare had been sighted, and the life-boats had therefore to be got ready, for Captain Wandelaar was going to lend assistance.

Lend assistance with a bucket-dredger? It seemed to them sheer madness, but they supposed the Captain knew what he was doing. They stumbled across to the boats and started uncovering them, peering at the horizon now and then in case there was anything to be seen. A quarter of an hour later another flare whizzed up behind the white wavecrests. The Captain ordered bo'sun Janus to fire a rocket for the dredger to give the poor devils over there some hope. The rocket nearly knocked bo'sun Janus off his feet when he fired it. A red streak of flame hurtled up towards the clouds, leaving behind it a trail of dark smoke which gradually flattened itself out into a black smudge above the water. The Captain took the wheel himself. He was the best helmsman on board and steered the *Frisia* up and down those mountainous seas as if he were driving a train on a scenic railway. She plunged and rammed her square bows into the waves with deafening thuds, she tossed and rolled so wildly that her stern was often out of the water and her propeller threshed the air. To prevent the Captain from being thrown headlong as the ship reeled Flip brought out the emergency-belt—a heavy leather band fitted with a hook which fastened on to a ring on the wheel casing. It was an odd sight to see him clinging to the wheel and ducking every moment to dodge the cataracts of water that deluged the ship, the brim of his sou'wester turned up like a cocked hat, his pipe turned upside down to keep the tobacco dry. Yes, the only one who really enjoyed himself was Bout, for now his engine really had a chance of showing her paces.

After two hours, during which another flare had flickered upon the horizon, they sighted a vessel: a white ketch with a clipper stern, riding the wild seas like a wounded gull. As they approached, the Captain let the dredger swing round, so as to get a full view of the stranded ship, but there was not a soul to be seen. He pulled the dredger hove-to again, and steered once more towards the ketch, but no one in her made any sign in answer.

She was a beauty of a ship, obviously a private yacht; mauled almost beyond recognition by the weather. Her mainmast had broken off to about the height of a man above the deck, and the top had crashed overboard, smashing the rail. The rigging, however, kept the mast from drifting clear of the ship, and now the force of the waves drove it in against the hull, like a battering ram. The thudding blows of it could be heard on board the dredger above the roar of the sea. It was obvious that the yacht was leaking heavily already, and if the mast wasn't cut loose pretty soon the ship would be done for.

After the Captain had come as close as he could without getting caught in the tangle himself, Flip, Bulle, Janus and Kees manned a boat, and put out for the yacht. While the boat was being lowered Bout came out to have a look. He pointed to the yacht, then at the wheel, and made a gesture of hauling a rope. When Jan nodded, he beamed, waved his hands delightedly, and crawled back down the hatch to give Coba the glorious news.

The boat started off on its hazardous crawl towards the listing yacht. The sea seemed even higher now that the black speck of the boat was tossed about on the mountainous wave crests, then plunged wildly down and seemed lost for ever. After interminable minutes, while the men on the dredger held their breaths, the tiny craft appeared again, scrambling up another of those watery peaks. And yet that journey was nothing compared with the job of making fast and boarding the ketch. To approach her luff would mean being smashed to splinters against her sides; and her lee, littered with the debris of the rigging, was as dangerous as a reef. They rowed towards her stern, hampered by the wreck of a lifeboat stuck half-way down its davits and battered to pieces against the hull. Obviously the crew of the yacht had tried to lower it, and failed.

Bo'sun Janus got on his knees in the bows, a line with a boarding-hook attached to it ready. They managed by skilful manoeuvring to get practically underneath the stern, avoiding the swinging wreck of the lifeboat. Then came the manoeuvre which is always agony to watch, no matter how often you've seen it happen. Janus flung the anchor on board where it caught on the rail, and with almost the same movement he jumped. He hung kicking over the boiling abyss, and though it couldn't have taken him more than two breathless minutes to haul himself up to the rail and swing over it, it seemed like hours. When at last he stood on the deck of the yacht and waved triumphantly, everybody watching him on board the dredger became delirious with relief and excitement. They shouted and cheered and waved their arms. Even the hooter gave a raucous blast to express the Captain's appreciation.

The moment Janus got on board, the deck of the ketch became alive with figures. They crawled from the hatches, from the skylights; one of them even bobbed up in the wheelhouse, where he must have been crouching ever since the dredger made her appearance. To Jan, watching them through binoculars, they seemed an odd crew for any ship. Most of them wore what seemed to be pyjamas, and after much peering and refocusing of his lenses, Jan came to the conclusion that there were women among them, for one of them was even wearing a hat. Later he caught sight of Flip making his way towards the rail. He had got hold of a signal lamp, and his first message was THEY WANT TO GET OFF.

Get off? They must be out of their minds! The worst of the gale was over. All they had to do was cut the rigging and the broken mast adrift and they would keep afloat and even make some way.

Jan was so surprised that he hesitated for a moment to send back an answer. In the meantime Flip signalled again CAN THEY GET OFF?

Jan then replied, BY ALL MEANS BRING THEM HERE THE LOT OF THEM. DO NOT LEAVE A SINGLE ONE. REPEAT NOT A SINGLE ONE. CONFIRM.

Flip confirmed, adding that there would be eighteen guests for breakfast, including two pekinese and a cat.

They came in two boatloads, seasick and miserable, their condition worse for the final torture of being hauled on board by ropes, as they were too ill to climb up themselves. A pathetic lot, but Jan had no time to pay them much attention. He left it to Bout to pilot them down into the foc'sle and see that they got something to eat. He had other problems to cope with. Night was falling and if possible the mess over there had to be cleared up before dark.

Now the yacht's crew were off, the boarding party got down to business. They cut the swinging mast adrift and disposed of the battered lifeboat. Then they hoisted a mizzen sail and managed to get the ship hove-to. It was blowing too hard and the seas were still running too high to pay out a hawser, and in any case a dredger wasn't equal to a tug. The best plan was to let both vessels ride within sight of each other until the morning, and if necessary until the following day.

When at last Jan went below, after giving Coba the helm with orders to keep within sight of the yacht's bobbing lights, he found a curious party in the foc'sle. Sixteen men in pyjamas and underwear were chewing chunks of bread, their unshaven cheeks bulging like monkeys'. Among them were two women, one elderly and one young. The elderly one had fainted and lay prostrate on the bo'sun's bunk; the young one sat on a stool, wrapped in a blanket, with a cavalier on either side trying to comfort her. It was obvious, however, that she didn't need any comforting. She took it all in with wondering eyes. She seemed to find it an exciting adventure now the immediate danger was over and she could relax with two faithful admirers to wait on her. She gazed with awe at the Captain coming down the stairs in torn oilskins and a sou'wester like a pirate's hat. He looked grim, but she ventured a coy smile and said "Hullo" when he glanced in her direction.

The Captain said nothing, but, looking round coldly, asked who was the skipper here, if there was one. A fat man got up, breathless and myopic, grabbed the Captain's hand and shook it violently, mumbling something about "Wonderful," "good sport," "human greatness." He was not the skipper, but the owner; and when he was asked to follow the Captain to his cabin, he put on a pair of oilskins and trotted behind him obediently, like a dog that's found its master.

In the cabin Jan was informed that he'd been fortunate enough to save the life of the great Mr. Michael O'Connor, the famous American lard manufacturer, whose name was a household word throughout the States. Mr. Michael O'Connor, who wasn't loath to blow his own trumpet, also informed the Captain that he was regarded by all those who knew him as a shining example of the business man.

Jan pressed the proffered hand absent-mindedly. Its back was hairy but it was small and surprisingly flabby for a man the size of a bison. Mr. O'Connor asked the Captain to take him and his party to Miami as quickly as possible, and he was put out and offended when he was told that he and his yacht would be taken to Pernambuco. Financial matters were not discussed; there would be plenty of time for that later. All Mr. O'Connor was asked to do that night was to sign a declaration that he had abandoned his yacht *Patsy* on the high seas of his own free will and without any pressure whatsoever from the boarding party, and that he would have taken to the boats and abandoned her if the dredger *Frisia* hadn't taken her over.

The next morning they made fast and started sailing. It was a strange reversal of the natural order for a dredger to do the towing, but it served the purpose, though their speed was only about two and a half knots.

Mr. O'Connor took to joining the Captain during the first watch; he sat on Bout's stool, leaning back against the rail with his arms spread on it. He told the story of the end of the *Patsy*; how they sailed in the most magnificent weather until the hurricane hit them unawares in the middle of the night; how the skipper was washed clean overboard; and how he was the only one who kept his head, probably because he didn't get seasick like the rest. He had never been seasick in his life. He crossed once from Frisco to Shanghai through a succession of typhoons and the only ones left in the dining-room were himself and the Captain. He disclosed too that the *Patsy* had cost the nice round sum of eight hundred thousand dollars to build, and that experts considered this a bargain, which pleased him because if there was one thing he hated in this world it was being robbed. It was not because he couldn't spare the money. He could afford to build a thousand *Patsies* and not notice it, but it was the principle of the thing.

That was probably why he flew into a towering rage when he met Captain Wandelaar's agent in Pernambuco and was told that the Dutch Harbourworks Company claimed a salvage premium of four hundred thousand dollars, being half the value of his ship, as the law decrees. Mr. O'Connor was so enraged by what he described as blackmail that he called on the United States consul, who merely explained that the Dutch Company were perfectly within their rights. Because he insisted on abandoning his vessel on the high seas, he had left her to the boarding party, and this meant that he'd have to part with four hundred thousand dollars if he wanted to get his ship back. But possibly those Dutchmen might be reasoned with.

They did, in fact, reason about it for days, over scores of drinks and cigars. But four hundred thousand dollars it was and four hundred thousand dollars it remained, and when the deadlock seemed permanent the agent had the *Patsy* chained to the quay and sealed by the bailiff, with a legal notice nailed to her broken mast. That was the last straw. Mr. O'Connor was so outraged by what he called this "act of flagrant piracy" that to save his precious yacht from further insults he paid up the four hundred thousand dollars.

The agent was one of the first to congratulate Captain Jan Wandelaar on his success. Jan afterwards called his crew together in a bar on the waterfront to tell them that their share in the premium amounted to fifty per cent, which was two hundred thousand dollars. As it happened, they were less impressed than they had been when they heard about the eight hundred pounds they were to get as their share in the premium for the *Cape Breton*. The present sum was too large for them to grasp. But the Captain knew how to translate it into more tangible terms.

"Boys," he said, "this means our own ship. I'm going to buy her as soon as we are home."

CHAPTER FIFTEEN

Even Bout had to admit that Captain Jan had figured it all out very nicely. They discussed the prospect of their own ship almost every hour of every day on the voyage home. They were sailing home on a coffee clipper, a lovely craft whose graceful lines seemed specially intended to foster romantic notions. Their favourite spot was the bowsprit net, where they used to lie on their backs and gaze up at the play of light and shadow on the inside of the flying jib, or turn round and watch the dolphin-striker slash the waves. As they gazed ahead at the blue horizon their imagination easily conjured up the vision of the perfect tugboat sailing on enchanted seas.

"Yes," Bout said, "I have to admit it. I never believed you'd ever really get her. But, by God, Captain, you did it. I take my hat off to you."

That was what Mr. Beumers van Haaften said in effect when the quiet young man was standing once more in front of his desk. "I take off my hat to you, Captain—but it's a pity you're going to leave us. I thought our little arrangement most satisfactory."

But when he heard that the Captain didn't want to leave him, but proposed towing the Company's vessels with his own tug, his smile became a little stony. For though Mr. Beumers van Haaften might be a bit of an amateur as far as the actual sailing was concerned, when it came to shrewd planning he was a wizard. He spotted at once what Captain Jan was driving at, and it came as quite a revelation to him. At last he realised what the quiet young man's ultimate objective was: he wanted to undermine Kwel and Van Munster's monopoly. Very clever, very shrewd, to offer to tow the vessels of the Dutch Harbourworks Company for the same price that he asked for sailing them across on their own power. There was one trifling condition attached to his generous offer. He wanted an option on any transport jobs the Company had to offer; he wanted the first pick of the lucrative contracts that any tugboat-owner would be glad to have. Naturally he wouldn't be able to make any profit if he stuck to his price; but then, of course, he wouldn't stick to it for long. Once he got his foot in, the rest would be easy. Well, well, who'd have thought it of the pathetic creature he went to see in prison? An option on all transport indeed! When old Kwel got to know he'd laugh his head off. It was so crazy, and at the same time so touching in its childlike innocence, that Mr. Beumers van Haaften could hardly prevent himself from laughing in the young man's face. He rubbed his chin and fiddled with his paper-knife and ended by going to the window to hide the smile he couldn't any longer suppress. He said, with his back to Jan:

"This is something new, Captain. I can't possibly make such an important decision without having first discussed it with my co-directors. I'll let you know in the morning."

But at the door, while he was seeing the young man out, he could not help saying: "My dear Captain—let's be sensible for a moment. We have anything from ten to sixteen big transport jobs on hand at the same time. How on earth could you, with your one small tug . . . ?"

"Small?" the young man queried, with a tone of resentment in his voice. "You haven't set eyes on her yet—nor have I."

After that, all Mr. Beumers van Haaften could do was to mutter: "No, indeed. Well, see you in the morning."

Bout was waiting outside, beneath the trees that lined the canal. "Well?" he asked. And Jan merely answered, "Wait and see," with a shrug of his shoulders. But in his heart he knew that he'd get the option, and that he'd struck the first blow against Kwel. For the man who got the towing contracts for the Dutch Harbourworks Company ruled the tugboat business.

That evening and the night seemed endless. But somehow they managed to survive till morning, and after hardly touching their breakfast they strolled along the canal again to the office of the Dutch Harbourworks Company, where they arrived about two hours too early. There they kept a look-out for Mr. Beumers. When eventually they spotted his carriage approaching at the far end of the quay they hid behind a tree until he had gone safely inside. They gave him a quarter of an hour to take off his coat and get settled at his desk. Then Jan climbed the marble steps with quaking knees. It seemed hours before he was finally admitted to the great man's room again. Mr. Beumers van Haaften was very busy that morning and not nearly as genial as he had been the day before. He told the Captain that he had discussed the matter with his co-directors, and that they had authorized him to offer the Captain a rise in his salary, an increased bonus, and the command of a large ocean-going tugboat which he might choose himself, although the Company would be the actual owners.

Jan received the offer impassively. He was very sorry, he

said, but it seemed that Mr. Beumers had misunderstood
him. He wanted to be his own master, and was prepared to
undertake towing jobs at the rates already agreed upon,
provided he was given the option on all the transport work
the Company had to offer, even if such work necessitated
the use of four tugs at a time.

Mr. Beumers was no longer smiling when he repeated
what he had said so genially the day before. "My dear
Captain, let's be sensible."

"I am talking sense," Jan answered, coolly. "If you don't
feel like accepting my offer, please yourself. Kwel and Van
Munster seem to have served you pretty well before I came
along and I dare say they'll serve you well in the future. In
any case I'd like to thank you now for the confidence you
have shown in me, in case this should mean the end of our
association."

"My dear Captain——" Mr. Beumers van Haaften began
once more. But the door slammed so loudly that it made
him jump.

Well—if that was the way the Captain wanted it, it
couldn't be helped. A pity though, for he was a nice boy. A
sailor right enough, but a dreamer. Compete with Kwel,
indeed! The poor chap had no idea of what he was letting
himself in for.

But Mr. Beumers van Haaften knew well enough, and for
that reason he was confident that the Captain would be
back within a year, at the most. All the same, he couldn't
help being worried by the thought of what this optimistic
youth was letting himself in for. He remembered the other
poor devils who had tried the same thing before, the small
companies, the solitary skipper-owners, with their single
tugs. There had been quite a few of them in the past; they
had all, sooner or later, been driven off the seas, invariably
broken and penniless, and all they achieved was to make
Kwel even stronger, for other men were impressed and
intimidated by his success and they measured his power by
the number of rivals he disposed of. To them, Kwel seemed
like a savage warrior ruling his tribe by reason of the scalps
dangling from his belt, or the heads impaled on his palisade.

Well, anyhow, Mr. Beumers decided, when the Captain
did come back he'd be welcome. He was a nice man, one of

the best. In fact Mr. Beumers had become quite fond of him, which was perhaps a little foolish for a shrewd-headed business man.

Next morning, after a melancholy breakfast in a café smelling of stale smoke, Jan and Bout went out for a walk to discuss what to do next. They decided they might as well go to the bank to arrange about that money, and they also decided to insert an advertisement in the *Nautical Weekly* to see if there were any tugs for sale. In due course they got seven letters in reply.

The National Company at Ijmuiden wanted to sell its *Groningen*; Meulemans in Flushing offered his *Agatha* and his *Christina*; Herder in Maassluis his *Almelo*; Kwel and Van Munster offered as a real bargain the first-rate ocean-going tugboat *Fortuna*, the sturdiest ship afloat. A shipwright in Kinderdyk sent an estimate for building a new tug at a special price owing to the slump in the business. And then there was an untidy letter from B. Kiers in the Isle of Terschelling:

> Sir,
>
> This is to inform you that owing to trade falling off, I can offer you my sea-going tug "Fury," at present laid up. The "Fury" is. . . .

Then followed a description of the ship that didn't sound too bad. But then, neither did the description furnished by the others. Kwel and Van Munster, in fact, were quite lyrical in their praise of that first-rate tug the *Fortuna*. All the replies ended up with the statement that the prospective purchaser could view the ship at any hour of the day or night. The slump had, it seemed, hit the business pretty hard.

After receiving these replies Jan started off on a tour of inspection, taking Bout and Janus with him.

The *Agatha* and the *Christina* turned out to be two sistership, tiny river-tugs of the oldest vintage. They were solidly built and well kept, but useless for deep-sea work. He met Meulemans, a good-natured man with shrewd eyes, and accepted his invitation to inspect the rest of his fleet. All good, but not quite up to the standard he wanted, a description which applied to all the other tugs he saw. He then considered the offer made by the shipwright in

Kinderdyk. Of course it was very tempting to have a ship built to your own specification, but it was much too expensive, notwithstanding the "special price." The only one left was Kiers. Jan decided to go and have a look at the ship he offered without the others, to save the possible waste of fares. If the tug proved worth considering he could always send a telegram to Bout and Janus telling them to come.

As the ferry swung round in the harbour of Terschelling he saw on the jetty an old man with side-whiskers and a peaked cap. That must be Kiers. When Jan introduced himself the old man mistook the name and started calling him "Mr. Davelaar" and Jan didn't bother to correct him. On their way to his moorings Kiers told him in a few terse sentences that the *Fury* had worked round about the shoals for nine years, that she was a good, willing ship, her only fault being that she was apt to get a bit lively when running with the tide. As they turned a corner he spotted the masts of a tugboat, and liked the look of them. "That her?" he asked. And Kiers grunted, "Um."

After he had stood looking down on the *Fury* for a couple of minutes, his hands behind his back, he said: "Let's take a look at the inside of her." Already he felt himself falling under her spell. For the *Fury* was a glorious ship, not big, but steady on the water. Strength, sturdiness, pluck; those were words that seemed to Jan to sum up her qualities. This was the only ship among all those he had seen that really won his heart. This was at last the real thing. Bout and Janus must come at once to see her, and the rest of the boys as well.

Kiers had been looking at him with keen eyes, a stump of a pipe clenched between his teeth. "Well, Mr. Davelaar——" he began. But at that moment a figure came darting out of the chart-room with a pot of paint and bumped into him.

"Damn you," Kiers exclaimed, reeling with astonishment, "can't you look where you're going? And what are you doing here anyway? Go home! Get yourself washed!"

When the figure turned round Jan nearly reeled with astonishment himself. It was the girl he'd rescued from drowning that night, the strange waif he had nursed back to life on the dredger. He recognized the solemn stare of those blue eyes in a second and he knew that she had recognized him too, although she turned away almost immediately and vanished down the ladder of the stoke-hole. "My daughter," Kiers said. "Don't mind her clothes, she's on a holiday and loves pottering about on board my ships. You know what children are."

They made the round of the ship. Jan inspected her from top to bottom, and what he saw surpassed his expectations. This was about the best tugboat he had ever set foot on, the *Jan van Gent* included, and she was kept like a bo'sun's dream. When they sat down in the messroom at last, the old man lit his pipe and asked in a casual voice: "Well, what do you say?"

Jan answered equally casually: "Well, not a bad ship. I'll ask my companions to come and have a look at her, and, if it is not too much trouble, I'd like to see her out of water and have a walk round her. I expect there's plenty of firm sand around here where she'd be safely beached at low tide?"

Kiers said he thought there was. And now was there anything else Mr. Davelaar would like to know? No? Well, then, that was all they could do in the matter today.

When they were back on the jetty again he invited Mr. Davelaar to a cup of coffee, and when Mr. Davelaar declined politely he was plainly relieved. They then said good-bye, after having fixed a time to meet again tomorrow for another inspection of the ship. After Kiers had gone Jan took a room for himself at an inn called *The Fisherman's Rest* and went to the post office and sent a telegram to Bout: GOT HER. COME IMMEDIATELY. JAN WANDELAAR.

When he had sat down for his solitary meal, with a sleepy cat on the window sill by his side, the door suddenly flew open and old Kiers rushed in. "Wandelaar! Why the devil didn't you tell me it was you who saved my daughter? And to think I didn't even get your name right. Wandelaar, the man who wrote to me for the job of Mate, after that trouble with Kwel. Boy, if only I'd known. Come home with me this moment. I insist on it."

Old Kiers dragged Jan by the arm into the street and they went together to the old man's house, which was situated in the middle of the sand dunes, where they sat round a bare table in a bare room like a barn. Jan drank bitter tea from a ship's mug, while Kiers' daughter sat opposite him, knitting. When her father asked occasionally: "Well? Getting on all right?" she answered bluntly, "No."

Strange girl, but old Kiers was proud of her. "She's knitting a sea cap for me," he explained. "Damned useful thing on the bridge in frosty weather."

It was obvious that the girl had been told to sit down and knit, to correct the bad impression she had made that afternoon, and she resented it.

When at last old Kiers had finished expressing his gratitude to Jan for saving "this foolhardy daughter," as he called her, he began recounting stories of the *Fury* and the jobs she had done. But Jan couldn't keep his attention on the stories. His mind was too occupied with the girl, though he was careful to avoid glancing much in her direction. She didn't look at him either but kept her head bent over her knitting. It was only when she reached for another skein of wool that she looked up, and then her glance was cold and contemptuous.

When Jan said good-bye he pressed Kiers's hand so heartily that the old man seemed quite touched by it. He promised to come back again the next day as soon as his mates arrived. He walked about a hundred yards across the dunes and his eyes were beginning to get used to the darkness when he heard footsteps. Surprised, he turned round. It was Kiers's daughter. The moment she came abreast of him she started talking. But she spoke so fast that he could hardly make out what she said.

"Just because you fished me from the harbour," she panted, "that doesn't give you the right to steal my father's ship! Yes, that's what you're doing, stealing! You may as well admit it because anybody with half an eye can see what you're up to. You come here, hoping to get it for a song because of my father's gratitude to you. But don't think you can fool me. I saw through you the very first time I ever set eyes on you. You're a scoundrel, if ever there was one. And the *Fury* of all ships! Not the *Cerberus*, that rotten old barge, oh no! You must have the best ship of the fleet, nothing less. Don't think I didn't realise what the game was when I saw you looking over the ship this afternoon, your eyes popping out of your head with excitement. You won't find another ship like this, not if you search till doomsday.

And I'll tell you something else—she's too good a ship for you, so keep your dirty hands off her. If I'd known the sort of person you were when you fished me out of the sea that night, I'd have rather let myself be drowned than give you this chance to filch my father's best ship. . . ."

Jan, who had walked on in silence, suddenly stopped and turned on her. His first feelings of anger had given way to cold, helpless misery. "I wish you had let yourself be drowned," he said slowly and passionately. "I wish to God you had."

She laughed so derisively, that it was only by an effort that he kept himself from boxing her ears. "Thank you so much," she said, with mock politeness. "Now I know for certain the sort of person you are." And she ran away into the night.

He wanted to call after her, but he couldn't think of anything to say. While he still hesitated he heard her footsteps die away in the distance. Dejectedly, he walked back to the inn.

When Bout and Janus arrived the next day Jan went to meet the ferry. He purposely said nothing about the ship, having decided in his own mind to throw up the whole business. When, however, Bout and Janus spotted the *Fury* they were clearly impressed. Bout was so busy looking at her that he forgot to light the pipe he had just filled, and Janus rubbed his chin with a dry, rasping sound. They stood there looking for so long that Jan said at last: "Well, come on, there's more to see."

They strolled up and down the quay, looking and musing. Bout measured the height of her funnel with one eye and the bo'sun stooped to look under her counter. Jan's resolve not to buy the ship began to weaken now that he'd set eyes on her again. When finally they stepped aboard Kiers came out of the chart-room to welcome them. Jan hoped fervently that the girl had stayed at home, but a moment later she crawled out of the stoke-hole, as black as a nigger. She had been stoking the furnaces since four o'clock in the morning in order to get up steam for the trial run. After they had thoroughly inspected her, old Kiers suggested them putting out to sea. Bout went down the engine-room hatch as if he were lowering himself into his grave. When the telegraph was put at "Stand by" he rang back almost sulkily. Kiers called: "Let go fore and aft!" and the girl cast off. The telegraph rang again: "Slow ahead," and the *Fury*, with a swirl of her propeller, lifted her bows and swung clear of the quay.

The moment she reached the open sea Jan and Janus exchanged a look. The ship was a beauty and no mistake. Yet that very fact gave him an odd, sinking feeling. There was to be no going back now. Soon the girl joined them on the bridge, and stood by her father's side at the wheel. When Kiers went to the telegraph again to put it at "Full Speed Ahead," she took over the wheel and held it with a sureness and an ease that proved she had done it before.

There was a silent party up on that bridge. The only sounds were the soft humming of the engine, the swish of the spray and the occasional rattle of the rudder-chain. The day was glorious, with the sky crystal clear, except for a single feather of cloud on the horizon, like a gull's crest, and the air so pure and bracing that it gave one a feeling of intoxication. Jan's hands itched to take over the wheel, for only when he felt how the ship responded to the helm could he really judge her. But the girl stuck to it as a matter of course. When he finally went to take over he felt as if he were seizing something that was hers by right.

She handed over the wheel at last, but she didn't go. She merely stood where she was, swaying to and fro with the movement of the ship, her hands behind her back, looking ahead. He felt the strength of the ship like the tingling of an electric current through his arms, but he couldn't concentrate on the course he was steering nor on the behaviour of the ship with the girl standing there beside him like a monitor. Then she said, without looking at him: "Port a little."

It made him furious, with a sudden blind fury. But Kiers turned round and repeated the order, by a motion of his hand, and Jan meekly obeyed.

They sailed on for a few minutes, silently. Then again the girl said: "Port a little." By God, it was enough to make a man's blood boil! He, the Captain of twenty ships, a seaman who . . . but again Kiers turned round, warning him with his hand. "We're right among the shoals," he said, "it's tricky here."

Then Jan let go of the wheel and surrendered it to the girl, who took it again without a word. When at last he ventured a glance at her face it told him nothing, and she was looking straight ahead. But triumph shone in her eyes.

The trial run took the best part of the day, for they beached the ship on a bank of hard sand and had to wait for the tide to float her off. While she was high and dry they inspected her hull and examined the propeller and the rudder. When they got back to the hotel for a late meal, Janus and Bout, who had scarcely spoken a word all day, vied with one another in their praise of the ship, both talking at once. It took them nearly an hour to say all they had to say and in the end they began calculating the value of the *Fury* with the aid of paper and pencil in order to get some idea of the price Kiers would ask. According to their estimate the ship was worth at least one hundred and twenty-five thousand guilders.

That night they received a pleasant surprise. When they were all sitting round that bare table again, with the girl knitting furiously in the corner by the stove, old Kiers said solemnly: "Wandelaar, I've got something to say to you. I can't use that ship any longer. She has been rusting away at the quay. I never planned to sell her, so I didn't count on the money. I'll offer to rent her to you for an indefinite period. You go ahead and sail her, and I don't care when you bring her back. My only conditions are that you pay the insurance and a rent of seven hundred guilders a month. Well, what do you say to the idea?"

Bout and Janus gaped at the old man as if he were a ghost, for the offer seemed too good to be true. But the girl threw down her knitting in a sudden fit of rage. "Damn you!" she said, jumping up and glaring at Jan with blazing eyes, and then, before anyone could say a word, she had slammed the door and disappeared. Kiers was as startled as the others, and very put out. He crushed a matchbox in his hand in his embarrassment, mumbling: "Never mind her, gentlemen, she's very fond of the ship, and. . . ."

But Jan had got to his feet, as if he were up for a fight

and had gone after her. Kiers called: "Hey, Wandelaar, listen . . ." but Jan was already outside and didn't hear him.

He found the girl leaning against the wall behind the rain butt, her face in her hands, sobbing. When he touched her she kicked at him and sobbed the louder.

"You silly girl," he began, "can't you see that I. . . ."

But she couldn't see anything; she only wanted him to leave her alone and go away. "Stolen her, that's what you've done," she cried, trembling with rage. "I knew it all along. You're nothing else but a common thief." On the other side of the house a door opened, letting a wedge of light into the night, and a voice called: "Rikki, Rikki! Where are you?"

Jan grabbed the girl's arm and drew her out of ear-shot. "Shut up!" he said ferociously. But the moment he touched her a strange tingling feeling shot through his arms, almost the same sensation as he'd experienced when he took the wheel of the *Fury* for the first time. "Tell me," he growled, "how much would you say that ship is worth?"

She stood motionless and silent in the darkness, pondering her answer. "How—how much?" she stammered at last.

"Yes!" he said. "Name the price and I'll pay it, and to hell with the old man."

Then she said: "At least—at least—a hundred thousand guilders."

Jan strode swiftly back to the house.

When Jan later told Kiers that he appreciated his offer, but that he didn't want to rent the ship, not even at that ridiculous price, the old man looked disappointed and shrugged his shoulders. "All right," he said. "Please yourself. If you want to buy her you'll have to pay a hundred thousand."

"That's too little," Jan said. "She is worth one hundred and twenty-five thousand at least. Gratitude is all very well, but I want to sail on a ship that I've bought honestly, not on one I've wormed out of someone as a favour."

"All right," Kiers said reluctantly, "if that's the way you want it. . . ."

Only then did they notice that the girl had been standing

in the doorway all the time. "Father!" she said, "it's a mistake! I must tell you something! I. . . ."

But Jan grabbed her arm. "You get on with your knitting," he ordered sternly. Without a word she sat down, beaten for the first time in her life.

Three days later the *Fury* sailed for Amsterdam where she was put in drydock and fitted out for a long trip. When the Captain called "Let go fore and aft!" and the telegraph rang out for the start of the first voyage, emotion almost got the better of Jan. This was the goal he had been heading for all these years.

As the *Fury* followed the coastline and he looked back at the island from the bridge, he saw a tiny figure running along the beach. He focused it in his glasses and discovered it was Rikki plodding through the sand.

He followed her with his eyes for more than a minute; then he lowered the glasses, went to the wheelhouse, and gave three blasts on the ship's hooter. When he looked again she had stopped and was gazing at the ship intently, her eyes shaded with her hand. He waved at her, and he saw that she waved back. He kept her focused in his glasses till she became a speck in the distance and disappeared.

CHAPTER SIXTEEN

EVERYTHING was ready for the battle against Kwel, and Jan had only to wait for Kwel's next move—the beginning of the torture.

He didn't have to wait long. Business was slack, the jobs in the market averaged about one worth-while tow a week. He tendered for all of them at carefully estimated prices, but didn't get a single contract. That was strange, for he was sure that his price was the lowest possible; anybody taking less must sail at a loss. And that somebody was Kwel.

He didn't see through the game straight away. After every contract he failed to get, sometimes by a margin of less than a hundred guilders, he sat up in his cabin into the small hours, trying to figure out how Kwel did it; and every time he came to the conclusion that he must be losing money deliberately. It was a mystery why a company of Kwel and Van Munster's size should waste so much money on the elimination of a single skipper-owner with only one small tug. The reason for it became plain enough after about two months. Kwel just wanted to starve him into submission; but why he was prepared to lose so much money by continually sailing at a loss remained a mystery. It was not the only mystery, though. Another puzzle was how Kwel got to know the prices at which Jan Wandelaar and Co. tendered. He must know them beforehand, or he couldn't undercut his rival so successfully. But how did he get his information?

At first Jan thought that Kwel's agents must be calculating too, on the same basis as he was. They knew the exact size of his ship, her bunker-capacity, her overhead costs; all they need do was to work out the lowest possible price and undercut it by a hundred guilders. Even so, it was a masterpiece of calculation, too consistently accurate to be the result of this method.

In a moment of exasperation Jan tried an experiment. A rock-crusher was offered for tow to Stavanger, and he tendered at the token price of three thousand guilders, about five hundred too low. The moment he had dropped the letter into the pillar-box he regretted it. This was probably exactly what Kwel wanted him to do—to start towing at a loss; for Kwel could probably tow at a loss without feeling it; but if Jan Wandelaar and Co. attempted the same thing it would be the beginning of a "voluntary Roman," as it was politely called. For two days Jan was on tenterhooks, certain the job would be his, and cursing himself for his stupidity. And then the job was given to Kwel and Van Munster's International Tugboat Company at a price of two thousand nine hundred guilders.

That settled it: there was shady work somewhere. Kwel must have an agent who informed him of his rival's price before he offered his own tender. At first the relief of having escaped from his ridiculous offer prevented him from realising the real danger behind all this mysterious scheming, but soon it dawned on him. Kwel would just go on undercutting him until he was almost bankrupt, even if it should take him a year; then Kwel would let him have one little job, some trivial, risky job, that amounted in fact to suicide.

There were jobs like that going occasionally—old pontoons or strings of dilapidated barges, offered for tow by some big contractor who aimed at the insurance rather than their safe arrival. Any expert would know at a glance that the job was a blind, and nobody ever accepted, for even if the ship herself escaped damage, the loss of a tow was the worst thing that could happen to a tugboat owner. It had the effect of putting up the insurance premium for his next sailing and of ruining his name in the business. One lost tow undid at a stroke all the goodwill laboriously built up with a hundred magnificently successful ones.

After the business of the rock-crusher a visitor came to see Jan. He was a little man, like a typical commercial traveller; a ship-broker, he said, and mumbled a name; he had come to make Captain Wandelaar an offer. It had become obvious to everybody, he said, that Kwel and Van Munster's were undercutting Jan Wandelaar and Co. as a matter of policy. But he had done some thinking and it seemed to him that this situation could be exploited to the advantage of both of them. The contractors were delighted at the rivalry between the two tugboat owners—imagine how happy the man must have been to get his rock-crusher towed to Stavanger for two thousand nine hundred guilders —it was ridiculous! Now if Captain Wandelaar would agree to tender for his next job at an even lower price, thus forcing Kwel to undercut him, the mysterious little man would see to it that the Captain got a nice percentage from the contractors who'd benefit—ten per cent, say, of the difference between the normal price and the token one.

It sounded quite an idea, but somehow the little man's eyes in the softly swaying oil-light were curiously like a rat's. The Captain said he'd think about it, and when the little man offered to come back the next night to hear his decision Jan said cautiously, "Please yourself."

That night, after the visitor had slunk out as furtively as he came in, Jan didn't sleep much. He lay awake thinking of the words that old Parson Gripper had once used at a Sunday-school class: "The great principle of our Christian faith, children, is this—the end does NOT justify the means." A preposterous thing to say to a roomful of kids in Sunday clothes cooped up behind the stained glass of the vestry with the glorious spring sun glowing in Jesus' scarlet heart and Mary Magdalen's blue petticoats; but the words had stuck. When he fell asleep at last he had decided to take the little man's offer; he would be a fool not to. But somehow he knew that, decide what he might, he wouldn't when the time came.

He was right, but it was not a moral victory. The next afternoon he got a letter.

> *Dear W.,*
>
> *I know it is none of my business, but I have been following your struggle with interest, and I must warn you not to enter upon any shady deals in connection with Kwel's manoeuvres. If a man of the name of Wouters calls, offering to give you a profit if you tender at token prices, turn him down. He is sent by Kwel. If you let yourself be trapped you'll find yourself with a major job on your hands at a price that won't even pay for your tobacco.*
>
> > *Yours cordially,*
> > *Beumers van Haaften.*

That night he waited for the return of the little man—in vain. He must somehow have got wind that his victim had been warned, for he never showed up. Jan's first impulse after getting the letter was to go and call on Mr. Beumers. But he decided to see the little man first in order to report the outcome of his visit. After waiting for over five hours and falling asleep on his bunk with his clothes on, he woke up with no desire to go and call on Mr. Beumers. The certainty that he would be offered again that subordinate post as resident tug-skipper for the Dutch Harbourworks Company made him decide not to. He merely sent him a picture post-card of a hydraulic bridge with *"Thanks, W."* All he could do was to wait for Kwel's next move. He could last out three months longer, and after that he'd have to sail, whatever the job, or sell the *Fury* in the market.

Those three months were nearly up when Kwel moved. On April 22nd Shipcoal Ltd. offered two coal barges for tow from Rotterdam to Batavia. Jan Wandelaar and Co. tendered at cost-price and got the job. Half a year before he would have been delighted with it; now he knew, even before he weighed the thing up, that it was a trap. It must be, or Kwel would have snapped it up as he had done all the other jobs before.

It was difficult to make out at first where the catch was. Shipcoal was a respectable firm, the two barges *Otter* and *Beaver* were sturdy, solid vessels. The insurance company, however, refused to cover the trip unless they went *via* the Panama Canal route. It was obvious why. If they sailed, say, during the first week of May, that would mean that if all went well they'd arrive at Aden about a month later; and by then the West Monsoon would be blowing at full force over the Indian Ocean. To cross from Aden to Cape Dondra during the West Monsoon was impossible for a tug with a tow. It had been attempted twice before, once by a tug owned by Kwel and again by one of old Van Munster's craft. In both cases nothing was ever heard of either tug or tow. Since then the crossing had been given up between May and September.

When Captain Jan tendered for the job he ran right into Kwel's trap. For he had calculated his price *via* Suez, whereas he ought to have realised immediately that he would have to go *via* the Panama Canal. He was too low in funds now to stand the loss and go the long way round; he'd have to sail *via* Suez and cross the monsoon region, and almost certainly meet with disaster.

In his panic he went to see Mr. Beumers and was admitted into the private office immediately, although he hadn't announced his visit beforehand. Standing in front of that desk again, cap it hand, he realised that he had nothing to say, that he was trying to run away from the noose he had put round his own neck. But Mr. Beumers seemed to think it was quite obvious why he'd come. His first words were: "Well, Captain, what can I do for you? Help you wangle your way out of that contract?"

"The news seems to have travelled fast, sir," Jan remarked sourly.

But Mr. Beumers didn't seem to be taking it too seriously; he beamed with geniality and confidence. "I appreciate it, Captain, that you have come to me for advice," he said, "and in a way I am glad that you didn't come before. I would have

251

urged you to strike your flag to Kwel and accept the arrangement I offered you some time ago. Now, however, I shan't repeat that offer. I think you're a lucky man, Captain. I am convinced that Kwel has made a big mistake. This is your chance."

"I'm glad to hear it, sir," Jan said. "But I must confess I can't see it myself. Do you realise that this is the season of——"

"Of course, of course!" Mr. Beumers waved away the monsoon with an impatient gesture of his beringed hand. "You aren't trying to tell me you'll let the monsoon worry you? My God, Captain! Surely you haven't lost confidence in yourself as a sailor?"

"It's not a matter of confidence," Jan said. "It's a matter of attempting the impossible. I may be able to improvise my way out of a tricky situation when I meet it unexpectedly, but I can't deliberately take a ship through the world's worst weather trusting just to luck. It would be little short of suicide."

And then Mr. Beumers got up and stood very close to Jan. "Young man," he said, looking at him with those curiously hard eyes, "if Kwel had gone on playing cat and mouse with you in high finance he'd have beaten you as sure as fate. But now he's challenged you in the one field where you have the mastery. Whatever may happen in the future, if you should ever get the better of Kwel now I'll know that he's got himself to blame for giving you battle as a sailor instead of as a business man. If you do sail through that monsoon and arrive safely and in time, you'll earn the admiration of all contractors at home and abroad. You'll be mentioned in every trade paper, and I for one will guarantee that whenever possible I'll give you important jobs that will prove to the world that you're one of the best seamen in the business, and a firm one can trust one's transports to with confidence. So go along and sail those two barges to Batavia. And if you get there, my friend, let me give you one piece of sound advice: compete with Kwel where he is open to competition—at sea, and let him fiddle about with figures until he's blue in the face. If a job is worth a hundred thousand, ask a hundred thousand and make it worth it; and I assure you that clients will bring their business to you, even if Kwel offers to do it for fifty thousand. Believe me, it's the only chance you've got of beating Kwel. His fleet's getting old, his crews are dissatisfied and apathetic. You make yourself the better seaman and you'll win. But don't try to be a better business man. You'll never be that, and I doubt if anyone else ever will be. So good-bye and good luck. I'll be waiting for the news, and I know it's bound to be good."

Jan didn't utter a word except a mumbled and sheepish "Thanks." But he was heartened to find that someone had confidence in him, even though that someone was ignorant of the real hazards.

Just before he sailed Jan was surprised to receive a letter. It was written in a childish hand and was full of smudges and mistakes.

"Dear Jan Wandelaar," the letter ran, "I must write to you, for I am sorry about the things I said and did and I don't know how to get rid of the feeling that if you bought the *Fury* at too dear a price it was because of me and that I didn't know much about the prices of tugboats although I know a lot about them otherwise. You will be surprised to hear that father has decided to send me to a cookery school and you will probably be going East with the *Fury* I suppose. Father says that you should go East for there are no tugboats there and a lot of business and no Kwel to bother you and if he was young he says that is what he would do, go East. All I ask you to do is to write to me sometimes at the cookery school, c/o Mrs. Hansma, Institute Libelle, Anchor Bark, Helder, Holland. Write what you like, but any news about the *Fury* will be welcome. Love from Rikki Kiers, a friend."

Jan intended to write a few friendly lines to the girl, to tell her he didn't bear any hard feelings and if she liked to write to him she would be welcome to do so. But after half a page he changed his mind and sent a picture post-card: "Dear Rikki Kiers, thank you for your letter. I cannot give you any bunker-stations yet as I do not know what our first trip is going to be. Good luck in your cookery school, and greetings to your father. Yours sincerely, Jan Wandelaar."

It was the evening of December 3rd, 1913.

CHAPTER SEVENTEEN

WHEN the tugboat *Fury* sailed from Rotterdam with the coal-barges *Otter* and *Beaver* in tow, heading for Suez, she was commanded by a bad Captain. For Captain Jan drank more than was good for him and went on writing letters which he tore up and secretly threw overboard with the empties, at the change of the Middle Watch.

But his crew didn't notice anything; his crew were happy, for at last the miracle had come true; they were sailing in their own ship, a wonderful future before them, free men on a free sea. They were blissfully unaware of the almost certain disaster that lay in store for them beyond Aden. Yet had they seen the weather chart with the annotation: *Gales up to hurricane force between May and September in hatched region,* and the pencil line of their prospective course running straight across that hatched region, they might have had some inkling of their fate. It was because Jan knew the facts and daren't divulge them that he had to endure the agony of this other loneliness. If only he'd had the courage to discuss the thing with Bout and Flip, to take them into his confidence and say straight out: "I have made a bad mistake. I signed that contract without realising it would land me in the full monsoon," his loneliness would have vanished, and they could have discussed the situation together in the messroom night after night, till they had found some way out. But he lacked the courage. Now all he did was to retire to the chart-room or to his cabin, with a bottle for company. All alone he pored over the weather and current charts of the Indian Ocean till the whirlpools and the eddies danced before his eyes. If only his bunkers were twice the size he could avoid the bad weather by sailing round it: he would go S.S.W. from the eastern tip of Socotra, then follow the one-and-a-half-degree track along the Equator, pass the Maldive Islands, and from there sail in a straight course to Sunda Strait. It would be the longest jump a tugboat ever made, roughly sixty-five days without a glimpse of land. But what was the good of thinking about it? His bunkers wouldn't even take him as far as the

Maldives, and below the line from Aden to Cape Dondra there were no stations.

It was an ironic situation—the ship was a beauty, the tow easy, the weather perfect, the crew delighted—and the Captain slowly going out of his mind with worry. For every mile was a mile nearer Aden, and after that, disaster and the end of everything.

In the Suez Canal they had to stop for twenty-four hours in the Bitter Lakes to allow a convoy to pass that took up the whole breadth of the canal. It emerged from the desert after sunset, a gaunt, black colossus among the quivering stars. A few lights twinkled on and around it; the signals and answers of hooters sounded forlorn in the vast emptiness, like the baying of dogs at night. It was the hulk of a sixteen-thousand-ton dreadnought being towed by six of Kwel's tugs from Singapore to the Tyne for scrap. When they glided past it had become too dark to read their names, but everyone on board recognised their silhouettes—the *Albatross*, the *Galebird*, the *Schouwen* and the *Jan van Gent*. It gave Jan a queer, aching feeling in the pit of his stomach to see these shadowy ships, like a slow procession of memories, drifting past. He wanted to hail the *Jan* just to hear Siemonov bellow back at him across the water, perhaps for the last time, but his voice failed him. And then, at the far end of the convoy, he made out the silhouettes of two other tugs, placed there at the dreadnought's majestic stern as course-keepers. One of them, he recognized, was the *Aurora*. Siemonov and Bas in one convoy—it was too much for him to bear. He hurried back to his cabin and shut the door, wishing he could relieve his feelings by bursting into tears like a woman.

When they had moored in Aden, a glaring white town bathed in ferocious sunlight, the harbourmaster had a letter for Captain Jan Wandelaar, which he delivered when the Captain was on his way to the coal depot. The Captain opened it in the hot shadow of the Jesuit Church. Five pages about the Institute Libelle, and then: "Father says you are about to cross a patch of bad weather down there. I expect you'll be ballasting your barges and. . . ."

But Jan didn't read any more. He merely stood and gaped; for a thought had suddenly struck him. Good God!—he had it! Here, on the steps of the Jesuit Church in Aden, steaming with sweat and assailed by the sickening smells of frying and smouldering incense from beyond the studded doors, he had suddenly got a wonderful idea. Yes, by God, he would ballast his barges! He'd ballast both of them right up to the top—with coal! Each of them would hold two hundred tons easily. His own bunkers held three hundred tons, so altogether he would have seven hundred tons of coal: enough to take him from Aden to Batavia, *via* Australia!

So simple was the solution, so glaringly obvious, that it seemed incredible that no one had ever thought of it before. Ballast your tow with coal, anchor in the lee of one of the Maldives, bunker at sea with your boats, and sail right round the storm area. It was as simple as that. So immense was his relief that he entered the Jesuit Church and said a prayer there in the smouldering darkness. When Jan came out into the open and had got his bearings again in the ferocious sunlight, the first thing he did was to let himself be rooked by one of the pedlars in the street. He bought a pair of Arabian bedroom slippers with red tassels for three times the price they would have charged him at Simon Artz's, and mailed them to Beumers with a picture post-card of "A Camel in Aden," saying: *Thanks for your confidence. I think I have licked him. Am setting out for a seventy days' jump. Think of me on your way to the bathroom in these, if they fit. Regards, J. W.*

Of course the wonderful feeling of elation at having discovered a way out didn't last long. In fact it only lasted until he got back on board ship; then he woke up. It was the most sobering awakening a man could have. He met Bout on his way to the engine-room, a swearing, sweat-blinded Bout, who asked: "Well, what next?"

"We're going to ballast the barges with coal and sail right round the monsoon," Jan told him.

"All right," Bout said off-handedly, "what of it?"

"You don't seem to realize what it means," Jan said, irritated at Bout's apparent lack of interest.

"What what means?" Bout asked, with a note of defiance in his voice.

"That we are going to ballast our barges with coal and sail

right round the monsoon, instead of letting ourselves be battered to glory in the Indian Ocean."

"Jesus," said Bout, "is that all? What else have you figured out—how to poach an egg?" Then he shuffled on, but turned again when his sweating torso was half submerged in the engine-room hatchway. "Sometimes you blokes on the bridge make me sick," he said. "Yes, sick. 'Sail right round the monsoon'!" And when only his head was above deck, he added as a parting shot: "What else could you have done, you blockhead?"

But Bout had an excuse: Bout was only an engineer and couldn't be expected to know the finer points of seamanship. Flip had no such excuse. Flip merely remarked, when told that they were going to ballast the barges with coal and sail right round the monsoon, "Well, of course."

The casualness of his tone infuriated Jan. "What the hell do you mean by OF COURSE?" he asked, with such fierceness that Flip raised his scarcely-visible eyebrows in injured amazement. "Sorry," Flip said. "You pencilled it on the chart as far back as Gib."

"I did what?" Jan asked, glaring at Flip, as if he could eat him.

But without another word Flip stepped into the galley and disappeared. Instead of calling him back and boxing his ears Captain Wandelaar stood gaping for a moment in amazement. Then he slowly turned and went to the chart-room.

The weather and current-chart was still lying open on the table, as it had been for weeks. Round the hatched region ran a faint line, a half circle reaching nearly from Socotra to the one-and-a-half-degree belt along the equator. At first it seemed to be an hallucination but when he took the chart outside and looked at the faint half circle again in the sunlight he saw what it was: a ring made by the bottom of a bottle, his sole companion in his hours of despair. Fate, in her inscrutable way, had indicated the course he should take, but the medium she used was brandy.

When the *Fury* sailed three days later, with her bunkers and her barges full of coal, for a hop of three thousand miles, her Captain was a calm, sober man. It took him a week to realise that the secret of his calmness was the complete absence of fear. He was the only one on board who was not being slowly undermined by fear, for the simple reason that he had experienced to the full fear already. As the *Fury* crept further into the vast solitude of the ocean the men became haunted by the old stories of the tugboat service, the stories of the giant bats, the sea-serpents, the waves as big as cathedrals.

They sailed round the hatched region all right, but still they got their share of the monsoon. They got the swell and the rain. The heat of the tropics began to have a strange effect on things. The bread was so clammy that it started to live almost the moment it left the oven. Wet clothes left on the floor at night grew little fungi in their folds by the next morning. Books taken from the shelf dropped out of their bindings because the glue had been dissolved by the dampness. Curious little insects and plants sprang to life in the most unexpected places. Pale weeds sprouted among the signal-flags and the fresh water tank became an aquarium. One night when the men were watching the moving ridge of phosphorescence that marked the course of the barges far astern, they saw below them a shoal of small fish, like a cloud of shimmering green. And then an enormous shape, like a luminous submarine, slowly floated past—a shark. The shark circled round them twice; twice the colossal luminous shape slowly crossed right underneath them, following the phosphorescing trail of its shoal of pilot-fish, then it was gone.

To ease the strain and loneliness of the trip Jan began writing to Rikki Kiers as he had once written to Nellie. Yes —the letter of the *Cape Breton* all over again. It was a comfort, that letter—his only comfort. Yes, it was a troubling reflection that nothing had changed in the game except the other player. It started him wondering whether he really loved the first one, or whether it was enough merely to have a woman sitting ashore waiting for him—any woman. Whether all this gush about 'love' and 'sweetheart' and all the rest of it wasn't just an illusion, a pathetic piece of make-believe. In the vast solitude of the Indian Ocean with luminous monsters slowly circling round and colossal clouds drifting overhead, he speculated on the purpose of life, the validity of moral scruples, the nature of conscience.

Jan wrote a great deal. He spent hours in his cabin

writing, trying to formulate a philosophy of life, to discover a plan behind the chaos. He wrote not only far above the head of the girl waiting in the Institute Libelle for another of those exciting letters from her hero, but also far above his own head as well. The only basic truth that seemed to survive in this great loneliness was the dictum that the end did not justify the means. But that was only a principle, not an explanation. It didn't provide an answer to those haunting questions about the significance of life, the point of love, the meaning of death and suffering. And then, as if to bring everything back to stark, uncompromising fact, Kees was drowned.

He was drowned after the first bunkering at sea, which went smoothly after forty days of uneventful sailing. It had taken them only one day to ferry the contents of the barges across, for there was no need to row the boats; all they had to do was to pull them backwards and forwards in a continuous line. The sea was smooth, the weather calm. The only disturbing thing was the sharks which gathered round the ship, glinting maliciously as they turned their white bellies over and streaked through the green, transparent waves. There had never been so many sharks round the ship before. Bo'sun Janus said, jokingly: "Bet you they're waiting for someone," and that someone turned out to be Kees.

After the bunkering was over Kees went to lean against the rail, forgetting that a portion of it had been removed to facilitate the work. He fell backwards with a scream, and before they could throw a line to him the sea was seething with ferocious life. They never saw it happen, the water was too churned up for that. But that night there were no swift, sinister trails following in their wake. The sharks had gone, and for the first time in forty days they were sailing without their sinister escort.

When, after seventy-six days, they sighted land again on the horizon, it felt like waking up from a deep, troubled sleep. Bulle got lost the day they touched shore; he vanished in the kampong and no one could find him again. "That's what always happens," said the tall Captain of the tug *Kali Mas*, which was moored alongside them in the harbour at Tandjong Priok. "Whenever you've got a couple of them, and one goes, the other is no good any more. I'd let him go, old chap. He'll find his end all right, like all stray cats in the jungle. No use hunting for him, he's gone to join his chum."

The tall Captain was called Rang, and he had pottered about in the Far East with his tug for over fifteen years. What he didn't know about sailing in the Malay Archipelago wasn't worth knowing. He was oddly frank about things most men usually keep to themselves. He took one look at the newcomer with the tired blue eyes and remarked: "Not easy, eh, a hop like that? Anyone go off his head?"

And when Jan asked what he meant he said: "You know well enough. I recognise the symptoms, old chap. No need to be bashful with me. I have made longer trips than anyone else round here. I know from experience that after about eighty days you start wanting to jump overboard—after a hundred you do. When you're the skipper, that is. The rest just revert to apes."

He threw back his head and drank like a cock, his profile black against the purple disc of the port-hole that framed the velvety evening sky.

The thin man put down his glass with a bang, wiped his lips with the back of his hand, and said: "Well, old chap, I'm glad you turned up. We may do some good business together."

It was at this moment that Jan knew that the man was no good.

But Captain Rang's first suggestion sounded straight-forward and innocent enough. It concerned a wreck on the shores of New Guinea.

CHAPTER EIGHTEEN

Without Captain Rang of the *Kali Mas* a lot of things would have been quite different. At first Jan kept him at a distance; whenever the thin man started talking about the wreck in New Guinea he was non-committal. "Let's see what else is going first," he said. "I prefer to go back north as soon as I can, and what I'm really looking for is a return tow."

Captain Rang laughed at his optimism. Captain Rang was right. Despite Beumers' high hopes and prophecies about Jan's name being mentioned in all the shipping papers, no one seemed to bother. He had sailed right round the monsoon and delivered his tow on time, with all the odds against him. But there was no eager crowd of contractors, giving dinner-parties for him and his heroic crew; no list of remunerative jobs to pick and choose from; not a thing. Oh, there were plenty of jobs in the market, perfect little jobs for one tug with an able Captain but, incredible as it may seem, they all went to Kwel. Even in the Far East that man was omnipotent, as Jan soon found out. Kwel's flag-ship, the *Walcheren*, anchored in Tandjong Priok, and when she sailed three days later she took in tow a small dredger, a job Captain Jan Wandelaar had been angling to get for a fortnight.

Captain Rang didn't say, I told you so. Captain Rang behaved as if he didn't care in the slightest what his friend Wandelaar did—Captain Rang came over for drinks at five and left again at seven, and he brought his own bottle. He was quite an interesting companion, and he imparted a lot of useful information about the East which would have been particularly useful to a tugboat captain who was planning to spend a couple of years towing in the Archipelago. But that wasn't Jan's intention. He hung on, waiting for a return tow with dogged stubbornness. Well, live and let live was Captain Rang's motto; if his friend Jan Wandelaar wanted to waste time waiting for a return tow, he wouldn't interfere.

In the meantime Captain Rang was very helpful and obliging; for instance, he procured a new cook to take the place of Kees. The man was called Blekemolen and was abnormally fat. He had had a tropical disease that left him with dropsical tendencies and when he waddled about the deck he was constantly on the look-out for somewhere to sit down. Captain Rang had given him the highest references. He was an ex-naval cook and exceptionally good at his job. He had sailed in the tropics for over fifteen years, and when he was invalided out, he had married an ayah. The ayah was dead now and so cook Blekemolen had nothing to do, and he was sick of life in the jungle. When cook Blekemolen came shuffling on board he was followed by a coolie staggering under a laundry basket full of patent medicines. He had a fainting fit in the doorway to the galley and started complaining about everything he saw the moment he came to. But when his first steaming dish was carried to the mess-room and put on the table with a curious reverence, everybody praised him to the skies. A man who could conjure up dishes like this one in the space of two yards by three was nothing less than wizard.

Captain Rang also found someone to take Bulle's place, a fair-haired giant with childish blue eyes and the largest pair of hands a man ever had. He was a Dane called Ole, with an unpronounceable surname. Ole spoke Dutch, German and pidgin English, an international type. He had sailed on ships of all nationalities down to Siamese and he had lost all notion of home. To him "home" was simply "the shore." He came on board with a huge, unshaven grin, carrying a tiny kitbag on his shoulder and a big, flat parcel wrapped in a tarpaulin under his arm. In the foc'sle, where he was at home the moment he had dropped his kitbag on to his bunk, he unwrapped the parcel under the awed stare of his shipmates and revealed a piece of cardboard in a frame. The edges of the cardboard had been crudely decorated with amatory scenes painted in water-colour, depicting naked male and female forms embracing on violently green and purple sofas. There were also two hearts, one in gold and one in silver, linked together by a garland of flowers and surrounded by the motto: *Life is a ship of beautiful dreams, but beware of her propellers*. All this, however, was only the setting for a carefully arranged collection of locks of hair, about three hundred in all. The pieces of hair were kept in place by strips of paper pasted across them. On these strips names, ports and dates were written: *Lola—Stavanger— 16.3.'09, Mimi—Havre— 22.6.'10*, and so on, but the difference, Ole explained, was more subtle than one would imagine at first glance. The quantity of hair in each exhibit was proportionate to the rapture its donor had given him. There were locks the thickness of a cigar, a pencil, a needle; there were even items consisting of just one hair, merely to complete the record. The whole ship was immensely impressed by this sample card of Ole's amorous adventures.

But Captain Rang was not so helpful and neighbourly for nothing. When after three weeks no return tow had offered itself, he said: "Well, Wandelaar, let's talk business. This beating about the bush has lasted long enough." And he unrolled a map on the chart table.

It was a rough, home-made map, like a pirate's chart. At a point in the centre of it there was a black cross which was marked MOIRA. "This is better than the *Lutine*," Rang said. "If we can bring it off, the job is worth half a million to each of us, but we've got to work together. I've had my eye on this treasure ever since she struck that shoal, but I had to wait till somebody turned up to help me; a chap with ingenuity and imagination, willing to take a risk—someone who wasn't squeamish. Actually the risk is small, if you and I team up. You are a master tugboat-man all right, or you wouldn't have got here at this time of the year with those barges, and I may be a bit of an optimist in some respects, but one thing anybody will have to grant me: when it comes to finding my way about on the uncharted shores of that bleeding island there's no one alive who can beat me."

The island was New Guinea, and the spot where the *Moira* struck her shoal was on the south coast of the Frederik Hendrik Isle. Jan, despairing now of getting the return tow he had once been so certain of, allowed Rang to give him all the facts about the *Moira*. She had been a brand new ship of six thousand tons on her maiden voyage; fire broke out in the engine-room and her captain ran her ashore. She burned so fiercely that her deck buckled, but only the mid-ships and the engines were damaged; the rest of her was unscathed by the fire. Of course the insurance company wanted to salvage her. They sent out a bunch of experts who came back with the verdict that at least four tugs, a suction-dredger and a crowd of fifty navvies were needed to re-float her, and the cost would be more than she was worth. Rang went to see the company's agent to find out what they would be prepared to pay if he salvaged the ship and delivered her in Melbourne. The agent's terms were half her break-up value. But Rang insisted that he should get three-quarters. In the end they agreed on that. A contract was drawn up, with Rang paying for the stamp. Rang showed the contract to Jan to prove his words.

Jan looked at it without making any comment. It seemed sound enough: three-quarters of the break-up value if delivered to Melbourne within three years from that date, all duly signed, witnessed and stamped and legalised by the consul. "Pretty," he said at last, handing it back to Rang, who had been looking at him closely with bleary, red-rimmed eyes. "But how do you know that the experts weren't right? Have you seen her?"

"The experts," Rang answered contemptuously, "were a pack of fools who didn't know their job. And, what's more, they hadn't specialized knowledge of local conditions. Anybody suggesting they could import fifty navvies there is a fool."

Although Rang hadn't seen the ship himself, he had got plans of her and a sketch of her position from the agent. These he now handed over for Jan's inspection. Together they studied the plans which, though only roughly drawn, gave all the necessary data. There seemed, in fact, a fair chance of getting the ship off, but a channel would have to be dredged and most of her gear would have to be hauled out and jettisoned in order to lift her. Although she could still raise enough steam to work the winches when the experts visited her, she was probably completely rusted up by now. And that wasn't all. When Rang produced the report of the experts the proposition turned out to be even tougher still. The terrific heat of the fire had not only buckled her deck, it had cracked her hull as well. Two large vertical cracks ran right down her freeboard, one on either side. To sail the vessel in that condition would be equivalent to scuttling her. The deck plates would have to be straightened and the cracks patched up, and to do that two lighters of material at least were needed. Rang must be mad.

Rang must be mad, but he was shrewd. He worked it all out, down to the last detail. Two tugs the size of his *Kali Mas* could do the job, if they sailed with a deck-load of stuff and a crew of twenty men between them. The only problem was the man-power needed to haul out her gear and fittings, and this man-power Rang guaranteed he'd round up ashore. "I'll get that hulk off its shoal, Wandelaar," he said, "if I have to drag it off with my teeth! And if I succeed, this will be my last trip. In that case you may buy the *Kali Mas* for a song if you want it, and I'll make you a present of the crooks that sail her." His beaky silhouette against the star-studded disc of the port-hole looked like an illustration of the devil in a children's Bible. That was probably the reason why Jan couldn't bring himself to like the man, though he had to admit that Rang had been nothing but helpful and considerate up till now. Only the occasional glimpses he had got of him on board his *Kali Mas* seemed disturbing. His crew consisted of Chinese; but the two engineers were Europeans: two little fat men, with pale, flabby faces that contrasted oddly with the yellow, impassive countenances of the Chinese. Rang seemed to be allergic to Chinese, for the moment his ship sailed and he saw the yellow bodies moving lethargically about the deck he flew into a rage and lashed about him with a whip, like a man possessed. Whenever his tug sailed to take a liner in or out of the harbour it seemed like the departure of a slave-ship, for the sound of whip cracks and the rattle of chains combined with the throb of the engine.

Rang's plan was risky, but Jan couldn't afford any more time to consider it. Another month of idleness, waiting for the next job, would mean bankruptcy for him. After a week of hurried preparations they sailed with their decks piled to the bridge with the necessary materials. But the strangest part of their cargo were three crates marked *"Fragile."* Three crates full of Christmas-tree ornaments—coloured glass balls, birds, silver stars, tinsel and so on. Rang had scoured Batavia for them with such persistence that the shop owners concluded he was a lunatic.

The two tugs arrived at last, after a non-stop voyage of two weeks. The great masses of material piled on their decks gave them a strange, unwieldy appearance and excited some curiosity on the way. Javanese djongs, grotesque and silent like prehistoric bats, with their huge matting sails, altered course to get a closer look at them; swift, slender prahus, racing across the deep blue of the straits between the islands, swerved around them like wild birds; a patrol ship of the British navy stopped for a while to scrutinize them, her low grey hull squatting on the lazy swell of the Banda Sea. But after passing Tanimbar and the Aru Islands all signs of human life disappeared. The Arafura Sea, an endless plain of the deepest blue under an unchanging sky, was lonelier than the Pacific. They only spotted two ships between Larat and Terangan; one, a white speck in the distance half hidden in a cloud of hazy smoke, which must have been a coaster of the Royal Packet Company sailing from Merauke; and the other was an old-fashioned steamer belonging to a Japanese shipping line that ran a service between Yokohama and Melbourne through the Torres Strait. When these had vanished they never sighted another ship until at last they came upon the *Moira*.

It took them the better part of the day to grope their way towards her, a day of continuous soundings in the scorching sun. When they eventually dropped anchor, night was falling. The dead port-holes of the *Moira* mirrored the sunset, giving the impression that the fire that had devastated her was still burning. On the evening breeze came the faint clank of loose chains and the rasping sound of rusty derricks swinging to and fro. That night the look-out men on the tugs were fully armed, in case the Papuans launched an attack. "Butter won't melt in their mouths in daylight," Rang said, "but at night they are out to cut your throat."

The Papuans showed themselves the next morning, a swarm of black shapes, at first just spying from the reeds, then dangling from the aerial roots of the skeleton trees. Later a flotilla of scooped-out tree-trunks brought hordes of them in amongst the tugboats. They remained there silent and motionless, but now and then they gave a jump and a yell, and something flickered ominously in the air and was caught again. Then they lapsed again into silent staring.

After an inspection of the *Moira* it was obvious why the Australians had estimated that they would need to employ fifty navvies to prepare the hull before refloating her. The devastation caused by the fire inside the ship amounted to absolute chaos. Everything combustible had been burned to a cinder. There was not a trace of woodwork left, and the heat had been so intense that the iron steps, the ribs and the bulkhead-plates had been buckled and twisted almost beyond recognition. The boilers had canted off their beds and were lying topsy-turvy in the holds; the engine was a rusty wilderness of broken steel. The plates of the hull had been subjected to such great heat that the rivets had sprung, and daylight showed through the cracks between. Obviously the only thing to do was to try and clear the ship as far as possible by gang labour, the kind of labour Rang was optimistic enough to think he could round up on shore.

When Jan, Bout and Flip returned to the *Fury* and smoked their pipes in the shadow of the wheelhouse they didn't say much, but their silence was gloomy. They hadn't expected to find things as bad as this. Since the Australians had made their estimate a good many months had passed, and in the meantime the sea had pushed the wreck still deeper into the mud. The hull, in fact, had served as a breakwater and collected so much silt in its lee that the suction would probably be terrific once they started trying to move the ship away.

However, when Rang came over for a visit in his shabby dinghy, with four dirty Chinese slumped over the oars like galley-slaves chained to the gunwale, he radiated cheerfulness. All they had to do, he insisted, was to clear the worst of the silt away and the hull would move as easily as a vessel being launched down a greased slip-way.

The next day they made their first attempt. The tugs were unloaded and the heavy hawser and the towing chains were got ready. Both tugs had been building up steam pressure over-night, and when they were ready for the manoeuvre plumes of steam were rising from their safety-valves. The idea was to see if they could get the wreck to move at all. If they succeeded they would know in which direction the channel had to be made. Normally such a channel would be scooped out by a suction-dredger, but if the mud was as soft as Rang believed, it could be done by the scouring action of the tugboat propellers.

The tugs made fast at nine, and began pulling at ten. They pulled for all they were worth until evening. They swung and churned about, throwing up waves of muddy water behind them. They tried every trick of the trade to shift the wreck, but when at last they gave up she hadn't budged an inch. So that was that.

But when Rang came over for a drink after supper again he was even more cheerful than he had been the night before. He chatted and laughed and indulged in a good deal of jovial back-slapping. He brought three bottles of gin with him, and drank most of it himself. When he was finally piloted back to his boat he was drunk, but happily drunk. He even kissed the yellow oarsman who picked him up after he had fallen flat on his face between the seats. "Tomorrow, boys," he kept shouting as he disappeared into the night, "tomorrow, boys, we'll do the trick." He talked as if it were only a matter of repeating some magic formula, and the wreck could be coaxed out of the mud as easy as winkling.

When he turned up again the next morning he was as sober as a judge. The sun wasn't up when he routed Jan out of his bunk and asked for two boats, complete with crews. Bout and Coba were ordered to go on board the *Moira* and make the hoisting gear strong enough to lift out the wrecked boilers. Jan himself was told to take up position with the rest of his crew on board of the wreck, and to arm himself and his men to the teeth. The bo'sun was ordered to load the three crates containing the Christmas-tree ornaments into Captain Rang's boat. Rang himself boarded the *Moira*, bringing with him his four boats manned with every soul he could muster, and all armed to the teeth, like pirates. As soon as he had ascertained that everything was as he wanted it, he set out with his fleet for the shore, taking with him two timber rafts that had been constructed the day before.

The moment the sun rose the Papuans in their log boats had swarmed out again, as inquisitive as cats. They had plenty to be curious about that morning, for Rang started to perform a veritable pantomime, as soon as it had become light enough for him to be seen from a distance. He staggered on to one of the rafts in waders, his arms full of shining toys, like a grotesque Santa Claus, and sprinkled the stuff about until the whole raft was covered with scintillating objects. When he'd finished he worked his way to the edge, his arms spread to keep his balance on the slippery planks, and scrambled back to his boat. Then he had himself rowed to the other raft, and went through the same performance there. When both rafts had been liberally sprinkled with these ornaments he turned to his own tug. Jan, who had been following his mysterious antics with a pair of binoculars, noticed a thin rope stretching out behind him, a steel cable which he secretly unwound, like an angler paying out a line. When he had boarded his tug again and fastened this cable to his main bollard, the rest of his crew rowed back to the *Moira* and joined Jan's men where they lay on her decks, with their guns at the ready, as Rang had ordered. "Keep everyone out of sight," Rang had said. "If you show a sign of life they won't bite." At first nothing happened, but after about half an hour the first canoe ventured past the surf, a canoe with six giants in it, who were daubed with bright colours and covered with amulets. They paddled like maniacs, as if they were chasing something. When they got nearer Jan saw that they were trying to catch up with a couple of glass balls that Rang must have dropped. They soon reached the mysterious things, but they didn't dare to pick them up straight away. They looked at them suspiciously for some minutes, then one of the men plucked up courage and grabbed the two glittering balls. In a moment scores of canoes with hundreds of dark men paddling rhythmically, like mechanical toys, came shooting out in all directions, heading for the rafts.

The men on the *Moira*, spying from their ambush, could scarcely repress their excitement and Jan had to swear to make them shut up. On the *Kali Mas* Rang peeped round the corner of the wheelhouse, and the head of his first engineer, which had been sticking out of the hatchway, vanished at once. The native fleet circled round the rafts suspiciously for a while, and a few of the helmsmen stood up and peered about, shielding their eyes with a hand. But as everything seemed quiet they climbed on to the rafts. The whole lot of them climbed on, or tried to, and when one raft was crowded they clambered on the other and began gathering up as many of the glittering toys as they could lay their hands on. Just then the engine-room telegraph of the *Kali Mas* rang out. The wash of the propeller thundered under her counter; the steel-line jerked taut, and the natives were rapidly pulled along with the rafts and out of reach of their canoes. The rest clung to the rafts, too terrified to move.

Rang sailed his catch round in a wide circle, and ended up by pulling them alongside the *Moira* directly beneath the rope ladders that had been thrown out by Jan's men. A few of the natives grabbed the ladders straight away and started climbing on board in an effort to escape. But as the rest seemed to hesitate and the rafts were in danger of drifting wide of the *Moira*, Rang let go his line, swung round and headed full tilt at the rafts with their load of terrified natives. The sight of those murderous bows cleaving the waves like a hatchet and racing straight towards them had the effect of driving the remainder up the ladders. So great was the panic that a number of the men lost their hold and crashed back on the rafts. But Rang was not a sentimentalist. He swung the telegraph back to "Full Speed Astern" only at the very last moment to prevent damage to his bows. The *Kali Mas* crashed right through the rafts, splintering the wood with a succession of reports like a volley of gunfire.

Jan heard it, but he didn't see what was happening, for the herd stampeding on the deck of the *Moira* was completely out of control. They rushed blindly from the poop to the foc'sle and back. Some of them stumbled through the gaps in the deck and fell among the rusty debris in the holds; others got pushed over the rail, or leapt blindly into the sea and fell victims to the sharks. Then Rang and his men came on board, armed with whips, and the cowering natives were beaten into submission. The men of the *Fury*, so boyishly excited while the hunt was still on, stood gaping at the scene, stunned. But the Chinese lashed out at the cringing, howling herd without a flicker of an eyelid, with the same impassive, inscrutable expression on their faces that they always had.

All the stories about the proud high bearing of the noble savage proved to be nonsense. These men behaved as a bullied crowd would behave anywhere else on earth. They didn't understand Dutch, and they had never been treated like cattle before, but under Rang's brutal treatment they became in a little while abjectly submissive. What looked at a distance like a crowd of fierce warriors turned out to be a herd of miserable human beings covered with sores and mutilations. Urged by the whip the dark bodies strained and pulled. When the first boiler began to shift in the depths of the ship there was a tremor that shook the wreck from bow to stern. Half an hour later this great weight of metal crashed over the side into the water with a thud that drove away the sharks like birds scattered by a shot.

In the distance the sun sparkled on the glass balls and the floating tinsel that were fast drifting out into the blue expanse of the Arafura Sea.

Never before had the *Fury* been so strangely silent as that night after sunset. Dark groups of silent men stood at the rail or squatted on the foredeck, staring at the fires in the distance, the fires on the wreck.

The Papuans seemed to be celebrating. A succession of great fires sprang up on the decks of the *Moira* and groups of wild figures danced round them, chanting ominously in the still night.

Nobody on board the *Fury* said a word, but everybody was thinking the same thought: What did these people, marooned on a burnt-out wreck, find to eat? They didn't bring any food with them, they couldn't get ashore; what, then, did they live on? The dancing and chanting grew more frenzied, till the wild savagery of it acted on Jan's men like a sinister spell. The *Fury* was a silent ship that night, manned by a silent crew who kept casting furtive glances up at the bridge, where the Captain sat in a deck-chair, smoking, staring across the firelit water at the dancing evil on the wreck.

The Captain sat and smoked, but he did not see what was happening on the *Moira*. The barbarism he'd already witnessed was still before his eyes. Not only had he witnessed it, he was in part responsible. Because Rang's brutalities served his own interests, he had acquiesced in them; he had made no move to interfere. Alone on the bridge he suffered the tortures of a bad conscience. This was his first real defeat. This was worse than anything that had happened before. Here, in a remote corner of the globe, beyond the reach of justice and civilisation, he had shown his crew the sort of man he really was—a brutal hypocrite. To see a bully deliberately crush helpless human beings to death with the bows of his ship; to see child-like men, mad with fear, hurl themselves to death in the rusty tangle of the holds or in the shark-infested sea; to see a gang of men kick and beat defenceless people into abject slavery; to see all this and lift not a finger—that was the worst crime he had ever been guilty of.

And there was no excuse. It was no good pretending to himself that he had never believed Rang capable of such a thing. He had known all along the kind of man he was. In fact he had expected that something would happen sooner or later, and in consequence he should have been all the more ready to prevent it. In the space of half an hour there had occurred the most shocking demonstration of human cruelty he had ever witnessed. And he had done nothing. He had stood by merely gaping, like the rest. If ever he won his fight against Kwel, the triumph would be marred by the memory of this cruelty, this utter nightmare of cowardice and defeat.

The Papuans danced and chanted round their blazing fires, their gigantic shadows swaying in the darkness. To these famished natives marooned on a burned-out wreck, cannibalism would be as natural as the frenzied rhythm that bewitched their feet. No man with any trace of conscience left could watch that spectacle without a feeling of horror. Jan got to his feet, knocked out his pipe and went down the steps to his cabin.

His cabin was hot and dank, with gouts of moisture streaming down its walls. On the lid of the wash-stand a child's exercise-book lay open. *I cannot see how the man imagines he'll ever be able to get this hulk afloat again, with the twenty-seven men we have. I am afraid, my girl, that I have let myself in for an adventure that'll end in disaster; but"* There he had broken off the previous night. At that point Bout had come in for a glass of gin and a breather for his three hours' task of stoking up the furnaces. If only Bout would come in again so that he could discuss it with someone, and get it off his chest. But no one came. Jan sat down on the stool in front of the wash-stand, planted his elbows on the lid and covered his face with his hands. "This is unbearable," he thought. "I can't face this again tomorrow, and the next day, and God knows how long after that." He remained there for a long time, trying to think of some other way of clearing the debris out of the *Moira* and getting the wreck afloat. But the only chance was to work the hoists by hand power, and there was no other labour available except that crowd of savages now dancing on her decks.

Were they still dancing? It was very silent now. The sound of stamping feet and voices chanting had died down. When Jan got up and looked out of the porthole the fires were glowing steadily, but there were no shadowy figures dancing round them. The moon had risen and the shore seemed to be nearer; the roots and the skeletons of the dead trees shimmered white in a cold, silvery light. The crew were no longer huddled in little groups against the rail, watching. They must be lying on their bunks now, awake, staring in the darkness, wondering what he was going to do. And of course they never doubted that he would do something, that he would find the right way out. They trusted him, and they had trusted him all along. He had sailed them round the monsoon, he had taken them safely through so many dangers, right back to the days of the *Cape Breton*, the *Ameland*, the *Scottish Maiden*. And there had been times when mere physical danger was nothing in comparison with other and more subtle dangers—those insidious threats to human decency and commonsense that arose in strained and difficult situations. Such a threat, they knew, hung over them now. If this went on, if the Captain put up with this merely to gain money, something inside them would be shattered, something precious, a kind of primal innocence, and that essential goodness of heart, without which they would be lost indeed.

Somehow the feeling that his crew believed in him made it easier for Jan to act. If there was a spark of divinity in human life, if a man possessed a soul at all to be preserved by moral principles, then there must be a way out of this, even though the way was anything but clear to him at that moment.

Jan must have slept, for the sun shone in his eyes when he opened them again. In the pink light of sunrise everything seemed simple and obvious. It was as if during the hours of sleep he had gained the moral strength he had lacked till now. The despair and weakness of the previous night seemed a childish thing. He washed and shaved, and then shouted for a cup of coffee. When cook Blekemolen came shuffling up with the tray and steaming cup on it, Jan said: "I won't be in for breakfast, but don't let the others wait. Get me the bo'sun."

When the bo'sun came he ordered the dinghy to be lowered, to take him across to the *Kali Mas* before work started. The bo'sun said "Aye, aye, Skipper," and called the men with a voice that made the birds ashore whirl up from off the trees in a frightened cloud.

As he was rowed across to the *Kali Mas* he discussed the condition of the dinghy with the bo'sun at the helm. They agreed it badly needed a coat of new paint to make it weather-proof. The bo'sun said he hoped to find time within the next day or so to do it. When they got alongside, the bo'sun said: "Mind your trousers, Skipper, she's filthy." He swung over the rail without smudging his trousers, and asked a Chinese face peering out of the galley where the Captain was. "Mistah Capp'n having breakfast, Mistah Cap'n suh."

Jan came down the messroom stairs as Rang looked up from his porridge.

"Morning," said Rang. "You're early."

"I know," Jan answered; "I've come to talk to you."

Rang's eyes didn't change. He just looked at him a second without speaking; then he said: "About those natives, eh?"

Jan nodded.

"I knew it," Rang said, with a kind of amused tolerance. He winked at his two pasty engineers and wiped his mouth with a dirty napkin; then he pushed away his plate. "I knew it the moment I saw your face yesterday. No point in telling you that you are just a bloody lot of tenderfeet, for that's obvious."

"I suppose so," Jan said. "But what of it?"

"All right," said Rang. "Thought of another way of getting those boilers out?"

"No, I haven't," Jan admitted.

Rang produced a needle and started picking his teeth. "Look here," he said, "there won't be any whipping today because it won't be necessary. They know now what's expected of them, and they'll be ready to jump to those ropes like lightning the moment I show my nose. So if that's what worries you, don't let it."

"That's not the only thing that worries me. I won't have them forced to stay against their will," Jan continued. "Let those who wish to, stay, and the rest go back on shore. And I want to pay them decent wages and provide them with food while the job lasts."

"Is that all?" Rang asked, smiling. "What about their life insurances and their old-age pensions? Have you worked that out yet?"

"Don't think I'm just talking," Jan said quietly. "If you or your crew lift a finger against those natives again, I'll drop the job and leave you to get her off alone."

"Don't be silly," Rang said. "You'd be broke."

"I know," Jan said. "But it can't be helped."

Rang picked his teeth again. The engineers sat with their spoons balanced in their podgy hands, and their heavy eyes fixed on Rang. When Rang had finished picking his teeth he wiped the needle on his sleeve and replaced it behind his lapel. Then he picked up his cap and put it on the back of his head. He looked almost surprised when, turning to go up the stairs, he found himself confronted with Jan. He seemed to have forgotten about him already. Then he said: "All right. Have it your own way, Jesus," and brushed past him on to the deck.

As Jan was being rowed back to the *Fury* he felt quite sick through lack of food, and the boat was rolling badly. It all seemed a lot of fuss about nothing now. He couldn't imagine why he hesitated a moment last night; this was the obvious thing to do. It just meant that he'd have to share out his food, and thus limit his stay here to about another week. After that he'd have to sail to Australia to stock up again. It just meant that he had chucked away about ten thousand guilders to appease his conscience. Well, it couldn't be helped.

On board the *Fury* he found his men ready to take to the boats and go back to the wreck. They hung about, obviously dying with curiosity to know what had been going on. He had better tell them, for it was their money too.

"Boys," he said, "I'd like you to know that I have just made it a condition for our carrying on with this job that those natives are fed and paid, and that there shall be no more whipping and kicking them about. That means we'll be down to emergency rations from now on, and that a watch will have to be kept on the wreck tonight to prevent them killing each other. What do you say to it?"

They said nothing at first. Then a voice grunted, "Hear, hear." It was Bout. And then they all repeated "Hear, hear" awkwardly, like farmers at a meeting.

"All right," Jan said. "Let's go."

They manned the boats and started out without saying another word. When they'd got half way Bout warned them: "It's going to be a scorcher again. Mind you keep your caps on, chaps. No point in getting sun-stroke."

The rest of the journey was completed in silence.

Afterwards Jan wondered if he'd been mistaken. Perhaps Rang was not such a brute after all. For Rang never referred to the condition imposed on him. It would have been understandable if he had treated the natives with a mock politeness, if he had shown them an exaggerated deference, just to score off Jan. But he did nothing of the kind. He made a little speech to the staring herd in some outlandish language, presumably telling them that those who wanted to go ashore were free to go. The others would be paid ten cents an hour and given three meals a day. He made his speech with a sour, unbending dignity, without betraying his disgust at this hypocrisy by so much as a look. After he had finished he paused a moment to give the natives a chance to express their wishes. Then he turned to Jan: "None of them seems to want to leave, so let's get on with it. It is understood, I suppose, that you provide the food. I'm willing to share in paying their wages, but I can't cut the rations of my crew. Chinese don't understand this kind of thing."

Jan agreed. Rang gave one crack of his whip, but it was only a token crack. At the sound of it the Papuans jumped to the ropes and began heaving on them with the same frantic energy they had shown before.

At mid-day cook Blekemolen was rowed across from the *Fury* with a hundred portions of stew, which he shared out, stripped to the waist, under an awning held up for him by two deck-hands. The natives filed past him patiently, as if they had been used to this routine all their lives. At night cook came back with soup and a boatload of bread, which was shared out this time by a stoker, while the cook fanned himself with the lid of the pot. After the food had been distributed, the Papuans filed past Rang, who paid them a new, shining guilder each, of which he had a dozen bags on board. When the day's work was over all the boilers had been cleared away and half the rusty debris from number three hold. In two more days the ship would be empty.

Flip, the bo'sun and two stokers volunteered for the night watch on board the wreck. That night there was no dancing round the fires and no chanting. When Jan flashed his morse-lamp at them at midnight, before turning in, Flip flashed back: "All quiet as a school dormitory. Happy dreams."

Everything worked out for the best, in a way, for after the holds had been cleared and they had cut a channel with their propellers, the *Fury* had six days' rations left and a fortnight's coal. If they wanted to bunker in Port Kennedy they would have to leave after six days anyhow, so sharing their food with the Papuans hadn't actually lost them any time on the job.

For six days they pulled at the *Moira* with all the power they could muster, on the long hawsers at high tide and the short ones at low. And they might just as well have pulled away at Bishop's Rock for all the difference it made. She just wouldn't move an inch.

They tried everything. They tried pulling at her anchor chains crossed over her bows. They tried pulling with her anchor chains crossed under them. They filled up the ballast tanks in hold number four, to make her lift her bows. They pulled with all their thirty-five hundred horsepower, sixteen hours a day for six days. They pulled until the hawsers frayed. But she still didn't shift an inch. In the end Rang said: "You'd better go and bunker as fast as you can, and be back before spring tide."

Spring tide was their last and only chance; if they couldn't get her off then they'd have to give her up.

Before the *Fury* sailed, at night, Jan went to see Rang on board the *Kali Mas*. He found him thinner and hoarser than ever, a bleary-eyed inebriate in a cabin smelling like a mouldy cupboard. His Chinese were singing on the moonlit foc'sle to a flute, warbling tunelessly with mournful persistence, like the wailing of cats. Rang couldn't stand it. "Shut up!" he shouted, "or I'll wring your bleeding necks." He slammed the port-hole shut and lurched drunkenly on to his couch. Jan said: "I'd turn in if I were you; you're getting a heavy list."

Rang nodded sheepishly. Suddenly he grabbed Jan's coat with his skinny hands. "Don't leave me in the lurch," he whimpered. "Don't leave me to perish all alone in this hell! Swear you'll come back! Swear it!"

Jan pulled him up without answering, and was shocked to find how little he weighed. Gradually Rang lapsed into a state of helpless blubbering. Jan told him: "The trouble with you is that you're overworked. I'll be back in six days. Take it easy in the meantime."

After he had lifted the thin body on to the bunk and shaken the pillow for him, he turned to go. "Don't forget to feed those Papuans, or there'll be trouble when I get back," Jan said, as he went out of the door.

Rang didn't answer; he just lifted a limp hand in what must have been intended for a reassuring gesture. "Blah," he murmured thickly; "Blah, blah, blah."

The trip to Port Kennedy was like a pleasure-cruise, a holiday everybody had deserved. Blue sea; blue sky; and a deliciously soft breeze. First the crew washed the ship, then they washed themselves. When the *Fury* came steaming between the islands of the Torres Strait she looked as if she were dressed with flags, so many bits of brightly coloured laundry fluttered from her lines.

The little harbour didn't amount to much, a fifth-rate coaling station for the big liners. But to the men of the *Fury* it stood for luxury and freedom. After slaving for three days on end in the coal dust within sight of the harbour, it was a bitter blow to be dragged back without even a look inside. Now they had to face again the grim loneliness of the sea, the stench of tropical mud and the oppressive monotony of the jungle. Janus and Flip kept alternate watches at the gang-way to prevent anyone from running away. When the bunkers were full and the anchor weighed, they sailed northward again. The atmosphere on board was as gloomy as if they carried a corpse. Bout asked: "Any hopes?" and when Jan replied: "Frankly no," Bout merely said, "I see."

"I think we are bankrupt again," Jan told him.

"I see," said Bout with a shrug. "I suppose it means a quiet funeral for us all. No flowers, by request."

After they'd left Port Kennedy the sea began behaving strangely. A heavy, rolling swell piled in from the north, but there wasn't a breath of air anywhere. The sky was the purest blue, with only here and there a yellow fluffy cloud like a duckling's feather. Jan and Flip stood looking at the sea in amazement, clasping the rail of the bridge to keep on their feet. Bout came up after his watch with plaster over his eye. In the stoke-hole a furnace door was jolted open by the shock of a wave and some embers fell out and burned one of the stokers.

They thought of many explanations for this mysterious swell, which eased off after an hour or so and left the sea as peaceful as it was before. Only when they sighted the coast of the Frederik Hendrik Island did they realize what had happened.

The beach, seen through a telescope, was completely desolate. The skeleton trees on the shore had been washed away. In some places landslides had formed creeks and shoals not recorded on any chart. The explanation was that an up-heaval of the sea-bed had caused a vast tidal wave. Everyone came on deck as the *Fury* sailed up and down the coast looking for the *Moira* and the *Kali Mas*. The spot where they had been was easily recognizable. The wrecks of the boilers had been thrown high on the shore and were surrounded by small dark shapes which when seen through a telescope, turned out to be a number of brown corpses lying on the beach.

The *Fury* sailed up and down that bit of coast three times. But no trace of the wreck was discovered—only the boilers and the dead Papuans. There seemed nothing left to do but to drop anchor and wait for morning; then sail home.

That night Jan was suddenly woken up by Ole and Janus

bursting into his cabin. "The guns, Captain! The guns!" Ole shouted. "Those bloody Papuans are coming for us. We've heard the splash of their paddles on the starboard quarter!"

Jan groped for cartridges for his revolver in the drawer of the chart table while Ole and the bo'sun ran for the guns. Then a shot barked outside followed by a weak echo from the shore. A voice shouted: "Stop! Stop shooting, you blasted fools. *Fury* ahoy! Friends!"

Jan stood on deck, peering under his hand into the inky darkness. He called: "*Fury* here! Who are you?" And a hoarse voice shouted from the darkness "It's ME, Rang. You idiots, can't you recognize my voice?"

"Where's the *Moira*?"

"Anchored in the Princess Marianne Strait, ready to sail!"

There was silence for a moment. Then Bout said, invisible in the darkness: "Well, I'll be damned!"

Rang told the story in a few words. As he told it, leaning against the wall of the chart-room, trembling, an exhausted victor in the wavering light of the oil-lamp, the men looked up at him with awe, for what he had done sounded like a saga. He told it with an indifferent shrug of the shoulders and a deprecatory gesture of his hand. He saw that tidal wave coming a long way off, for the tide had run so far out that the *Moira* had been lying high and dry, separated from the beach by the deep water behind the shoal. He had chased the Papuans off the wreck and had made them collect the timber of the rafts and haul it on board. Then he had fastened every hawser and rope he had to her poop and had stayed waiting for the tide to reach him. The tidal wave came at night. The sea, glowing with phosphorescence, looked like a great wall of fire as it rolled towards him. He gave his engine all the pressure he had, even cutting off the safety valve. As the great mountain of water lifted his ship he held the wheel himself and managed to keep her right side up. The force of the water lifted the *Moira* off her bed, and by tugging at her like a bulldog he had managed to keep her off the shore. Then the water started running back with her, and now she was lying on a hard shoal in the Princess

Marianne Strait, afloat at high tide and aground at low, ready to be fitted out for the tow to Melbourne.

They drank to the successful outcome of the affair, clinking glasses with Rang, in solemn ritual. Afterwards Rang said it was about time he went back to his ship and turned in, as he could scarcely stand up for exhaustion. Before he went, Jan who was taking off his boots for the night, asked him: "By the way, what exactly happened to those Papuans?'

Rang, on his way out, shrugged his shoulders. "How the hell should I know?" he said. "We're rid of them, that's the main thing."

"I counted about two hundred corpses on the beach," Jan said. "How did they get there?"

Rang looked at him with a nasty glint in his eyes, and said: "Looks as if they were drowned, doesn't it?"

Jan pulled off his left boot and put it by the side of the right one. "Looks like it," he admitted. Then he got up to turn down the lamp. "Weren't they on board the wreck when the tidal wave came in?"

"No," said Rang, "they were standing on the shoal. Now you mention it, I must have clean forgotten them."

"It looks to me," Jan said, "as if you took in your ladders purposely and left the natives there to drown."

And then Rang suddenly became very nasty. A cunning light flickered in his eyes. "And what if I did, Jesus?" he said threateningly. "Suppose I had drowned them in cold blood? Suppose I had never told them in that little speech of mine that those who wanted to could leave, and the others would be paid ten cents per hour? Suppose I had told them that my men were too tired to use the whips; that anybody who slacked for a moment at those ropes would be shot; that everyone would be given a piece of silver each day, to be handed in at the end of the job, so that I could discover who'd played truant simply by counting the pieces handed back? Or suppose that I don't speak Papuan at all, that I just made up a language as I went along? Or suppose anything you like, Jesus. It doesn't matter to me. But I'm curious to know what you propose doing about it. Will you hand me over to the police or to the nearest priest? Or will you pocket your half million and mind your own business?"

"I suppose," said Jan, "I'll have to leave you to God."

That nearly finished Rang. He laughed till tears rolled down his cheeks, making an odd kind of cackling sound, like a chicken being carried by its wings. "God!" he cried; "Can you beat it?" Then he wiped his eyes and patted Jan on the shoulder. "That's right, old chap, leave me to God, that suits me fine. Just you go off and be a good little Christian. Say your prayers and go bye-bye, and leave naughty little Rang to God."

"I think you'd better go and turn in," Jan said—"Good night."

"Good night," Rang said, still wiping his eyes. "And don't ever do this to me again; it just kills me." Then he went out, slamming the cabin door.

For four whole days the men of the *Fury* and the *Kali Mas* worked on the *Moira* patching her up as she lay on the shoal. They scarcely had a chance to get their clothes off, but no one grumbled. The work was too urgent. The noise of continuous hammering and the roar of the surf echoed back from the impenetrable wall of the jungle. The fourth day was the crucial one; it was the day when all the riveting had to be done. At low tide then every available man would have to rivet like a woodpecker, six hours at a stretch, for if the wreck should be lifted off her shoal again by the high tide without all the repair plates being fixed, the ship would break her back again and be lost for good.

It was a race against the tide, and they won. It cost them ten years of their lives in anxiety and effort, but they did the job with time to spare. When the sea lifted the *Moira* off her shoal again a number of the new rivets sprang out with an ominous twanging sound that was amplified a hundredfold in the bare iron holds. But the plates and stanchions held. That night Rang and his engineers came over to the *Fury* to celebrate, fouling the air of the chart-room with the smell of gin and very bad cigars. "She's seaworthy, boys!" Rang said, winking across his seventh glass, as if he was about to bathe his eye in it. "Tomorrow we can start the towing. Here's luck to us."

Next morning at sunrise she moved off. She sailed slowly away from the coast which had held her a prisoner so long, bound for Singapore. On her poop six deck-hands waved farewell to the jungle as they watched it disappear in the grey haze behind them.

The route they planned was through the Banda, Flores, and Java Seas; and from there, through Karimata Strait and the Riouw Archipelago, to Singapore. On July 30th, the night after the thirteenth day they passed Gunungapi Island. So far the trip had been child's-play. The weather was consistently fine, the sky cloudless, the sea like a mill-pond. On the fourteenth day, fifty miles west of Gunungapi, they spotted a wind-jammer on the starboard bow. She was a European vessel, a schooner. At first she seemed to be crossing their bows, but when they got nearer they saw that she was tacking all the time. Everybody on board the tugs and the *Moira* stood looking at her. Every time she seemed to be going about and her sails began to flutter, she drew away again. Then men trained their binoculars and tele-scopes on her, and saw no one on her decks or at her wheel. When they got her on the beam Rang hoisted signals and sounded his hooter, but there was no response. They stopped the tow, and a boat put out from the *Kali Mas* to investigate. Through his binoculars Jan saw that Rang was the first on board the schooner. He could make out her name now—*The Rising Hope*. In a little while the schooner came in closer, crossing the bows of the tugboat, with Rang at her wheel. As Rang swung past the *Fury* he hollered "Not a soul! Corpses!—Prize! Hang on to her!"

An abandoned ship on the high seas, rigging complete and cargo undamaged—the men cheered wildly. This was a colossal windfall. *The Rising Hope* was tied up to the *Moira* by Rang; her sails were furled and her royal- and topgallant-masts were lowered. Four of his Chinese stayed on board as an emergency crew, commanded by Rang's Mate. On his way back from the ship Rang rowed past the *Fury*; but in the meantime the swell had increased, and there was wind be-hind the horizon, so he didn't come on board. He shouted the information that there wasn't a soul on board; only two corpses partly decomposed and a lot of dead rats, but her cargo of copra was sound as a bell. They had caught her in the nick of time, if indeed the wind was coming from the horizon. When he had gone bo'sun Janus came to the bridge to protest on behalf of the men that there were only members of the *Kali Mas* crew on board the schooner, and they were afraid they might be swindled out of their share of the prize. But Jan calmed him down, promising that he'd see they got their share when the time came. Flip wanted to be rowed out to the schooner just to satisfy his curiosity, but Jan forbade it. They would have to get ready in case the wind blew up suddenly.

The wind came during the night, a regular gale of it. When the next morning the sun rose in a yellow sky there was a lot of cursing and pointing aft on board the *Fury*, for *The Rising Hope* had vanished. Only the *Moira* sailed with them, huge and gaunt on the choppy seas. Rang flashed out a morse message to the effect that the men put aboard the schooner must have cut loose. Probably the Chinese had murdered his Mate and then taken possession of the ship. Bo'sun Janus and Flip were furious. If only the Captain had allowed them to go on board the schooner, this wouldn't have happened. They knew all along that the scum on the *Kali Mas* wasn't to be trusted.

Everybody developed a blind hatred for the *Kali Mas*. Luckily she was too far off to board, or there would have been trouble. Now they'd have to bottle up their rage until they got to close quarters again, and that would take twenty days at least. But they had a chance to show their disgust when two days later Rang signalled that his cook had died during the night and asked for a volunteer from the *Fury* to take his place. Jan had to reply, "No cook available," for nobody would volunteer. They clustered together in small groups on the deck between the bridge and the foc'sle, shouting curses and shaking their fists at the *Kali Mas*.

The next day Rang signalled again asking for volunteers. Two more of his men had died: a stoker and a sailor, victims of the curious form of pneumonia that his cook had died from. Again there were no volunteers; but when a boat came from the *Kali Mas* making a special request, one of the stokers said he'd go if he was paid extra for it. He was standing ready to jump into the boat when suddenly one of the Chinese oarsmen had a frightening fit of coughing. He clasped his throat and all at once slumped forward with a cry, dead as mutton. That made the stoker change his mind. He wouldn't get into that boat for all the tea in China. The boat went back dejectedly, with one man less at the oars.

It was Bout who uttered the word first, the terrible word that made every sailor's blood run cold. He had been looking out of the hatch-way and had seen the Chinese seaman die at his oars. When the boat was on its way back he came up on the bridge, wiping his greasy hands on a plug of cotton waste. "Did I hear him say 'pneumonia'?" he asked with a peculiar kind of smile. "Yes," Jan answered: "What of it?" "Nothing," Bout said; "Only we used to call it the plague."

For ten days more the *Kali Mas* sailed on without reducing speed. Almost every day another corpse was thrown overboard. Then Rang signalled: "We've broken the back of it. Epidemic subsiding. Only a few sick left, and they are recovering." With a depleted crew they sailed on. But Rang was over-optimistic, for none of his men recovered. The *Kali Mas* passed the Tukangbesi Islands, the Tiger Islands, the Postillon Islands. If she managed to make Surabaya she would be safe. But fate was against her; within sight of the Kangean Islands, the *Kali Mas* gave up. Rang signalled: *Four men left alive. Am dropping anchor. Get help Surabaya.* Jan signalled: *Try to make Singaradja. Will anchor tow there and take you to Surabaya.* Rang signalled: *Cannot. No pressure left. Have to drop anchor, chief engineer dying. Greetings.*

That was the last signal. After that he didn't answer any more. Jan attached the *Moira* to his own hawser and steamed towards the *Kali Mas*, approaching her luff. The ship looked quite normal. Only there was no one to be seen on deck. On the roof of the engine room three bodies were lying side by side, as if asleep. On the foc'sle Rang was struggling with the anchor-winch. When Jan hailed him with his megaphone Rang waved back and pointed at his throat, indicating that he was unable to speak. He walked with difficulty, supporting himself on the rail of the winch. But he managed, by crawling, to knock out the peg, and when the anchor dropped with a violent rattling of the chain, he fell prostrate in a cloud of rust.

It was a grim experience to watch a man dying at fifty yards distance, and not be able to do a thing. All the men on the *Fury* stood watching, horror-struck. Rang pulled himself up until he was almost standing upright; then he made a weak gesture, as if to say, "Go away, go away! What business is this of yours?" Then he started walking away as if he were ashamed of himself and wanted to behave as if there was nothing the matter. But he was too weak now. He stood with his legs giving way under him, on that bare foc'sle where there was nowhere to hide. He sat down on the winch with his back to them, and tried to make that gesture of dismissal once again, but failed. It looked as if he was trying to scratch his head and found his arm too heavy. He remained like that, sitting quite still, for a long time. Then he took off his jacket with slow, weak movements and tried to pull it over his head, like an ostrich. But when he had almost succeeded he suddenly stiffened; the jacket dropped on to the deck, and a faint gasping sound broke the silence, the sound of a man struggling for breath. A moment later his body toppled over, with the sound of boots scraping iron, and he was dead.

A believer in a Higher Justice would say Rang had got his deserts. However that may be, it was Jan who benefited from Rang's death. Now all the salvage money belonged to him, and with that sum behind him he could successfully challenge Kwel on the open sea.

But when the crew of the *Fury* brought their tow into the harbour of Surabaya, they heard that a world war had broken out while they were struggling with the *Moira* in the jungle. That meant that the *Fury* would have to stay in the Far East until the war was over and the great battle with Kwel would be postponed indefinitely.

In the end the *Moira* was handed over to the agents and Jan put the salvage money in the bank, gave the *Fury* a new coat of paint, and bought himself a pipe and a musical box with a stuffed parrot on it. The musical box, however, didn't last long. The parrot began to moult and the works disintegrated somewhere off the coast of Dirk Hartog Island while the *Fury* was towing a cable-ship to Melbourne. It remained on the top of the wash-stand cupboard in the Captain's cabin until it was slung overboard at last, half-way to Antofagasta.

The *Fury* sailed on without it, a lonely buccaneer of the Pacific Ocean.

CHAPTER NINETEEN

IN THE summer of 1919 the tugboat business was enjoying the biggest boom in its history. Hundreds of thousands of tons of shipping had been sunk during the war and on all the beaches and reefs of the seven seas the damaged hulls of ships were waiting to be salvaged. Projects for new harbours which had been shelved for the duration were now put into effect, and the busy little boats of the Dutch tug-boat companies were scattered all over the globe, towing pontoons, sluice-gates and dredgers to various destinations.

In the summer of this year Kwel and Van Munster's International Tugboat Company tried by every means at their disposal to force the privately owned companies of Louw, Herder, Kiers and Meulemans into a merger. Nobody understood why. Business was booming; there was more than enough work for every ship—why then this pressure for a merger?

It was a mystery to everyone—even to Connie Stuwe, who was the intimate friend of Nol Kwel, the director's son. She was a person who was usually in the know, for she owed her position as shipping-correspondent for the *New Rotterdam Courier* entirely to Nol and in return she handed over to the Company any useful information she picked up. But even she, with all her information, hadn't the answer to this particular riddle.

The answer lay hidden behind the doors of Father Kwel's private office, and the mere fact of its being hidden there made her all the more anxious to possess it. At last she asked Nol outright. "You know darling, father doesn't approve of my discussing business matters outside his office," the young man answered rather nervously. Obviously the need for discretion had been strongly impressed upon him. But he was a weak young man and a little judicious flattery would open him up as easily as heat applied to an oyster.

"Your father is perfectly right," Connie agreed. "One can't be too careful in business matters. But you're a man of the world and you know the sort of people you can safely trust."

She gave him a look that clearly indicated that she was one of the people he could safely trust. And by way of reassurance she added with a smile, "After all, Nol, thanks to you, I'm practically one of the firm."

"I know," he said, flattered by her look. "Well, I'll tell you in confidence, that the reason for that merger is Jan Wandelaar." She raised her eyebrows. "Who is he?" she asked.

"Jan Wandelaar is a sea captain," Nol informed her. "He's the captain of a tugboat, and that's the reason why father wants to get the whole business under his thumb before this fellow comes home."

"I see," she said in a tone of bewilderment. "But why should this mysterious Captain Wandelaar worry your father?"

Nol hesitated a moment, as if he felt his father's reproving eye upon him. "I'll tell you on one condition," he said at last; "that you won't tell anybody, not a soul."

"Whom could I tell?" she asked innocently. "Who would be interested?"

"His friends," Nol said. "And practically every seaman sailing on a tugboat nowadays is his friend. He is the most dangerous man father and I have ever had to deal with—he'll stop at nothing, the scoundrel. But one's got to grant him this: he's about the best sailor in the business. Father and I tried to squeeze him out just before the outbreak of the war—he had just got a tug of his own then, and we collared every job that was going, even at a loss, in order to force him into the little trap we'd laid."

"Trap?" asked Connie with a sudden flicker of interest.

"We wanted to squeeze him so hard," Nol said, "that he'd be forced to take any job that was offered, perhaps some risky job that would finish him for good."

"What a charming idea," Connie remarked, icily. "And did he fall into your beautiful little trap?"

"He snapped up a risky job all right," Nol said sourly.

"And he managed it, I suppose."

"Yes," he admitted. "Instead of breaking him, it made him. He landed up in the Far East and towed anything he could lay hands on during the war, and he got himself a little nest-egg of capital. We felt certain he'd come back sooner or later, and by Jove, we were right. We hear on good authority that he's due back tomorrow."

"And now Kwel and Van Munster's International Tugboat Company is afraid that Captain Wandelaar with his one tugboat will torpedo their precious monopoly—is that it?" Connie asked mockingly.

"Oh, we're not really afraid of that," Nol said; "But he's a tough nut to crack all the same. He's not just another owner, trying to make money. The fact is, money doesn't interest him, and his sole aim in life is to get the whip hand of us. That's why he's so dangerous. Now he's started buying up our best men. His first move was to get hold of a Russian, the Commodore of our fleet, who had been sailing the *Jan van Gent* for over fifteen years. Some time ago this Russian suddenly asked father if he was willing to sell the *Jan* to him, and when father very naturally refused, the fellow handed in his resignation. Almost at the same time, Maartens, another of our best captains, handed in his resignation, and after that resignations poured in—engineers, cooks, bo'suns, deckhands. Father made inquiries and found out that all the men had been engaged by Wandelaar—the complete crews for two ocean-going tugs. But he also discovered that nobody had sold Wandelaar any tugs. That put the idea of a merger into father's head: if Mr. Wandelaar wants to buy tugboats to put his crews in he'll have to buy them from us. Now are you satisfied?"

As far as the bare facts were concerned, she was, but Nol had told her so little about Captain Wandelaar, the person, that she couldn't resist looking through the newspaper files in the *Courier* office to find out more. She had quite an exciting morning pulling out old files and hunting him down in the pages of the newspapers.

Captain Wandelaar salvages the wreck of the P. & O. steamer Moira, burnt out on the reefs of the Frederik Hendrik Island; Dutch tugboat Fury meets the German raider Mowe in the Pacific Ocean; Captain Wandelaar picks up survivors of the Eugenia in Polynesia; Crew of the tugboat Fury cheered in Shanghai as they tow in the training ship Iquique, presumed lost.

It was a veritable Odyssey, but apparently no picture of the hero had ever been published. All she could track down after hours of careful searching was a very old photograph, printed in 1910 and captioned: *The Dutch sailors who equalled Columbus in daring, commanded by Captain Jan Wandelaar (indicated by arrow) in front of the light-ship Cape Breton in the harbour of Esbjerg.* The arrow pointed to a blurred face under a peaked cap, impossible to distinguish. So what a pity that it was still a mystery; she still did not know what he looked like. It was no secret, however, that the captain was a widower, with two children in Helder.

When your special correspondent went to see the Captain at home in Helder his silver-haired old mother-in-law opened the door and whispered: "Don't disturb him, sir—his wife has died, and he's only just heard the sad news." It was a moment of tense tragedy. Your correspondent stood there, in that humble doorway, sharing the sorrow that had befallen this happy home. . . .

To satisfy her curiosity she even went along to the Poland Hotel where she knew the Captain was staying and asked if she could interview him on behalf of the *New Rotterdam Courier.* When the page-boy whom she sent upstairs to get hold of him came back with the message that the Captain wouldn't see any visitors, not even journalists, it meant five guilders down the drain. All she could do was to take up a strategic position near the revolving door and wait until he came down.

After hanging about there for nearly an hour she saw a girl enter the hall and heard her ask for Captain Wandelaar. She was a young, pretty girl with high cheekbones and a curious hat on top of an untidy bun of fair hair. She looked as if she was wearing her Sunday-best clothes, and her shoes squeaked horribly. In reply to her question the hall-porter said: "Sorry madam, Captain Wandelaar is not seeing anybody."

She looked at him with very blue eyes and said: "Oh—I didn't know that. Good afternoon." And she disappeared through the revolving door.

Connie decided it would be rather fun to play the spy, and she hurried out after the girl. She found her standing on the pavement in a state of indecision. "Did you want to see Captain Wandelaar my dear?"

The girl looked her up and down with interest and said:

"Yes." Connie said: "That's a pity—I am waiting for him as well. We have arranged to meet. Perhaps I can give him a message."

The girl's blue eyes remained fixed on her with disconcerting steadiness. Then without a word the girl marched off, shoes squeaking irrepressibly as she went. Suddenly a voice bellowed from overhead: "Hi, Rikki." The voice belonged to a man leaning out of one of the hotel windows, a man in shirt-sleeves and an open collar, who was waving a fiery red tie like a signal-flag.

The girl stopped and looked up. The man shouted: "Wait, I'm coming down" and disappeared. A few moments later he came dashing out of the hotel and joined the girl who was waiting for him in the street. The two of them then went off arm-in-arm.

At this point Connie was half inclined to call off the chase; but her feminine curiosity got the better of her. She decided instead to follow at a discreet distance. Across the canal opposite the Central Station was a little bar that looked out on to the flat, featureless back of a bronze bust erected there in memory of Prince Frederic. It was to this bar that Captain Jan and the girl directed their steps after hesitating on the pavement for a while, trying to make up their minds. The bar consisted of a long, narrow room partitioned off into a series of little boxes, each containing a bench and table. Connie managed to slip into a box adjoining the one where the Captain and the girl were seated. She heard the Captain say: "I nearly fell out of the window in surprise when I spotted you in the street. Whatever were you doing there?"

"I'd just been with father to a meeting," said the girl.

"Meeting?"

"Yes, a meeting of tugboat owners that had been called at Kwel's request."

He laughed. "Old Kwel still doesn't let the grass grow under his feet, does he? He wants to put the lot of them in chains, I presume?"

"Yes," she said. "He has offered father, Louw, Herder and Meulemans a merger. They have to hand in their decision tomorrow."

"That's cheek," he said. "A damnable piece of cheek."

Then there was silence for a moment. Then he said: "How did you know I was staying at the Poland?"

"'Bout told me."

"Did he know? Have you been on board?"

"This morning. She looks all right. But you've got her a nasty dent on the starboard bow, haven't you?"

"Yes," he admitted. "I got that at Corunna." There was silence again. The girl said: "Why are you looking at me like that?"

"I was just thinking," he said.

"Thinking of what?"

"Oh, various things. About our letters."

"Well—?"

"It suddenly struck me that mine weren't letters at all. Just pages from a diary forwarded to you from various places. I only wrote them for my own satisfaction, with no idea of anyone else reading them."

"Don't be silly," she said. "If you'd only written them for your own satisfaction you wouldn't have sent them. You wanted an answer, didn't you?"

"Yes," he said. "I wanted an answer. But somehow . . ."

"Well?"

"Somehow I never felt that you were really the person who answered them."

"You wrote those letters to a girl who only existed in your imagination, and now I turn up and you're disappointed. Is that it?"

"Don't be a fool," he said. "Of course not."

"Well, what is it, then? Didn't you visualize me sometimes when you wrote?"

"No," he said. "I didn't. At least I don't think I did. I wrote those letters to . . . to . . . well, I don't know how this sounds to you—but I wrote them to someone who doesn't exist. That's the nearest I can get to it. Can you understand?"

"Yes, I think I can," she said. "You mean you wrote them to someone who's dead, to your wife, in fact."

"I suppose so," he answered. "I know it's wrong to think too much about the dead. Life has to go on, and all that; and yet I just can't help it. I still feel in a way that I belong to her. God knows, a day may come when I'll say 'Let's get married and have done with it.' For the time being, however, leave

292

me alone with the job I came home for. Let me deal with Kwel and finish him off if I can. Let me write to you, talk to you, if you like; let's be friends, the best friends in the world, but don't expect me to marry you, for I can't. You have been wonderful all these years, and if ever I marry again it would be you every time. But just now, what I need is to have things go on as they were: you at home and I at sea, and an exercise book to write to you in and a letter from you waiting for me in every port."

"My God," she said. "You certainly make me grow up."

"I'm sorry," he said. "Let's be friends. It's my fault, I know, but that's how it is."

"You make me grow up so fast that it hurts," she said. "But I suppose I'll have to take it or leave it. Let's go. There's no point in talking now."

"No," he said. "Don't go away now. Let's thrash this out, it's important."

"I'd rather not," she said. "I've had enough of this. I don't think I can stand much more of it or I'll do something desperate."

A few moments later they got up and went out. This time Connie didn't attempt to follow them. She felt suddenly ashamed of having played the eavesdropper, of having pried into the lives of these two people. And for some reason she couldn't help feeling overwhelming contempt for the House of Kwel.

CHAPTER TWENTY

WANDELAAR'S mysterious behaviour made the Kwels apprehensive, especially when they heard that two new tugboats ordered by him had been launched in Norway. No details of the ships were disclosed, but it was said on good authority that the design of the vessels would revolutionize the industry. Kwel and Van Munster had used this phrase too often themselves, in connexion with newly built tugs, not to take it with a grain of salt; but the fact that Jan Wandelaar had bought new ships convinced them that he was about to launch a battle for supremacy. And his chances would not be bad, for there was so much business about that the old tactics of squeezing him out by undercutting wouldn't work. All they could hope to do now was to grab as many of the plums as possible, but in order to do that they would have to bring under their control every ship they could lay hands on. They put pressure on the other tug owners, and on 23 July, 1919, the merger was announced. On 26 July the tugboat *Fury* sailed from Ijmuiden for an unknown destination. On board were Captain Maartens and Captain Siemonov, accompanied by their crews.

On 27 July Nol Kwel went to see Mr. Louw, and they had a heated discussion behind locked doors. Next day Mr. Louw declared in an interview with the *New Rotterdam Courier* that he wouldn't enter into a merger with anybody if it was against the interests of his company and his employees.

On 30 July Mr. Beumers van Haaften, director of the Dutch Harbourworks Company, was asked outright by young Kwel if he intended to grant Wandelaar an option on any jobs the Company had to offer. Mr. Beumers van Haaften replied that he did not consider giving anybody an option, no matter who, if it was not in the interest of his Company and its shareholders. Kwel and Van Munster were so anxious to find out what Jan had up his sleeve that Nol Kwel asked Connie Stuwe if she would, in her capacity as shipping correspondent, put a few exploratory questions to Miss Kiers. At first Connie refused, but in the end her own curiosity and a present from Nol did the trick. So she went along to an address on the waterfront where she was told Miss Kiers was living.

Young Kwel had warned her not to make her questions too direct. He had suggested that she should go under the pretext of collecting material for an article on the future of the tugboat business. But to show her contempt for young Kwel and his stratagems, she came to the point at once.

"I've come to find out what your—what Captain Wandelaar's plans are," she said.

"That's easy," Miss Kiers answered. "He plans to run his company as if Kwel and Van Munster didn't exist." And when she was asked what she meant by that she gave a frank explanation. Nowadays, she said, clients didn't bother about prices; all they worried about was getting their stuff towed to its destination safely and quickly. And because speed and safety were now the main consideration Mr. Kwel with his fleet of sixty-eight tugs was in a worse position than Captain Wandelaar with his three, for his vessels were brand-new, and he had the lowest accident record in the business, whereas Mr. Kwel's sixty-eight were old and he had a record of one tow in ten a total loss, three in ten delayed or damaged, and only two in ten arriving on time and in good condition. So it was obvious that Captain Wandelaar would have the pick of the market and at his own prices, and if it interested Miss Stuwe, she might as well know that Captain Wandelaar would be charging twice Kwel's price, on principle. "Is that the information you wanted? Very well, then, good day."

When, a fortnight later, Jan Wandelaar's two brand-new tugs, the *Captain Van der Gast* and the *Chief Engineer Bevers,* came steaming into the harbour of Ijmuiden, they caused a sensation. All day long people stood gaping at the ships moored side by side at the quay. And it wasn't only the ships that caused a sensation; the names painted on their sides were a kind of challenge to the Kwel dynasty, commemorating as they did two brave men who had died in Kwel's service. The quayside bars buzzed with the news and the press gave the new fleet a lot of publicity. It was soon common knowledge that the well-known tugboat owner Jan Wandelaar had acquired a small fleet of tugs of the most modern design, manned by crews who were experts in the business. It wasn't long before important trade inquiries began to come in.

The Spanish Government had ordered from America a salvage-vessel for submarines, and they were so proud of the new toy that they didn't want to run any risks in getting it across the Atlantic. They were therefore anxious to entrust the towing of it to Captain Wandelaar. The Russians wanted to charter him for five years to force the northern passage round the continent. The Dutch Harbourworks Company were disappointed at not receiving a tender from Captain Wandelaar for the transport of a tin-dredger to Billiton. Mr. Beumers sent a polite little note saying that this must surely be an oversight on the part of Captain Wandelaar, and that he'd keep his list open a week longer to enable the Captain to tender at his convenience.

And during these eventful weeks the Captain sat gloomily immured in a single room at the Poland Hotel in Amsterdam, and was not at home to anybody, not even Miss Kiers, who called daily. He sat in his room, smoking and reading old letters, tattered log-books and a volume called *The Miracles of the Ocean*. For three weeks he sat there and brooded, inaccessible to everybody—even to his Captains. He gave the hall-porter strict orders to show no one up to his room. "Nobody, not a soul, do you hear?" he gruffly insisted. "The only person I'll see is the gentleman whose name I gave you on a piece of paper. If he turns up, let him in, even if it is past midnight."

The name he wrote down for the hall porter was MR. BEUMERS VAN HAAFTEN. But this privileged gentleman didn't arrive. The hall-porter had to consult the little piece of paper occasionally, when a Mr. Bakkers or a Mr. van Manen or a Mr. Heuvers asked to see Captain Wandelaar—but no Mr. Beumers van Haaften. Why did the Captain want Mr. Beumers van Haaften so urgently, and no one else?

Because, after that polite little note inquiring why Captain Wandelaar hadn't tendered for the tin-dredger to Billiton, another note arrived in an envelope marked "Private and Confidential." *Dear W, the note ran, If you tender for that dredger I'll be very disappointed. Bide your time until you get a really first-rate job that will put your name on top for good. I am sorry that I myself have no such job to offer but I know there is one coming. The British Navy will soon have a thirty-thousand-ton dry-dock ready for towing from the Clyde to the Falklands, and although it sounds to me like a four boat job I think it may be just the thing you need. My advice is: start estimating now; put your price as high as you can within reason, and tender AS LATE AS POSSIBLE. I am no prophet, but I feel sure that you will get the job. Don't give yourself a headache trying to puzzle out why I give you this piece of advice which probably seems contrary to the interests of my Company. It isn't. Yours cordially, B. van H.*

Jan answered on a picture of the Central Station, Amsterdam: *Dear Mr. B. van H., thank you for your communication. I've decided to take your advice, but should like to know more. I wonder if you would be kind enough to come and see me at the Poland Hotel, or drop me a line saying where I can meet you. I am not giving myself a headache, I've given myself enough already. Yours gratefully, W.*

But Mr. Beumers van Haaften didn't come to the hotel, nor did he write suggesting another meeting place. Confidence was put to a severe test during those endless weeks of silence. Not a word from Mr. B. Not a word from the British Naval authorities. It took Jan two days to estimate the cost of towing that dry-dock. After that he sat and brooded, thinking about Rikki. And he came to the conclusion that he was really incapable of loving her, was incapable of loving any woman. Then afterwards he would tell himself that his indifference towards women in general merely sprang from the fact that he didn't love this particular one because he thought her too domineering and possessive, and was afraid he'd be as helpless in her hands as a trussed chicken. It was his liberty he wanted. Yet he wasn't sure. All he knew was that the idea of feminine love and domestic cosiness repelled him. That kind of life would make him as miserable as sin. He had been born a sailor and would die a sailor, like Siemonov or Maartens or Van der Gast. He hated the idea of being absorbed in a domestic routine, of spending his evenings dozing in an arm-chair by the fire. No, he wouldn't resign himself to that. The evenings he pictured were of a different sort. He saw himself standing on the bridge with his feet firmly planted on the swaying deck, while the dim shape of the look-out reported: "All's well, Skipper; lights burning brightly."

All he needed to be happy—as happy as any man with his tendency to brooding could be—was a woman ashore, who would act as a prompt and sympathetic correspondent. But he knew now that Rikki would never consent to be merely that. She would try to make him stay at home with her and forsake the sea, and she'd go on trying until she found out at last that he never would. Then she'd drop him, and, after a short period of utter misery, find someone else, someone younger and less complicated. Alone in his room at the

Poland Hotel, waiting for news he sometimes despaired of getting, he pondered these things till they seemed as meaningless as a dream.

On 13 October, 1919, the British Admiralty invited tenders for the transport of a dry-dock of thirty thousand tons, from the Clyde to Port Stanley, Falkland Islands, a voyage of seven and a half thousand miles, the longest distance a dock of this kind had ever been towed. And the dock itself was the biggest ever to be transported overseas in a single piece.

The press was all agog; articles appeared for and against the risky enterprise. Kwel and Van Munster's International Tugboat Company, an old friend of the British Navy, tendered at a low price—a suspiciously low one. The experts at the Admiralty shook their heads. How could a job of this kind be done for so little? And why was there no competition?

The competition came all right. It was late, almost too late. When the Kwels got to know through their agents in London the price at which Jan Wandelaar and Co. had tendered, they were cock-a-hoop. His price was so much higher than theirs that they never doubted they would get the job.

On 25 October the British Admiralty awarded the contract to Jan Wandelaar and Co. As soon as the Kwels had recovered from the first shock of the announcement they began a whispering campaign which hinted at shady practices at the Admiralty, at departmental corruption and bribes. But the battle was already lost. Kwel did himself more harm than good by these insinuations. When, in answer to a question from the opposition, an imperturbable First Lord of the Admiralty explained why the contract had been awarded to the Wandelaar Company, despite the difference in price, Kwel's weapons were turned against himself. For the First Lord compared the records of the two competing companies, and wound up by saying that His Majesty's Government would not have been justified in trusting this important and hazardous operation to a company that had lately seen its insurance premium doubled owing to an alarming increase in losses. And the company in question must have been aware of the decline of its reputation, otherwise—the First Lord declared roundly—it would not have tendered at a price well below the actual cost. Captain Wandelaar's price was, in the view of naval experts, a high one, but not unreasonably so; Kwel and Van Munster's price on the other hand was unreasonably, if not suspiciously, low.

"Unreasonably low" was a phrase that got a good deal of publicity; one school of thought took it as an example of the postwar contempt for sound economic principles, another school of thought hailed it as marking the beginning of a new era in which quality would be the prime consideration, not price. This view was shared by Mr. Beumers van Haaften, director of the Dutch Harbourworks Company, who referred to the phrase in his speech to the shareholders at their yearly meeting. "The perfect expression," he called it, "of the truth that cheapness never pays, and that competition inevitably leads to economic disaster."

Mr. Beumer's speech was another blow to Kwel and Van Munster; for it clearly implied that price considerations did not weigh with him. In fact, he made it clear in what he subsequently said, that, after their towing contract had expired, the Dutch Harbourworks Company would not renew the option they had granted to Kwel. And whoever had that option ruled the tugboat business.

Although Kwel and Van Munster's International Tugboat Company had suffered a resounding defeat, it was by no means beaten yet. It had ruled the seas for over twenty years, and faced with this crisis in its affairs it did everything in its power to win back its old supremacy. Connie Stuwe hardly caught a glimpse of young Nol during the weeks prior to Wandelaar's sailing date. He sat behind his desk from morning till night, carrying out his father's orders. He was in constant communication with foreign countries, and received many callers, sometimes at strangely late hours. On occasions he worked twenty hours out of the twenty-four. Connie, in fact, found him quite a changed man—hard, efficient and completely unromantic.

When at last he took her out to dinner one night, he refused to discuss anything to do with business or Wandelaar, and merely dropped the remark: "Our only hope is that something will go wrong with that transport."

It sounded innocent enough, the kind of remark a tired

and harassed man might make. But Connie, however, caught the implications. "You aren't planning to make it go wrong, by any chance?" she asked, casually.

He looked at her in pained surprise. If he had looked a little less pained she might have dismissed the idea from her mind. "Don't talk nonsense," he said. "The Company's name stands too high for that kind of thing."

"Of course it does," she said. "Only the thought just struck me." She spoke with a note of gay unconcern that belied her real feelings.

"My advice is, don't let such absurd ideas enter your pretty head," he said. "And remember I have a personal stake in the high reputation of our Company."

"I don't doubt for a moment you'll be able to keep the Company's name clear," she said, laughing. "It might be awkward if you couldn't."

Nol said nothing, but just sat smiling his foxy smile and fingering his wine glass while he waited for his *omelette paysanne*.

"How do you think you'll go about it?" she asked, as off-handedly as she could.

He went on smiling, but didn't even look at her when he answered very quietly: "Don't be a fool."

"It seems to me an impossible thing to do," she went on, feigning a tone of secret admiration. "The British Navy, I imagine, isn't a thing one can easily hoodwink."

He looked at her with an expression of displeasure. "I took you out because I was tired," he said. "I came here to amuse myself. If you can't stop talking this nonsense I shall have to leave."

"Don't be ridiculous," she said. "Anyone would think you didn't trust me."

Nol was silent again, and his eyes had a hard, unpleasant glint. Ignoring the warning, Connie repeated her question. "Tell me, how do you propose to go about it?" she asked.

A sudden wave of anger swept over him. "Excuse me," he said, and got up. She was so taken aback she didn't move. She just sat gaping at him, wondering if it was mere bravado. She saw him pause at the door and beckon the waiter. He pointed to their table, thrust some money into the waiter's hand with a keep-the-change gesture, and disappeared.

She remained staring after him for some moments. Then she put her cape round her shoulders and went out. While she was waiting for the hall-porter to call her a cab she caught sight of herself in a mirror near the door. The figure that stared back at her from the gilded frame was tall and elegantly weary. No one would have guessed that the bored, pretty face hid a secret that concerned the fate of eighty men and the destruction of a thirty-thousand-ton dry-dock somewhere in the Atlantic. She told herself that she was jumping to conclusions, that she was letting her imagination run away with her. The Kwels might be scoundrels, but they weren't madmen. To blow up a dock belonging to the British Royal Navy, merely to oust a trade rival, was something no firm in its senses would attempt. Yet it might happen simply because there was so little chance of anyone discovering the facts. The actual sabotage would be the work of experts and the secret would be shared by only a few tried and trusted friends. The rush of conflicting thoughts left Connie dazed and bewildered.

The cab was taking her along the Prince's Canal now, though she couldn't remember having given the man her address. A sightseeing boat, with coloured lanterns wobbling in the wind and three people huddled in the bows, made its way through the black, gleaming water, its wash rocking the dark coal barges moored along the quay. The sight of it seemed somehow to emphasize the need for making a decision. If she didn't act, if she just let this thing happen she'd have it on her conscience all her life. Yet what could she do? She had no facts to go on; only a vague suspicion, a feeling somewhere at the back of her mind. When she arrived home she began a letter: *Dear Captain W.*, but got no further. In the end she took a couple of sleeping-tablets and went to bed, still undecided.

Next morning she was convinced she'd seen things in too lurid a light. The Kwels would certainly do all they could to delay the dock. They'd probably instruct their agents abroad to make things as difficult as possible for Wandelaar. But they wouldn't be so utterly crazy as to start any real sabotage. That would be risking their own necks.

Yet as the time went by the fear that Kwels would attempt something more desperate began to grow on her again. After all, there was so much at stake. If that dock got to the Falkland Islands on time and without damage the firm of Kwel and Van Munster would be virtually finished. And rumour had it that in the past Kwel's record was not exactly irreproachable. Yet her fears and the prompting of her conscience were not sufficient to inspire that letter. She still didn't get any further than *Dear Captain W*. It wasn't that she didn't know how to word it, but rather that she was reluctant to get herself mixed up in the affair. What she needed was just something to help her make up her mind, something to break the spell of that reluctance. And when it turned up that something proved to be a trivial incident that ninety-nine times out of a hundred would have gone unnoticed.

Jan Wandelaar had invited journalists to a press conference at the British Consulate. The Consul made a few introductory remarks, speaking with a strong English accent. After that Jan Wandelaar began describing his plans for towing the giant dry-dock. The three tugboats he intended to use were the *Captain van der Gast*, the *Chief Engineer Bevers* and the *Fury*. The distance was seven thousand, four hundred and fifty miles; but the voyage wouldn't be interrupted for bunkering; instead the tugboats would cast off in turn and slip into various ports along the route to bunker separately. By this method, he reckoned, he could do the voyage in eighty days.

Up till then Connie hadn't been particularly interested. She had taken this opportunity of scrutinizing the Captain closely and she wasn't much impressed. Stolid, clumsy, self-conscious, and at the same time as immovable as a rock—a typically Dutch mixture: that was how she summed him up. He was straightforward and sincere, of course, but those qualities in themselves didn't inspire her to get mixed up in his affairs. There he was, immovable and stolid; let him fend for himself—that was how she felt.

While he was talking he absent-mindedly took a biscuit from a plate and dipped it in his tea. For some reason that homely gesture did the trick. Connie suddenly forgot the stolid, clumsy Captain and saw only a rather simple, childlike man. At that moment she decided she would have to write that letter after all.

When she got home she took pen and paper, and made another start. This time, however, she addressed the letter to Miss Kiers. *Dear Miss Kiers* (she wrote), *whatever you do don't let him sail. I'm sure the Kwels are planning to sabotage that dock; though I don't know how. Of course it's none of my business, but I feel I must write and warn you of the danger before it's too late. Yours, C. S.*

Early next morning, before Connie was fully dressed, there was a ring at the door-bell. It was the girl. "I've come about that letter," she said.

"Letter?" Connie echoed, half inclined to deny that she had written it.

"The letter you sent me yesterday. I want to find out how much you really know."

"Let's go into the kitchen and make some coffee," Connie said, wanting a chance to collect her thoughts.

They went into the kitchen and the girl filled the kettle while Connie lit the gas. In this domestic setting, Connie felt, they ought to be discussing clothes and love affairs, not the chances of sabotage in a thirty-thousand-ton dry-dock.

"I don't know anything for certain," Connie said. "But I have an instinctive feeling that they're out to break that transport. In fact I'd stake my life on it."

"I have that feeling too," the girl admitted gloomily. "The question is, how will they go about it?"

"God knows," Connie answered with a shrug. "I've thought of all possibilities, and by the look of it the Kwels have a pretty wide choice." She began to shiver a little. "You watch the kettle while I get dressed," she told the girl. "I shan't be a moment."

But the girl didn't stay and watch the kettle. She followed Connie into the bathroom and stood leaning against the door in her skimpy raincoat. They exchanged a few casual glances and remarks while Connie brushed her teeth and combed her hair. Then they went back to the kitchen and drank their coffee seated in armchairs by the stove. As they sat there Connie enumerated all the possibilities of sabotage that had occurred to her—a formidable list, that ranged from mutiny on the high seas to the planting of explosives. The girl stared at her with those worried blue eyes, like a child listening to a ghost story, terrified, yet unable to resist hearing the end. She looked pale and thin and unhappy, and love was absent from her eyes. When Connie had finished relating the things that Kwel might do, there was silence between them.

"Why did you write that letter?" the girl asked at last, still staring hard.

"Made me feel better, I suppose."

"Why to me? Why not to the police or to him?"

"I don't know. Probably because I thought you'd understand the situation better."

"I see," said the girl in a rather hopeless tone.

"If I had anything to go on apart from just my personal feelings it might have been easier, and then we could inform the police or the naval authorities. Remember, I don't know anything for certain. I may be completely wrong, after all."

"No," the girl said, grimly, "you aren't wrong. I knew it from the beginning. For over a week I've been trying to get in touch with Beumers. I wanted to talk to him, to warn him, but. . . ." She broke off as if afraid of saying too much.

"Where is the Captain now?" Connie asked.

"In Helder. Seeing his children before he sails. I wish I could keep him back," the girl added, "but I can't."

"It might be worth trying," Connie suggested.

The girl shook her head. Then, after a pause, she asked: "Are you sure you can't find out?"

"Quite sure," Connie said. "At least not from young Kwel. He trusts me about as much as I trust him. If your Jan Wandelaar takes action now, young Kwel will know that I've let the cat out of the bag. He suspected me the moment I started angling for details."

The girl frowned and bit her lip. "There's only one thing to do," she said, speaking in an undertone, as if she were thinking aloud.

"And what's that?" Connie asked.

The girl looked at her searchingly for a moment.

"That's my affair," she answered, with a wan attempt at a smile.

CHAPTER TWENTY-ONE

NEVER before had Jan longed so much for the moment of sailing. He counted the days, as he did when he was in prison. Only five days more, and the last great battle with Kwel would be on. In the meantime he had to decide how best to ensure the safety of the transport.

He had examined the problem from every angle. The safest thing, of course, would be to hand all arrangements over to the Navy who would see to it that Kwel got no chance of doing any mischief. They would make the convoy's fuel and victuals their responsibility throughout the trip. They would keep an eye on the wireless operators and intercept all messages transmitted and received, and they might even add a destroyer to the convoy for that purpose. And they would post anti-sabotage officers on the dock who would comb every inch of it before sailing. The dock would arrive safely and on time but Holland's reputation in the towing business would suffer. What was more, Kwel might get cautious and never play into his hands like this again. If he could only get proof of Kwel's intentions; if he could catch the saboteurs red-handed, and force them to sign confessions; if he could pin down the coal-merchants and the ship-chandlers and force them to disclose their secret instructions, he would have Kwel in the palm of his hand. This was the second time Kwel had made the same mistake in tactics, the mistake of challenging him as a sailor rather than as a business man. It was too good a chance to be missed.

He thought of calling his crews together for a meeting the day before they sailed, but didn't. If there were agents among the deck-hands, which was more than likely, they would warn Kwel that his plans had been discovered, and the chance of catching him in the act would be lost. Jan decided instead that the best moment for the meeting would be when the dock was anchored in the Clyde, waiting for high tide. There would be no chance then of anyone slipping ashore again. As a precaution against any hold-up in food supplies he packed the ships' store-rooms with cases of emergency provisions. He also sent cables to the various coaling stations on the route, asking for telegraphic confirmation that they would supply him with grade "A" coal only, and he had their replies registered and legalised by the British Consul. He added to the ship's articles, to be signed by each member of the crew, a clause which stated: "It is agreed that any act of sabotage or wilful damage will be considered as mutiny." This gave him the legal right to take away their lifeboats—a fact he would make known when he called that meeting on the Clyde. He insisted that his tugboat Captains and their Mates should go through a quick course of wireless telegraphy at the local nautical college before they sailed, just as a precaution.

With so much to do, it seemed a miracle that they actually sailed on time. However, in the grey light of dawn on the appointed day three small ships nosed their way down the North Sea Canal. The three of them passed through the locks together, fretting at their moorings in the turbulent water, like stabled horses eager to be free. When eventually they swung out into the open sea and rode the choppy water with triumphant ease, the pilot exclaimed: "By God, you've got some good ships here, Cap'n." Then at last the moment came for dropping the pilot, and the tugboats roared farewell to him with blasts on their hooters. In a matter of seconds the pilot's boat was a dancing speck in the distance, carried quickly shorewards by the strong wind that lent a double power to the spidery little oars. With the dropping of the pilot the link with the shore had gone. To Jan it was a relief to watch the lighthouse recede in the distance and to feel once more the spray against his face and the rocking motion of the swell. The doubts, the worries and the heart-ache of the shore were swept away like cobwebs and he lived again in the free world of sky and sea.

Towards the end of the watch, when they seemed to be swinging along on a sea of pure silver, with the spray tossed in the air like clusters of diamonds, Jan was surprised to hear the panting voice of Cook Blekemolen calling in the distance: "Captain . . . Captain." A moment later Blekemolen himself staggered on to the bridge, clinging to the handrail with one podgy hand and pressing the other to his heart. "Captain," he gasped, "there's someone in the pantry. . . ."

"Come on, out with it," Jan snapped. "What's up in the pantry?"

The cook rolled his eyes and paused a moment to get his breath. "A stowaway among the potato sacks," he managed to blurt out at last.

Jan pushed the panting figure of the cook aside and jumped down the steps of the bridge. In response to his call, the bo'sun, Bout, and five deck-hands from the foc'sle came running up.

"Stowaway in the pantry," Jan shouted. "Get him out, but mind how you go. He may be armed."

The bo'sun and a couple of deck-hands lowered themselves into the pantry. "Take him to the chart-room," Jan ordered. "I'll deal with him there." As he turned away he heard the sounds of blows and screams coming from the pantry.

So Kwel had begun making his moves already, had he? Well, better now than later, Jan thought, as he got ink and paper out for the purpose of taking down a signed confession. While he was fumbling in a drawer the door of the chart-room suddenly opened and Bout appeared. "Jesus, Skipper —make 'em stop," Bout shouted. But before he had time to explain a huddled figure was dragged into the room by three panting deck-hands and flung against the wall, where it collapsed on its knees, protecting the back of its head with its hands.

"Got him, Captain," one of the men proudly announced. "Bit me bloody hand, he did, but I got him."

Jan stood motionless, staring at the cowering body. It was Rikki. "Get out," he told the men hoarsely.

They filed out, mumbling to themselves. Bout said: "Let me get some water."

"Clear out," Jan said—"all of you."

"I swear I knew nothing about it," Bout said. "I never thought she would be this mad, to stow away."

"Clear out," Jan repeated. And after a moment's silence he heard the door being shut, reluctantly.

They remained where they were for a moment or two—she cowering on the floor with her hand on the back of her head, he standing motionless, looking down at her. The throb of the engine and the faint rattle of the lamp glass broke the silence. "Get up," Jan said at last.

But she didn't move. She just lay where she was, without uttering a sound.

"Come on," Jan said again. "Get up."

As she still didn't move he took her by the shoulder and pulled her to her feet. She stood swaying a moment, then her knees gave under her and she sank again to the floor, pressing her hands to the back of her head.

"What's the matter," Jan asked, "are you hurt?"

She didn't answer. He sat down beside her and tried to take her hands away from the back of her head; but they wouldn't move. With an effort he managed to release them and found they were wet with blood.

There was no need to call for Bout. When Jan opened the door he found Bout waiting outside. "Get that water," he said. "Quickly." Bout hurried off and Jan knelt down beside Rikki to examine her wound. It was a deep gash that seemed larger than it was on account of the blood oozing through her hair. In a very short time Bout was back bringing a pail of water and some cotton wool. "Get a bandage," Jan said, "and iodine."

"Aye, aye," Bout answered, very nervous and very pale.

She didn't move or utter a sound as Bout bathed the wound, but her face was haggard with pain. Bout muttered and fussed, patting her hands and wincing when she should have winced. "Poor child!" he kept muttering. "Poor child!"

"That'll do," Jan said at last. "Now get along."

"But you can't leave her like that. She'll have to lie down and be kept quiet for a while."

"I know," Jan answered. "Go and clear your cabin out. She'll have to stay there till we get ashore."

"My cabin?" Bout queried.

"You can have mine. I'll sleep here on the couch."

"If that's the way you want it, let me take the couch," Bout said. "I don't mind a bit."

"All right," Jan answered impatiently. "Only clear off."

"God almighty!" Bout exclaimed. "You're a difficult cuss to get on with."

"Sorry," Jan said. "Now leave us alone."

Bout went out, muttering to himself as he closed the door. Rikki sat, propped up against the wall, her face looking grey in contrast to the stark white bandages.

"Why did you do this?" Jan asked when Bout had gone. She didn't answer but sat staring straight in front of her with a tense, pained look.

"You have lived on the sea all your life," Jan went on, "you know its unwritten laws and traditions. Don't tell me you didn't know that this is unforgivable."

She tried to shake her head, but only succeeded in moving it very slightly.

"Then why did you do it? Why?"

She didn't answer and her eyes stared into the distance as if he didn't exist.

"Why, in God's name?" he persisted. "Everything might have worked out all right if you'd only let me play a lone hand."

"Yes," she answered vaguely. She was on the point of fainting, but he still persisted with his question. "Then why did you do it?" he asked again.

"Because you need me," she answered simply.

He couldn't say anything to that. All he could do was to look at her and shake his head and sigh. On the deck overhead slow steps could be heard pacing up and down. Flip must have taken over the watch.

"A pity," Jan said at last. "Well, it can't be helped."

He went to the corner cupboard and poured out a drink. The noise of the lock being turned and the squeak of the cork sounded strangely loud in the heavy silence.

"Here," he said, "take this."

But she wouldn't drink it. "Don't worry," she managed to say. "Everything will be all right. . . ." Then her voice tailed off, and she lost consciousness. Jan caught her before she collapsed on the floor. He took his oilskins from the wall and rolled them into a pillow for her head and fetched her a blanket from his cabin. When he opened the door of the chart-room he found Bout waiting outside, reproachful and worried.

"Everything all right?" Bout asked.

"No," Jan answered. "I'm at the end of my tether."

"Never mind about you," Bout said. "How's the girl?"

"She's just fainted," Jan said. "But she'll come round all right. You'd better sit by her till she's fit enough to be moved. I don't want to set eyes on her again before we reach Glasgow."

"Very good," Bout replied. There was an expression of hostility on his face which hadn't appeared before.

When Jan returned to the bridge the sea and weather hadn't changed, and the *Bevers* and the *Van der Gast*, with their red pennants fluttering in the breeze, were following him at precisely the same distance astern. But the sight no longer held any magic for him. He paced up and down the bridge with a face black as thunder for the better part of an hour, while such phrases as "seaman's honour," "age-old tradition" and "abused trust" obsessed his mind and roused him to a state of seething anger. It took him a day before he was sufficiently sobered and exhausted to accept the verdict of his common sense. Never mind if she was right or wrong in doing it. The reason why he'd been tramping up and down this bridge for nearly eight hours was simply because he couldn't bring himself to face unpleasant facts. It might be accepted—honoured tradition—for seamen to make a hell of a mess ashore and then clear out, leaving someone else to bear the consequences. But this time the responsibility couldn't be shelved. Though by degrees he came round to an attitude of common sense, he was still left posing the question in his mind: why did she do it? Hadn't she enough sense to realise that, whatever happened, he would never take her further than Glasgow? To tow a dry-dock the size of a cathedral, liable to blow up any minute, from one side of the globe to the other, was enough of a headache in itself. To carry on a love-affair at the same time would be like trying to knit while one swam. Only a silly, totally irresponsible woman could have hit on such a ridiculous idea. Yet, whatever one said about her, she wasn't that. So the question had to go unanswered.

When the helmsman coming off duty called him for his watch and he opened his eyes in the blue darkness of the starlit night, he was quite himself again. He was once more the Captain of the ship, dressing to take over the watch. He lit his pipe before going out and a swirl of sparks was blown from it as he climbed the stairs to the bridge. The sea was a dim, hazy plain beneath an enormous starlit sky. The swell had died down to a mere surface ripple and there was no spray tossed up by the bows. As he came on to the bridge he saw that Rikki was there already—a dim figure leaning on the rails, gazing into the night. She must have heard him coming but she didn't turn round. He went across to the helmsman and checked the course; then he leaned on the rail beside her.

"Better?"

"Yes, thanks."

They stood like that for a minute, side by side, leaning on the rail and looking out over the dark sea at the blazing brilliance of the sky. Then she said: "Sorry I had to do this. But there was no other way."

"To do what?"

"To come with you on this trip and help you."

"Help me?" he repeated ironically.

"Over the past five years I've helped you quite a bit and you seemed to be grateful enough then."

"We exchanged letters," he admitted.

"I realized all along that this was going to be a crucial trip in more ways than one. It wasn't only the fate of a dry-dock and the lives of eighty men you held in your hand, it was the whole future of the tugboat industry as well."

"I'm quite aware of that," he said.

"You'll have to make up your mind now, before you get to Glasgow, what the future of the business is going to be, or wash your hands of it altogether."

"Why?"

"I have been re-reading your letters lately, the ones that explain your plans for reorganizing the tugboat business. I found that you dropped the subject about two years ago. After that your letters mention only the future of Jan Wandelaar. When I realized that, I decided to come aboard. I'd toyed with the idea before, but now I saw it was the only chance I had of getting you to thrash this question out."

"So?"

"You have been writing and talking a lot about eliminating Kwel and then going back to being just an ordinary seaman. Are you serious about it, or is it only something you wanted me to believe?"

"Of course I mean it," he said.

"Then what do you intend to do? Suppose you eventually get the tugboat business into your hands, how will you deal with it? Leave it at the pawnbroker's and run off to sea again?"

"Reorganize it on a co-operative basis, like this Company, appoint a director I can trust, and. . . ."

"When you say 'on a co-operative basis like this Company', what do you mean? At the moment you're managing your business with about as much co-operative effort all round as Kwel is."

"Nonsense. Every man has, apart from his salary, a share in the profits."

"But did you ever pay that out?"

"Certainly. They decided, of their own free will, to sink it in the new ships. But every man has a share in the profits which he can claim whenever he likes."

"But your profits have been sunk in the ships. Suppose Janus comes to you tomorrow and says, 'I want to get out. Give me my share in the profits', what would you do then?"

"He won't."

"You mean you hope he won't. If you really ran this Company on a co-operative basis your fellow partners would be entitled to a say in all decisions concerning the Company's policy. For one thing, you wouldn't have locked yourself up in the Poland Hotel for three weeks, and then, without consulting a soul, have submitted a tender for the towing of this dock. Your so-called partners had as much say in the matter as the sparrows in the trees."

"If I had left it to them they would have snapped up the first towing job offered them."

"Well, what if they had? The Company is as much theirs as yours."

"If they had taken the first job offered we shouldn't have got as far as this."

"And is that so very far?" she asked contemptuously.

He seemed about to answer, but refrained. They stood looking at the stars for a while, without speaking. Then she said: "Look, Jan, it is very simple. You have got forty deck-hands on that dock, of whom you can trust about ten. The rest, for all you know, may be Kwel's agents. In any case they've got no particular reason for being loyal to you because when it comes to the point you've got nothing more to offer them than Kwel. Now you know the men as well as I do. They won't be intimidated by threats or coercion. You may take their boats away, you can threaten them with the police or with gaol, and they won't care two pins. All you'll do is to put their backs up. If you ask me, you have no hope of preventing any attempt at sabotage unless you convince the men that the success of this trip means that in future the business will be owned by the men who sail the ships, and not by the financiers. If you can win them over you'll nip the threat of sabotage in the bud. If not, you'll lose the dock for sure."

"I might sack these deck-hands and man the dock with English ones."

"Don't be silly. You know as well as I do that it is a specialized job. You might be able to man a coal-barge with a crew of beachcombers, but not this dock. The success of this trip depends on the men even more than on the ships."

"I wouldn't say that."

"Of course it does. And you know it does as well as I do, or you wouldn't have been so careful in choosing them. Every man on that dock is an expert at his job; but a possible saboteur at the same time—and an expert one at that."

"I wonder, you know, if we aren't worrying about this sabotage question too much. After all, what have we to go on? Only a woman's suspicions. And to start turning the whole of the tugboat business upside down on that account seems rather unwise."

"I don't think that's really the point. What worries me is that sooner or later you'll find yourself with the whole tugboat business in your hands and you won't know what to do with it. In the end you'll just turn yourself into another Kwel or, more likely, turn someone else into one. You've only got five days in which to think out your plans. I don't want to make them for you, but I'll argue with you till you see the issues clearly in your own mind. In a sense I've been in the tugboat business ever since I was a child and I know as much about it as you or anybody else. I'd rather risk making you hate me than let you spoil the business and turn it into a new monopoly. If that happened I should never forgive myself."

"I see," he said in a strange, impersonal voice. Then he added after a moment's silence: "You'd better turn in now, you must be tired. I'll think about what you said, and let you know tomorrow."

"All right," she said. "See you in the morning." And she was gone.

He didn't sleep until sunrise. When Flip came to take over the watch he went down to the chart-room, poured himself out a drink, and sat down in the shabby swivel-chair with his feet on the table, thinking. The ship was so steady that she might have been in port. The only thing that moved was a pencil that rolled at intervals across the chart from Portsmouth to Le Havre.

He sat, staring at the pencil, forgetting to drink. He was thinking of the discussion he'd had with Rikki on the bridge that night. He wasn't surprised at her grasp of things —he had realized she was an intelligent girl by her letters. He was only surprised at the way she knew him, even better than he knew himself. She was right about the deck-hands, of course. The only way to make sure there would be no sabotage would be to turn this trip into a kind of crusade. But did he want it to be that?

The pencil rolled and paused; then rolled again. And as he watched it he decided that he didn't want that crusade. The years of aloofness, the years of authority, had changed him. He didn't believe in his boyish ideal any more. To hand the tugboat business over to the men who sailed the ships would end in disaster. To let Siemonov, Verwoert and Bo'sun Janus decide on the policy of a Company involving millions of guilders and hundreds of men would be as senseless as handing a wireless transmitter to a herd of monkeys. The men themselves wouldn't want it that way either. It would burden them with a responsibility they were unfitted to take, and it would make them thoroughly unhappy into the bargain. Even he himself, who knew the ropes, was reluctant to shoulder such responsibility. That, of course, was at the bottom of the vague desire he had to throw up the business side and become just a Captain again, once he had settled with Kwel. But she was right on insisting that he'd have to make up his mind now. He had never realised before how near the goal he was; somehow he had always regarded it as something he would never attain. But now within a couple of months, if all went well, the apparent mirage would become a proved reality. And then?

The pencil rolled backwards and forwards on the chart. He heard the sound of footsteps mounting the bridge, and he knew it was the look-out reporting. He recognised from long experience every sound on board his ship. He could distinguish, for instance, the peculiar metallic ring that came from the engine-room when a stoker dropped a shovel, or the hollow thud that announced the closing of a furnace door. Nothing happened on the *Fury* without his knowing it, and he was prepared for every eventuality. But if Kwel were in command he'd be as helpless as a baby—just as Captain Jan would be if he were seated behind Kwel's desk. If he didn't want to bring disaster to the tugboat industry he must find someone of Kwel's ability and experience in business to take over the management of the fleet. And the only one he knew was Beumers.

At first he was quite pleased with the idea. It was the obvious solution. Force Kwel to sell up, combine the fleets, appoint a management committee chosen from the men who sailed the ships, and let Beumers run the business. Then suddenly an idea occurred to him which made him gape. He remembered the note he had received from Beumers which had ended with the words: *Don't give yourself a headache trying to puzzle out why I should give you this piece of advice which probably seems contrary to the interests of my Company. It isn't.*

Suddenly he saw it all. He saw Beumers's plan as clearly as if he had made it himself. The little man had realized that sooner or later Captain Jan Wandelaar would have the whole of the Dutch tugboat business in his hands, and wouldn't know what to do with it. In fact he had manoeuvred Jan unobtrusively into that position with the help of little notes and some friendly words at the right moment, not out of admiration for him and dislike of Kwel, but simply because he saw the chance of reaping an advantage for himself. Let this sailor undermine Kwel, he had thought, and the tugboat business will fall into my lap.

It took him a long time to get over the shock of that discovery. In the end he realised there was only one way out. That night he planned it, sitting in his swivel-chair in the chart-room, staring at the rolling pencil.

CHAPTER TWENTY-TWO

WHEN the dry-dock was anchored in the Clyde, ready to be towed out to the open sea at the turn of the tide, Captain Jan called the men together in the steel canyon between the towering walls, and made a speech.

He stood on a crate, facing a silent, hostile crowd that watched him in the flickering light of smoking torches. He had to raise his voice occasionally to make it heard above the sound of ships' hooters and the clatter of cranes and steam hammers on the wharves across the river. At first the men were restless and bored, thinking it was just going to be another of those speeches that captains make at the beginning of a long trip. But it wasn't. He riveted their attention at the start by declaring that he knew there were men amongst them who had been bribed to sabotage the dock. He even said he knew who they were, but that he wouldn't take any measures against them. All he wanted to do was to make them realise what they were doing: that they were throwing away their last hope of breaking the strangle-hold the owners had on the tugboat business.

The speech lasted almost half an hour, but the men listened to every word. Their Captain told them briefly the history of the tugboat business, how he himself had fared in it, how he once made a pledge, when he was still a Mate, that he would not rest until he had seen the business handed over to the men who made it. He told them that if this dry-dock got to the Falkland Islands safely and on time, the moment for that handing over would have come. If, however, it was delayed or damaged, things might go on as they were for years. He told them that instead of having the dock searched and the saboteurs arrested, he would do nothing but make another pledge. He pledged himself to see to it that, if all went well, the business would from then onwards be controlled by the men who sailed the ships, and that he himself would retire from the management and become a Captain again and nothing else.

It was all he could promise them now. But what he'd outlined could be done if the dock arrived on time, and if he could prove, beyond question, that an attempt had been made at organized sabotage. That was the reason why he wouldn't do anything against the saboteurs, apart from opening their eyes to what they were doing. If the men came to the conclusion that he was right and if they trusted him, he expected them to divulge their secret plans on a signed declaration that was to be given to the officer in charge of the dock. The future of the tugboat industry, he ended by reminding them, was now in the hands of the men who sailed the ships.

The dry-dock RN 26 sailed at night, a dark colossus slowly edging its way down to the sea along the lane between the flickering lights. All traffic on the Clyde had been stopped to give it passage. When they reached the open sea at sunrise they passed the grey shadow of a battleship on which the white ensign was just being hoisted. The battleship ran up a signal: T. D. L.—I WISH YOU A PLEASANT AND SUCCESSFUL VOYAGE.

The *Fury* answered with X. O. R.—I THANK YOU.

The first stage of the voyage, between the Clyde and the Scillies, was like a triumphal procession. The Irish Sea was full of ships; they all saluted with their flags or ran up signals as the dry-dock sailed slowly past, huge and forbidding. The *Fury* led the convoy, flanked by the *Bevers,* commanded by Maartens, and by the *Van der Gast,* commanded by Siemonov. It was an impressive sight to see these three powerful ships breasting the waves, with the foam whipped up from beneath their counters sparkling in the sun. When they strained too hard on the hawsers they would heel over until the sides of their hulls ploughed the seas, leaving a furrow of milky foam. Destroyers on manoeuvre crossed their course, weaving wide circles around them. The Liverpool to Dublin mailboat stopped to let them pass, her decks black with waving people. It would have been a real joy, this first stage of the trip, a heart-stirring experience, if only some news had come from the men on the dock—any news. But they took a long time to make up their minds. At last, when Jan had almost given up hope, the dock hoisted a signal: J. C. Q.—Come at once.

When he had been rowed to the dock he was received by a very nervous Flip and a grim committee of five deck-hands. When he asked Flip: "What's up?" Flip answered, in an agitated whisper: "God knows—they won't tell me."

They spoke their minds to the Captain, however. They told him to go up to the starboard quarters and see for himself. Accompanied by the five deck-hands, he climbed the ladder that led to the men's quarters, a wooden shed erected on top of the huge steel walls. Up there all the men stood waiting, a silent, hostile crowd. "Well," said one of the men, nodding in the direction of the table; "there you are."

On the table a number of objects had been neatly laid out, a miscellaneous collection that included drills, hacksaws, crowbars and blasting-charges. Some of these objects had scraps of paper beside them which bore clumsily worded statements such as: *I, Willem Band, deck-hand on the dry-dock RN 26, declare that on the evening of October 24th I was approached by a gentleman in Poppy's Bar in Amsterdam. This gentleman offered me one thousand guilders if I would do the following: take charge of the tools he would give me, hide them until the dock was midway between the Scillies and the Azores, then place the explosive charge I would find in the parcel between the girders of the floor of the dock.*

Jan remained in the men's quarters for more than an hour, reading the statements and examining the strange assortment of gear. In the background the men stood watching him, a silent, hostile crowd. As he climbed over the rail and made his way down the ladder some of the men expressed their disapproval by spitting loudly.

Flip was waiting for him below, pale and very worried. "Well," he asked, "what the devil have they been up to?"

"It's all right," Jan said. "They've given up their stuff and written their confessions. You might as well go up and collect the lot."

"You aren't taking the stuff with you?"

"No, better not. They're sure to have kept some of it in reserve, in case they want to get their own back on me. To leave it here is the safest thing."

"Well, I suppose it's all right," Flip admitted grudgingly, "but I might as well tell you that as far as I can see three of them are missing."

"Where are they?"

"God knows," said Flip. "If you ask me they've been slung overboard."

"Don't be silly," Jan said. "Count again."

Flip counted again, and made the total thirty-seven. When he made inquiries from the men themselves they told him that thirty-seven was the number they had sailed with. "Those three must have got lost in Glasgow," Jan said jokingly.

"Well," said Flip, "I expect they must have."

And that was the last they heard of Kwel for the rest of the trip—at least as far as the dry-dock was concerned.

With the tugboats it was a different story. The first twenty days were all right. They made good progress; the coal was excellent, and so was the food. The only doubtful element on board the *Fury* was the wireless operator, a pale, weedy youth with pimples. The future of the tugboat business didn't concern him because he'd been hired from a wireless company. This was his first trip on a tugboat, and he didn't seem to like it. He considered himself a cut above the rest of the crew and avoided them by spending most of his time in his little cubicle behind the funnel. He had to share their meals of course, and by doing so he made himself easily the most disliked man on board. He came down to the mess-room in a green and brown check dressing-gown, and talked very loudly about the comfort of the officers' quarters on ships of the merchant navy.

Bout, who seemed to dislike him less than the rest, suggested that his curious behaviour had something to do with a tendency to sea-sickness. Rikki and the wireless operator were at loggerheads from the beginning. She was always going into the wireless-room at odd moments, where she used to stand watching him at his work, not saying a word. It made him nervous, and he expressed his irritation by slamming down his notebook whenever she appeared. At last he requested her politely to leave him alone as he hated being watched while he worked. As she still persisted in worrying him he went to see the Captain, togged up in full uniform to give his visit an official character, and lodged a complaint. The Captain said he'd look into the matter, but at the same time he must point out that these were exceptional circumstances. He was sure, however, that once they had reached the Falkland Islands everything would be all right. The wireless operator was very annoyed, and wrote a long letter to his company complaining about the treatment he was getting.

The other newcomer on board the *Fury* had a happier life: Paarlberg, the Mate who had taken Flip's place. He was an old friend of the Captain's, he said, for they had met years ago in Brest, when he was Mate on the *Texel*. He was an amiable man, like a St. Bernard dog, and he was far too good-natured to bear the Captain any grudge for having got so far ahead of him. The Captain was now almost the most powerful man in the business, and Paarlberg was still exactly what he'd been in Brest: a Mate, and not a very bright one at that. He felt uneasy the moment he was left alone on the bridge, which was not often. The Captain slept in the wheel-house and only went down for meals; and while he was absent the girl took his place—or so it seemed to Paarlberg. He preferred the Captain to the girl, for the Captain, though keeping a strict eye on him, left him more or less alone. But the girl was always asking questions. She asked him the names of constellations and of lighthouses, not because she wanted to know them (she knew them perfectly well), but because she wanted to test his knowledge, like an examiner putting a pupil through his paces. If he gave the wrong answer or failed to produce an answer at all she raised her eyebrows in a peculiar way and said, "I see." Once when his reply was hopelessly wide of the mark, she said: "You're lucky it's me, and not the Captain, aren't you?" Paarlberg grinned sheepishly and muttered "Yes," though in his secret thoughts he would have preferred it to have been the Captain every time.

Paarlberg it was who invented the joke about the Captain naming his ship after his fiancée. It wasn't a particularly good joke, but the ship enjoyed it hugely. Soon after that she was given another nickname, though no one knew who was responsible for it. But suddenly the whole ship began calling her "Crikey." It was a good thing, that nickname, for it helped the crew to accept her. Now, automatically, she'd become one of them. For Jan, too, her status on the ship had changed. For some reason she had lost all the physical attraction that used to make him so uneasy ashore. She looked as pretty now as she did then, if not prettier, yet she was somehow so much part of the ship that she seemed a different person. Only once during those first twenty days did he feel any of the old desire; it occurred when he was writing up the log one evening after supper, and she was sitting opposite him. He paused, thinking about the next sentence. Their eyes met. At once her look became stern and admonitory, as if to warn him that emotions were out of place at this time. One night while he was calculating their position in the chart-room and she was washing her hair in the cabin next door, he shouted through the partition: "We'll get married when we get home, I take it." And she shouted back: "That's right. Have you got a clean towel somewhere?"

At that moment it was a tremendous temptation to answer: "I'll get you one," and to go into her cabin and take her in his arms; but somehow he resisted it.

The first port of call was Funchal, where the *Fury* berthed to take in stores and coal. She was the first of the tugboats to leave the convoy. If everything went according to plan she would rejoin it in four days, after which the *Van der Gast* would cast off to bunker in Las Palmas; then finally, when the *Van der Gast* returned, the *Bevers* would cast off and nip into St. Vincent to replenish her bunkers before the whole convoy made the long crossing between the two continents. Funchal, Jan realised, would be the test. If Kwel was going to show his hand he would show it now, and his most likely plan would be to attempt some shady business in connection with the coaling and victualling of the ship.

But Jan had planned his counter moves carefully. Bout would check every single basket of coal that went into the bunkers, and he himself would inspect the stores before they left the warehouse. The moment he and Rikki set foot ashore they made a bee-line for the ship-chandler's office, which they found in one of the narrow, steep streets, and at the top of three flights of stairs. When they entered the office the ship-chandler looked up from his ledger with an expression of sour distrust. In a corner a fat, swarthy secretary was typing away on an antique machine. Jan explained that he had come to see if the arrangements for the delivery of the stores had been completed, and when the man said, "Of course," Jan asked if he could just check them over in the warehouse. The man said "Of course" again, but after a moment's hesitation. He mumbled something to the secretary in Portuguese, put a hat on his oily head and led the way to the warehouse.

The warehouse turned out to be a dark, untidy basement that smelt rather like the lion's cage at the zoo. The stores for the tugboat *Fury* were found after a good deal of stumbling about, and peering at labels by the dim light of a lantern. Eventually the stores were located; the man said:

"You want to count them, I suppose?"

"No," said Jan, "I want to open them." Before the man had time to protest, Jan had whipped out a chisel from his hip pocket, rolled one of the barrels marked MEAT into the passage between the walls of sacks and prized open the lid. It was only the work of a moment to discover that the top layer alone was good quality meat, the rest merely skin and bone. "I protest," the man spluttered. "If you want to do this, do it on board your ship. I can't have this mess in my warehouse; this is outrageous."

"Potatoes next," said Jan. He pulled a sack out from the pile and ripped it open. About a quarter of the contents were sound, but the bottom of the sack was nothing but a mass of rotten pulp. "Now we'll go back to the office," Jan said, pushing the indignant ship-chandler out of the warehouse.

When they got back to the office the man began murmuring something about "an unfortunate mistake."

"All right," said the Captain, "don't let's waste time on explanations. I happen to know the facts. I'll take no further action in the matter on condition that you give me A.1

stores instead, and you hand me over the letter in which you got your instructions."

"Letter?" the man repeated, trying to look surprised. "My dear sir, I haven't the faintest notion what you're talking about."

"That letter from Kwel and Van Munster," said the Captain calmly. "If you don't hand it over I'll have to call in the British Consul. This dry-dock belongs to the British Navy, remember, and I happen to be in possession of certain facts that might have awkward consequences for you if they came to official ears."

"There's no such letter," said the man doggedly. "I don't know what you are talking about."

"Very well then," said the Captain. "I'll search this office till I find it." He brushed past the man and began scattering the papers on the desk. But the threat was enough. Muttering under his breath, the man went to a file marked "F-K" and pulled out a letter which he tossed at the Captain's feet.

"All right," said the Captain, pocketing the letter. "Now see that A.1 stores are delivered to me by two o'clock this afternoon. Every barrel and every sack will be opened on the quay, in the presence of the British Consul. Good day."

Outside in the street he and Rikki read the precious letter.

Dear Friend,

At the beginning of November a dry-dock will pass your way which is, for various reasons, not being towed by our Company this time. On one occasion in the past you have seen fit to serve us in a particular fashion, which became the basis of our arrangement, as you may well remember. We trust that you will give the customer in question, who is a good friend of ours, the same service as you gave us then. Our representative will be visiting you during the course of next month, and we are sure that you will find his visit rewarding in many ways, provided this matter has been arranged to our satisfaction. Yours truly, N. Kwel.

When they got back on board they found Bout beside himself with rage, which was extraordinary for so even-tempered a man. "Look at this," he said. "By God, *LOOK* at this, just *LOOK*," and he held out a piece of coal in a trembling and dirty hand. "This is what the bastards wanted to chuck down my bunkers! This—this—this cow-dung!"

Jan took the piece of coal, looked at it, and as Bout spluttered: "Pinch it—here, pinch it!" he crushed it in his hand. It crumpled into dust almost at a touch.

"Well?" Bout asked. "What do you say?"

"Good," Jan said. "Have you loaded any of this?"

"I?" roared Bout. "I load any of—this! What do you take me for?"

"Where are they now? Alongside?"

"No," said Bout. "They came and wanted to hurry and when I saw this I told them a thing or two. And so they went home again. What are you going to do?"

"Don't worry," said Jan. "Everything is going beautifully. Come on, Rikki."

And back they went on shore, making their way once more through the maze of steep, narrow streets, to the coal merchants. The coal merchants were a lot grander than the ship-chandler. They had to pass various secretaries before they were admitted into the private office of the local director: a suave young man with oily hair, and the eyes of a vulture. The young man was extremely sorry about the slight misunderstanding in connection with the coal. He was afraid, however, that the Captain's engineer had been unduly rude and had put his men's backs up. "We Madeireans, you know, have a great sense of pride, and——"

The Captain cut him short by asking two questions: "Do you remember you promised me first-quality coal? And do you realise that I am representing the British Navy?"

The young man smiled radiantly and said, of course, of course. He was very sorry, but the coal he sent the Captain was the best he had in stock. "Madeira, you know, is rather far away and in consequence I often have to take what I can get. Unfortunately the last lot was of very poor quality. . . ."

The Captain asked if he might use his telephone.

Certainly he might, but what number did he want?

"The British Consul," said the Captain.

The young man paused ever so slightly, before he talked

rapidly into the instrument. "My secretary is getting him for you," he said. "Cigar, Captain? What about a drink, Madame? A small glass of our famous Madeira wine, yes?"

They waited a long time, but there was no news of the Consul. "I'll enquire again," the young man said, and started babbling into the telephone. "Sorry, the British Consulate seems to be continuously engaged. But I have been thinking, Captain—what about you coming with me and looking at what we've got in stock? You're free to pick any lot you like. If you find something better than the stuff we offered you this morning I shall be very much surprised, but you're welcome to it."

The Captain said it wasn't a bad idea, so they followed the young man through his offices and out into the street, down to the quay, where he whistled to a longshoreman who took them to the coal wharves. They made the round of the coal wharves with the young man babbling away merrily as he picked his way carefully among the coal heaps in his spotless tropical suit, like a white cat. When the Captain indicated a lot and enquired: "What about this?" the young man said: "Ah, I know. But that's sold, Captain, I'm sorry to say."

All the best-quality coal was sold, it appeared, and only the rubbish was left. When asked who the buyer was, the young man smiled radiantly and said: "I'm sorry, Captain, but for business reasons I can't divulge the names of our customers. A rule of the firm, you know."

But the Captain would not be put off with anything but the best. Even when offered a moderately good lot, he refused it. "I want A.1 stuff," he said, "and if I can't get it, I'll take it." At which the young man smiled even more radiantly, and said: "Now who said that we Madeireans were a hot-blooded race, eh? You are just like my Pancho, Captain, all roses and dynamite."

Jan went back with the young man to the office, and in spite of a long delay got on to the British Consul, who promised to come at once. That made a difference straight away. For one thing it made the young man's smile a bit less radiant. "You don't believe, Captain, that all the best quality coal has been sold, do you?"

"I do," said the Captain. "And I think I can even tell you

whom you've sold it to—Kwel and Van Munster's International Tugboat Company."

"Ah," said the young man.

"And I'll tell you something else," the Captain went on. "The Consul may be here any minute now. As I've said before, you're virtually sabotaging the British Navy. . . ."

"Sabotaging!" The young man's smile was gone now. "I'll thank you, Captain, to remember——" he began.

"All right," said the Captain. "I'll let the matter drop if you'll show me the contract."

"Contract?"

"Between you and Kwel; an agreement relating to the sale of that coal."

The young man thought a long time, and then pressed a bell. When a secretary came in he whispered something to her in English, not in Portuguese this time. After a few moments she came back with some papers. The young man read them through before he handed them to the Captain. "Here you are, Captain," he said. "As you see, it is all absolutely above board."

He was right, it was. It was a contract by which Kwel and Van Munster's International Tugboat Company bought at a high price all available stocks of first-quality coal held by the merchants between the dates of October 31st and November 14th. All entirely above board, except in one small detail. The confirmatory telegram sent to Captain Jan Wandelaar by the Company, in which he had been assured that he would be served with A.1 coal, had been dated October 2nd. When the young man murmured that the Captain must be under a misapprehension, Jan showed him a copy of that telegram, bearing a statement to the effect that the original was in the possession of the British Consul in Amsterdam, who had duly stamped and legalised it.

At that moment the British Consul in Funchal was ushered into the office, a dapper old gentleman in spats, wearing a boater which he put on top of his cane as he sat down. The dainty old gentleman looked like a superannuated thrush, but he was as hard as nails. After a little chat with him the young man's radiant smile completely disappeared, and his concern for the affairs of Jan and the British Navy knew no bounds. And as a result, showers of rich, gleaming coal went thundering down the hatches of the *Fury*. As Bout looked on, leaning over the rail, his eyes seemed to caress every piece as it rattled down.

It was so dusty and hot on board while the bunkering was going on that Jan and Rikki went for a walk. They climbed up to a little café on the mountain at the very edge of the town, a tiny building full of flies and the smell of hot food, and remarkable for the number of earwigs wriggling over its flowered tablecloths.

A woman brought them gin and lime in tumblers and a plate of salted biscuits. It was pleasant to sit out on a verandah that looked over the town and the harbour, nibbling a biscuit and discussing a good day's work.

While they were talking Rikki suddenly put out her hand, palm upward, on the flapping tablecloth. After hesitating a moment, Jan rather self-consciously put his hand in hers, and they sat like that for a while, looking at each other and at the sea. It was odd, but he no longer felt like taking her for a walk round the park, as he had planned to do. He didn't want anything more just now than this: to sit among the flies on that verandah, looking at the sea, hand in hand with her. Her hand was small and firm, and somehow he couldn't help thinking of that occasion years ago when he had held another hand, small, warm, soft, incredibly feminine, the hand of Agnes of Rio de Janeiro, as he had called her. How he had cursed himself later for letting that wonderful chance slip by. Cowardice? Loyalty? A mixture of both, probably. At this moment, too, he thought of Nellie. He felt a sudden sense of the uncertainty of life. As if for reassurance, he pressed Rikki's hand and said, without looking at her: "Do you ever have that feeling?"

"What feeling?"

"That anything good never lasts."

"No."

That was her all over. Any other girl would have turned this into a lovely, whispered conversation—a little sad, a little wistful, something to be remembered. But not she, oh no. Not Rikki Kiers. He asked a question and she gave a straightforward answer, and that was that.

"Want that last biscuit?"

"No, thanks."

So he ate it, munching slowly, gazing at the sea. "You know," he said, "I wonder what would happen if we gave in."

"To what?"

"That feeling."

"Nothing, I think. What could happen?"

He turned his head and looked at her. "What do you mean?" he asked.

"Well," she said, "it seems to me that the only thing to do is to be happy while you've got the chance and let tomorrow take care of itself."

"What are you talking about?"

"That feeling of yours that nothing good ever lasts."

"Oh," he said, "I meant that feeling of wanting to make love to you."

"Oh," she said. "I see."

When he had paid, they made their way back to the town, walking arm in arm down the steep, narrow streets, but although there were dozens of corners that seemed made for lovers, they went on without pausing, feeling rather tired and depressed. When they got back to the ship they found cook Blekemolen inspecting the stores that had arrived. When he was asked what they were like he made a gesture of blowing a kiss from his fat lips and exclaimed: "Perfect!" Bout was in good spirits too, now the bunkering was finished. "I've turned over every bit they tipped down my bunkers," he said, "and it's a dream." Everyone on board seemed pleased with life, except the Captain. "Well, let's get going," he said after he'd made a final tour of inspection. An hour later the *Fury* nosed her way out of Funchal harbour in a glorious sunset.

When they sighted the dock next evening everyone came on deck. Seen from afar, the colossal monster looked like a floating factory, or a block of houses that had somehow got adrift. Every man watching it across five miles of the Atlantic Ocean asked himself, what would happen if that vast, unwieldy hulk ran into a storm? All the things they had towed before bore some resemblance to a ship—even tin-dredgers. But this couldn't be called a ship by any stretch of the imagination; it was just a vast, floating mass of steel. The men weren't exactly apprehensive, but somehow this view of the dock had been a kind of eye-opener and they were more interested in the weather now than they had been before. For each one of them had, some time or other since that occasion, lain awake in his bunk and imagined what would happen if they should ever run into a proper old gale with that hulk; it wasn't a very pleasant subject to think about last thing at night, but at least there was always the comforting knowledge that the wireless operator could pick up the weather reports and warn the Captain what to expect, provided the ship wasn't too far from the shore. They'd already changed course several times on account of these reports, but on the long jump to Pernambuco they'd have to do without them and trust to luck.

The weather reports had been scrutinised by the Captain very, very carefully, more carefully than seemed really necessary, and in consequence the wireless operator had become extremely touchy. Once again he donned full uniform to lodge a formal complaint with the Captain. He wasn't trusted, he declared. Not only did that young woman practically sit on his lap all the time to see what he was doing, but even the Captain himself seemed to question the accuracy of his reports. "All right," said the Captain, "complaint acknowledged." And the wireless operator went to his little box behind the funnel to take off his full dress uniform and put on his green and brown check dressing-gown again, and that was that.

In point of fact the Captain was reassured by that complaint. If the fellow was up to any tricks, he argued, the last thing he'd do would be to focus attention on himself by these "official" visits. He was even more reassured when, during his visit to the *Van der Gast* and the *Bevers*, two days after his return from Funchal, he compared the reports of the other wireless operators with those of his own. Of course, that those boys had flashed their reports to each other every day and brought them into line was always a possibility, so one could never be quite sure. Anyhow, Rikki reported that she'd found nothing suspicious, which was the most reassuring thing of all.

The visit of the Commander to the Captains of the two other tugs wasn't solely on account of those weather reports. Jan told them exactly what had happened in Funchal, so they'd know what to expect when their turn came for bunkering. The reactions of the two Captains were characteristic: Siemonov, whose turn it was next, hardly listened. "Yes, yes," he said, "I see, borother," and poured out two tumblerfuls of vodka. His cabin looked exactly like the one he had on the *Jan van Gent*: socks soaking in the washbasin, bedclothes scattered on the floor, and a patch of soot over the icon in the corner of his bunk with the words SUSPENDERS written in it with a finger—obviously a reminder to himself to buy suspenders in Las Palmas, though why he should want to buy them was a mystery, since he never wore them.

Siemonov scarcely listened when Jan told him how to handle the ship-chandlers and coal-merchants he'd be up against in Las Palmas. "Yes, yes, borother, you leave it to me, ha? You be happy, leave it to me." And then he slipped out a pack of filthy cards from some pocket underneath his beard, looked at Jan with big, pleading eyes, and said: "Before you go—just one game, ha? Just one game of Squinting Tom, for old times' sake." He won, needless to say.

Maartens, as usual, was the complete opposite. When Jan came to see him in his spotless cabin, which smelt of furniture polish and mothballs, Maartens listened attentively to what Jan had to say and even wrote down his advice in a little pocket-book. While he was busy writing, Jan looked at him and wondered if he was still wearing the same cap he had worn years ago, a cap limp as a rag and bleached to a drab, bluish-green by long exposure to sun and sea. Maartens was very impressive, in a slow taciturn way, much more impressive than the smelly Russian. But when it came to dealing with the crooks, Jan's bet was on Siemonov.

He was right. When Siemonov returned after bunkering, with black smoke belching from his funnel, Jan knew he'd done the trick: only tiptop coal could produce such black, oily trails. And when he went aboard his ship to find out how he had fared with the ship-chandlers, Siemonov said: "Oh, all right, borother, all right—I opened one barrel when he came to deliver the stuff, saw it was bad, called out the boys, went to his warehouse and helped myself."

And when Jan, alarmed, asked: "I hope you didn't get into trouble with the police?" Siemonov pursed his hairy lips by way of reassurance and said: "No, no, oh no, quite the reverse."

Jan looked at him for a moment, then said sternly: "The police ran into trouble with you, you mean?" Siemonov grinned and nodded his head. But when he saw Jan's face he added hastily: "I've got the papers, though. The letters you wanted. I've got them—here!" And he pointed to a bundle under the chart-table.

Maartens, however, was a day overdue when he returned from the Cape Verde Islands, and received Jan with a worried face. "I got everything straightened out in the end, I think," he said, "but it took me some time."

He had managed to get a decent lot of stores, but he wasn't too happy about the coal. It was a bit of a mixture—fairly good stuff, but some slag and grit amongst it. Trouble with the police? Good God, no! He had got everything he wanted by quiet reasoning, so there was no need for any desperate measures. The only thing he couldn't get by quiet reasoning, it seemed, was the letter from Kwel to that ship-chandler who tried to monkey with the stores. But then he was doubtful about that part of the business from the start. "One just can't take a thing like that," he said. "I mean, one can't unless one's a pirate."

"Yes," said Jan, "I suppose you're right."

Rikki, of course, was all for Maartens, simply because she couldn't stand Siemonov. "You wait," she told Jan, "till you have to foot the bill for your wonderful old shipmate. I bet he damn near wrecked the whole town carrying out your instructions."

As it turned out, she wasn't far wrong. When the *Fury* arrived in Pernambuco for bunkering, Captain Wandelaar received a letter, *via* the Consulado d'España from the Prefect of Police in Las Palmas, which ordered him to pay damages amounting to seven hundred pounds sterling, ten shillings and ninepence, in accordance with the enclosed assessment, a fine of fifty pounds sterling, imposed by His Majesty's Court in Las Palmas, plus another twenty pounds sterling costs. The Captain would be allowed one month to pay, after which the matter would be pursued at diplomatic level. The details of the assessment made alarming reading. It was almost unbelievable that a mere fourteen men could wreck so much in so short a time. Whole taverns seemed to have been razed to the ground, and a vast number of policemen taken to hospital. Well, there seemed nothing for it but to pay the bill and hide the letter from Rikki. Yet, expensive though it was, this little escapade proved in the end to be well worth the money.

At first Jan could hardly believe it, but then the wonderful truth began to dawn on him: the crooks of Pernambuco had somehow got wind of what had happened in Las Palmas, and they'd decided to take no chances. This time the coal was all first-rate, the meat perfectly fresh, the potatoes sound and healthy. Well—if that wasn't worth seven hundred and seventy pounds sterling, ten shillings and ninepence, what was? But Rikki was furious with Siemonov and expressed her disapproval by retiring and sulking in her cabin. Even Jan was in her bad books. To give her time to cool off he went ashore and bought himself a drink, then another drink, and another after that. And he ended up by buying something for Rikki too. It was only after the *Fury* had sailed, under the command of a very nervous Paarlberg, that he sobered up sufficiently to realise that the present he'd bought her was a monkey.

Yes, by God—a monkey. A live, three-foot-tall male monkey swarming with vermin and with a piece of insulation tape clapped round a sore on its tail. It was sitting at the foot of his bunk when he opened his eyes, blinking its pale eyelids in the lamplight. At first Jan thought he was suffering from delirium tremens and shouted for help. A moment later cook Blekemolen, who must have been hanging about outside the door, came hurrying in with a cup of coffee. He merely grinned when Jan demanded: "Who brought that filthy thing in here?"

"You did, Captain," answered the cook. "You wouldn't have it put anywhere else. You said you wanted Miss Kiers to come and get it."

"Oh, yes, of course," Jan murmured feebly. "I just forgot."

When cook had gone he got up and dressed. As he did so, he kept staring at that blessed monkey, trying to remember how he came by it. He remembered in the end, but that didn't solve the problem of what he was to do with it now he'd got it. He remembered standing a lot of people drinks, and seeing the monkey on the shoulder of a man who was wearing a hat with feathers in it. He remembered, too, making his way with a crowd of people through the dark, echoing streets with the monkey on his own shoulder; then kissing them all goodbye on the quay and trying to prevent the monkey from kissing them as well.

When at last he went up to the bridge, he noticed something lying on the table as he passed through the chart-room; it was a hat with feathers. He picked it up gingerly between his finger and thumb, and dropped it overboard before he climbed the stairs to the bridge.

Paarlberg was there to meet him. "All's well, sir," Paarlberg said. "Course east-south-east. Wireless contact with the convoy established."

"All right," Jan said. "You may turn in."

He didn't see Rikki that night. If she had come to the bridge that night she would have found him miserable and humiliated. But she did not come to the bridge. In fact, they didn't meet until breakfast. A pity, in a way; for by then he had time to think: if I had come home in that condition ten years ago, Nellie wouldn't have left me to the tender mercies of cook Blekemolen.

"Morning," he said.

Coba and Sparks said: "Morning."

She said nothing, but she had lost.

When Rikki brought him his coffee on the bridge later in the day, she behaved as if nothing had happened, and so did he. They didn't discuss the stores; they didn't discuss Siemonov; they didn't discuss anything but the weather, which was beautiful. She was all sweetness and light, and later in the day he saw her on the poop, washing the monkey with soap and a brush.

The monkey became quite popular once he had got used to his new home and had broken the ice, as it were, by throwing an egg at cook Blekemolen's head. He was called "Frits," and that egg was the first of a long series of pranks which amused everyone on board vastly—everyone, of course, with the exception of the wretched victims.

Frits sucked the oil out of Bout's oilcan and spat it on to bo'sun Janus's clean laundry. He dipped his paw in the wireless operator's inkpot and smeared all the sheets of his weekly report. He dangled from the pulley over the wheel-house and sounded the hooter. He stole Bout's dentures and bathed in the soup. But he was forgiven all this because he provided so much amusement. Rikki laughed most of all, and he seemed to single her out for his affection. She couldn't show herself on the bridge without Frits jumping on to her shoulder, and he followed her about everywhere. Whatever he did was funny—even down to being seasick when the weather became rough off Bahia.

A seasick monkey was a comic enough spectacle in itself, but when it began imitating the wireless operator who was in the same plight, it was the funniest sight on earth. The men slapped their thighs with mirth. They leant back against the walls, convulsed and helpless. The chorus of their laughter even drowned the noise of the great waves that came pounding in from the east. It looked like a proper gale brewing, but the men didn't worry about that. If the high, shallow dock couldn't be kept on its course they'd have to heave-to and ride the waves until the gale blew over. As a precaution the hawsers had been doubled hours ago. There was nothing else to be done now but to wait and hope for the best. And they had too much experience of dirty weather to be unduly worried by the threat of it.

But Jan felt less happy at the prospects. Siemonov had cast off two days before to go to Bahia for bunkering, so now Maartens and he had to face the gale alone. That wouldn't be too bad if he hadn't in the back of his mind that nagging worry about the coal that Maartens took in at St. Vincent. He signalled: "How long will your fuel last at full pressure," and the *Bevers* answered: "Four days." This answer made him swing round the tow at once. In fact, Maartens's last signal was still flying when the *Fury* hoisted P.Y.T.: *Heave-to.* For if Maartens had only got four days' fuel left at maximum speed, the wisest course would be to save as much fuel as possible, and the only way to do that was to ride the wind. If the wind didn't increase they'd be able to keep the dock stationary by running at moderate speed. But if it increased to the velocity predicted by the weather reports, that was from 40 to 45 miles an hour, the pressure on the dock would grow to about nine thousand pounds per square foot, and in that case they'd be driven back, towards the shore, even if they gave their engines every ounce of power.

While the men slapped their thighs and screamed with laughter at Frits and the wireless operator being sick in unison, their captain had to make a grave decision: whether to take a risk and keep the dock stationary once it had been swung round, or to assume at the outset that the wind would increase, and meet that eventuality by getting as far away from the shore as possible before the gale actually set in. If he chose this course, there was the risk that he might get beyond the range of Siemonov's wireless transmitter. If that happened it might take Siemonov several hours longer to locate the convoy, perhaps even a whole day.

Jan waited until the dock had been swung round, which was easily done, before he made his decision. He then hoisted the signal, O.S.T.: PROCEED AT HALF SPEED, and sent Rikki to give the wireless operator a message for the *Van der Gast*, if he could reach her. The message indicated the position of the convoy and ordered the *Van der Gast* to join it at once. If the wireless operator failed to get in touch with the ship, he was to pick up the nearest vessel and to ask for the message to be passed on to Bahia; Rikki returned after five minutes to report that the wireless operator was pretty ill. However, he had managed to get the message off, sending it via an English ship, but she was doubtful if he'd be capable of dealing with a reply. Jan asked her then if she knew enough about the job to take over herself. She said she thought she did—at least, she could receive messages but not transmit them. "Very well," Jan said, "you hang on to that wireless till you get a message back."

"Right-o," she answered, making her way to the little cabin behind the funnel. She had to keep a tight grip of the rail to prevent herself from being knocked off her feet by the rolling of the ship.

They sailed at half speed for an hour and twenty minutes; then the wind increased so much that they had to run the engines at full speed again to save the dock from being swept back by the wind. Now they had no choice but to pull for all they were worth. If they had run full speed into the wind an hour and a half ago, they would be by this time another three miles clear of the shore, but Maartens would have been out of action an hour sooner. If Siemonov sailed at once and the wind didn't get over fifty miles an hour, they'd have nothing to worry about. It was a bad stroke of luck that the weather should have hit them on this particular stretch of coast. There was no shelter anywhere, at least no shelter that would have been much good for a dry-dock of this size. When Rikki came back to the bridge, struggling against the wind, she reported that Siemonov had replied: SAILING AT ONCE. DON'T WORRY. And the Englishman who passed the message on had added: SHALL I STAND BY?

They were then one hundred and fifty miles east of the coast. Even if they started running back at the rate of three miles an hour—which they would if the wind increased much more—there was still a good margin of safety. Jan asked how the wireless operator was, and she said he seemed worse. "Don't worry," Jan said. "Tell him that the Captain orders a message to be sent to the Englishman, acknow-ledging with thanks their offer to stand by, but declining it. And, whatever happens, don't let that fellow lose touch with Siemonov. Make him realize that he's now the most important man on board this ship. If we lose contact with Siemonov we're going to look damn silly."

"Right-o," she said again. "I'll do my best."

Holding tightly to the rail, she made her way back to the wireless cabin, her oilskins flapping violently in the wind.

Jan hoped the gale would lessen at nightfall, but it didn't. It got worse. The ship rose and fell with a steep, lurching movement; when the towing hawser was suddenly jerked taut everyone was flung forward with the shock. The dock seemed to be pulling with the force of the moon. Jan didn't worry about the hawsers too much; he was more worried about the dock itself. If it broke loose it would race towards the coast like a windjammer with a gale behind her. Or it might get cross-seas and capsize almost at once. By four o'clock in the morning he knew what measures he'd have to take as soon as daylight came. The dock would have to be partly submerged so that a large portion of it was below the water-line, like an iceberg. In the meantime he had to spend most of his time ducking behind the sprayshield to escape the deluges of water that kept breaking over the ship. In spite of everything, Rikki went to and fro between the bridge and the wireless cabin; she reported any news she had got from Siemonov with the regularity of a watchman. But she didn't mention the wireless operator, and Jan guessed that the wretched man had reached the stage of wishing he were dead. By the look of things he wouldn't have to wait long. The helmsman was hurled from the wheel at every dive and then flung violently back when the towing hawser jerked suddenly tight. Jan kept a sharp look-out for any signals from the *Bevers*; but all he could distinguish now and then were the three swinging toplights an immense distance away. But as soon as the first pale light of dawn appeared in the sky and he could make out the *Bevers* clearly in the distance, he saw a string of tiny flags go fluttering up her mast: THIRTY-SIX HOURS' COAL LEFT. Thirty-six—why the hell hadn't Maartens banged that coal merchant's head against the wall until he got first-rate coal? If anything went wrong now, the responsibility for the loss of the dock would rest on Maartens.

Jan hoisted the Yellow Jack, the signal calling the dock. It was half an hour before they acknowledged it because the visibility was still so poor. The moment they acknowledged the signal Jan hoisted X.G.W.: SUBMERGE YOURSELVES.

It seemed to take them quite a time to make out what he meant. He was forced to lash himself to the rail in order to have his hands free for keeping his binoculars trained on them. When at last he saw the acknowledgment go up their spidery mast he was so completely drenched that his clothes seemed to weigh a ton, but he hardly noticed it. He was too busy wondering how the men were going to handle that dock. If he had manned it with a scratch crew from Glasgow they would have submerged it right enough—in fact, they would have sent it to the bottom like a stone. As it was, he couldn't be sure that the men he'd picked would be capable of tackling the job in the teeth of a raging gale. But they succeeded. It seemed an immense time before Jan noticed any reduction in the height of the dock above water. They submerged it so gradually (using the valves and gauges with such skill that they did the job by inches) that it was only by looking away for a while and then looking back that Jan was able to estimate their progress. When, after three hours, they signalled: SUBMERSION OF DOCK COMPLETED, Jan realized with feelings of pride and relief that the men on that great mountain of wave-tossed steel had performed a consummate feat of seamanship. Twenty-five thousand tons of water had been let into the ballast tanks until only a third of the huge steel walls showed above the surface. Now Jan could signal Maartens to slacken speed and save his precious coal, while they waited for Siemonov to catch up with them. But the trouble was that it would take them a good twenty-four hours to empty that colossus again— another twenty-four hours added to the forty-eight they were already overdue. And it was a tradition of the business that a tugboat must always arrive on time. If a tugboat happened to arrive three days overdue after a voyage of eighty, there was always someone to shake his head and say reprovingly: "I had expected better of you, Captain."

At noon the gale turned into a hurricane. The height of the waves increased from about twenty feet to thirty. The tugs, which had managed till now to hold their own against the wind, were completely at its mercy. The *Fury* herself was being driven back at a speed of three miles an hour. The *Bevers* hoisted a signal: AERIAL BROKEN, and the top flag of the three was torn to shreds before they could haul it down. Jan, who had been on his feet for twenty-four hours now, sent Paarlberg to the wireless cabin with a message for Siemonov: *Bevers* WIRELESS OUT OF ORDER. RUNNING BACK FAST.

When Paarlberg returned he was flung past the door of the wheelroom three times before he managed to get in. The news he brought was bad. The wireless operator was so ill that his mind seemed to be affected, and Rikki couldn't transmit that message to Siemonov. "All right," Jan said, "take over. I'll be back in a minute."

When at last he had managed to battle his way to the wireless cabin he found the wireless operator in a state of collapse on the bunk and Rikki fumbling about with the wireless transmitter. The rancid stench of vomit, mixed with the smell of acid for the batteries, was enough to make anybody sick, but Rikki seemed unaware of it. "Can you handle that thing?" Jan asked. She shook her head.

Jan seized the wireless operator by the shoulders and shouted: "Get up, you!" The man stared at him with bulging eyes. Jan took hold of his clothes and dragged him out of the bunk, shaking him violently. "The ship's in danger," he shouted. "Go back to that set!"

The man gulped and stammered feebly. "Can't—I'm done for. . . ." In a sudden fit of rage, Jan began slapping his pinched and bloodless cheeks. "Don't!" Rikki shouted, trying to catch Jan's arm. The two men became locked together against the wall, with Rikki struggling desperately to separate them. They were thrown from one end of the tiny cabin to the other, staggering and lurching with the movement of the ship. All at once, the wireless operator broke away from Jan's grasp, seized the stool that lay overturned on the floor and with three flailing blows shattered the transmitter. A plunge of the ship made him lose his balance and he staggered backwards, striking his head against the wall. He lay where he had fallen, his limp body rocking to and fro.

Jan stood swaying on the floor. Then he bent over, grabbed the rolling body by the collar and would have strangled the man if Rikki hadn't pushed him aside with all her strength. What brought him to his senses was not this unexpected show of force, but the terror he saw in her eyes. They looked at each other speechless for a moment, then he went back to the bridge.

At five o'clock, just before nightfall, the *Bevers* signalled: HAVE THREE HOURS' COAL LEFT. The log indicated a negative speed of four miles per hour. Their position was twenty-five miles east of the shore. And there was still no sign of Siemonov. Now that contact between the *Van der Gast* and the convoy was broken, the odds were that Siemonov would never find them in time—never in this weather and in this pitch darkness.

At five-thirty a flare shot up from the *Fury*; three minutes later the *Bevers* sent one out, too. They went on shooting off flares every quarter of an hour, but there was no answering signal on the horizon. At seven-thirty the log indicated a speed of well over six miles astern; the *Bevers* stopped pulling. This was the end.

Bo'sun Janus got the order to make the boats ready. They were racing towards the coast at such speed now that the men must be got off the dock somehow. It was suicide to attempt it in these seas, but the boats were made ready. At ten past eight a morse-lamp flickered through the haze. It was a signal from the dock: TAKE US OFF. And still there was no sign of Siemonov.

Jan gave the wheel to Paarlberg; he wanted to supervise the lowering of the boats himself. He buttoned his oilskins and tied the tabs of his sou'wester under his chin. When he placed his hand on the door handle Rikki threw her arms round his neck and pulled his head down and kissed him with a long, anxious kiss, salt with sea brine. "Good luck, my dear," she said. Then he went out.

Before he gave the command to lower the boats he shot off one last flare. It was a failure, showing no more than a dim, flickering spark that hardly reached the height of the masthead before it spluttered into the sea. But suddenly, like the emblem of hope itself, a ball of fire rocketed up on the horizon, shattering the blackness of the sky with a blaze of light, right on the starboard beam. And then another and another. Old Siemonov on the *Van der Gast* seemed to be enjoying his own firework display.

Bout, exhausted and black with oil, stumbled to the speaking-tube when the whistle blew, cursing as he grabbed it; but when he pressed his ear to the instrument a broad grin spread over his grimy face. "Boys," he shouted, "that bloody Russian has arrived!"

Then he flung open the door of the stoke-hole and yelled: "Feed her, boys! Chuck it under! The Russian has come!" The stokers cheered; and then he ordered Coba—he, that sane, cautious man—to give him a hand at screwing down the safety-valve.

The whistle was left dangling from the speaking-tube, which occasionally spurted water.

The *Van der Gast* was probably the best tugboat in the world, but if Captain Siemonov hadn't been in command of her she would never have made it. She came rearing out of the night like a ghost vessel. She cleared the *Fury* by what seemed no more than a foot when she crossed her bows, more under water than above it, smothered right up to her bridge with seething foam. She swung round alongside the *Bevers*, shot a line across to her, and ran out her own hawser for Maartens to hold and make fast to. It was a manoeuvre no ordinary man would ever have attempted, let alone achieved; and it cost Siemonov four dead.

The glory of what Captain Siemonov did that night on the murderous seas off the coast of South America was not commemorated by the erection of a statue or the naming of a street. Its only memorial was the gratitude of the fifty-two men whose lives he had saved. Jan had never embraced a man before in his life; but when, after the storm, he went aboard the *Van der Gast* and was received with open arms by old Siemonov, he just tumbled into them and threw his own arms round a neck the size of a bollard, and had the breath slammed out of his by a hand patting his back, until he had to sit down and cough.

"Borother," Siemonov roared delightedly, "this calls for a drink!"

It called in fact for a good many vodkas and for a card party that lasted six hours—six hours during which the dry-dock, like a rusty monster in the flaming sunset, slowly rose out of the sea. Not a single man on it was missing, although the living quarters had been swept clean off the walls and underwear was left dangling among the anchors.

The wireless operator was still alive, too. The man had been locked up in his cabin by the Captain, who kept the key in his pocket. Every now and then the man beat on the door with his fists and screamed: "Let me out! Let me out!"

Rikki said: "Why don't you release him? He can't get off the ship, can he?" But Jan insisted that the man should remain locked up on a charge of insubordination and sabotage.

The night after the *Bevers* had returned from bunkering, the man started yelling again in his cabin: "Let me out! Let me out! I'm ill."

He began pounding on the door with something hard, and there was a succession of heavy thuds, as if he were flinging himself against the panels. He made such a commotion that Jan went to the door of the cabin and shouted at him to keep quiet. But the voice went on screaming: "Let me out! I'm suffocating!"

When the man heard Jan's footsteps retreating from the door he yelled out suddenly: "Now I shall take things into my own hands. Don't say I didn't warn you."

By the time Jan got to the bridge the noise had ceased. The monkey sat scratching himself on the roof of the wheel-room and Rikki was leaning on the rail, looking at the sea. "I think you are wrong to keep him locked up," she said. "Believe me, he's. . . ." She was interrupted suddenly by a noise that sounded like a distant shot. They stood looking at one another for a moment, motionless. The sound came again, now much nearer, and they knew it was a shot. At the same time the monkey, who'd been sitting on the roof of the wheelroom, toppled down with a thud at their feet. Jan swung round and came face to face with the wireless operator standing on the stairs of the bridge with a revolver gleaming in his hand. Quick as lightning, Rikki leapt at him. There was a sudden flash from the gun and Rikki stumbled forward on to her face. She lay huddled in the corner of the bridge rail, so small that Bout didn't even notice her when he came running on to the bridge. The wireless operator stood terrorstruck, with the revolver dangling from his hand. "No, not that," he stammered. "I didn't want that. . . ." Bout wrenched the gun from his limp grasp before the men overpowered him and dragged him back to his cabin.

Nobody was allowed to touch her. The Captain carried her to his cabin himself. He laid her gently on his bunk, and cut open her jersey with the bo'sun's knife. The wound was so small that it was hard to find it—a dark spot between her small, white breasts. When Bout came in, too, they were all standing very still, looking at her and at the Captain. She lay there quite peacefully, her mouth a little open. Only her eyes were strange, the whites showed and no one dared to close the lids. The Captain closed them himself in the end.

When they all shuffled out at a signal from Bout, they blinked in the bright sunlight that glinted off the sea. They stood a moment without quite knowing what to do after they put their caps on again. Then the bo'sun said: "Well, we'd better lower the flag, I reckon. And tell the others."

At least that gave them something to do. Five minutes later the *Fury* ran up the signal M.E.L.: YOUR FLAG HALF MAST.

The *Van der Gast* answered with K.O.N.: WHO IS DEAD?
The *Fury* answered: Z.H.M.: WOMAN.

Three days later she was buried at sea—a bundle in tarpaulin poised on a plank against the rail. The convoy had been stopped. On the dry-dock the men stood looking on, a row of black dots high up on the wall, beneath the small Dutch flag that fluttered at half mast.

The crew stood cap in hand, while the Captain prayed. "Our Father, which art in Heaven," very slowly and clearly. Only at the last command, "One—two—three, in God's name," did his voice falter. Then bo'sun Janus and Bout lifted the plank and the body slid off; there was a faint rushing sound, a splash, and she was gone.

> *It is our sole relief*
> *That on some distant shore*
> *Far from despair and grief*
> *Old friends shall meet once more.*

Before they'd finished singing the hymn, Jan hurried away to his cabin with bowed head, Bout following him.

As he didn't come back, Mate Paarlberg gave the signal to proceed. The engine-room telegraphs rang, the propellers began churning again, the hawser rose dripping from the sea and the convoy sailed on once more, its flags fluttering now from the mast tops.

On the evening of the eighty-second day, while they were waiting for the pilot to take them into Port Stanley, the wireless operator committed suicide by hanging himself with the belt of his dressing-gown. When the police came on board to arrest him, he was found hanging from the ceiling. They cut him down and carried him ashore, shoving him into an ambulance, like a loaf into an oven. Thus ended a little melodrama of the sea that was hardly mentioned at the time and was soon forgotten.

But when, in after years, Captain Wandelaar sat at official

343

banquets, listening to speakers who flatteringly referred to him as the greatest figure in the Dutch tugboat industry, he hung his head as if he were ashamed to hear it.

For somewhere on the bottom of the Atlantic Ocean rested the body of a woman to whose courage and foresight the men of the tugboats owed so much.

CHAPTER TWENTY-THREE

WHEN he got home after his great triumph with the dry-dock convoy, he paid a call. After the ships had berthed at Ijmuiden he went ashore, leaving Paarlberg in command. An hour later he rang the bell of Kwel's house. A footman opened the door and informed him that Mr. Kwel was not at home. As he brushed the man aside, a door opened at the end of the corridor and a girl came out whom he had never seen before but who seemed to recognize him. "Oh, Captain," she began, "let me take your coat." And she whispered to the footman: "Tell Mr. Nol that Captain Wandelaar is here."

"I don't want to see just the young one," Jan said. "I want to see them both."

"Of course, of course," the girl said, opening a door. "Go in, please. Shall I take your brief-case?"

"No, thank you," he replied, and went in. She hesitated, but did not follow him.

The room he entered was a large one, with a log-fire at one end, and an enormous crystal chandelier in the centre of the ceiling. He was standing with his back to that fire, his hands clasped behind him, when the door was opened and an old man came in. An old man with a small white beard and gentle eyes. Kwel! It ought to have been a moment of triumph, but it wasn't. For he had lost all desire for power or revenge; he had lost everything except a longing to be back at sea again. It would pass with time, probably, his feeling of emptiness, of wanting to sail on and on till he reached some distant shore. He felt no emotion when he shook Kwel's hand, only a strange sense of pity and the urge to be back at sea. All he had to do tonight was to arrange things so that he and his comrades could sail with their minds at rest.

"You realise the position, I take it," he said. "I won't waste any words, for you know the situation as well as I do, probably better. The fact is I can break you if I want to. In this brief-case I have enough documentary evidence to get you put in gaol."

Kwel said nothing, but smiled, a tired, gentle old man, amused by the earnestness of youth.

"And even if they don't put you in gaol," he went on," I am now in such a position that I can ruin your Company within a year. Well, I won't."

"That is very kind," said Kwel. It was the first time Jan had heard his voice. It was an old man's voice, thin and soft.

"I've got it all worked out in here," Jan said, opening his brief-case. "Here is a draft of what I propose."

He handed the draft to Kwel, and the old man took it with a delicate, veined hand, pulling out a pair of gold pince-nez from his breast-pocket with the other. When he put the pince-nez on he looked very distinguished—like an old senator reading a petition.

"You'll see from that draft that I'm not even pressing for a merger. You're welcome to buy my ships at valuation price and take over all my contracts. All I want is to sail as a Captain in your Company, on two conditions."

"Yes?" said Kwel, reading.

"That you resign as a director, and that all demands of the Union of Tugboat Workers are met."

"I see," said Kwel, still reading. "I have just come to that."

"It was the only alternative," Jan said, "to handing over the tugboat business to Beumers."

At the mention of Beumers, Kwel looked up sharply. For a split second it was no longer a mystery how this gentle old man could have done all he had done—but then he smiled again, with kindly, amused eyes behind his gold pince-nez, at the impetuousness of youth. "So," he said. "So, Captain. That gives me plenty to think about. You'll realise that I can't, at a moment's notice, tell you precisely what I think of your proposals, but if you give me time. . . ."

"No," Jan said. "If you don't sign that draft now, while I am here, I'll hand in my documents."

"To the police?" Kwel asked, smiling.

"To Beumers," Jan answered. "Let the wolves devour wolves—that's the conclusion I have come to at the end of the road."

"I see," said Kwel. "Well, if you don't mind waiting a few minutes, Captain, I should like to discuss this with my son."

"By all means," Jan said.

After Kwel had left him alone in that room, he felt very tired and dizzy, as he always did for his first few hours ashore. And he felt, too, the need of some companion who was somebody friendly and sympathetic, somebody who'd make a cup of tea and hum in the kitchen and listen when he described how the dry-dock looked after the hurricane, or how the bo'sun secretly buried the monkey in a laundry bag at dusk, thinking he wouldn't see it from the bridge.

He sat down on the couch in front of the fire and smelt the odour of old plush, and watched the glint of the fire in the polished brass fender. The despair was over; the yearning for her kiss, and the touch of her hand. Now he faced the months, the years of being on his own, of being tired and lonely, with a vague longing for somebody sympathetic to chat to while he sipped a cup of tea, his back on a sofa, his feet up, looking at the ceiling and at the flies round the lamp.

He leant back on the cushions now and studied Kwel's ceiling, a great expanse covered with stucco garlands and cupids, and dominated by the imposing chandelier in the centre. When at last the door opened, he sat up with a start; but it was the girl. He got to his feet.

"I—I should like to speak to you for a moment," she said, "if you don't mind. I am Connie Stuwe."

"How do you do," he said.

"I know how things are," she said. "I heard what you and he discussed. And I heard what they discussed, just now. What I want to ask you is—don't decide anything tonight. You must trust me. Your—your friend trusted me before, and I believe. . . ."

"Yes," he said. "I have to thank you for that. Without your information a lot of things would not have happened."

"You'll win," she added hurriedly, "but don't decide tonight. Turn left as you go out of the front door. There'll be a cab waiting on the corner. I'll be waiting for you in the cab."

Before he could think of something to say, she was gone.

"Yes," she said, "she was brave. That morning she came to see me and sat just there, where you are sitting now, I felt very fond of her. It must be terrible to go through this kind of thing for the second time."

"No," he said. "It is easier the second time. You know what's coming."

He looked very big in that low tub chair, much bigger than anyone had ever looked in that room before. She hadn't felt any particular tenderness for him so far, only sympathy and respect. But when she saw him sitting there, turning his sherry glass in his hands and staring at it, she felt again that sudden wave of affection that had overcome her at the British Consulate that time when she saw him dip his biscuit in his tea. He sat now stolid and matter-of-fact, but because the chair was so low his trouser legs had got pulled up high above his boots and his underpants showed above his coarse black socks. Pathetic pants, bus driver's pants, and somehow they expressed a terrible, clumsy loneliness.

"Another drink?" she asked. But he said: "No, thanks," hastily. "This will do me fine."

"Well, she said. "Let's get down to business. To start with, let me tell you what I heard them say, after you had spoken to him. I. . . ."

But he looked so uncomfortable in that chair, so heart-breakingly clumsy and awkward, that she just couldn't go on. What the devil did one do with a bus driver in a thick blue suit and long drawers and thick woollen socks, sitting practically on his heels in a doll's chair? And then, in a flash of inspiration, she asked: "Would you like a cup of tea?"

"Oh, no," he said. "Don't bother. I'm quite happy, thanks." But his face would have melted a heart of stone.

"Won't take me a moment," she said. "Take off your coat, and get out of that mouse-trap. Here—sit on the sofa. Make yourself at home." And when he hesitated, embarrassed, she added: "Come and fill the kettle, if you like. I'm dying for a cup."

She went to the kitchen, lit the gas, got the tea-caddy from the mantelpiece and the teapot out of the cupboard. There was the sound of hesitant steps in the passage, an awkward cough. "Can I help you with anything?" he asked.

"Yes," she said, without looking round. "Fill the kettle, will you?"

"Here you are," he said.

"Thanks. Have you got a cigarette?"

"No—sorry, I never smoke them. . . . Can I get you one?"

"Don't bother, thanks. What do you smoke—cigars?"

"No, a pipe."

"Well, light one if you like, I love the smell."

She poured out the tea. "How strong do you like it?" she asked.

"As it comes," he said.

She had put in four big spoonfuls, enough to poison a cat! Her intuition hadn't failed her, this was the sort of brew he wanted. They chatted over tea-cups till a clock in the hall struck twelve. The striking of that clock seemed to break his train of thought, for when the last stroke died away he paused for some minutes, puffing thoughtfully at his pipe.

"What are you thinking about?" she asked suddenly.

"Nothing in particular," he said. "I was only wondering why you should have done so much to help me."

He was surprised at his own lack of self-consciousness. He had never set eyes on this person until some three or four hours ago, and yet he was more at ease with her than with any other woman he had ever known in his life. Tea, a pipe, a fire, a friend to talk to; it was almost too good to be true. Three hours he had known her, and already she seemed a better friend than Bout, understanding him better, and somehow cheering him up by not taking his troubles too seriously. It was perhaps one thing she said that served more than anything else to put them on this footing. They were talking about Rikki, and he had referred to her death as a "tragedy." She looked at him quizzically and said: "I wouldn't call it a tragedy. I'd call it damn bad luck."

By saying that she seemed to lift a burden from his mind.

She was the first person he'd been able to discuss it with in human terms. Not a tragedy, but damn bad luck. Yes, that was how he ought to look at it. "Mind if I take my coat off?" he asked.

ded: "What made you
I was merely only helping
r?"

taking off his coat; "I just
d put it on an empty chair.
at what it boils down to is that I
. I liked you even before I set eyes
ol told me, that night you came home

wered gravely.
ped you this far," she continued, "I think I'd
on helping you. For one thing I'll write to you
y when you're at sea to keep you informed about
ngs here. I dare say I may be able to give you some first-
hand information."

"I still don't understand why you should take all this
trouble," he said, "but it's very kind of you."

"Don't worry," she laughed. "I feel it's something you
deserve."

At four o'clock in the morning he was still there. But the
teapot was empty, and they'd switched to brandy. He had
told her nearly all his story and she felt she knew by now all
there was to know about the steep streets of Funchal and the
details of that dock.

"I think it's about time we turned in," she said when he
showed signs of getting drowsy at last. "Have you got anywhere to go?"

"Yes," he said, "of course. I'm sorry; I didn't realise it was
so late."

"Don't worry about the time," she said, "you can stay
here if you want to."

He settled down to talk again, blissfully happy, in the glow
of brandy and the company of a willing listener.

The next morning, after breakfast, she made him do the
first wise thing—the first, she hoped, of many. She told him
not to go and see his kids, not to go and see old Kiers, not
to waste his time wrangling with the Kwels. They drew up
a kind of contract between them, and after that she packed
him off to France.

To France of all place▮
knew that the Dutch Har▮
dredger ready for towing. She▮
desperately anxious to get sor▮
mand of the convoy in the even▮
them. She felt pretty certain they'▮
he'd be able to go on board the flag▮
Brest. She had to be very careful not to l▮
taking his affairs in hand. She contented h▮
forward suggestions and then, with a little tact▮
leaving him to make the decision. Jan didn't rea▮
was best for him to go away. He didn't realise that h▮
still in a weak and vulnerable state; in consequence he w▮
an easy prey for anyone who wanted to get the better of
him.

She arranged all his business papers with him; that side
of the tugboat business she knew backwards. She bought
his ticket for him, new underwear, new socks, a raincoat,
handkerchiefs, and a writing-case as a present. It was a
leather writing-case, with lots of ruled writing-paper, big
envelopes and a blotting-pad. He was so overjoyed with it
that she realised with a pang that he'd probably never
received a present from anyone in his life.

When at last the train carried him away, she stood looking
into the distance long after it had vanished round the bend.
As she turned to go, a thought struck her that made her smile
a little grimly to herself. The Kwels were child's-play to deal
with; it was little Mr. Beumers who might give trouble. Well,
she could manage him, she felt, as long as he didn't realise
who was the new power behind the great Captain Jan.

When the news became known that Jan had gone over to
Kwel and Van Munster with his ships, to be Commodore
of their fleet, after he had forced them to accept all the
demands of the Union and pensioned off the old tyrant himself, and that he would command the big tin-dredger convoy
to Billiton, everybody was anxious to seek him out. Everybody—the newspapers, the organisers of charities, the
advertisers and, of course, the director of the Dutch Harbourworks Company. But nobody knew his address: his mother-
in-law didn't, old Kiers didn't, nor did his friends. All the

could say was that

"Go ahead," she said. Then she a ...me *Fury,* which would
wonder about me? Did you think mmand of Captain Flip
to get something out of it mysel... would join the convoy

"I don't know," he said,
wondered." He folded it an

"I think," she said, "th... small hotel on the Breton coast:
just happen to like yo...med to be writing a lot in his room
on you, from what N...g walks by himself along the beach.
from the Far East ...om noon till sunset, took bread and a

"I see," he ans...wine with him in a haversack, and was

"As I've be...n by the crab-fishers sitting on a rock, shading
better go o... his hands, and looking out to sea. Or else on his
regularl...er the shade of a bush on the dunes, his hat over
th... face and an empty bottle by his side. The men of the
village, with whom he chatted occasionally in the village
café, called him "Yann"; when he left the village they drank
his health and wished him "bon voyage."

He went off like a pilgrim with his kitbag over his
shoulder and a stick in his hand. At Brest, he asked for a
bed in a sailors' hostel on the water front and had to pay in
advance before he was allowed upstairs, because he looked
such a tramp. He lived in the hostel three days—*"ce matelot
Hollandais."* Then a huge convoy anchored in the bay: six
tugboats towing a tin-dredger from Rotterdam to Billiton.
The town turned out to look at it.

A boat from the *Fury* took him on board, and only when
all the ships hoisted the Blue Peter did the guests of the
"Hotel l'Océan" realise that they'd been sitting at the same
table with *"l'illustre capitaine Vandelaar,"* and had cursed
him for not passing the salt.

When the convoy sailed, a large crowd of sightseers
watched it from the shore. It was a bright day, and the ships
were visible a great distance out to sea. On the bridge of the
Fury Captain Jan stood, as he had always stood, his hands
behind his back, his feet planted firm—a stalwart figure
gazing hopefully towards the horizon.